Kay Louise Cook
14352 37th Ave NE
Seattle WA 98125

RETURN TO THEBES

BY ALLEN DRURY

Fiction

ADVISE AND CONSENT
A SHADE OF DIFFERENCE
THAT SUMMER
CAPABLE OF HONOR
PRESERVE AND PROTECT
THE THRONE OF SATURN
COME NINEVEH, COME TYRE
THE PROMISE OF JOY
A GOD AGAINST THE GODS
RETURN TO THEBES

Non-fiction

A SENATE JOURNAL
THREE KIDS IN A CART
"A VERY STRANGE SOCIETY"
COURAGE AND HESITATION, *with Fred Maroon*

RETURN
TO THEBES

Allen Drury

DOUBLEDAY & COMPANY, INC.
GARDEN CITY, NEW YORK
1977

ISBN: 0-385-04199-3
Library of Congress Catalog Card Number 76–23757

Sitting or standing, as the mood or the ritual occasion dictated when they posed for the royal sculptors millennia ago, they stare pleasantly out upon the long green snake of Egypt—which they called Kemet, "the Black Land"—and the desert wastes of "the Red Land" beyond.

They have been there, some of them, five thousand years and more.

If there is an Earth five thousand years from now, some of them will doubtless be there still.

Smiling, happy, confident, serene, ravaged no longer by the fierce ambitions and violent passions that often moved behind those deliberately impervious formal masks, they have a satisfaction, not given to many, which they will never know but seldom doubted:

They always said they would live forever.

And as forever goes in the lives of men, they have.

INTRODUCTION

In the novel *A God Against the Gods,* to which this novel is sequel, there is related the early life and rise to supreme power of the Pharaoh Akhenaten, tenth god-king of the Eighteenth Dynasty, who thirty-four hundred years ago ruled the "Two Lands" of Upper and Lower Egypt.

Akhenaten, husband of one of history's most beautiful women, his cousin, Nefertiti, was the son of Amonhotep III and Queen Tiye—"the Great Wife," who for many years directed (or thought she did) the destinies of Egypt while her amiable but indolent husband enjoyed his luxuries and let his country's tenuous grasp upon its poorly defined and loosely held "empire" in the Middle East gradually slip away.

The slippage was not helped by Akhenaten, who, after suffering in early youth what we now know as Frölich's syndrome, a disease of the pituitary gland that left him malformed with sagging belly, woman's hips, thin arms and elongated neck and face, became Co-Regent with his father at the age of fifteen, sixteen, seventeen or eighteen. (Egyptologists differ, as they do on so many other things. A novelist must make choices from among their conjectures, adding here and there a few of his own. This I have done, trying always to remain within the bounds of what seems *humanly logical* and eschewing those intense arguments over fragmentary details that understandably make up much of the world of professional Egyptology.)

Quite soon after his coronation as Co-Regent, Akhenaten changed his original name, Amonhotep IV, to Akhenaten, which means "Pleasing to the Aten," the Aten being the traditional Sun God in the form of a bright and visible disk. He also established a new capital halfway between Thebes and the Nile Delta that he named Akhet-Aten, meaning "Horizon (or Resting Place) of the Aten." And he began a lengthy attempt to establish the Aten as the sole god of Egypt—the first such attempt at monotheism in recorded history—thereby seeking to supersede all of Egypt's myriad animal- and bird-headed gods, and doing particular violence to the powerful and deeply entrenched priesthood of Amon-Ra. Amon-Ra was another form of the Sun God, his very essence, hidden and mysterious. His priests had for a century and a half been inextricably entwined with the fortunes of the Eighteenth Dynasty.

Thus Akhenaten began what is now known as the "Amarna Revolution," Tell-el-Amarna being the present Arabic name for the empty plain halfway up the Nile which is all that remains of the briefly flourishing city he established there.

For more than a decade, according to the version I have set forth in *A God Against the Gods,* the "revolution" proceeded in desultory fashion while Akhenaten, Nefertiti and their six daughters attempted to win over the people of Egypt, rather more by example than by any strong overt insistence on Akhenaten's part, to the worship of the Aten. Finally convinced that this easygoing policy would not work, and enraged by the continuing opposition of Amon, Akhenaten became more active.

At the conclusion of *A God Against the Gods,* Amonhotep III has died and Akhenaten has assumed full power. He has also by that time fathered three daughters by his three oldest daughters, in a vain attempt to produce sons who could succeed him and carry on the cult of the Aten. In addition he has alienated most of the members of the royal family ("the House of Thebes,") including his mother Queen Tiye and his powerful uncle Aye; he has raised to power his cousin, the scribe and general of the army Horemheb, who eventually became the last Pharaoh of the Eighteenth Dynasty; he has finally turned in full fury upon Amon and all its fellow priesthoods; and he has begun the emotional and physical relationship with his younger brother Smenkhkara that has resulted in estrangement from Nefertiti and the beginnings of the final break with both his family and his people.

At that point, with his father mummified and entombed after the ritual seventy days of mourning, with Smenkhkara named Co-Regent and destruction loosed upon his fellow gods, Akhenaten and Smenkhkara set sail from Thebes to return to Akhet-Aten and *A God Against the Gods* concludes.

Here, three years later, in 1362 B.C., begins RETURN TO THEBES— which means, in essence, "return to the city of Amon," who will eventually win their bitter battle and, with the assistance of many powerful court figures including Tiye, Aye, Horemheb and Akhenaten's youngest brother, Tutankhamon, (born Tutankhaten) be restored to all his powers and privileges.

Again, I am indebted to the friends mentioned in the Introduction to *A God Against the Gods* who have assisted in gathering books and research materials, who have provided delightful company on two invaluable visits to Egypt, and whose ideas, bouncing off mine, have helped clarify my approach to a tangled but hypnotic subject. Once again I am particularly indebted to the great British Egyptologist Cyril Aldred, until retirement Keeper of Antiquities of the Royal Scottish Museum in Edinburgh. His book *Akhenaten, Pharaoh of Egypt* (London: Abacus paperbacks, Sphere Books, Ltd., 1968), has been my desk bible throughout. In an extensive and cordial personal correspondence he has been unfailingly kind in answering my questions and politely adamant in opposing some of my conclusions.

He tends to discount with some vigor the thesis, in which I am not alone among those familiar with Ancient Egypt, that there was a contest between Horemheb and his father, the Pharaoh Aye, for the throne. In this Mr. Aldred is characteristic of many Egyptologists who find it difficult, if not downright distasteful, to bring their serenely sculpted friends down to human reality. Yet these *were* human beings, and they were contending for the greatest prize of the ancient world, the Double Crown of Egypt.

Better a rendering giving due weight to human desires and emotions on a scale to match the prize, than an account as serenely bland and lifeless as the paintings on the walls.

There is much blood in RETURN TO THEBES, as there is in *A God Against the Gods;* but where the prize is great, and where those who seek it really care and have at hand the means to express their caring, blood is apt to follow. I have opted to have my Ancients bloody and human rather than emptily—and often falsely—smiling faces on the wall.

For these views of mine, and for others expressed in the two novels, Mr. Aldred and his fellow Egyptologists of course bear no responsibility whatsoever. Taking a leaf from the book of my complex protagonist, who prided himself on "living in truth" in all things, I have tried as clearly as possible to present the truth of this fascinating period as I see it. Others disagree, and more power to them. In the world of Egyptology, one conjecture is as good as another, providing it stays within hailing distance of the few scraps of known fact we have. I have tried to remain reasonably well in range of all the matters covered in the two novels.

I should perhaps repeat here the general principles which I have followed in constructing RETURN TO THEBES and *A God Against the Gods,* particularly in so far as they apply to dates, spelling of names and certain familiar locutions that the Ancients did not know but which I have adopted for the ease of the modern-day reader. For instance:

Estimates of how long Ancient Egypt had been an entity prior to the events of *A God Against the Gods* and RETURN TO THEBES range from a minimum of one thousand to a maximum of almost three thousand years. I have chosen arbitrarily, on what seems the main burden of the evidence, to put it somewhere approaching two thousand years. We do not know: only the sands of Egypt, which cover all, know; and until there is time and money to dig to the full beneath them (assuming that might be physically possible, in itself an optimistic conjecture), we will never know with any degree of certainty. Somewhere in the neighborhood of two thousand years would seem to encompass logically and comfortably the earliest beginnings, the seventeen dynasties recognized by the Egyptian historian Manetho (who himself did not come along with *his* arbitrary guesses until 305 B.C., more than a thousand years after the events of these novels), and the so-called "Hyksos invasion," which preceded the Eighteenth Dynasty.

In the same fashion I have chosen 1392 B.C. as the birth year of both Akhenaten and his wife and cousin, Nefertiti. It was somewhere around that time: there are as many guesses as there are Egyptologists. I have grounded my time frame on that arbitrary date and have anchored it at the far end to somewhere in the neighborhood of 1330 B.C., which allows sixty or so years for Akhenaten's birth and adolescence, his co-regency with his father Amonhotep III, his co-regency with his younger brother Smenkhkara, the reign of his youngest brother Tut-ankhamon, the reign of their uncle Aye, and much of the reign of Horemheb, last Pharaoh of the Eighteenth Dynasty. Some professionals may dispute this, but anyone who delves into Egyptian history soon finds that his own guess is just about as good as anyone else's—providing it allows sufficient elbow room for the generally agreed-upon lengths of these various kings of the Eighteenth Dynasty. This I have sought to do.

Similarly with names. Horemheb, for instance, is "Har-em-hab" to Mr. Aldred; "Harmhab" to the first great historian of Ancient Egypt, James H. Breasted; and appears elsewhere variously as Horemheb, Horemhab, Haremhab, Haremheb, Harmhab, Harmheb, Heru-em-heb—somebody has to make a decision, and in this case I'm it. "Hor-emheb" has a solid ring to me, so "Horemheb" he is herein.

This decision, as with many other names, is based on what to me seems easiest and most euphonious for the present-day reader to articulate and understand. Akhenaten's father was known to the Greeks, Romans, and to modern-day Egyptians who follow their lead, as "Amenophis III." Aldred renders him "Amon-Hot-pe." I have chosen the third most popular version, "Amonhotep," as the simplest for the modern reader's purposes. Similarly the Sun God himself appears in many texts as "Re," pronounced "Ray" or "Reh." I prefer the simpler rendition "Ra," pronounced "Rah," which seems to fall easiest on the tongue. He is also "Amon," "Amun" and "Amen." "Amon" seems the simplest, both when standing alone and when used as a part of a name.

I have also adopted the practice of breaking down into their components, for the first three times they appear in the text, the more difficult names of the Eighteenth Dynasty. If one gives to *a, e* and *i* (which were unknown to the Ancients and only introduced in Greco-Roman times for much the same purposes of convenience that I am striving for here) the sounds "ah," "eh" and "ee," it becomes relatively easy. The name of Akhenaten's (Akh-eh-*nah*-ten's) third daughter, who appears in *A God Against the Gods* as a little girl and plays a major role in RETURN TO THEBES, is a real jawbreaker—Ankhesenpaaten. But if the reader will take a moment to sound it out slowly— "Ankh-eh-sen-pah-*ah*-ten"—the going becomes much easier and the name quite beautiful. And so with Nefer-Kheperu-Ra, Ankh-Kheperu-Ra, Neb-Kheperu-Ra (the brothers Akhenaten, Smenkhkara and Tutankhamon) and the rest.

For easy reference by the modern reader I have also, in common with many Egyptologists, adopted certain recognizable locutions. For Amonhotep III to refer to his family as "the Eighteenth Dynasty," for instance, is a complete prolepsis, since Manetho and his list did not come along until more than a thousand years later. And yet the Ancient Egyptians were a time-minded and orderly people and undoubtedly (to use a word beloved of the professionals) had some sense of what went before, and in their own minds must have had some cataloguing of the royal houses that preceded theirs. Accordingly I have them refer to their own "Eighteenth Dynasty" and their own "House of Thebes," because this makes it easier for us to understand what they are talking about.

By the same token, they did not know the terms "Valley of the Kings" or "Valley of the Queens," although they did have some general way of referring to the royal necropolis on the west bank of the Nile opposite Thebes. "Beneath the Peak of the West" is one with some historical foundation, and I have used it fairly often; but, for us, "Valley of the Kings" is more instantly recognizable, and so I have often used it too. "The blood of Ra" is a locution for the blood royal that they may not have used, but it is understandable here. They did not know the terms "mother-in-law," "brother-in-law" and the like. They did not know that millennia later we would refer to the oddly elongated skulls of Akhenaten's family as "platycephalic." But we know that, and it simplifies understanding in the text.

One name I have retained in its original form is Akhet-Aten, the name of Akhenaten's new capital. We know it more readily as Tell-el-Amarna, yet it seems fitting to keep the name he gave it—and to syllabify it throughout, so that it will not be confused with his own.

For those who wish to delve further in the period, I have appended at the end of *A God Against the Gods* a partial list, headed by Mr. Aldred, of some of the authors who have been most helpful to me in constructing *A God Against the Gods* and RETURN TO THEBES. I offer them as a very modest introduction to a vast and ever growing literature, and I repeat the warning I gave in *A God Against the Gods:*

Once enthralled by the Ancient Egyptians, you will be enthralled, as they themselves said so often about so many things, "forever and ever —for millions and millions of years."

ALLEN DRURY

THE HOUSE OF THEBES
Family Relationships of the Later Eighteenth Dynasty
of Ancient Egypt

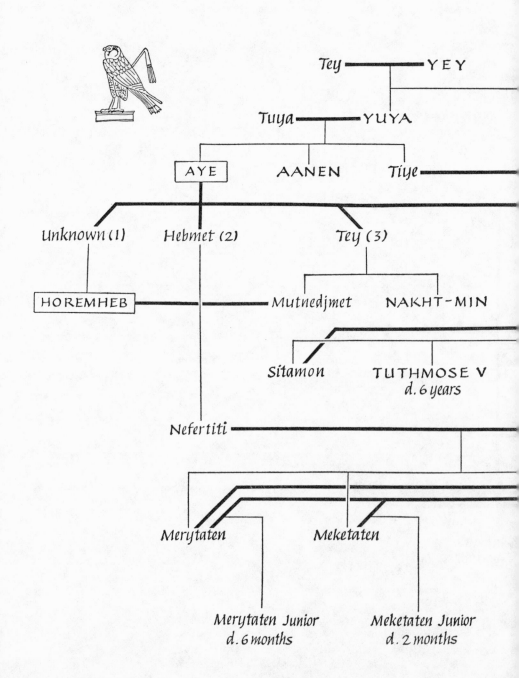

Tey ——— YEY

Tuya ——— YUYA

AYE   AANEN   Tiye ———

Unknown (1)   Hebmet (2)   Tey (3)

HOREMHEB ——————— Mutnedjmet   NAKHT-MIN

Sitamon   TUTHMOSE V
d. 6 years

Nefertiti ———————

Merytaten   Meketaten

Merytaten Junior
d. 6 months

Meketaten Junior
d. 2 months

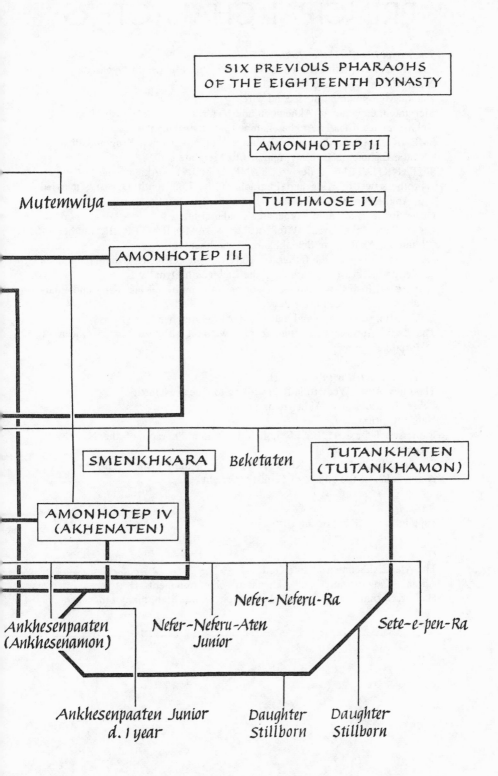

BOXED CAPITALS : PHARAOHS   CAPITALS : MALES
talics : Females   ━━━━MARRIAGES   ────ISSUE

SIX PREVIOUS PHARAOHS
OF THE EIGHTEENTH DYNASTY

AMONHOTEP II

Mutemwiya   TUTHMOSE IV

AMONHOTEP III

SMENKHKARA   *Beketaten*   TUTANKHATEN
(TUTANKHAMON)

AMONHOTEP IV
(AKHENATEN)

Ankhesenpaaten
(Ankhesenamon)   *Nefer-Neferu-Aten*
Junior   *Nefer-Neferu-Ra*   *Sete-e-pen-Ra*

Ankhesenpaaten Junior
d. 1 year   *Daughter*
Stillborn   *Daughter*
Stillborn

LIST OF
PRINCIPAL CHARACTERS

The Royal Family ("the House of Thebes"):

AKHENATEN, tenth King and Pharaoh of the Eighteenth Dynasty

Nefertiti, his cousin and Chief Wife

Kia, of Mesopotamia, his second wife

Merytaten, daughter of Akhenaten and Nefertiti

Ankhesenpaaten (later Ankhesenamon), another daughter

SMENKHKARA, Akhenaten's younger brother, eleventh King and Pharaoh of the Eighteenth Dynasty; married to Merytaten

TUTANKHATEN (later TUTANKHAMON), Akhenaten's youngest brother, twelfth King and Pharaoh of the Eighteenth Dynasty; married to Ankhesenpaaten

Queen-Princess Sitamon, Akhenaten's older sister

Queen Tiye, "the Great Wife," widow of AMONHOTEP III, mother of Sitamon, Akhenaten, Smenkhkara, Tutankhamon

AYE, her brother and father of Nefertiti, successor to Tutankhamon as thirteenth King and Pharaoh of the Eighteenth Dynasty

HOREMHEB, his son and successor as fourteenth and last King and Pharaoh of the Eighteenth Dynasty

Nahkt-Min, son of Aye and half brother to Horemheb

The Lady Mutnedjmet, daughter of Aye, half sister and later Queen of Horemheb

Others associated with the Court:

The Lady Anser-Wossett, lady in waiting to Queen Nefertiti

Bek, chief sculptor to Akhenaten

Hatsuret, priest of Amon

Ramesses, later RAMESSES I, first King and Pharaoh of the Nineteenth Dynasty

Seti, later SETI I, second King and Pharaoh of the Nineteenth Dynasty

Amonemhet of the village of Hanis, a peasant

Abroad:

Suppululiumas, King of the Hittites

Gods:

The Aten, Akhenaten's "Sole God"

Amon, "King of the Gods," Akhenaten's chief opponent

Hathor, Sekhmet, Isis, Osiris, Sebek, Hapi, Thoth, Ptah, many others

Book I

LOVE OF A GOD
1362 B.C.

King of   Ankh-Kheperu-Ra,   Son of the Sun,   SMENKHKARA
the North
and South,

Bek

I am the apprentice of His Majesty, I have been taught by the King; and now that I come to die—for I am dying, they cannot fool me however much they attempt it—I feel that I have served well him whose creation I have been . . . as he has been mine, for it is as fellow artisans, almost more than as ruler and subject, that Nefer-Kheperu-Ra Akhenaten, tenth King and Pharaoh of the Eighteenth Dynasty to rule over the Two Lands of Kemet, and Bek, his chief sculptor, have labored all these years.

Now my duties pass to my principal assistant, Tuthmose: and it is better so, for I am old and ill and much disheartened by these recent days. Ever since His Majesty returned from the funeral of his father, the Good God Amonhotep III (life, health, prosperity!), in Thebes three years ago, I have been asked to do things I would never have done were I in a position to refuse. Of course I have not been, and it has not been a happy time for me. I am not sorry it is ending, though I could have chosen some better means, had it been left to me, than this steady weakening that thins my flesh and brittles my bones and withers into uselessness the strong hands that carved so many wonderful things for him in the years when we were younger.

I hardly feel that I know His Majesty now. I thought I did, so closely were our thoughts and projects intertwined. But this, I suppose, only proves how slippery is the slope on which humans meet and pass one another—particularly when one of them is a god and answerable only to his own conscience for what he does.

I suppose the Good God Akhenaten (life, health, prosperity!) has a conscience, though of late it has not been visible to me. In the North Palace the Chief Wife Nefertiti lives her life alone, unmolested but, as nearly as we in the Court can determine, unloved. With her resides Queen Kia, native of Mesopotamia, second wife of His Majesty, small, dark, quiet, friendly to all save him, and observant—always observant. I have sculpted them both, and both have befriended me. I grieve for the separation, particularly for the Chief Wife, who has, I think, loved His Majesty greatly all her life, and now must live out her days without

his presence to enliven them; even though I think she had decided,
quite some time before he sent her from his side, that she must go.

With her also resides the Prince Tutankhaten, just a week ago entered upon his eighth year. He is growing into a reserved, quiet,
thoughtful little lad. We used to see him toddling about, fat, happy, always gurgling with laughter. Now he is thinner, less happy—rather
sickly, in fact—and now he walks more solemnly, forcing a dignity beyond his years, as though he feels already the weight of the Double
Crown he may someday have to wear . . . someday not too far off, I
am afraid, unless His Majesty decides to live his life much differently
than he has in recent times.

In the North Palace also reside three of His Majesty's four surviving
daughters by the Chief Wife: Ankh-e-sen-pa-a-ten, thirteen, who is to
be married to the little prince later this year; Nefer-neferu-ra, nine; and
Nefer-neferu-aten Junior, eleven, named for her mother when her
mother bore this name. This was before His Majesty took the name
from her and gave it to His other Majesty, his younger brother the
Prince Smenkhkara, now Ankh-Kheperu-Ra Smenkhkara, Co-Regent,
King and Pharaoh also, in the union that has all of Kemet, and espe-
cially all of us here in the Court, saddened and dismayed that such
things can be.

That is why I say the little prince may come to wear the Double
Crown "someday not too far off." Akhenaten flies in the face of all
right and reason: he overturns *ma'at,* the eternal order and fitness of
things that has existed in Kemet from the Beginning. He affronts the
gods, whom he has hurled from their temples and driven from the land.
And he hurries their return, for they live in the hearts of the people
where his vengeance can never reach them, and wait patiently for their
time to come again. As it will, for His Majesty's time is no more than a
ripple on the Nile when matched against the eternal calendar of theirs.

Yet I should not be happy to see his downfall, and so in a way I am
just as pleased that I shall probably not live to witness it. Because His
Majesty and I have known great days. We have performed many "wonders," as he calls them, together. I shall never regret, though I live in
the afterworld forever and ever, for millions and millions of years, that
I was at his side and was given the privilege of assisting him, in the days
before he went beyond us into his strange world and left us all behind.

Have you been to Karnak and seen the three colossal statues of him
that I sculpted there? They guard the entrance to his first great temple
to the Aten, which he built in the days before he established this city of
Akhet-Aten. Have you noticed how I captured him, the very essence of
his being, the long, narrow eyes, proud and arrogant and yet hiding

such pain—such pain!—the pain of his awful ailment, which came upon him as a youth, and whose bitter gifts I also captured in the stone: the sagging belly, the woman's hips, the spindly shanks, the skinny arms, the elongated neck, the pendulous lips, the high cheekbones, the face that Kemet has called "Horse Face" for almost twenty years. All, all, I captured in the stone. And he approved my doing it, he urged me to do it. When I demurred at first, he said, "Bek! Bek! I live in truth, and you must too. Make them see me as I am, and they will know what a wonder they have as Pharaoh! I command you, Bek. Make me as I am!"

And so I always did . . . until lately, when it has become more important to him to try to keep pace with one whose favors from nature he can never match, than to live in truth. And so he no longer cries, "Make me as I am!" but rather indicates, "Make me as I wish to be, to equal him!"

And so obediently Tuthmose and I have begun to round out the cheeks, smooth out the hollows, make him look younger, more conventional, more perfect in the style all Pharaohs before him have favored. I have tried to help him match Smenkhkara's golden beauty, which of course he can never in reality do, and becomes thereby, to all who see him as he actually is, pathetic in the trying.

Pathetic and more than pathetic: for in these past three years he has ordered me to sculpt and paint things that not only have offended me as a man but have violated my honor as an artist. And for that, since I of course have had no option but to do as he wished, I think I cannot find it in my heart to forgive His Majesty.

Statues of a king embracing a king—paintings of a king kissing a king —stelae of a king fondling a king!

I hope they may all be destroyed sometime. I hope they may never see the light of day in after years. But they will last our time, I know that, for he has ordered them created without shame, and he has ordered them displayed without shame, and without shame he has forced upon Kemet the spectacle of himself and his brother almost as man and wife. And shame has come to the House of Thebes because of it, and because of it great sadness and foreboding lie upon the Two Lands.

I know the pretense he used to offer, though in recent months he has abandoned even that—the pretense that because the Chief Wife is no longer beside him (and why is this, one may ask, if not that he himself decreed it!) therefore King Smenkhkara stands in her stead and takes her place as his helper in the worship of the Aten, and so must have her titles, her power and (who dares guess how fully?) her wifehood as well.

Who believes such madness? It is folly, self-delusion. It is worse: it is insanity, though none dares call it so for fear of His Majesty's vengeance. Or perhaps I should say: none outside the Great House dares call it so. Because, as one who passes quite freely in and out and is able by virtue of his skills to spend some time in both the North Palace and the South, and sometimes in Queen Tiye's Palace of Malkata in Thebes as well, I sense that there are some within the walls who have more freedom to speak their minds than we do—though even they, I think, hesitate to challenge him direct, but instead satisfy themselves with doing what they can to conceal the record of his folly.

Thus the matter of the "coronation durbar" which has now become such an issue in the Palace. . . .

When he returned from Thebes after his father's funeral—never, to this day, to leave Akhet-Aten again—he held a "coronation durbar," as he called it. At first he proposed that he should crown King Smenkh-kara and that King Smenkhkara should then crown him. One can only imagine the arguments that took place in the Family. There must have been some, because presently it was announced that fierce old Pinhasy, chief servitor of the Aten, would crown them both, chanting His Majesty's Hymn to the Aten for the first time directly to His Majesty, as though His Majesty now embodied the Aten and should now be worshiped *as the Aten.*

(No priests of Amon dared protest. None, at least openly, are to be found. Amon's temples stand desecrated and deserted from one end of Kemet to the other. Only an occasional whisper indicates that the young priest Hatsuret and some of his closest friends still move in hiding through the land. Once I came upon the Councilor Aye—who now styles himself "Divine Father," meaning "father-in-law of the God," namely Akhenaten—and General Horemheb talking in a corridor at Malkata. "—suret,"—I thought I heard that portion of a name as the general spoke to his father—"is now near Memphis where I am sending him gold and sustenance." "Good," Aye said. "Tell him to be of good heart. Tell him that soon we will bring him—" Then abruptly they became aware of my approach and turned away with a sudden burst of talk about innocuous things. I pretended I had not heard, though I am convinced that the full name Horemheb spoke was *"Hatsuret."*)

So the coronation durbar was held, a tragic spectacle for all who love the eternal *ma'at* and fitness of things in the Two Lands—and that is everyone, I think, except Their two Majesties, who care neither for *ma'at* nor for the feelings of their people.

Side by side they sat upon their thrones, King Smenkhkara at his brother's right hand where the Chief Wife should have been, no others of the Family anywhere about. Pinhasy put the crowns upon their heads and chanted the Hymn to Akhenaten as the embodied Aten. Smenkh-kara rose from his throne, stepped forward, turned, bowed low, offered sacrifice and formal worship to his brother. Akhenaten raised him up, kissed him, handed him gravely to his seat. A dutiful shout went up from the scanty crowd of court sycophants gathered before the King's House to witness this sad proceeding. A straggling little line of emissar-ies from abroad—Mittani, Naharin, Byblos, wretched Kush—all that cared, or could be commanded, now in these days when our possessions fall away from the slack hands of His Majesty—jostled one another by with meager gifts: this was the "Parade of Tribute." Akhenaten clapped his hands. Trumpets blew, a chariot race began, youths dutifully leaped into athletic contests, a forced air of gaiety covered all. Within the hour the games and envoys were gone, the two kings had withdrawn, the crowd had dispersed, the palace grounds were deserted. Ra moved on impervious through an empty sky, over an empty scene.

As quickly as possible, all was forgotten—until a week ago, when both Huy, the chief steward of Queen Tiye, and Meryra, the chief stew-ard of Queen Nefertiti, reached that point in the building of their tombs where they wished to pay tribute—which one still must do, of course, on fear of death—to His Majesty. Then arose the question of how they should best do this. To me, who am still consulted graciously though I give my advice from a bed I do not think I will leave alive—and to Tuthmose, who now actually carries out my suggestions and his own skilled ideas—they both proposed that they use the scene of the corona-tion durbar.

"As it was?" I questioned, startled that they should make such a choice.

"Without the Chief Wife and the Family?" echoed Tuthmose, equally aghast.

"His Majesty lives in truth," Huy said, a smug look on his face. "He will want it exactly as it was."

"If we, too, are to live in truth as he wishes all men to do," remarked Meryra with similar superiority, "then you must portray it as it hap-pened."

"I would suggest," I remarked, I am afraid quite dryly, "that you consult your mistresses and see what they advise."

"They need not know," Huy said, though here in Akhet-Aten, where the tombs along the northern and southern ridges bounding the city are open to public view at all times, nothing is concealed.

"I would rather risk their anger at being told than risk their anger if things are hidden from them," I said with sufficient severity to stop their

flippant attitude and sober their smug faces. When they spoke to the
Great Wife and Nefertiti later that day, their carefree approach ended
altogether. And now we have the bitter controversy that flares within
the Palace and seems to have produced some sort of culmination in the
continuing crisis we have all lived with ever since Akhenaten sent his
wife to the North Palace and installed his brother in her stead.

In the cities and villages of Kemet, no one knows that this battle
rages. But it is not in the cities and villages, of course, that the fate of
Their Majesties will be decided. It is always from within the palaces
that changes come in the rule of Kemet, for the people have never
rebelled in all our nearly two thousand years of history. Even now,
ruled by the One who is increasingly, if still with great secrecy, called
"the Madman" and "the Criminal," they will not rebel. He is still the
Good God, and it is unthinkable to them that they might ever rise
against him.

Unhappily for him, such superstitious acceptance does not prevail
within the Family.

Yesterday the orders came down, almost simultaneously, from his
palace, from Queen Tiye's and from Queen Nefertiti's, to poor unfortunate Huy and Meryra. It will be quite a while, I think, before they find
life a subject for smug jesting again.

His Majesty commanded: portray the coronation durbar exactly as it
was, himself and his brother alone (fondly entwined!) the paltry "Parade of Tribute" straggling by.

The Great Wife and the Chief Wife commanded: portray the coronation durbar as the eternal traditions and *ma'at* of Kemet dictate, as it
has always been throughout our history—Nefertiti seated beside Akhenaten, their daughters (even those who are dead, for this is royal
myth, not royal fact) around them, a lavish and fawning Parade of
Tribute maintaining the dignity of the Double Crown—not exactly
truthful, of course, but as truthful as most of the pictures of royal triumphs that have come down to us from ancient days.

Now the battle rages. I do not care what the outcome is, for I am
now, ironically, in a position where I am privileged to watch—a privilege I would gladly yield were it possible, but one which I do not think
the gods will permit me to evade. Tuthmose is a little more in the center
of things, but he too is safe. We exist to carry out orders, not give
them. There is much stirring in the palaces. Horemheb and his chief
aide General Ramesses have hurried back from Memphis, where they
had gone to attend to the government's business in the Delta. Aye and
his sister, Queen Tiye, have come down from Thebes. Amonhotep, Son
of Hapu, that sainted scribe whose wisdom becomes more universally

respected as he learns to express it less, is bustling about. Tuthmose is keeping me informed. I feel the wind, though I am no longer able to be at the center of the storm. And storm it is, I am afraid, for His Majesty.

I fear for him and weep for him, because I think in his own strange way he has always meant to do right, and to live in truth. It is his tragedy that his truth is unlike the truth of any other. In that, I think, His Majesty has found the seeds of his downfall, at last.

Amonemhet

I am Amon-em-het the peasant, and you will remember how I saw His Majesty with the Prince Smenkhkara—whom we must now call "His Majesty," too—sailing downriver to Akhet-Aten from Thebes, golden in the torchlight against the dark bosom of Hapi, god of the Nile, chanting His Majesty's Hymn to his god the Aten, on that night three years ago when my wife and I frolicked too much and wound up with child number three. Not that I mind him, or the method of his getting, which is always pleasant any time, but he does have to be fed, of course, and that poses a problem. But we love children, and we manage. Number four will be here in another two weeks. Then, I suppose, will come five, six, seven, eight—may the gods stop us!

Ho, *ho!* Let them try!

Anyway, I told you on that night when I saw His Majesty that it did not matter much to us here in the village what happens in the great cities among the great men. But in this I think I spoke too easily and too fast, because it has come to matter much in these last three years.

It used to be that we would hear distant reports that all was not going well in Kemet. Before His Majesty's father died—Amonhotep III (life, health, prosperity!), that good man who governed us so well and looks better all the time compared to what we have now—we used to hear rumors, sometimes, about troubles in far-off places. It was said our allies, or countries we owned, or were friendly with, were not friendly any more. But this did not bother us in the village. It was all far away.

It was also reported—particularly by old Sahura, he who once was a scribe and went to the cities before he came home to sit in the square all day and demand that we listen to his old man's warnings of disaster —that there was trouble in the whole government. He said order was breaking down, *ma'at* was being violated, bad times were coming to the Two Lands because of the Pharaoh Akhenaten. And even though we did notice that the priests of Amon were worried and seemed not quite so powerful, and occasionally a tax collector tried to take more than what seemed to us to be our fair share of taxes (the last such wound up that night in the bosom of Hapi and nevermore was seen again, may the Forty-two Judges of the Dead keep him drowning forever in the jaws of Sebek the crocodile god!), still it all seemed far away and not much of our concern.

But now that His Majesty Akhenaten is King, with His Majesty Smenkhkara beside him on the throne (and somewhere else, too, so everyone says), I have to admit it: there is real trouble in Kemet. It is not far away now, it is in the village. Now it concerns us because it is in our own place. Now we must pay attention—although there is not much that we can do about it now, of course: it has gone too far. It has got away from us almost before we knew it was happening. And of course we are only ignorant peasants who must obey the will of His Majesty in all things, as has ever been the way of the Two Lands.

But, I tell you! Now we have tax collectors who come, not in ones or twos who can be killed or cheated, but in gangs and bands who rove through the village and demand great sums and call in soldiers to help them destroy our dikes and fields if we will not pay. Who gets these sums we do not know, but we do not think they can go to His Majesty, or that His Majesty knows of this, for surely he would not permit it, being just and good and a father to us as Pharaoh has always been. But somebody gets this money. Somebody sends the thieves and the soldiers. Who is it? Who is to protect us?

And now we do not see priests of Amon any more, who also used to take taxes from us, but who gave us in return food and shelter when we needed it, and helped us from their granaries if we got a low Nile and the Inundation did not flood our fields properly with water and new soil. Now the priests of Amon are all in hiding, and the new priests of the Aten lord it over us. They too take our money and seize our crops and even take our children away to place them in the service of the Aten, who is His Majesty's god and not ours, and whom nobody in the village wants. Is this done at His Majesty's command? We do not believe it. But somebody commands it, for it is done. And whom can we look to for salvation from these crimes? It should be the duty of His Majesty to protect us, but he does not. What are we to do?

Now we talk, all up and down the river, from village to village in the ancient way that carries the news of Kemet swiftly from the Fourth Cataract to the Delta. Now we are all aware of what is happening, because it is causing trouble for us, and for our wives and children. We did not pay attention when His Majesty was Co-Regent with his father, because we knew his father and the Great Wife still had some power in Kemet to see that we were well governed, which is Pharaoh's charge. We knew they were trying to look out for us.

We could ignore his god the Aten, which we did, because Amon and the other gods we have always worshiped were permitted to continue much as they had always done. Now all has changed.

Now it is known to us that His Majesty is not interested in keeping the faraway lands that brought wealth to Kemet and helped us all. He is not interested in caring for his people when they go hungry and need assistance. He is not interested in maintaining *ma'at* and the eternal order of Kemet which has always given us a contented life along the Nile, in good years and lean. He is not interested in protecting us, as the Good God should.

He is interested in three things only:

His god the Aten.

His brother the King Smenkhkara.

And himself.

We would never do anything to harm His Majesty, for he is the Living Horus, Son of the Sun, King of the Two Lands, Good God and Pharoah, and we are his people, as has ever been the way in Kemet. But we no longer believe in him, nor do we love him any more, since he does not love us. And we think—nay, I will go further since I am saying my thoughts secretly and in private, and say *we hope*—that this will weaken him enough so that someone *can* do something to save us from him.

Save us, his own people, from Pharaoh!

How sad that it should come to that! How sad for Pharaoh, and for us, who wanted only to love him had he but kept his trust with us and made it possible for us to do so.

Now from the Fourth Cataract to the Delta we know this is not to be. And this is sad and frightening for Kemet, because we do not know what will happen to us, and in the village we all go fearful and uneasy because of it, and even in the midst of frolicking with my wife I find I cannot stop thinking of it, which makes me pause so that she cries out angrily and blames me for being a weakling and no man, when it is really His Majesty she should blame.

Kia

Poor Naphuria—whom I still call that, as we do in my native Mesopotamia, because in ten years as his second wife we have never been
close enough so that I could comfortably call him Akhenaten.

Poor Naphuria, who thrashes about in the grip of his futile love and
his unloved god and wonders why the Two Lands slip away from him!

Or does he wonder? Sometimes I think he cares not at all, so
recklessly does he conduct himself, with so harsh and contemptuous a
disregard for the traditional ways of Kemet. They were not my ways
when I came here, and it has taken me awhile to understand them, but I
have learned that they are good for Kemet. They have kept this ancient
land in relative peace and stability for almost two thousand years, saving only the invasion of the Hyksos and a few weak kings here and
there, and two millennia is not such a mean record for a country. I
know, in fact, of no other like it. But such a heritage apparently means
nothing at all to him.

Nefertiti and I have been living in the North Palace ever since our return from Thebes after the funeral of the old Pharaoh three years ago. I
did not have to go: Akhenaten did not banish me from his side because
I have never really been there. But I thought it best to go with her
whose strength and courage I have always admired. There was nothing
for me in the palace of men.

We have with us brave little Tut, no longer the happy child he used
to be. The intimations of the adult world have turned him old before his
time, and the knowledge that he may be called upon at any moment to
replace his brother weighs heavily upon him. I think he still loves and
stands in awe of his brother—of both brothers, in fact—and the
thought that he may be used to do them violence troubles and shadows
what was once a sunny personality. No one has ever said, or indicated
openly, that violence is what may be done: but it is implicit. Implicit in
the air, and implicit, let us be honest about it, in the situation.

Thus does the corruption of the Aten, confused and confounded yet
more by the unhealthy love of the brothers, spread and poison the happiness of the Family, as it spreads and poisons the happiness of the
land.

Yet I do not think Tut sees it in these terms, being still a child, nor does the Chief Wife, nor her three daughters who also live with us. To Nefertiti particularly, whose powerful personality influences all of us who live closely with her, the Aten remains, I think, the perfect ideal to which she would like to see all Kemet aspire. She has never wavered in her faith in the Sole God, and she still, I think, loves the Sole God's prophet. The habit of love, ingrained in them both by their parents from earliest childhood, remains unbroken in her in spite of all. As it does in him, I think, because he has made no move to "disgrace" her as those who fall from favor in Kemet can be disgraced—by the destruction of her portraits and cartouches everywhere in the land, the smashing of her statues, the abolition of her name, and thus of her very *ka* and *ba,* the soul and essence of her being. (Only one cartouche, on a "sun-shade" on the Nile that he has given to Merytaten, has actually been replaced, of all her thousands.) Nor has she "disappeared," except that she now occupies a separate residence and is no longer portrayed officially as being at his side.

It is true that he has given his brother one of her names, Neferu-neferu-aten, "Fair is the Goodness of the Aten," has conferred on him the titulary "Beloved of Akhenaten," and has had the two of them portrayed together in poses more than brotherly. But she lives on, unmolested and well maintained, in the North Palace scarce three miles from his. Sometimes they even see one another when they proceed in their separate chariots to the Great Temple of the Aten to do worship, though both make every attempt to assure that their visits will not coincide. When they do, no glance is exchanged, no word is spoken. All fall silent and, oblations done as swiftly as is decent, they hastily remount and speed away to their separate palaces. But, for a wife the gossips of Kemet would have you believe is "disgraced," Nefertiti manages to live on very well.

Such, it seems to me, is token enough that somewhere in the strange world to which he has gone from us the Good God retains some sense of sanity and balance, at least on that particular subject; and also, I believe some memory of love, if not its actual being, which will not permit him to be fatally harsh to her.

Partly because of this, but more, I believe, because she truly believes in the concept of one universal god, the Chief Wife remains true to the Aten. And so all of us in her household remain true to it too: Tut-ankhaten, who himself may yet rule in the name of the Aten; healthy and determined Ankh-e-sen-pa-aten, who will become his Queen; sickly Nefer-neferu-aten Junior and sickly Nefer-neferu-ra, both of whom give promise of soon following into the afterworld the sixth little sister,

Set-e-pen-ra, who withered and died, like a lotus taken from the river's edge and planted in the open desert, scarce six months after the move to the North Palace.

The oldest princess, tough and ambitious little Merytaten, Queen of her uncle Smenkhkara, now lords it over the King's House in the stead of her mother, whom she apparently despises, for no kind word to the Chief Wife ever comes from her. She seems content with her lot, even though her marriage is known in the palaces to be simply form without substance. I believe she has no desire to have children, and indeed cannot, since she was injured in the delivery of her father's daughter, Merytaten Junior, another feeble infant who perished several years ago after an uncomfortable and mercifully short existence. (Why is it that Akhenaten can beget only girls, most of them sickly? Is it some punishment of Amon, perhaps, who has never forgiven him and bides only the time when his priests can reclaim their power?)

To Merytaten, being the only Queen at the side of the two Pharaohs is evidently quite enough. She supervises her father's household, attends him at ceremonies, travels with Smenkhkara on his frequent visits to Thebes. He has returned to the compound of Malkata and established a palace there, which he occupies quite frequently, almost as if he considered this some form of appeasement of Amon—though he rarely goes near the deserted temples at Karnak and Luxor, and always hurries back to his brother to make public show of his devotion to the Aten. To me this seems very typical of Smenkhkara, who remains a charming, golden man as he was a charming, golden youth, but who seems to suffer from some inherent weakness that keeps him always indecisive and seeming to hang between two divergent paths of action. Perhaps this accounts for his relationship with his brother. Weakness usually seeks strength, but in a certain kind of mentality weakness seeks weakness.

Yet perhaps in this I am being unfair to Akhenaten, because I do not think "weakness" is exactly the right word for him. Certainly one who has had the character to defy the awesome weight of the ancient gods and traditions of two thousand years, who has finally declared and conducted open battle against Amon, the most powerful of them all, who has dared to "live in truth" in ways that are shocking and affronting to his people, who has defied the powerful members of his own family who oppose his policies, who has deliberately placed himself beyond the reach and understanding of ordinary men, even more than the god-kings of the Nile *are* beyond the understanding of ordinary men—such a one is not exactly "weak." He has a powerful personality and a powerful will, my husband, poor Naphuria; and it is only in the fact that the word "poor" comes automatically to my mind, and to that of many others, when we think of him, that there is indication of how weak, in the most fundamental sense, he is.

He is weak in that he *is* beyond the understanding of mankind. He is weak in that he no longer has a foot on the common ground, he is no longer in touch with reality as it is perceived by most who tread the earth. He has moved ever more steadily into a world of his own, a world unique to him alone—an insane world, if you like. Not even poor Smenkhkara, I suspect, can truly follow poor Naphuria where he goes.

We wonder, in the North Palace and at Malkata—where the Great Wife still prefers to live, though she comes often here to see her sons (and always, with complete impartiality and lack of fear, sees Nefertiti and the rest of us, as well)—what Smenkhkara makes of all this and what he feels about the strange things Naphuria does. Does he bear the name, title, and aspect of wife to his brother willingly? Does he approve when Naphuria orders Bek and Tuthmose to make Naphuria steadily younger and more beautiful in his statues, abandoning that "living in truth" that touched his earlier portraitures with near grotesquerie, so that he may try to match (pathetically, we all think) the gifts nature has conferred on Smenkhkara? Does Smenkhkara approve of the stelae and statues that show the two of them in intimate and candid embrace? Does Smenkhkara ever wonder whether he, too, is leaving sanity to live in his brother's world? Or is he content to bask in the favor of the Good God, accept his gifts along with his attentions, and appear unabashed and unashamed in a relationship that most would accept were it kept private, but which none in tradition-bound Kemet can accept when it is flaunted before them officially by Pharaoh? And does he truly believe in the Aten, or is that, too, just a convenience to help him stay where he is?

These are questions that are now suddenly inescapable as the Family gathers to do battle over the paintings of the coronation durbar in the tombs of Huy and Meryra. Normally you would not think two paintings on two stone walls would cause such furor, but you must understand that in Kemet things that are pictured *are*. They *exist* because they are painted, and they exist *only* as they are painted—and they exist, you must remember, not just for a year or two but for all eternity in this preserving desert air. Therefore it is considered very important, in the Family, how things are portrayed, because this becomes the official history that will go down forever to those who come after. It is no wonder they are concerned about the tombs of Huy and Meryra, for in them the story will be told for all time—*not necessarily as it was, but as the Dynasty wishes it to be.*

So, the battle of the durbar, which has brought them all to Akhet-

Aten. Queen Tiye is the last to arrive, her state barge having docked shortly after noon today. We understand she went directly to her own small palace. Already she has sent word that she, Aye and Horemheb will visit us in the North Palace this evening, "before we see Their Majesties." This means the three who must ultimately decide the Family's position wish to take counsel with the Chief Wife, and possibly me as well, before they act. It is flattering and it is also dangerous, for it may well invite the open wrath of Akhenaten, whose temper is becoming steadily more erratic and unpredictable. But we are not afraid. When we received the messenger, Nefertiti merely read the Great Wife's words aloud to me and then turned to the waiting servant and said quietly:

"Tell the Great Wife that Her Majesty Kia and I will be most happy to receive her, the Councilor, and General Horemheb at the evening hour that suits them."

Then when he had swiftly gone she turned to me with a slight smile and a level glance from those steady, beautiful eyes, now filled with so much sadness, and said, with a trace of wistfulness in her voice:

"Poor Naphuria, as you would say. Once again he flirts with fate and invites the wrath of the Family. We must try to give our judgments fairly."

"Yes Majesty," I agreed. "I believe we can do so."

"I, too, believe it," she said, "though, once again, it will not be a happy time." Her eyes widened in thought and almost to herself she added, *"Why does he always persist in making life so hard for himself?"*

This I could not answer; although in fairness it must be said that on this occasion the responsibility is equal. It is Naphuria who wishes to tell the unadorned truth about the pathetic little coronation durbar. It is the Chief Wife and the Great Wife and the rest of the Family who want to tell the official lie.

It is, as usual, a head-on clash of opposites such as he always seems to invite. Poor Naphuria, indeed—and poor Smenkhkara, too; because this time, I think, the results may be very serious. The confrontation that is coming has been building for three years. It could have come over almost anything but, rather absurdly to me who am still, and will always be, essentially an outsider, it has come over something as seemingly trivial as two paintings in a couple of tombs.

The feeling must have been growing in the Family for some time that a turning point would have to come. Nefertiti and the Great Wife have deliberately helped to precipitate it by their orders to Huy and Meryra. They could only have done so, I believe, at the direct suggestion of Aye and Horemheb. Naphuria's order came first—that made him vulnerable. The decision seems to be that now is the time to make use of this.

Poor Naphuria and poor Smenkhkara! I do not like either one, particularly, but as a disinterested party I do not enjoy seeing them so willfully rush headlong into what may prove to be great disaster for them, for Kemet, and for us all.

Smenkhkara (Life, health, prosperity!)

I wonder what is happening here. My mother landed at noon today, and already, so my brother and I are told, she has notified Nefertiti that she, Aye and Horemheb will visit the North Palace this evening before they see my brother and me. I do not understand it. Simple courtesy would dictate a call upon the Sons of the Sun before seeing a castoff wife (two, for Kia of course has chosen, in her spiteful way, to go with her) whose only purpose must be harm to us.

Perhaps the purpose of my mother, my uncle and my cousin is also harm to us. If so, we are ready for it. It does not frighten us. We are strong together and we will defy them. Not all their spiteful plottings will drive Akhenaten and me from the path of love and glory for the Aten to which we have decided ourselves. We defy them.

I have been Co-Regent for three years now, and have been many times in Thebes, never failing to visit the Great Wife dutifully on each occasion. At times she has tried to argue with me, as mothers will, but I have not paid much attention. I have turned it all aside with a laugh and a joke, as I long ago learned to turn aside everything hurtful and unpleasant. Or did I have to "learn" this? As far as I can remember, it has always been my nature, save for the occasion when my brother and I first became one, many years ago. Then for a few days I did feel a terrible remorse and sadness, a terrible regret for what I seemed to be "doing" to my cousin Nefertiti and to my mother. Soon, however, my brother convinced me that whatever was being done, *they* were doing, since they were attempting to interfere with a union ordained by the Aten and intended only to strengthen my brother so that he might better conduct the Aten's worship and better carry his faith to the people. Since that time I have never worried, regretted or looked back. And I do not intend to now, whatever they may be plotting in the North Palace.

On my visits to Thebes I have now and then investigated the temples of Amon at Luxor and Karnak. The few remaining priests there, those gaunt-eyed, starving ones who scuttle about the silent corridors and peek out at me from behind deserted columns as I pass, obviously think my brother has sent me there to spy upon them. And so he has, and why should he not? They spy on us all the time, those few who are left openly, and those many who hide among the people and make their futile plans to overthrow us. We still have not caught Hatsuret, though our spies report him here, there, and everywhere from Karoy to Memphis and back. The people secrete him among themselves and not all my brother's threats of vengeance serve to bring him out. But he only plots: he does not put plots into effect. We can suffer that, as long as he does not receive help from those who are closer to us.

This may now be about to happen, though I would prefer it not, for it will only mean great danger, and perhaps death, for my mother, for Nefertiti, for Aye and Horemheb. We cannot suffer *them* to plot against us, breeding treachery in the Two Lands, the army, even in the palaces. That would violate the very *ma'at* of Kemet, because an attack upon the Sons of the Sun is an attack upon the soul of the land itself. My brother and I are the guardians of that soul: indeed we *are* that soul, as Pharaoh has always been. Were the hands of the Great Wife, my uncle, my cousin and the Chief Wife to be lifted against us, then, surely, would the people rise in our behalf. And sad would be the fate of the Family.

I do not want this to happen and I do not believe Akhenaten does either. Therefore we must hope, very desperately, that good sense will prevail and keep them from this folly. Anything else would be sad— very sad, because we would have to take vengeance, and we would not hesitate. And the people, rallying to our cause, would make their names anathema in Kemet forever and ever, for millions and millions of years.

I know Akhenaten has wished Merytaten to convey this warning to the Chief Wife before it is too late, but I do not believe she obeys her father. She told me with a sniff, "Why should I go out of my way to see *her?* I am the mistress of the Great House and the King's Palace. Let her come to me, if she wishes to be warned!"

That is one of the many reasons why I do not like Merytaten, who is my niece and my wife and who despises me just about as much, I think, as I despise her. We have never been close, there has always been a prickly truce between us. The way she treats her mother has always appalled me: she positively preens herself upon the way she now lords it over her. As far as I know, she has never gone near her since Akhenaten sent Nefertiti to the North Palace three years ago. And on the one occasion, a year ago, when Nefertiti finally found sufficient forgiveness in her heart to attempt a reconciliation, Merytaten dashed the basket of fruit and gifts from the hands of Nefertiti's messenger and drove him out of the Palace, shrieking threats and imprecations against her mother which the terrified fellow had to promise he would swiftly carry back.

Two minutes later, of course, Merytaten had gathered together all the gifts—some of them quite ornate, including two golden pectorals and a lapis lazuli scarab bracelet from Nefertiti's own private collection—and was sitting on the floor placidly eating one of the pomegranates she had sent, spitting out the seeds in all directions and humming a satisfied little song to herself.

"Why are you so cruel to her?" I could not help blurting out. "She has done you no harm."

"She does me harm just by living," she said in a flippant tone. To which I could not resist:

"I think she did us all harm by giving *you* life."

Thereupon, of course, she screamed and shrieked at *me*, casting various aspersions upon my character and manhood which I chose to suffer in patient silence, as there were servants about in the outer hall and I have some respect for the dignity of the Double Crown, if she does not. She did not quite dare go so far as to attack what makes her most jealous, namely the perfect understanding that exists between her father and me, but she made enough unpleasant insinuations so that I am sure the servants had another good gossip that day, as they often do at our expense. This is largely because of her, however: Akhenaten and I of course make no secret of our union, because we live in truth, but we conduct ourselves with dignity as Father Aten wishes us to do. It is only Merytaten who lowers the aspect of everything.

I have suggested upon occasion to my brother that he discipline her for this, but he seems curiously listless about her effronteries as he does about so many things these days. I think he is not in very good health; his energies seem to be declining; the strain of maintaining the cause of the Aten against the growing opposition of the Family, the still virulent hatred of the dispossessed priests of Amon, and the general apathy (if not outright hostility) of the people toward the Sole God have inevitably begun to take their toll.

Lately there has been added to this a growing arthritis that attacks and weakens his always vulnerable frame. As if defying it, he has asked Bek and Tuthmose to portray him in a fashion ever younger and more handsome in their sculptures, stelae and paintings. I do not know really why he has done this, unless it is to impress the people, who now see him no longer save here in Akhet-Aten, and even here on increasingly fewer occasions. I asked him once why he, who has always prided himself on living in truth, should now be engaged in a deliberate lie about his appearance. He looked at me in the strangest, most stricken way, and asked, in the emotional croak his voice becomes in moments of tension, "You mean you do not know?"

"No," I said, I am afraid in a somewhat offhand manner. "You are always handsome to me."

He cried out, some harsh, inarticulate sound: his eyes filled abruptly with tears. Apparently I had hurt him deeply in some way I have never been able to understand, no matter how many times I have gone back over it. After a moment he composed himself, clearly with great effort, and reached out a hand to comfort me, because his stricken countenance had of course turned mine stricken too.

"It does not matter," he said then. "It does not matter."

And he refused to discuss it with me, ever again. But his physical glorification in the sculptures continues, so that if one were to see only the portraits of these later years in Akhet-Aten one would believe he had always been as handsome and as virile as any other Pharaoh.

Apparently, as I say, he does it to impress the people, since he goes no longer among them very much. He has not left this city since we returned here after our father's entombment in Thebes, and even here his appearances are becoming more and more infrequent. Occasionally still he will worship the Aten in the Great Temple, occasionally he will still dispense gifts from the Window of Appearances, now and again he will still visit the ledge along the Northern Tombs from which one gets such a commanding view of the city and the plain (and where so many significant things, including our own understanding, have happened, over the years). But all of this is becoming steadily rarer. Increasingly he worships in his private chapel in the King's Palace; it has been six months since he held a ceremony at the Window of Appearances; even longer, I think, since he ventured to the Northern Tombs. And to Memphis, our northern capital in the Delta, and to Thebes, he ventures, in these recent years, not at all.

He has become increasingly what I overheard our cousin Horemheb remark to his faithful shadow Ramesses one day—"the Prisoner of Akhet-Aten."

(I let them see that I heard it, and did not like it, but our cousin Horemheb did not look impressed by my annoyance, and Ramesses, not knowing which of us to fear the most, only gave me a sickly smile as I brushed past with a deliberately imperious air. They are always huddling together, those two, planning I know not what: though

Horemheb continues faithfully to execute my brother's orders against the priesthoods, and Ramesses apes him dutifully in that as in all else.)

"The Prisoner of Akhet-Aten"—and therefore, of course, my own frequent travels. "I want you to be my eyes and ears," he said soon after we established our joint household in the South Palace with Merytaten three years ago. I did not know then that he intended to isolate himself—or rather, perhaps, that the Aten would further cripple his already crippled form, perhaps so that he could concentrate more upon the Aten's worship without the distractions of travel. I knew only that he wished me to do this to assist him. In the same loving spirit in which I have always assisted all his enterprises, I of course said I would.

My first move was to return to Thebes and secure my mother's permission to construct a small palace for myself and Merytaten—who, insufferable as she is, is still Pharaoh's daughter and my Queen, and has her birthright of official honors—within the compound of Malkata. I then began the regular round of travels which takes me three times a year to Thebes and three times a year to Memphis. Thus am I able to supervise those activities of government with which he has entrusted me, and to act truly as his Co-Regent and helper in ruling the Two Lands.

I think I do these things very well. And I also am able to fulfill some of the public ceremonial demands that he no longer cares, or perhaps is unable, to perform. I always take his latest statue with me and place it, in full regalia, beside me on the platform: and I suspect that in the minds of our younger people, and among the elder who have not seen him in many years, and whose memory grows hazy with time, there is a gradual replacement, by this handsome and sturdy figure, of the awkward, misshapen, shuffling reality that once was known everywhere in Kemet. Thus do I assist him in that aim of his also.

I really do think I conduct the government very well for my brother. And although at first I was made somewhat hesitant and confused by the foreign policy, for instance, conducted by our Foreign Minister, Tutu, I think I have come to understand it quite sufficiently. It consists of trying to maintain those alliances we still have in the far north toward Mittani and Naharin. Tutu gives me copies of the dispatches that come in from there. I read them and report on them to Akhenaten. We discuss them from time to time and I report back to Tutu his instructions: keep trying to warn off our enemies and keep trying to satisfy our friends, who always clamor for gold and also, of late, beg us to send troops to protect them from their neighbors.

This last I am unable to have Tutu promise, because my brother does not have the inclination or now, perhaps, the strength, to make the

show of force that held our possessions secure in the days of our fore-
bears, beginning with our great-great-grandfather, Tuthmose III (life,
health, prosperity!) and lasting down through our grandfather, Tuthmose IV (life, health, prosperity!). Our father abandoned this practice
in his later years, and now it seems almost too late, in some areas, to
revive it. I might enjoy, myself, going on expeditions to distant lands to
re-establish their awe of Kemet and the holders of the Double Crown
but, without my brother's agreement and active support, I cannot do it
by myself. And he does not seem to desire this. Again, energy flags and,
with it, the will to do in time what might save us much trouble later.

But I do not worry overmuch about this, because all my life I have
worshiped my brother and have believed that what he decided about
things was right. He believes that Kemet's wealth and strength should
be devoted to the worship of the Aten, to the establishment of the Sole
God, to the banishment of magic, misery and old, evil things from the
lives and minds of our people.

"If people everywhere," he has said to me often, "will but believe in
the Hymn and worship the Aten as I do, then the teachings of the Aten
will make them happier than they have ever been."

At first I was young and flippant, even with him, and asked:

"Has the Aten made you happy, then, Brother?"

He looked at me for a very long time and finally replied quietly, "In
my heart, I am happy."

And I never dared question him thus again.

And, in fact, I have never really wanted to, because I too have come
to believe in the Sole God, loving all men and all nations, who can
make us all happy. Certainly the Aten has made me happy, for he has
placed me at my brother's side and made me, too, Living Horus, Son of
the Sun, King and Pharaoh of the Two Lands: and I know there is no
higher happiness a god such as I could have.

I know this, as I know that it is only some passing melancholy now
that makes me worry about the gathering of the Family, about this ridiculous and unnecessary quarrel over the tombs of Huy and Merya—
which of course will be decided in truth, as Akhenaten and I desire it—
and about the uneasy feeling I have that my mother, my uncle Aye,
Nefertiti and our cousin Horemheb plan some unpleasantness for us if
we persist in the course Father Aten has told us to follow.

It is melancholy only, of that I am certain . . . though I could wish
this night were past us, and all decided happily for all of us, as we
desire.

Hatsuret

They do not know, the two besotted fools, how closely at hand wait the instruments of their destruction. They do not know that I am in Akhet-Aten, yea, even in the Great House itself. They do not know how well this is known to others, who also wait, and how secretly and subtly I am being helped to my tryst with them . . . for tryst I have, and all signs now point that it will not be long in coming.

When I was given assurance of my safety and was aided in my hiding by General Horemheb and the Councilor and Divine Father-in-law, Aye, I did not know at first the real meaning of their assistance— though I have been sure for ten years, since I first became an acolyte in the most holy ancient temple of Amon-Ra at Karnak, that eventually the Pharaoh Akhenaten would have to die for his sins against Amon and his betrayal of the *ma'at* of Kemet. When my brilliance and shrewdness took me up to become chief aide to doddering old Maya, Amon's High Priest, this conviction grew. When Akhenaten ordered Maya's murder and desecrated the temple on the day of the entombment of the Good God Amonhotep III (life, health prosperity!), I had no further doubts. Such monstrous evil as Pharaoh did that day can have only one final repayment, however long we must wait and plot to secure it. For never was there such a dreadful thing!

He ordered General Horemheb to batter down the doors. He ordered Maya and myself to be killed as we faced the soldiers and their battering rams, our arms outspread across the ancient planks. At the last second I leaped aside, to be spirited instantly away by many willing hands among the crowd. Maya, less nimble, died. Then Pharaoh directed the soldiers to seize the sacred statue of Amon-Ra, King of the Gods, and hurl it into the Nile, which they did, and called down eternal curses upon any who would seek to recover it. Of course a team of divers recruited by Horemheb recovered it that night, after Akhenaten and his brother the new King Smenkhkara had sailed downriver to Akhet-Aten; and it, too, is in hiding, safe until the day when Amon may rule again in his rightful place in the Two Lands.

Now I am in Pharoah's house itself, having been presented to His

Majesty six months ago by General Horemheb as a slave captured in some skirmish in Canaan. Horemheb had directed me to grow a beard, which is almost unheard of in clean-shaven Kemet, so this made me look foreign enough, and to that I added a reddish dye to my glossy black hair, and also affected a noticeable limp in my right leg, which served to disguise me further. Horemheb explained that my perfect tongue for the language was due to my actually being a native of Kemet whose family lived close to the border. I was kidnaped by a marauding band of Canaanites when I was twelve years old, he explained, and spent ten years in captivity before being retrieved. My leg, he said, had been deliberately broken by my brutal captors, and thus the limp.

His Majesty, who seems to pay so little attention any more to what is actually going on in the land of Kemet that he barely glanced at me, accepted all this without question. My very oddity was my safest disguise. The only break in his indifference came when Horemheb called attention to my limp. Then he asked me to walk up and down before him, which I did with an easy awkwardness, since I have practiced this handicap until I am now almost afraid that I shall not be able to walk normally again after His Majesty has been removed.

"Ah," His Majesty said, a genuine sympathy in his voice. "I, too, know what it means to limp. You are welcome to my household, Peneptah (for such is the false name I have taken). We shall limp about the Palace together, you and I, and keep each other company."

And he gave me for a moment a smile of quite extraordinary sweetness, which, did I not hate him so and were I not so dedicated to his death, might well have made me pause, ashamed by what we are doing to betray him. But even as I teetered for a dangerous second on the brink of this fatal precipice, he destroyed my mood by abruptly turning away.

"Where is Ankh-Kheperu-Ra?" he demanded in a high querulous voice, using King Smenkhkara's coronation name. "He was supposed to wait upon me half an hour ago, and still he does not come. Cousin, fetch him!"

"Yes, Son of the Sun," Horemheb said smoothly. "At once. It is all right, then, for Peneptah to be assigned to the ranks of your household scribes?"

"Take him to Amonhotep, Son of Hapu," he said impatiently. "Tell the old man to put him to work. We'll find something for him to do."

"Thank you, Majesty," I said, bowing low and feeling a great relief surge through me, for had he suspected anything I should have been dead upon the spot. But he turned his back upon me and shuffled away to a window where he could look out over the city, resting one clawlike hand against the wooden lintel, long bony fingers drumming insistently while he waited for his brother—a rasping, scratching, anxious sound in which all his uneasy yearning was expressed.

General Horemheb led me away before I could witness their touching reunion, which I am sure, now that I know them, came after a separation of no more than an hour at most. Since then I have seen them together many times. The younger King treats the elder with a deferential yet self-confident air, joshing, good-natured, patient and obviously deeply affectionate. The elder receives his confident deference with a gratitude so humble and self-effacing that it is almost embarrassing to see. It is but one more reason why the rule of Nefer-Kheperu-Ra must come to an end. It is the thing that will make its ending easier, perhaps, than we now think.

These past six months I have been working as a scribe with that wise old man, Amonhotep, Son of Hapu, probably the most honored of all the commoners of Kemet. Across the Nile from Thebes in the necropolis, his mortuary temple, given him by grateful Amonhotep III (life, health, prosperity!), has now been completed and is open for worship. He still, though in his sixties, supervises many of the architectural and public works. He continues to head the corps of scribes who assist Their two Majesties, and his opinion is almost always sought in the counsels of the Family.

"If Amonhotep, Son of Hapu, takes a liking to you," Horemheb told me, "all your plans will be greatly assisted." A fleeting smile touched his shrewd, sharp-featured face. "He has assisted mine, and I know. . . ."

But somehow I have never been quite able to establish such a relationship with the old man. He knows who I am, but he has never revealed it to anyone else by so much as a hint. He could betray me and have my head in an instant if he would, but he does not do so. I assume this means that he agrees with my purposes, but I can never be sure. Perhaps he wants it this way, because it means, of course, that I cannot move without his agreement. No more can I move without the agreement of Aye and Horemheb. Together these three, and possibly the Great Wife as well, whom they all consult, will decide the timing of my vengeance—and theirs.

I had been working for Amonhotep, Son of Hapu, two months when he discovered my secret. He caught me with the simplest of ruses. We were alone in the writing room, he at one side, I perhaps fifteen feet away. He lurched suddenly against a table, tipping it just sufficiently so that a pot of black ink began to slide toward a pile of pristine papyrus lying on the floor.

"Oh!" he cried in well-simulated anguish. "How stupid of me! *Catch it!*"

And instinctively, abandoning my carefully nurtured limp, I sprang to do his bidding.

"Thank you very much, Hatsuret," he said serenely when I had secured the ink and returned the table to its upright position. "I am getting *so* stupid in my old age."

But I would not say Amonhotep, Son of Hapu, is stupid at all.

Aside from an involuntary start at the sound of my name, which I could not suppress, I made no response. Nor have we ever discussed the matter. But Amonhotep, Son of Hapu, keeps a very close eye on me: I *think* for Aye and Horemheb, though he never reveals in the slightest where his sympathies lie. So I conduct myself with extreme care at all times, understanding that it is apparently my task to wait until I am needed, and that I will be told when that time is, and what to do when it comes upon us.

In the meantime I can only watch in anguish the desecration of the gods and the ruin of religion throughout the Two Lands. There are many among the palace servants who are still faithful to Amon, and very cautiously, little by little, I have let it be known to a few trusted ones who I am. Through them I am able to keep in touch with my principal priests in exile, and thus am I able to know most of the news of Kemet. So I know that from the Fourth Cataract to the Delta the temples of Amon lie in ruins, that the priesthood is dispersed and mostly in hiding as I am, that all the other principal gods, including Osiris whose rituals and customs for the dead His Majesty has abandoned, are in equal despair and desolation.

Never has there been such a great overturning of the gods as has happened under this Pharaoh, not even in the days of the Hyksos kings. Even they honored Amon-Ra and his fellow gods, even they associated the temples with their ruling. Not so the Heretic of Akhet-Aten, the Criminal, the Madman. Not so His pathetic Majesty, who shuffles about his palaces here as in a dream world, sacrificing to his false god the Aten, still trying to convince the people that one god can be so great and so all-embracing that he can know and respond to all the infinite needs of mankind, which is absurd on the face of it.

I serve discreetly, I listen, I observe. I see two foolish lovers trying to pretend that they are rulers of a great country. I see all, all, religion, civil government, Empire and all, falling away around them.

I see a man of thirty, so crippled in body and so discouraged in heart —for I believe he is greatly discouraged at last, though he still pretends he is not and tries to put a good face upon it—that he seems almost to have no energy left to rule.

I see a man of twenty, strong and vigorous and, yes, let me admit it, handsome, generous, kindly, and appealing, though of limited brain, wishing harm to no one, friendly to all—I see this amiable but inadequate man trying to administer the Two Lands for his listless brother.

Was there ever such a pair tried to lead a modern nation? And will it not be right and fitting in the eyes of Amon, and of all the gods, when their puny and pathetic charade is put at last to end?

So do I believe, and for that day I work. Now there is battle in the Family—they conceal it from the servants, who learn all things—over the tombs of Huy and Meryra. It would be a minor issue in any reign but this. Now, I think, it has suddenly become a symbol of everything, the issue on which the Living Horus may be brought to ground.

I am ready when they need me.

Hatsuret, who will yet be High Priest of Amon in the temple of Karnak when the great days return, is here.

Sitamon

My mother Queen Tiye invited me to go with her this time to Akhet-Aten, and I was bored in Thebes, so I came. But she has not invited me to accompany her to the North Palace tonight, so I can only speculate what is going to happen there. At first I was annoyed by this, but then I thought: One more family row, this one probably the most bitter we have ever had with my peculiar brother. I am probably well off out of it. I have had enough wrangling and disputation over the years. The last battle of wills can proceed without me. At thirty-eight the Queen-Princess Sitamon is beginning to reach an age where she is just as happy not to be involved in angry things. I shall hear the results soon enough.

Sometimes I look back on these three years since my father died and marvel at what has happened in the land of Kemet. Partly I suppose it began with him, who married me when I was very young in order to secure his own legitimacy to the throne (the Double Crown passing, as it does, through the female line, though I sometimes wonder what good that does us, who have no real right of our own to happiness but must always be subject to whoever marries us). He spent most of his life enjoying the luxuries our ancestors handed down to him and managed by his amiable ways to persuade the people that this was good government. Already Kemet looks back with heavy longing to the "golden age" of the Good God Amonhotep III (life, health, prosperity!). They call him "Amonhotep the Magnificent" now, forgetting how he lolled away the Empire and let civil government slip, beginning all the things my poor brother has carried grimly on to the point of near destruction. But in retrospect, as with most rulers whose people perceive their personal foibles and are so astounded to find them human that they gladly forgive them all their trespasses, he has emerged in an increasingly favorable light.

"We loved your father!" they shout at me when I pass in procession, adding commendation for him to the obvious love I can truly say they bear for me. I have never quite shouted back, "So did I!"—such informality does not become a royal princess and Queen to Pharaoh—but they can tell from my expression that our sentiments coincide. Their shouts of joy redouble and they always conclude by looking sad because he is gone forever and they cannot have him back.

Such unity with the people as our father had, Akhenaten has never achieved, except in the very early days when he first returned to public view after his ailment, and when he married Nefertiti. For a brief year or two they had such adoration as only my father and mother enjoyed, excepting one difference: my father and the Great Wife had it as long as he lived, and she has it still, whereas poor Akhenaten—and poor Nefertiti, whom I have come to feel dreadfully sorry for in these recent years—enjoyed the people's love for a fleeting moment and then lost it forever.

I suppose I have become so sympathetic toward my cousin Nefertiti because to some extent my situation parallels hers. You will remember that for many years I and he who turned out to be my cousin Horemheb have been lovers. I helped him keep this secret, bore him three children whom I had to dispose of, since I was married to my father (in name only, but nonetheless irrevocably) and it was thus impossible for us to acknowledge one another openly, however open our secret eventually became in the Court and, I suppose, in the Two Lands. Then Horemheb ("Kaires," as we knew him then) declared himself to be Horemheb, son of my uncle Aye; my father died; and I assumed—naïve girl that I was at thirty-five!—that all was now clear for us to announce our love and be married by my brother, who gave me his blessing after enjoying the pleasure of frightening me for a moment with possible refusal. But when I took the glad news back to Horemheb it was suddenly no longer as simple as it had always seemed. Horemheb, I began to perceive, had other plans.

He was, I found, not so eager as I to rush into marriage. He was not, in fact, eager to rush into it at all. He preferred, he said, to keep "our loving relationship," as he called it, exactly where it was—officially secret, officially unacknowledged, officially no restriction upon *him* at all. He told me this was necessary because his duties as general and chief scribe of the army took him too often from home. These journeys had never interfered with us before, and I could not see why they should now. But he was adamant, and although I perhaps could have tried to insist, we both knew it would probably not succeed. It would require my brother's full support, and Horemheb and I both know I do not have it; and Horemheb would have to be much lower than my brother has raised him for my brother's command to be effective. Above all, my brother would have to be a much different and more powerful Pharaoh than he is. He would have to be more like Horemheb.

In fact, I said almost as much the other day and apparently hit closer to the mark than Horemheb found comfortable.

"You treat me as though you were some Pharaoh!" I shot out angrily in the midst of our most recent quarrel on the subject. For a second he looked at me with complete and almost ludicrous dismay: he actually turned pale. He grasped my arm so tightly that it hurt, which is what he meant it to do. I cannot be quite so melodramatic as to say he hissed at me, but it was certainly a furtive and emphatic sound.

"Don't you ever say that again!" he ordered in a savage whisper. *"Don't you* ever *say that again!"*

I gave him stare for stare, since I am daughter and wife of a Pharaoh, but I must admit that for a moment I was genuinely frightened by the enormous suppressed anger in his voice. I have been his wife in all but name for almost fifteen years, borne him three children—and now I no longer think I even really know him.

Except that I know one thing now, after that exchange.

He wants to be Pharaoh and fully intends to be, if he can.

Somewhere down the years we have lost Horemheb, too—bright, cheerful, willing "Kaires" who came mysteriously and unexpectedly to the Palace of Malkata and charmed us all with his enthusiasm, diligence and idealism. He loved Kemet then, and I think he loves her now; but down the years he has also become enamored of power. I think he thinks he wants it only that he may better serve Kemet. And perhaps this is true: but, men being men, perhaps it is not, entirely.

Power for its own sake is enormously attractive, particularly when, as is the case with my headstrong brother, it is being so sadly misused by those who have it.

In any case, the quarrel did not advance the cause of our marriage, for which I have now almost abandoned hope. If he will not marry me, he will not, and there is little I can do about it. He talks vaguely of marriage "later, when it is more fitting." But when is "later," and when will it be "more fitting"? In the meantime, he says firmly, we will continue as we are. Unfortunately this, too, I will accept, because I suffer from the same disease as Nefertiti: I love him, as she still loves my poor, misguided brother, against all fitness, logic and common sense about what is best for *us,* not them.

There was a time long ago when I rather made fun of my perfect cousin Nefertiti, always so steady, so cool, so icy calm and self-contained in the face of all adversity. No hair was out of place on that beautiful head, no trace of consternation ever creased that perfect brow. Each eyelash was in perfect order above those lovely, contemplative eyes. Nothing seemed to disturb the serenity of the remote and impregnable fortress of her being. But I learned, in time, that a woman as vulnerable as any lived inside the fortress, and I came to admire her for the great dignity with which she conducts herself in the very difficult situation in which she lives now.

My brother is in his special world, my younger brother has followed him there, and now only the youngest of all, solemn little Tut, stands between the House of Thebes and extinction. Tut—and, of course, my mother the Great Wife, my uncle Aye, and my cousin Horemheb. But Tut carries the blood of Ra in direct line, and he it is who will rule next . . . if, as now seems steadily more possible, some move is made to remove our two brothers from the throne.

I feel sorry for Smenkhkara, who goes smiling and amiable through the world like our father, but without our father's genius for abiding by the eternal order and *ma'at* of Kemet. Our father also had Queen Tiye, of course, and Smenkhkara has only sour little Merytaten, who tries to lord it over us all and pretend that she is a greater Queen than any of us. This is nonsense, and I hope the gods will render her suitable justice when the time comes. Why Akhenaten permits it I do not know, unless it be some lingering feeling that it looks more fitting to have a woman in the King's House. He does not seem to feel the necessity in other respects, but it may be he wants her there for ceremonial reasons. And in her waspish little way she does have a good head for household management. Par-en-nefer, the major-domo, is a careless old man behind whose back all sorts of thieving and cheating goes on among the servants, particularly in the purchase and distribution of foodstuffs for the palaces. I do not know how much is spirited away to the servants' families every day, but it must be an enormous amount. At least Mery-taten tries to keep that under control. Her nagging voice is often raised to Par-en-nefer, and he can then be seen bustling busily and angrily away, protesting as he goes that he will "set all to rights—set all to rights!" These reforms last a day or two and the pilfering begins again. I do not envy my niece her task, though this is the only sympathy I can find in my heart for her pinched and spiteful personality.

So Smenkhkara has no one to help him keep his balance in a situation in which I do not think he has ever really wanted to preserve it anyway. I think he has been quite content from the beginning, being lazy and easygoing and also adoring his older brother, who did not hesitate to take advantage of this. Now they pretend to rule the country, though actually it is the Great Wife, our uncle Aye and Horemheb who carry out the orders, and indeed originate them, half the time.

Were I Akhenaten I should be disturbed by this, but as nearly as he shows us, he does not appear to be. He drifts along: Smenkhkara drifts along: the Two Lands drift along. Smenkhkara makes some pretense of running things, makes his trips to Thebes and Memphis, issues proclamations and decrees in Akhenaten's name, prides himself on being, as he confided to me recently, "our brother's eyes and ears." Real power resides where it has resided for many years, with my mother, my uncle and, lately, Horemheb.

They do not quite dare challenge Akhenaten openly, for he is after all the Living Horus, Son of the Sun, King and Pharaoh of the Two Lands. By adoption, as it were, Smenkhkara has comparable, if somewhat lesser, stature. It takes much—very much—for anyone to openly challenge Pharaoh. It has been done, in our history, but only after the most grievous and long-continuing provocations. And it has not been done until those who did it were sure they could win. The vengeance of Pharaoh, even such a generally peaceable one as my brother, does not fall lightly on those who fail in such a revolutionary and awesome attempt.

Now, however, I suspect the attempt may be made. It is a possibility I hardly dare think about, so terrible are its implications and so awful its consequences, no matter who wins. To overturn a Pharaoh is to shake to the very foundations the being of Kemet, for Pharaoh is all things to Kemet. Such an act violates the very *ma'at* of the Two Lands. Only a Pharaoh who himself has violated *ma'at* could ever be threatened with such a thing.

Tonight, I suspect, may be the start of it, though I do not expect the event itself to occur then. There will be a last attempt to reason with my older brother, who is responsible, and with my younger brother, who is not responsible but only the amiable and appealing dull-wit he has always been. If that fails, then I shudder to think what may happen next in the land of Kemet.

The argument at hand is very small: two paintings on two tomb walls. Around them rise issues so grave and great that their settling can convulse the earth from the Delta to the Fourth Cataract.

Knowing my mother, my uncle, my cousin Horemheb, Nefertiti and my two dreaming brothers, I expect the worse.

But I do not want to be there.

I shall walk by the Nile and try to think of peaceful things; though I think it will be long, now, before peace returns to the Two Lands. . . .

Ramesses

I have never known him to be so intent, so silent, so secretive about his plans, his purposes, his feelings. Always up to now Horemheb, my dearest friend and most trusted comrade in arms, has confided all to me, things he would never confide even to Sitamon, to whom he has been husband in all but name these many years. I have known him myself for thirty years, ever since the day of Akhenaten's birth when I brought to Thebes the news of the murder by the priests of Amon of his older brother, who was the then Crown Prince Tuthmose V. We were young scribes together, young soldiers together, traveled the length of Kemet and from there north to Mittani and Naharin, south to Nubia and wretched Kush, in the service of His late Majesty Amonhotep III (life, health, prosperty!). In the past fifteen years we have faithfully served (though with many profound misgivings which we have expressed only to one another) Nefer-Kheperu-Ra Akhenaten. Horemheb has been a part of my family, he is godfather to my son Seti, who now stands tall and sturdy beside us, ready for whatever the future may bring. He and I might be brothers, even twins, so closely have our lives, our thoughts, our hearts run together: and even I do not know what inner pressures move him now.

I do know that something must be done. I say this bluntly and without embellishment, for I am not a clever man, I admit it. I am simply a fair scribe and a very good soldier who does not concern himself over-much with policy. But policy is everyone's concern now. Nefer-Kheperu-Ra has made it so.

The Empire is almost gone, the Two Lands slip away into chaos and confusion. Robbery and corruption, murder and mayhem fill the cities and plague the villages. The temples of the gods stand ruined and deserted, the priests who helped administer government are dispersed, dead or in hiding. Many civil officials cannot be trusted unless they are directly supervised by the army. Even in the army itself Horemheb and I must be constantly on the alert to guard against corruption and betrayal. Men look only to their own self-interest: the love of Kemet wanes because the heart of Kemet no longer beats. Akhenaten is the heart, and he is no longer interested in Kemet. Sad days haunt the kingdom because of this.

Horemheb and I do what we can. Together with Horemheb's half brother, the Vizier Nakht-Min, we strive to keep all on even keel while Akhenaten lives in his dream of the Aten and Ankh-Kheperu-Ra Smenkhkara plays at directing the government—an easygoing, empty-headed boy of twenty, for such a task! It would make one laugh aloud were it not so tragic. But what to do about it? There we are frustrated and do not know.

I know there are some who whisper that there are plots within the Family against the two Pharaohs, that the Great Wife, the Councilor and Divine Father-in-law Aye, Horemheb, even Nefertiti, may be planning some action looking toward their removal. I do not believe it, for how can it be done? They are the Sons of the Sun. It would violate the eternal laws of Kemet. It would desolate the very *ka* and *ba,* the very soul and essence of the country would be destroyed by it. I, a simple soldier, would go mad with the rending of the world. So would most of our five millions of people. We would be lost and wandering in the eternal darkness of the universe and Ra would no more smile upon us. It could not be.

And yet—and yet . . . we must be relieved of this burden. Somehow the Two Lands must be restored to their glory. Somehow the people must be protected from the corrupt, the murderous, the avaricious and the hurtful. Somehow the Double Crown must regain its splendor in the hands of decent and honorable men. *Somehow the gods must be restored. . . .*

Horemheb asked me to return with him to Akhet-Aten from Memphis, where we were seeking to strengthen the hands of a few faithful servants in the northern capital. He did not tell me why, except to say, as he always does, "Because I need you with me—I must have one man I can trust at my right hand." I do not know his plans, his purposes, his feelings: but I know, as always, that I must be here to help him in whatever he intends.

He tells me there is some argument over paintings in the tombs of Huy and Meryra. Akhenaten wants them one way, the Great Wife and Nefertiti want them another. Evidently there are deep feelings aroused in the Family about this. I sense, though he does not tell me, that Horemheb considers it to be a major issue; though being a simple soldier, I do not really see why.

I asked him as much.

"Because it is time," he said. And that is all he would say.

I cannot believe it will change things. How could it? The Living Horus, Son of the Sun, cannot be toppled by such a paltry thing. The people would not permit it, unhappy and fearful though they have been made by the strange misrule of Nefer-Kheperu-Ra and Ankh-Kheperu-Ra. And how could any of us who love Kemet lend ourselves to so dreadful an overturn of all her traditions that hold us together?

Horemheb

Simple Ramesses is baffled by me, which I would like to think is more a tribute to my cleverness than his stupidity. I fear it is not, however. I think it is only because he is honest, dull and blinded by lifelong loyalty that he does not perceive my purposes; and so I try to conduct myself with extra circumspection in the sight of others, less close, who observe me more objectively.

In this I think I have succeeded very well up to this moment of final conflict with my irresponsible cousin. For fifteen years I have gone faithfully about his business in the Two Lands, and beyond. He has raised me to be chief scribe and general of the army, has used me with unhesitating trust to perform his will, has required of me that I do terrible things: and I have done them. From the murder of our uncle Aanen in the temple of Amon at Luxor to the murder of Maya—the desecration of Amon's holiest place at Karnak—the hurling of Amon himself into the waters of the Nile—and the ruin and dispersion of all the other gods and their priesthoods—I have done them. And somehow, although I have been the instrument, I have secretly been able to convince the victims that I am their friend and, like them, am biding only the time when all can be put right again. And so I have come through unscathed and still popular with the secret priesthoods and the people.

It is as though I had acquired something of the aura that Pharaohs have: that whatever seemingly false I do is blamed on someone else (as rightly it should, in my case), and that to me is accorded a great forgiveness such as is not given other men. Particularly such as is not given Akhenaten, I think; and again, rightly so.

All of this has required great subtlety, great cleverness, the ruthless leading of a shrewd and implacable double life. It has also required great courage, because not even such a listless and uncaring One as Nefer-Kheperu-Ra could afford to countenance such behavior, if he knew it. He would have had my head on a dozen occasions had I not been able to advance my purposes with the requisite amount of grace and bravery. That I have been able to do so safely has convinced me further, if I needed to be convinced, that the gods have in store for me great things in Kemet.

Many years ago—thirty, how the time rolls by!—Amonhotep, Son of Hapu, said to me when he first became my friend that he thought I did indeed have "purposes" in Kemet. I was only fifteen then, newly come to Thebes and all the dazzle of the Court. I knew I possessed great brains, a stout heart, wit, charm, a lightning intelligence—and the skill to dissemble, which I did not at first employ because I did not see any particular reason why I should. But as I rose higher, I learned. My father Aye was secretly guiding me, more by example than by direct admonition. Amonhotep, Son of Hapu, as he moved more and more securely into the position he now occupies (which is really "the official Sage of Kemet," so widely is he known, loved, listened to and revered), gave me many direct and helpful admonitions that greatly eased my way. My father's support guaranteed me position, his example schooled me in skill and statesmanship. From Amonhotep, Son of Hapu, I received the intimate guidance and warm day-by-day friendship my father's high position and remote austerity made impossible. I owe them both very much: and will continue to owe them much, I think, as I move closer to the destiny whose shape the gods have made clear to me beyond all doubt in these last few troubled years.

Sitamon knows. Her shot was in the dark, but I could see she sensed instantly how shrewdly it had gone home. I do want to be Pharaoh: I, Horemheb, say it secretly to myself and not yet to any other. But the day will come when it can be proclaimed to the world. When it does, I will be ready.

How this will come about I do not yet see, for at the moment the

path to the Double Crown is not open to me, who am the illegitimate
son of Aye, who is only uncle and father-in-law to the King and is not
able, himself, to confer upon me any rights to the throne. He has given
me the right of legitimacy, and he has given me the right to be a
member of the Family. Both have been great advantages: but he cannot
give me the right to the throne. Yet I feel that somehow the gods will
work on my behalf, as I work secretly and shrewdly on theirs. Somehow
I shall not go unrewarded—this I believe. In that belief I live and govern and do great things, though always, up to now, at the command,
and in the shadow of, my strange cousin and his amiable, empty
brother.

Suppose the day comes when they are removed—yes, that too I dare
say secretly to myself, though it is treason to even think it: *when they
are removed.* What will happen then? Solemn little Tut, who used to be
such a happy child before he became old enough to sense that the world
of Kemet is deeply in trouble around him, will succeed. He will be married to Akhenaten's second oldest daughter, sweetly ambitious little
Ankh-e-sen-pa-aten (another Merytaten but with much smoother
edges); and from his loins will no doubt spring many sons to revive the
House of Thebes. And what will happen to hopeful Horemheb then?
Will he succeed his father as councilor, when that good man goes? Will
he continue to run the army and govern the country while Tut remains
a child, and go finally to the afterworld, gray with honors, after Tut
takes full command and presently permits an old and faithful servant to
retire?

This is a future most men would greatly envy: but it is not enough
for Horemheb.

Still, as I say, that is what appears to be the likely outline of the future. I see no other path logically before me. *Yet I still believe the gods
will come to my assistance and make me Pharaoh.* How, I do not know.

For the present, I suppose, I am not intended to know. I am intended
only to play my part in the crisis that is now upon us, and to have my
just share in whatever must be done to save the throne and the Two
Lands, which now suffer so greatly under my cousin's misrule. That is
enough for me, right now—or so Amon and his fellow gods inform me.

I pray often to Amon, whose statue I ordered to be recovered
secretly from the Nile after Akhenaten ordered him thrown in. Hatsuret
—my father—the Great Wife—Amonhotep, Son of Hapu—Ramesses
—we six alone in all the world know where Amon is, for after the special group of divers I commanded had brought him up from the bottom
of the Nile, I had them slain so that there would be no witnesses.
Ramesses and I then took him to a secret place in the necropolis of

Sakkara, near Memphis, where he stands in an empty tomb carved more than a thousand years ago for some noble who never occupied it. It is at the end of a tiny passage leading off from my own, which has been under construction in Sakkara for many years. After I had the passage dug, the tomb enlarged a little and suitably decorated as a shrine, and a concealed doorway fitted cleverly into place, I had those workmen slain also. Now, as I say, only six in this world know where Amon is; and only I, who have the pretext of visiting my own tomb from time to time to supervise its progress, ever have the chance to visit him. But I take the offerings of the others, and he knows that all of us work toward the day of his restoration, and he favors us in our endeavors and guides us in what we do.

So does he guide us now as we come finally toward the day of reckoning with the treacherous Aten and his foolish servitors. My cousin has tried for fifteen years to make the Aten the Sole God of Kemet, he has persecuted Amon and all the other gods, he has had his subversive and ridiculous Hymn to the Aten inscribed on a hundred stelae throughout Kemet—and still the people do not love the Aten, any more than they love him. But this does not stop him: he continues, and will continue, to worship his Sole God and try to inflict him upon the rest of us. He will continue this to his death: for such is the nature of my cousin Akhenaten.

In a curious way, it is almost possible to admire such stubborn determination, however foolish and self-defeating it has been. His whole life since he became Co-Regent with my uncle Amonhotep III (life, health, prosperity!) has been a deliberate challenge to all the ancient traditions of Kemet. He has defied the weight of history: he has risked the wrath of centuries. And now that he nears the end of his rule and his life, for certainly he does, one can only ask: for what? Has he really had a purpose? Has he really known what he was doing? Or has he been simply the creature of an automatic and increasingly insane compulsion, without strategy, without aim, without sense?

I believe, myself, that he *is* insane. I have believed this ever since the day of my uncle's death when Akhenaten assumed full power, ravaged Amon, put aside Nefertiti and sailed off to Akhet-Aten from Thebes with silly, bewitched Smenkhkara singing the Hymn to the Aten at his side. I think on that day he relinquished whatever shreds of reason still remained in him. I think on that day the gods sealed his fate, and that everything thereafter has been simply preparation for the final ending of his crazy dream.

In this ending I have much part to play. I do not know yet exactly what it will be, what the Great Wife and my father will wish of me; but

I feel, though neither has talked to me about it, that both know well what they intend.

The army is in my hand, though it would take almost impossibly much to make my superstitious soldiers rise against the Living Horus— and so I know it is not by that means that we will bring him down. But bring him down we will. Of that I have no doubt.

And then in due time—somehow, someday, in some fashion the gods have not yet revealed to me but which I know they will, for I am their faithful servant—the way will open for Horemheb and he will lead Kemet back to what Kemet was when he first arrived, an eager lad, in then flourishing Thebes, so many years ago.

Aye

My sister thinks it time, my son thinks it time, I think it time, Amonhotep, Son of Hapu, though he confides nothing direct to any of us about it, indicates the same. We do not know what my daughter Nefertiti thinks but tonight we intend to find out. Then, perhaps, will indeed come the time—to act.

Yet what do I contemplate when I say "the time to act"?

My mind shudders away from it.

We say we are talking about two carvings in two minor tombs of the pathetic coronation durbar and what they should represent to posterity. In reality we are talking of something else.

Behind them lies the face of death.

So far we have come along the road with Nefer-Kheperu-Ra and his bemused and fatefully willing brother . . . my two little nephews, who so short a while ago laughed and tumbled at my feet! Of *them* I use the word "death!" May Amon and Aten and all the gods forgive me the thought . . . and may they understand, in horror and compassion, why it is that Aye, Private Secretary, Councilor, Divine Father-in-law, must now face the fact that for him, as for others, it is a thought that can no longer be put aside.

It is not enough to catalogue the wasting of temples, the withering of empire, the corruption of the land. It is not enough to talk of gods destroyed, of brothers shameless in public spectacle, of old ways thwarted and traditions upside down. It is more than that. It is *ma'at, the fitness of things* in all its aspects, that Akhenaten destroys with what he does. . . . It is this he destroys now simply by continuing to exist, simply by continuing to be the living symbol of all that he has done against *ma'at* and the safety and preservation of the Two Lands.

I have tried for a very long time to follow him, rationalizing much, excusing much, justifying much. When he asked me to stand at his right hand years ago as assistant high priest of the Aten, I did so, thinking I could thereby modify and guide and in some measure control his course. When I publicly recognized my son Horemheb and advised him to accept the honors and responsibilities his cousin desired to heap upon him, I did so in the thought, which Horemheb shared, that this too would be a modifying, guiding and controlling influence.

It has not proven so, in either case. Were it not that Kemet long ago came to respect and revere my integrity and intelligence—not giving me love, but giving me something I value more because in my mind it is more important, namely respect—I should now myself be suffering the secret grumblings, the growing fear and hatred that surround Pharaoh in the minds of his people. Were it not that Horemheb, too, has been universally respected and admired for his diligence, his loyalty, his great shrewdness and his obvious deep love for Kemet, he would be suffering in the same way.

Fortunately we have been able to escape opprobrium, retaining both the people's confidence and Pharaoh's, and it is this which not only gives us the opportunity but imposes upon us the obligation to assist in whatever is decided tonight. We will, in fact, assist in the deciding itself, for we are come now to the moment when all must be decided so that Kemet may be reborn and go on in the eternal glory that is rightfully hers.

We have wasted too much time: the Two Lands have drifted too far. Now, very late, we must pull them back.

In this enterprise my sister is the guiding force, as she has been the guiding force in so many things for the good of Kemet for so many years. I doubt if even now, confronted though we are by so many failures and misdeeds of Akhenaten, we should dare to even think of deposing him were it not for his mother's indomitable character and implacable will. I can only imagine the endless hours, days, nights of torment she must have gone through these past three years to reach the point she has: for she was always a loving mother, and she, too, has traveled far, very far, with Nefer-Kheperu-Ra and Ankh-Kheperu-Ra before coming at last to the conclusion I think she has: that, for the good of Kemet, they must go.

What form this will take we do not know—do not dare express as yet, though I think tonight we will.

Possibly the gods will come to our aid and it will happen naturally, for Akhenaten is not well, that is obvious to all. He seems to be suffering not so much a sickness of the body, though of course he has never been really strong since his illness, as a sickness of the spirit. He is listless, more erratic, more uncaring. With it comes a sharper tongue, an inward-turning sarcasm, a more savage bitterness—when he rouses sufficiently to respond at all.

Much of the time he stays alone and broods; now and again he calls me or Horemheb or my younger son, Nahkt-Min, whom he has now appointed vizier, to his side for halfhearted discussions of policy and government. More often he goes to worship the Aten with Smenkhkara and then they retreat to his favorite aerie, the ledge along the Northern Tombs overlooking the city and plain. At regular intervals Smenkhkara —I will say for him that he takes his "duties of government" with an almost touching earnestness and sincerity—travels upriver to Thebes or down to Memphis, makes his appearances at those two secondary and now half-deserted capitals, performs the ceremonies of the Aten and transmits a few desultory "orders" from his brother, so vaguely phrased that only ancient habits of obedience bring them even a semblance of response. "That canal for His Majesty's commerce near the oasis of the Fayum might be deepened," perhaps. Or, "It might be that an expedition to the western desert would find items pleasing to His Majesty."

Not—the canal *must* be deepened, you see. Not—an expedition *will* go and it *will* find *thus, thus* and *thus* for His Majesty. It is all a half formed hint, a delicate, weary suggestion—almost, if you will, a dying suggestion.

This is not how Pharaohs get things done.

It is only in the realm of his religion and his household, unfortunately, that he still remains vigorous and demanding. The temples of the Aten flourish, though they have few worshipers. The wealth of Amon and the rest flow into their coffers, and from there directly into his. The compromise I once suggested—that the wealth and priesthoods of the two great gods be equally divided—vanished with the blaze of rage in which he destroyed Amon at Thebes on the day of his father's entombment. It was not a very good compromise, probably, but at least for a year or two it did what I had hoped, prevented open conflict, preserved a semblance of uneasy peace between the two, re-established a little the mystique of Pharaoh as the impartial father of the land. But he was never impartial, really. Too long ago he became the slave of the Aten. And now he permits no other god to reign in the Two Lands, as he permits no other god than likable, amiable, stupidly easygoing Ankh-Kheperu-Ra to reign in his heart.

Is it any wonder we of the Family feel so torn about them both? Akhenaten has a great residue of love and pity to draw upon in our hearts, for he was so perfect a youth and became so pathetic and unhappy a man. Smenkhkara has always been everyone's favorite, because of his own sweet nature and because the blessings the gods gave him were never taken away. In many ways he is a replica of his father, tolerant, friendly, outgoing, lovable.

I have sometimes thought it, never dared speak it even to myself, but now I do: it is a pity the terrible illness did not take Akhenaten and leave us Smenkhkara to succeed to the Double Crown. There would have been no problems with Amon, no problems of personal relationship, no problems of any kind. He would have married, had sons, done his duty; he might even have taken to the field and restored the Empire, for he has his venturesome streak and sometimes talks longingly of the campaigns he would like to go on if only his brother were not too jealous of his safety to permit it. He would have been good, kind, reliable, dull: just one more greatly popular, greatly respected, greatly loved Pharaoh, easily managed and easily controlled, taking his place in the eternal unchanging parade of Kemet's rulers.

Instead came Akhenaten. . . .

And here we are.

I do not know exactly what my sister has in mind for this evening, but I think in the family council that will be held before we confront the two Kings the basic question will have to be put: are they to be removed, and if so, how and by whom?

I know that in the King's House there are two instruments, once the decision has been reached. Hatsuret waits, carrying in his heart Amon's burning desire for vengeance. And at the right hand of His Majesty stands my son Horemheb, whose ambition at last is beginning to frighten me, so boundless does it appear to be despite his outward dissemblings.

It is not often that Sitamon and I make occasion to speak on an intimate basis: she is a good niece, I am a good uncle, our friendship is always amicable, we leave it at that. It is seldom she seeks me out for counsel or advice. Two weeks ago she did, however, telling me of her strange little exchange with Horemheb, which she thought—and I agree with her—revealed his desire to be Pharaoh. Yet how can he be Pharaoh? The line of succession is firm and clear, going straight to solemn little Tut, more uneasy every day as he senses the concern of his elders increasing about him.

"Uncle," he said to me just yesterday, when I was visiting the North Palace—climbing up on my lap as he used to do, which is no longer quite so easy, as he is growing rapidly heavier and I am in my sixty-fifth year—"must I be Pharaoh very soon, when Nefer-Kheperu-Ra and Ankh-Kheperu-Ra die?"

For a moment I was so taken aback by this childish candor on a subject his elders have never yet expressed aloud to one another that I am afraid I must have looked a little foolish.

"They are going to die, aren't they?" he repeated with a bright insistence that suddenly frightened me so that I instinctively clapped a hand over his mouth. His startled eyes stared at me with such terror that I knew I must drop my hand instantly and hug him protectively to my chest.

"You must never, never, *never* say such things, Nephew," I said, managing with great effort to make my voice calm and soothing to stop the trembling of his body and the surprised and terrified little noises that were beginning to whimper from his throat. "Nefer-Kheperu-Ra and Ankh-Kheperu-Ra are the Kings of the Two Lands. They are well and no one wishes them ill. Someday far, far off when you are a grown man and are married and have a family"—a thought I try to instill in him every chance I get, since we do not want any repetitions of what is going on now—"it may be that the god will call them to the Western Peak—"

"Which god?" he demanded. "The Aten or Amon?"

"Perhaps both," I said soothingly.

"I should like the Aten," he said with a surprising firmness that brought a sudden terror to *my* heart. *That* repetition I had not foreseen. But he is only eight, and no doubt will presently forget it, and so I made my tone again deliberately hearty and comforting.

"Perhaps the Aten, perhaps Amon, perhaps both," I said with a studied indifference. "One does not know what the future holds, except that, as you truly say, you will indeed be Pharaoh when Nefer-Kheperu-Ra and Ankh-Kheperu-Ra are no longer on this earth. But that will be many, many years from now, and you must never discuss it with anyone, ever again. It does not become one who will one day be Pharaoh that he should gossip thus about his brothers."

This did what I intended it to do. He straightened up abruptly and slid off my lap, standing straight as a little soldier at my elbow.

"The Pharaoh Tutankhaten," he said solemnly, "will never gossip about his brothers to anyone again."

"That is good," I said with equal solemnity. "Have I the word of a Son of the Sun on that?"

"You have the word of a Son of the Sun," he said, still with great solemnity. Then he gave a sudden sad sigh and became a little boy again. "But, Uncle, I *do* wish we could all be happy together in the Family as we used to be."

"So do I, Nephew," I said, meeting the honesty in his eyes with honesty in mine. "But until the god—or gods—allows us to be so, we must all be strong and brave and show the world nothing and say nothing about it, not even to one another. Do you not agree?"

"I agree," he said, sounding much too old and tired for eight. "But I *do* wish it so."

"Come," I said then, rising and taking him by the hand. "Let us go and look at the lion captured last week in the Fayum. They tell me he has a marvelous growl that says, 'Tut-ankh-AAATTTEN! Tut-ankh-AAATTTEN!' "

"Uncle," he said, breaking into the sunny smile we do not see very often of late, "that's *silly*. But let us go anyway and see him."

And so we did, and the subject, I hoped, was forgotten; though I am very much afraid it was not, for I saw him just this morning being taken in his chariot to the House of the Aten to do worship, and the look he gave me was once again knowing and troubled and far too old for eight.

How Horemheb can contemplate that he will ever become Pharaoh under these circumstances, I cannot for the life of me see. It is as absurd as though I myself were to entertain such a thought. The succession is established and preordained. What we must all be thinking about now is how to bring it about as rapidly as possible, with as little disturbance to Kemet and with (I still hope with all my heart) as little hurt as possible to Akhenaten and Smenkhkara.

There is a possibility—a very remote chance—that they might be persuaded to leave the throne. No Pharaoh has ever done such a thing —voluntarily—in all our history. But I am not talking of voluntarily. Perhaps we can trade them the throne for retirement together here, suitably housed, suitably honored, remaining as guardians of the Aten in the Aten's city, while Tut returns to Thebes to re-establish Amon and restore the *ma'at* and power of the Two Lands—

But what nonsense am I talking?

Smenkhkara the easygoing lover of ease and luxury might agree. But embittered and unyielding Akhenaten?

Never.

What ever persuaded Aye, who has seen so much of tragedy and unhappiness in the House of Thebes (and I am afraid will yet see more), to entertain for even a moment such blithering thoughts!

My desperate desire for compassion and compromise runs away with me.

There is no easy way around this situation for any of us.

We gather in my daughter's palace an hour from now, and there we decide how best to go straight through, hoping we may somehow come out safely on the other side.

Tiye

I am getting old. I find that I am thinking often now, with frequent tears and deepening sadness, of the old bright days before trouble came upon this House. We were happy then. All was laughter, gaiety and pleasure. Nothing clouded our sky, from which Ra smiled benignly on us all. The world was filled with life and love and brilliant colors everywhere. Contentment—real contentment—blessed the House of Thebes and the fortunate people of our dear Two Lands.

I see the contrast in far too many things today. To take one example: the temples. "Colors everywhere," I said. Do you, too, remember how the great pylons looked, the giant figures of Pharaoh and the gods striding across the stone, painted in vivid reds and blues and yellows, with lovely gold and scarlet banners flying from every aperture? The palaces were lovely too, corridors, floors, doors, ceilings painted with a thousand scenes of gods, of Pharaoh, of comfortable domestic things and carefree hunting and fishing along the Nile. And on the river the bright sails going up and down, and in the streets the busy, happy bustle of our handsome people, the men dark and deeply tanned, the women fair, protected from the sun, gracefully languorous as they were carried by in litters and couches or, if assigned by the gods to a lower station in life, yet moving gracefully about their burdens with happy smiles, quick laughter, warm welcoming faces.

All, all has changed. A drabness has come upon the land. Since my son closed all the temples save those of his jealous Sole God, the work crews that once kept all bright and shining with their constant attentions have been dispersed. Care and love are gone from the world. The colors of the giant statues and paintings on all temples but the Aten's have faded and become splotchy, the banners are long since taken down and destroyed, the palaces themselves have been allowed to fall into shabby disrepair save in a few places where the orders of myself and Nefertiti have been able to preserve some semblance of former beauty. (She built her own temple to the Aten at Karnak. He did not dare object. It stands alone, a single note of brightness in the ruined surround.) On the river there is less and less color as if the boatmen were afraid to show it, and in the streets few smiles, little laughter, no longer the constant happy chatter—mingled so often with the sound of music, which also has almost vanished from our world—that used to fill Kemet with good will and laughter from Memphis to Karoy.

A sullen sourness grips the land, a deep unease. Joy has fled from Kemet and with it the air of well-being that used to be the principal distinguishing feature of our divinely ordered life.

It is because there is no order that this is so. It is because order— *ma'at*—the eternal fitness of things—has been destroyed. It is because my son has remade our world in his own sad image and that of his hurtful, vengeful god.

Long ago when his father and I first decided that we would dedicate him to the Aten, we intended the Aten to be a counterweight to then overweening Amon. We never contemplated that out of Akhenaten's illness would come his great hatred for Amon and the other gods, or that out of his worship of the Aten would come his final decision to overturn them all and make the Aten, alone, supreme.

Now the Aten is inescapable. His round, empty face and long spidery arms, ending in tiny hands conferring ankhs and gifts, look down upon us everywhere; and to him my son has given titles heretofore reserved for Pharaohs alone when they have celebrated jubilees of their reigns:

"Live, Ra, ruler of the Horizon, rejoicing in the Horizon, in his role of light coming from the Sun's Disk, giving life forever and to all eternity, Aten the living, the Great, Lord of Jubilees, Master of all that encompasses the Sun's Disk, Lord of the Heavens, Lord of the Earth, THE ATEN."

So high has he raised him.

I know he still conceives the Aten to be a sunny, bright and loving god. But seeing what has been done in Aten's name, it has been long since the Aten has appeared that way to our people. In Akhenaten's eyes—for he has told me so on many occasions—his "Father Aten" still gleams happy and beneficent above us all. In the eyes of the people he is a dark and vindictive god whose jealousy and intolerance of all others make him forever impossible to love.

Such is the tragedy of my son Akhenaten. And such is the tragedy of our House, which now must deal with him, since the people cannot— and will not, so deeply instilled in them lies the fear and worship of

Pharaoh, even when they know—*know*—what he is doing to the land. They would never dare rise against him; they would never dare risk the vengeance of centuries. In the land of Kemet, *this is not done.*

Yet it must be done; and I, his mother, for many years Pharaoh in all but name of the Two Lands, must now perform a terrible service for my people. Nothing will be done unless I give the word: the Family waits upon me. So I must give the word, because there is no one else to give it, and nothing else left to do.

I see them both, in those early happy days: Akhenaten running and leaping down the sandy pathways of Malkata, ten years old, shortly before the illness struck; Smenkhkara the newborn, crooning in my arms, suckling at my breast, beaming upon all the world with happy smiles and welcoming gurgles. They were such happy children. All my children have been happy children, though Sitamon is on her way to becoming a soured and disappointed old woman because marriage to her no longer has a place in Horemheb's ambitions . . . and Tut is aging rapidly before his time as the weight of the Double Crown comes ever closer . . . and Beketaten goes about a shy and frightened little girl because she, too, senses gathering storms . . . and Akhenaten and Smenkhkara are far, far now from the innocent and carefree days when we all laughed and loved one another in harmony and happiness in the Palace of Malkata. . . .

I envy my husband, sleeping peacefully in the Valley of the Kings beneath the Peak of the West, because he does not have to make the decision I must make. Were he alive, of course, he never would, because he was always weaker than I. He would flinch and smile and ease away from it, as he did from so many unpleasant things that, looking back, were clearly unmistakable warnings. We used to worry about these things, sometimes sharing our worries, sometimes not, but each sensing the other's concerns. From time to time it would come into the open: I would urge upon him some course of action—insist upon it, finally, for the good of Kemet. Sometimes he would comply and sometimes not. When he did, things righted temporarily; when he did not, they continued their downward slide. Never could he control Akhenaten, and as his health failed so steadily in those later years, he lost even the desire to try.

So came the awful and disgraceful day of his entombment, the destruction of Amon and the other gods, the final ascendance of Akhenaten and the Aten, the putting aside of Nefertiti, the shameless enthronement of Smenkhkara in intimate co-regency with his brother, the full impact, at last, of all Akhenaten's crazy dreams upon the Two Kingdoms. Because I think he *is* crazy—literally insane, and far gone now from any place where we who love him can reach him any more.

I blame myself for this, as I blame us all—but myself most of all, for I am his mother and it must have been my failure, somehow, that started it all: though I cannot honestly see how. I tried, I did my best. I have always thought to love and save him: but I failed. . . .

The hours I have wept for him, the Niles of tears I have shed! Even now, as I make ready to leave for the North Palace, I am shedding more. But something cold lies deep inside, at last. It is not my son—my sons—I weep for any more. It is for two alien beings, and for us who at last must regard and treat them as such if Kemet is to be saved from their infinite and awful folly.

I believe I have the support of my brother Aye, my nephew Horemheb and of Amonhotep, Son of Hapu. I am not so sure of my daughter-in-law, for I think her love still lives as it used to do, with something of the happy innocence of Malkata still alive beneath all the unhappy bitterness of these recent years. I think she also still believes in the Aten, which I have come to regard, I think realistically, as an experiment that failed.

Had Akhenaten been stronger, more insistent, had he moved from the beginning to impose his will as a Pharaoh should, instead of being so gentle, so cautious, so anxious to win the people to Aten through love instead of fear, then he might have achieved the religious revolution he sought and rid our House forever of Amon. But he wanted the people to come to the Aten of their own free will and he waited too long for them to do it. Then when he finally became enraged and decided to force them, it was too late and he went too far. And so the Aten's temples stand empty save for fawning priests who flatter him, and the nobility and sycophants of the Court who must worship as Pharaoh directs if they would keep their positions, wealth and power. Among the people, Hatsuret and his spies tell us—we think accurately —the time is ripe for Amon and his fellows to return.

But before Amon can return my sons must go: the bargain of the gods is as simple and as ruthless as that.

Later tonight we will confront the two Kings, ostensibly to argue out the question of what is to be placed in the tombs of Huy and Meryra to depict the coronation durbar. On the surface it will be an argument decided before it is begun, for Akhenaten of course will have the final say as long as he is Pharaoh. If he wishes to depict the durbar in all its pathetic "living in truth" reality, instead of as a dignified and opulent ceremony designed to strengthen and preserve through all eternity the hitherto glorious image of the Eighteenth Dynasty, then he can order it done. But before we argue that we will have met at the North Palace and there other decisions will, I think, have been reached; and they may influence him far differently than he now dreams.

My tears are drying as I prepare to go. They may never flow again for my sons or for their mother, who will perform her last service for her beloved land of Kemet though it kills her heart forever in the breast that nourished them.

Anser-Wossett

I have been first lady in waiting to Queen Nefertiti since we both were girls, and steadily in these past three years my heart has been wrung with pity for her, as hers has been wrung with sadness for her husband and the happy times they once knew together.

I have watched her age, something I never thought could happen when we were younger; and at the same time seen her become more beautiful, as maturity and suffering have eroded the youthful roundness and arrogant prettiness and transformed her into a stately, grave and truly beautiful woman.

Bek's rising young assistant Tuthmose has captured this best, I think, in the portrait bust he has just completed. Wearing her blue conoidal crown, looking out upon the world with a subtle sadness, a knowing but indomitable serenity, she gazes quietly into the eyes of the beholder as I have often seen her gaze in these past three troubled years. Only once have I caught that gaze direct, and then it was to look into such depths of sorrow that I quickly found a pretext to excuse myself and went away to weep in private for the beautiful woman who has come, only to find that all has crumbled and turned hopeless in her hands.

For this I can never blame the Queen, for it is only Pharaoh who must bear the responsibility. Her fault, if any, has been in loving him too much, and continuing to do so long after all evidence and common sense said such devotion was foolish and fated to end in emptiness. She has refused to believe it—refuses, I think, even now. Of all the Court—perhaps in all Kemet—she is the only one who still clings to the hope that someday, somehow, they may be reunited.

But suppose they were, what would it profit her? Nefer-Kheperu-Ra has not much longer to live, I think, and it is better that she be far from his side when the vengeance of the gods falls at last upon his head.

This I believe it will, for I do not believe that even the Good God can so long and so outrageously challenge the gods and the very *ka* and *ba,* the very soul and essence, of the Two Lands, without coming eventually to judgment. In my opinion, though I know the Queen has always supported him in his heretical ideas (something it took me long to forgive her, and only my deep love for her gentle person and my ever growing admiration for her indomitable character finally persuaded me to do so), judgment is long overdue. Vengeance will come, and it will destroy both Pharaohs. So are we told who still believe in Amon: and our number is as the sands of the Red Land, however much the Good God may have tried to discourage us and force us to worship his way during the strange unhappy time he has been on the throne.

Fifteen years—fifteen years! To think we have had to suffer him for fifteen years! They have flown so fast it seems impossible to believe it has been so long—were it not that the weary sorrow of my lady is as nothing to the weary sorrow of the land. We carry a constant depression in our hearts because of him. Laughter and joy are gone from Kemet. It has been long, too long, and retribution for it has been long, too long, in coming.

I speak occasionally with him who is known in Akhenaten's Southern Palace as Peneptah, meeting him casually at an appointed place in the market, appearing to the unnoticing passers-by to be chatting easily of ordinary domestic things. Secretly we exchange gossip and information as we seem to stand innocuously talking in the sun. I do not reveal to Hatsuret any of the private affairs of the Queen, for my loyalty is first to her, which he respects; but he knows me as a loyal follower of Amon, and so he tells me something of the whispers that are running through Kemet. We talk also of hidden things within the Family, which both of us are in position to overhear and to know. Vengeance is coming, he says; and he told me only yesterday that it will come "from those closest to Pharaoh, whom he does not suspect." He also told me that when I receive the sign from him—"which before long I think you will"—I should be prepared at once to disguise myself and the Queen—as if one could disguise that classic face!—and flee to hiding in one of the villages south, toward Aswan.

"Our quarrel is not with Her Majesty," he said, "though Amon knows she has abetted and encouraged the Heretic enough, through all these years. But Amon will forgive her if she will go quietly and nevermore appear upon the public scene. A modest house and a quiet living will be prepared for her and for you, and for three or four suitable ser-

vants to attend you. There you may live out your days unknown and
unmolested. But she must not hesitate. When I tell you, and you tell her
—*go*. Do not look back, either of you. Else will she, too, feel the vengeance of Amon, which is terrible and will devastate the land."

"Must there be more devastation?" I asked, embittered. "Have we
not had devastation enough? Must Amon compound Aten, and bloody
us all in the process? Why will you not be content, Hatsuret—Peneptah"—correcting myself as he gave me a hasty glare of warning—"to
simply reclaim the temples and the Two Lands from the Heretic? Must
you run the risk of ruining everything as he has, in the bargain?"

"Vengeance will not be complete until he is dead and all his doings
laid waste as he has laid waste Amon and the other gods," he said in a
harsh and unforgiving tone.

"You men love vengeance too much," I said. "Why must there be
more weeping in the Two Lands?"

"So that the Sole God will die forever," he said in the same cold way.
"Forever and ever, for millions and millions of years—so that no man
hereafter will ever again dare to blaspheme and say that there is a single
universal god supreme above all others. This is the reason we will destroy the Aten, and the Aten's worshipers, and the sick cripple who has
conceived blasphemy, and all his works of all kinds, forever."

"You cannot destroy what is in men's minds, Peneptah," I said, "and
though many condemn what he has planted there, not all will be able to
forget it. It may outlive us all, for all your vengeance."

"First we will have the vengeance," he said with a grim assurance,
"and then we will see."

"I shall try to persuade Her Majesty as you suggest," I said, dropping
the subject because I could see that he could not and would not accept
my prediction, which I think to be, unhappily, more likely to be true
than his. "But I do not know that she will listen to me. It is not in her
nature to flee."

"Then she will die with him," he said with a cold indifference. "And
you, too, unless you abandon her and return to Amon in time."

"I shall never abandon Her Majesty!" I exclaimed, shocked into a
loudness of tone that brought his hand instantly clamped upon my arm.

"You will have the chance," he said softly, "because you have been a
loyal daughter of Amon. But it will not be offered twice. At the moment
you receive word from me, in that moment you must decide. And so
must she. There will be no second chance."

"You do not frighten me, Hatsuret," I said in a whisper that trembled
despite my attempt to keep it steady.

"Amon is not interested in whether or not anyone is frightened," he said. "Amon is interested in justice."

"Vengeance!" I snapped. "Vengeance only, not justice!"

"The two are the same," he said with an indifferent shrug, and turned away to leave me staring after him with too much dismay on my face, for I soon became aware that several were giving me curious looks. I quickly gathered up the two earthen pots with their characteristic blue-striped design which were my excuse for being in the market, went to my waiting litter and was carried home to the North Palace through the city's bustling streets.

As we passed the King's House there was a sudden stir, a blare of trumpets, a hurried falling away of crowds before the entrance. Out *they* came, arms about one another's waists, no doubt on their way to worship at the House of the Aten. Pharaoh Akhenaten seemed sicklier than when I glimpsed him last, a month ago; it seemed to me that he leaned more heavily than usual upon Pharaoh Smenkhkara. Their chariot dashed past, the crowds instantly resumed their chatter and bustle, we all went swiftly on about our business. Oddly, it was almost as though the two Kings had never passed, so quickly did life resume its pattern and close over them like the Nile over a handful of sand.

I returned to Her Majesty much troubled, both by Hatsuret's warnings and by this new sign that the Good God and the young Pharaoh really have no support at all among the people to sustain them: for I do not really wish them ill, knowing how terribly Her Majesty would be hurt if harm came to her husband. Knowing me so well, she of course perceived my mood and demanded to know what had disturbed me in the city. But I had neither the heart nor the courage to tell her of either thing. I passed it off with some story of seeing a child slip and fall fatally beneath the wheels of a passing donkey cart, but I do not think she believed me. In fact I know she did not, for she responded with a searching look from the lovely thoughtful eyes and remarked only:

"It is a time when many things trouble us. Let us pray to the Aten—or you to Amon, if you like—that all will come well for the Two Lands."

"And for you, Majesty," I said fervently. "Particularly for you, who have endured so much."

"And with yet more to come, I think," she said in a faraway tone, as if to herself, ". . . with yet more to come."

Since then she has been lost in thought, withdrawn, remote, not participating as she usually does in the games and prattle of her daughters and of Tut and Beketaten. Now as we prepare for the arrival within the hour of the Great Wife, Her Majesty's father Aye, her half brother Horemheb and Amonhotep, Son of Hapu, she remains silent, unresponsive, almost listless under my skilled hands as I assist her once again with the unguents and oils, the kohl for her eyes, the ocher for her cheeks, the sweet perfumes, all the familiar beautifications with which I have helped her prepare for appearances so many, many thousands of times.

She will rise to this occasion as to all others, of that I am certain; and I know even more certainly than I did when I spoke with Hatsuret that she will never flinch or flee from the vengeance of Amon, which now seems to be coming very close and surely will not be long delayed.

Nefertiti

"Fair of Face, Joyous with the Double Plume, Mistress of Happiness, Endowed with Favor, at hearing whose voice one rejoices, Lady of Grace, Great of Love, whose disposition cheers the Lord of the Two Lands."

So did he have me described on the boundary stelae that ring the city and still carry these endearments, undisturbed.

Nefertiti, which means "A Beautiful Woman Has Come"—so was I named by my mother on her deathbed, in the hour of my birth.

And what is the object of all these brave and flowery words now, as faithful Anser-Wossett works diligently to hide my sorrow with lotions and ointments, sweet perfume and pretty things? What of the "Mistress of Happiness" now, when it is another's voice at which the Lord of the Two Lands rejoices, and another's disposition that cheers him in his lonely life? What remains for her who was "Great of Love" when love is denied and sent away to an empty and distant place?

For three years I have lived in the North Palace, nevermore seeing the Lord of the Two Lands save only on those rare occasions when we happen to meet unexpectedly while passing to or from worshiping the Aten. We do not speak, our glances hardly cross. I am afraid I cannot keep some lingering entreaty out of mine when they do: in return I receive nothing but a frozen stare. Whether this truly represents his feelings or whether he looks thus to avoid showing more genuine emotion, I do not know and probably will never know. I like to think it is because he dares not look at me naturally for fear of what his eyes would show. But that may be pretending to myself. It may all be as dead as my heart so often feels.

Beside him always is my cousin Smenkhkara, performing the weak pretext of government that Akhenaten no longer favors with his attention. But though he is still diligent about his visits to Memphis and Thebes, Smenkhkara is growing a little indolent as he grows more secure in his brother's affection. He is tending to become increasingly like his father, a lover of luxury, indulging himself—and being indulged —in fine food, fine wines, fine jewelry. Another year or two and he will no doubt begin to grow a bit fat, the golden perfection will soften and bloat: give him five years and he will waddle. But I do not expect even that to turn my husband from his obsession, so closely have their lives become entwined.

Nor do I expect it to have any effect on my selfish and hateful daughter Merytaten, who lords it over the Southern Palace as though she were the Chief Wife, or possibly even the Great Wife herself. Nothing suits her better than to have things stay exactly as they are, for she exercises my rights, my privileges, my honors with none of the responsibility—and none of the concern for Kemet—that always marked my conduct when I was at her father's side. She was always ambitious, always grasping, always shrewish, even as a child. Now she has it all, and makes sure that I know it. Possibly this is because I used to punish her from time to time, used to impose a stern and evenhanded discipline upon all the girls but particularly upon her and Ankhesenpaaten, who has many of the same characteristics but has learned under my tutelage to modify them to more subtle and more skillful ways. I do not know: I know only that she is hurtful to me and encourages both her father and her uncle-husband to continue in their foolish and fateful lives.

Thereby she invites upon herself the retribution that may fall upon them. I hope she will be happy with her bargain, if that time comes.

I suspect that my mother-in-law intends that it come fast, else she would not have called us together in family council tonight. She is looking much aged, tired and worn; the plump-faced girl who sits smugly beside smug Amonhotep III (life, health, prosperity!) in the colossal statues that still guard the deserted temple of Amon at Luxor now walks the earth a wrinkled old woman while he lies beneath it a shriveled mummy. But the indomitable character that made the Great Wife Pharaoh in all but name of the Two Lands for so many years remains indomitable still; and now I fear that she has decided at last to turn irrevocably against her sons.

I do not know what she contemplates: I do not know yet how I shall respond to it. Many things in me cry out for vengeance: many cry equally for forbearance and compassion. Smenkhkara is an amiable fool who may have to be sacrificed, but Akhenaten is another matter. His life has been so hard, beginning so brightly, turning so sad. Many and grievous are the crimes he has committed against *ma'at,* but many and grievous have been the compulsions driving him to it. And he did create out of his own heart and mind—the only Pharaoh in our two thousand years of history who ever dared defy the pattern—the decision to raise the Aten to be the Sole and Only God, a beacon to light Kemet's way from centuries of superstition and darkness toward a new and glorious freedom . . . which Kemet does not want, and which I am afraid the Great Wife, my father and the others have finally decided can never be.

But the Aten still lives in my heart, as love still lives there; which is one of the reasons I approach with such great apprehension our conference tonight and what may flow from it. In my house the Aten lives, as it does in his; and I am raising the children, particularly Tut and Ankhesenpaaten who may eventually reach the throne, to know the Aten's truth and loving kindness. I am determined that neither the Aten nor his principal prophet will be forgotten. Perhaps Amon and the others must be restored someday, but modestly—modestly. I intend to make certain that the Aten never loses the dominant position to which Akhenaten has raised him, for the Aten is bright and shining and good. The old darkness of Amon must never return to dominate the Two Lands with fear as it used to do. This I shall always try to prevent, and I believe Tut and Ankhesenpaaten will help me should they be called, as I am afraid they soon might be, to the Double Crown.

It is for this reason that I ordered three years ago, shortly after he put me aside, my own temple to the Aten to be built within the confines of the enormous one he built just east of Karnak soon after he became Co-Regent fifteen years ago. This temple I commanded to consist of nothing but glorification of me and our daughters (in a happy unity we do not, of course, possess) worshiping the Aten and being strengthened by him. I did this as an act of homage to the Aten, so that it would be understood that I was still loyal to the Sole God no matter what might happen to my husband; and also as an act of defiance toward my husband, so that he would know that he could not break my spirit or my loyalty to the god, whatever he might do to me. I did not try to have it built here in Akhet-Aten, for he could have prevented me here and probably would have done so. By ordering it built at Karnak I secured the assistance and support of the Great Wife. She confirmed my orders, and he did not dare countermand them. In any event, I doubt that he even noticed, or if he did, remained uncaring, because he has never returned to Thebes since the day of his father's entombment. Perhaps he even pretends to himself that my temple does not exist, since he has never seen it and apparently never intends to. But there it stands within the confines of his, lovely in colors and brightness—a temple to the Aten and *a temple to me,* whom he can never destroy for all his unfairness that hurts me so bitterly in my heart.

Tonight we have an issue on its face small, by implication and timing great: the depiction of the coronation durbar in the tombs of Huy and Meryra. Those two gentlemen, properly cowed, slink fearfully about their business, caught between the conflicting commands of Pharaoh that the scene be portrayed exactly as it was in all its pathetic sparseness and more than fraternal indignity, and the demands of the Great Wife and myself that the honor of the Dynasty be maintained for all time by depicting it as it should have been: myself and all six girls, alive and well and happy at the side of Akhenaten, receiving the fulsome tributes of our allies and vassals, blessed through eternity in the rays of the Aten.

I believe it may be the Great Wife's intention that we should present our demands (I doubt if I shall attend that session, but she wants my consent) to the two Kings as a united family; and that then, if Akhenaten and Smenkhkara refuse to comply, move swiftly to take some action we will have agreed upon here before they are confronted. What action does she have in mind? It is this that frightens me. I sense an end of patience in the air—perhaps even an end of love, as duty to Kemet persuades both the Great Wife and my father that they must put aside personal feelings and move at last to challenge Akhenaten's unhappy rule.

In this I do not know where I shall stand or what I shall do. I may not know until the moment actually comes. I cannot conceive of turning against him irrevocably myself; love ingrained in me since childhood—ingrained, ironically, by the very ones who may now wish to put love aside forever—would seem to make it impossible. Yet I agree with them: the Two Lands cannot go on like this. Somehow there must be a stop.

Anser-Wossett puts the final touches, for the many-thousandth time, to the changeless perfection of my face and hands me the mirror. Together, as always, we survey what her handiwork has accomplished with the gifts of the gods I received at birth. My eyes meet hers in the mirror and we exchange smiles: in my own, I am afraid, but a ghost of the delighted satisfaction with which I performed this little ritual in happier times.

As our eyes meet, there comes a sudden disturbance in the courtyard, a hurrying down the corridors, the distant sounds of arrival. My eyes widen and, despite my firmest attempts, grow frightened. Instinctively she places a reassuring hand upon my shoulder, a familiarity she has never dared before in all our years together: but these are not usual times. I place my hand upon hers, exert a grateful pressure in return. I hand the mirror to her carefully, rise slowly to my feet, turn with a careful dignity toward the door, take a deep breath and lift my head to its proudest height upon my long, graceful neck.

"Do not be afraid, Majesty," she says hurriedly at my back. "The gods will not desert you this night."

"I pray not," I say over my shoulder as I leave the room, "for I need their strengthening now as I never have before."

Tiye

My daughter-in-law greets us gravely at the entrance to her rooms in the North Palace. No outward sign of nervousness or apprehension touches that perfect face. Yet it is she, I know, whom we must convince before this night is over. I may have to give the word, but without her support the attempt can fail and accomplish nothing but more confusion and uncertainty for the Two Lands.

We have had enough of these.

Amonhotep, Son of Hapu

I have watched this family many, many times, and never have I seen its principal members so stern and troubled as they are tonight.

We come now, I believe, to the beginning of the end of the rule of Nefer-Kheperu-Ra Akhenaten, that strange boy we all regard with such sadness because there was a time when we all regarded him with love.

I shall soon be sixty-five years of age, Aye and I having marched the years together and having, in some degree, together been responsible for the creation of the complex character that has brought such disaster on the Two Lands. I wonder now if we could have done it any differently, produced some different end: I do not think so. I think it all came originally from his illness. I think it was all decreed by the gods.

I think, perhaps, it was decreed by Amon, though I have tried valiantly for fifteen years now to convince myself, as Akhenaten would have us convince ourselves, that Amon is no more and only the kindly Aten shines over all. Perhaps my lack of success in sustaining this conviction is that I know Amon has not left us. He is hiding in a secret corridor off Horemheb's tomb in Sakkara, awaiting only the proper day to reappear. Now the day approaches, I think. I know in my own heart, as I know in the expressions of the faces I see before me, that it is almost here.

The Great Wife is older, too, beginning to shrivel and wrinkle as the years march on. Her face, ravaged by time and worry for her sons and for the Two Lands, carries only a trace of its girlish beauty and self-satisfaction; long gone are the days when she and Amonhotep III (life, health, prosperity!) ruled contented over a contented and unthreatened kingdom. Now all that is gone, save for one thing: alone of them all, she still holds the undivided and unshaken love of the people of Kemet. They respect Aye, they admire, and secretly, perhaps, fear a little, Horemheb; they are deeply fond of Sitamon, they look with anticipation and approval on youthful Tut, they pity and still retain some lingering affection for Nefertiti; but only Queen Tiye do they still simply and unreservedly adore. To them she represents "the great days," as they have already come to call them, looking backward with a wistful regret. To them she still remains their Queen—and their Pharaoh, too, in a profound emotional sense that neither Akhenaten nor his too amiable and slow witted brother can ever match.

Therefore if she has finally decided, as I think she has, that the time has come when they must go for the good of Kemet, the people, though momentarily shocked and perhaps even horrified (though little feeling remains for either Pharaoh), will speedily embrace whatever happens if it is felt that she approves it. Particularly is this true if one adds to it the fact that this will be a mother's terrible judgment on her sons.

"If the Great Wife, *their mother,* feels that way," the whisper will run, "then who are we to question?"

And no one will. All will unite in unanimous joy that relief has come at last to the Two Lands.

Yet it is not an easy thing for this to happen; it is no light matter. It is tragedy such as Kemet has rarely seen and can hardly remember. Its

burden weighs upon us like a thousand stones as we take our seats in
Nefertiti's throne room facing the Great Wife, who by our instinctive
courtesy and deferral occupies the dais. She is dressed in her full golden
garments and wears her distinctive delicate and beautifully worked
golden crown, set with carnelian, turquoise and lapis lazuli.

Aye is frowning and stern, Horemheb is grim and, as always, wary;
Queen Tiye herself is sad, tense but determined. Only Nefertiti, as always, remains outwardly calm and unemotional, though we all know
the tensions that must be swirling inside. It is perhaps in hopes of
releasing these at once so that Nefertiti can join in what may have to be
done that Queen Tiye begins so bluntly.

"The time has come," she says, and though her voice quivers she
continues without flinching, "when for the good of the Two Lands
Nefer-Kheperu-Ra and Ankh-Kheperu-Ra must be removed from the
throne."

There is terrible silence for a moment. Then Aye speaks, a heavy
emotion dragging on his voice, but he too saying what he must:

"Sister, I agree with you."

We look then to Horemheb, who for a second makes some show of
hesitating. Then he bows gravely to the Great Wife and says firmly:

"And I, Your Majesty."

They look then to me, wanting to unite all of us before we demand of
Nefertiti her compliance and support. And so I too bow and say simply:

"It is for the good of the Two Lands."

Then we turn together to the Chief Wife, who has listened in silence,
only the widening of her beautiful eyes and the dead white paleness beneath her make-up (which now looks suddenly garish and obvious,
something we have never seen with her before) disclosing her emotion.
But what emotion? We wait for her to say.

A long moment passes. The silence grows more terrible still. At last
she speaks, very slowly, very carefully, as if seeking time against a
judgment she dreads but cannot contradict.

"Why does Your Majesty say this?" she inquires finally; and with a
sudden impatience, not unkind but not yielding either, Queen Tiye
says:

"Niece, you know as well as I."

Again the terrible silence, and again the very slow, very careful response, while we all stare fascinated, not wishing to watch her bitter
struggle but unable to keep our eyes away.

"What will be Your Majesty's excuse?"

"The excuse of the paintings in the tombs, Niece," the Great Wife says. "You know that, too."

"He will be given a chance to agree about the paintings?" Nefertiti inquires, and we can see she is clinging to some last hope, inspired by a lifelong love.

"He will be given the chance," Queen Tiye says grimly, "but you know as well as we what his answer will be."

"Perhaps not," Nefertiti says with a sudden beseeching eagerness that we all know springs from hope, not reality. "Perhaps he will agree, and then—"

"Then there will be more misrule," Horemheb says with a sudden bitterness. She turns on him like a lioness.

"You relish this! You wish him dead! You hate him as you always have!"

For a moment he does not reply. Then he looks her squarely in the eyes and replies softly:

"Do I, 'Little Sister'? Does 'Big Brother' hate 'Little Brother'? It was not so when we were playing together in the happy days at Malkata."

" 'The happy days at Malkata,' " she repeats, very low. " 'The happy days at Malkata!' I wish the gods had never let us leave Malkata!"

"They did not take us from Malkata," Aye remarks quietly. *"He* did. There was nothing but sand where we sit tonight before he brought us here. That you know also, Daughter."

"But he will be given the chance," she repeats, not replying to her father, seeming to speak from some inner world. "And if he says no, as you all expect—"

"And you expect," Aye says gently, but again she ignores him.

"—then what will become of him?" she concludes. And suddenly, frightening us all, her voice rises almost to a shriek. *"What will happen to my husband?"*

"We shall try," Queen Tiye replies, and her voice again trembles but she does not flinch from the import of her words, "not to hurt him. We shall try not to hurt either of them. But if they continue as they are— and we have all decided, Niece, that this is the final test—*then they must go.* There is no other way."

"You will not strike down Pharaoh!" she cries. "You dare not strike down Pharaoh! The people would never allow it!"

"No," Aye agrees, "they would not—not even this Pharaoh, with all his sad misrule—if they knew in time. But who is to tell them, Daughter? Horemheb's troops surround your palace. They have orders to let no one go out who is not approved by the Great Wife or by me. No one will arouse the people."

Again there is a silence as she stares at him with unbelieving eyes, the lovely face no longer serene but shadowed with a terrible fear and dismay.

"I am a prisoner, then," she says in a broken, pathetic voice. "I am a prisoner, then, and cannot even go to him."

"You are a prisoner for a little time only," Horemheb says; and adds, his tone more gentle than his words, "And besides, Sister: what makes you think he would *want* you to go to him?"

To this she replies with a sudden sharp, strangled cry, wordless but filled with pain—because it is true, and she knows it as well as we. She begins to weep, a racking, painful, awful sound; and on her throne Queen Tiye begins to weep in sympathy. But her expression does not yield, and presently Nefertiti rises and half walks—finally half crawls— to the foot of the dais. There she raises her hands in supplication.

"Can it not be done," she asks between her sobs, "can it not be done —in—in such a way—that it will not—not—hurt him? Can he not be given a warning? Can there not be one more chance?"

"What warning?" Horemheb asks sharply. "What chance? He deserves nothing from the Two Lands, or from us who are their guardians!"

"The gods did not make you their guardians!" she cries with a sudden savage bitterness, turning on him through her tears. *"He* is their guardian! He alone!"

"And Smenkhkara," Horemheb answers softly. "Do not ever forget Smenkhkara."

Instantly her expression changes: inspiration flashes across the now ravaged face with its make-up striggling, its hair at last disheveled, disturbed as we have never seen it. She turns back to the Great Wife, again raises her hands in supplication. I think all of us know instinctively what is coming now. Her voice is suddenly cold, clear and steady.

"Smenkhkara!" she says, with a softness as still and serpentine as Horemheb's own. *"Smenkhkara!* Would not that be warning enough, Majesty? Would not *that* bring him to his senses?"

For several moments no one speaks. We are figures frozen in a frieze, captured in our moment of revelation, devastated and enthralled as she is by the prospect she—and Horemheb (perhaps inadvertently—who ever knows, with Horemheb?)—have opened before us.

At last, because no one else seems able, I clear my throat and venture to break the silence.

"It would save a direct attack upon Pharaoh," I say cautiously.

Aye agrees, face grim.

"It would have that advantage."

"I do not think it will succeed," Horemheb says at last. "But if the Great Wife agrees, I am willing to try it."

We all look at Queen Tiye. Her tears have stopped, she is staring far away into some distance place—Malkata, I think, in the old days, with little boys running and laughing through the corridors. Almost she does not breathe, so intensely and so tragically is she thinking. Almost do we not breathe either, waiting upon her word. The silence lengthens . . . lengthens . . . until at last she utters a great sigh and returns to us.

"Let us see what they say a half hour from now," she says, her voice firm, a decision of some kind obviously reached. "Then we will know better what to do."

"You do agree with me!" Nefertiti cries with a rising excitement. "You will try what I suggest! Oh, Majesty, Majesty! Tell me you will do as I suggest!"

Queen Tiye stares down upon her still prostrate figure with a look both wondering and compassionate. Gently she rises, steps forward, reaches down and brushes a fallen strand of hair from the Chief Wife's sweat-drenched forehead.

"Do not worry, Niece," she says gently. "I shall try to be fair to all. Though the gods help me"—and suddenly she gives us a wild look, almost as though we were not there, swept away again into the world of our terrible decisions, twice as terrible for her, their mother—"though the gods help me, *I do not know how!*"

"Good!" Nefertiti cries, leaping to her feet like a girl, wildly excited and happy, while the old Queen gropes blindly for her brother's arm and with his help blindly descends from the throne. "Oh, thank you, Majesty, thank you!"

And she rushes to the door, flings it open, forgetting—probably for the first time in her entire life—how she will appear to the servants— and claps her hands furiously.

From all sides they come running.

Two minutes later we are in the chariots on our way across the still busy nighttime city—past the brightly lighted shops and bazaars where buyers and shopkeepers haggle over bread and meat and vegetables, past the shrilly whistling hawkers of candy and fine linens, the donkey carts pushing through with their loads of straw, the casually strolling soldiers, hand in hand, who know nothing of the terrible drama our hurried passage represents as we race by, scattering them momentarily before they close placidly behind us—on our way to the South Palace to see the two Kings.

Behind us in the doorway Nefertiti stands watching, a strange mixture of triumph, terror and sorrow on her face. Tears are once more running unheeded down her cheeks.

In the savage light of the torches she looks like an avenging goddess —ecstatic, but shaken to the heart in her moment of victory.

She is still a very beautiful woman.

Akhenaten (Life, health, prosperity!)

"Brother," he says nervously, standing close by the window in the South Palace, peering to the north across the low jumbled roofs of the city, "I see a little group of torches moving this way. They come quickly, as if on horses or chariots. I think they come our way."

"So?" I inquire dryly, for you and I have learned, Father Aten, that this is the way to calm this simple child who is Co-Regent, King and Pharaoh of the Two Lands as I am, yet at many moments is still just my worried and uncertain little brother in need of my comforting. "So? Are the Lords of the Two Lands to tremble like women thereby?"

"I do not tremble like a woman!" he says, half indignant but turning to smile at me. "It is just"—his expression changes abruptly again to one of nervousness and concern—"that I do not like the thought of having to do battle with our mother."

"There will be no battle," I say, raising myself awkwardly from my throne, hobbling carefully down the steps of the dais, shuffling over to stand beside him, my arm reassuringly around his waist.

"She is the Great Wife," he says uncertainly, leaning close against me as if for protection.

"And I am Nefer-Kheperu-Ra Akhenaten, King of the North and South, Living Horus, Son of the Sun, Great Bull, King and Pharaoh of the Two Lands, He Who Has Lived Long, Living in Truth—and all the rest of it," I say, trying to josh him from his mood. "And not even the Great Wife, I warrant you, will dare to attack me."

"But I am not these things," he says with a little shiver I can feel run through his body. "I was not born so, I am not so, save by your grace."

"Or if I should die," I say, still lightly. "Then you would be all this by full right, for it is all yours by blood as next in line, should I no longer be here."

He gives me a long, searching, sidelong glance, his face completely serious, determined, young.

"I will never let anyone harm you," he assures me solemnly.

"And I," I respond, my voice croaking suddenly with emotion, "will never let anyone harm you, either."

Suddenly we kiss, not lingeringly and lovingly as we often do, but with a terrible desperation.

Yet why should we *both* be afraid, Father Aten? We are under your protection, and all we do is guarded by love.

Below the guards come jangling to attention. Horses' hoofs ring on pavement, the sweating animals snort and puff. Bustle fills the corridors, shouts and sounds of arrival echo through the South Palace.

Reluctantly we release one another and he assists me back to the dais. Leaning heavily on his strong right arm, yet still having to drag myself painfully and by sheer force of will, as I must increasingly do in these recent months when my body seems to weary along with my mind, I remount the throne.

"Her Majesty the Great Wife, the Divine Father-in-law and Councilor Aye, the General Horemheb, the Sage Amonhotep, Son of Hapu!" the Guardian of the King's Own Room shouts from beyond the door.

"In a moment!" I call back sharply. "When the Good God is ready!"

Quickly Smenkhkara hands me the crook and flail, adjusts the pleated kilt over my knees, settles the golden headdress more gracefully about my shoulders, adjusts the towering blue linen Double Crown more firmly on my head, makes sure the uplifted cobra head of the uraeus is centered exactly above my forehead. Then he quickly adjusts his own regalia, exactly similar to mine, and takes his seat on the throne at my right hand.

Then, and only then, when all is ready, do I raise my voice and, aided by your loving strength, O Aten, and his, call out in a strong and commanding voice that miraculously does not fail me but sounds strong and steady:

"Bid those enter who wish audience with the Kings of the Two Lands!"

Amonhotep, Son of Hapu

They greet us like two golden statues, seated on their double throne. In
spite of all we know, all we think, all we plan, it is impossible not to be
awed by the ancient mystery. Aye, Horemheb and I fall to our knees,
touch our foreheads to the floor in ritual greeting. Only the Great Wife
remains standing, rigid and unyielding in her golden garments, crowned
head high, eyes staring fearlessly into theirs.

"You have not provided chairs for us, my sons," she says in a clear,
level voice. "I did not rear you to show such discourtesy to those to
whom courtesy is due."

She pauses expectantly while Aye, Horemheb and I rise. No expression crosses Akhenaten's face, and after a lightning sidewise glance to
see what he should do, Smenkhkara sets his face in the same unyielding
pattern. The silence lengthens, begins to turn awkward. Anger, for her
and for us, begins to fill our hearts. Once again Nefer-Kheperu-Ra has
misjudged the world in which he lives.

"You wished to see me about something?" he inquires, ignoring her
question. For a split second we can sense her debating whether to force
the issue, order Aye to call up servants with chairs—which I do not
think even Pharaoh, lost as he is in dreams of the Aten and arrogance,
would dare countermand. We can also sense Smenkhkara's instinctive
protest at this brutal treatment of their mother, even as we sense his immediate helpless resignation as he realizes he cannot defy his brother.

Then we sense her decision: *No, let him act like this, if he is fool
enough. It will only strengthen our resolve.*

"Very well," she says, and with serene grace turns gravely and
beckons us forward. Not looking at the two Kings, we advance, Aye at
her right hand, Horemheb and I respectfully a half step behind, he on
the right beside his father, I on the Great Wife's left.

"Are you comfortable now?" Akhenaten asks with a biting sarcasm;
and serenely she replies, "Yes, my son, and we thank you for your courtesy in granting us audience this night."

"What is it you wish to discuss?" he asks; and as she did with Nefertiti, Queen Tiye decides to be blunt. Her resolve, we realize, goes even
deeper than we imagined.

"Your shameful order to Huy and Meryra that their tombs should depict the durbar solely with your brother and yourself, instead of in the traditional way with the Chief Wife, your daughters and the tribute of the Nine Bows and all our vassals and allies, *as befits the dignity and honor of this House,*" she says calmly, biting off the concluding phrase with an emphasis that shows she does not desire to take any nonsense.

Neither, of course, does he.

"Mother!" he says sharply, hunching forward awkwardly on his throne and glaring at her from his slanting, wide-set eyes. "Madam! The dignity and honor of the truth are more important than the dignity and honor of this House. And do you not forget that this is what my Father Aten tells me, and this is what I believe."

"Then you are a fool," she says coolly, and instinctively we gasp, for no one has dared talk to a Pharaoh like this before, not even a mother. But the Great Wife has made up her mind at last, and there is no mistaking, of course, where his iron comes from. She gave it to him: it is only natural that she should get it back. Which she does.

"Not as great a fool as those who would deny the truth!" he says with a sharpness equal to hers. "In which category, Madam, I find you now. I have given my order to Huy and Meryra that the durbar shall be pictured *as it was,* Ankh-Kheperu-Ra at my side, the few paltry tributes we had—"

"And whose fault is that?" she interrupts angrily. "Who has let the Empire dwindle to nothing? Who has been so lost in his games with the Aten—and with his brother—"

"Careful, Madam!" he cries angrily, his voice beginning to get its emotion-filled croak. "Mother, *be careful!*"

"So lost with these things that he has paid no attention to keeping Kemet strong, he has let all slide, he has abandoned all, he has been no Pharaoh but a play-King doing futile things for empty and futile purposes!" she shouts above his bitter protest, and then, womanlike, begins to cry. But there is no question of this being weakness. They are tears of anger, and she dashes them angrily from her eyes as she hurries on, permitting him no chance to reply.

"You have let the Two Lands fall into chaos and corruption! You have made a mockery of government! You have made of Kemet, and of yourself and your poor brother, a laughingstock to the world! You have lowered this House and this Dynasty to the ground! You have debased not only yourself but all of us with your foolish Aten and your wild crazy doings! And it must stop."

And, breathless, *she* stops, continuing to cry, continuing to dash away the tears with a furious, impatient anger. Only her heavy breathing and his fill the room: the rest of us, including poor Smenkhkara, who now looks scared to death and even younger than his twenty brief years, scarcely dare breathe at all.

It is obvious that he is going through an intense inner struggle. Tentatively at last his brother reaches out and grasps his arm, with something of the same soothing gesture we used so often to see Nefertiti employ with his rages in his younger days. But he is much older, the rages go deeper and last longer: it will take more than Smenkhkara's frightened little gesture to calm him now.

"Majesty," he says at last, words barely distinguishable in the harsh croak of his terrible emotion, "I think you had better go and take your fellow traitors with you. I shall not punish you as you deserve, for you are my mother, and all of you are—" He hesitates for a second and then changes the word as he appears to be swept by a sudden gust of feeling—can it be regret and sadness, can those actually be tears in the eyes of our strange, strange Nefer-Kheperu-Ra? "Since all of you are— my—my family. But I do not want you come near me again, or try to communicate with me in any way, or defile and defame Father Aten, or Ankh-Kheperu-Ra, or me, ever, ever, *ever* again. Go! Go! *Go!*"

Again there is silence while he stares at us like some wounded animal cornered and filled with bitterness and hate. We are stunned, we do not move. He is pale and quivering with the emotion and effort of it all, looking suddenly as though Anubis, guardian of the grave, were touching him urgently on the shoulder and might not long delay calling him to the West. At his side his brother looks equally stricken, but in a way typical of poor Smenkhkara, who must now pay the penalty we have decided upon for his brother's intransigeance: he looks stricken for his mother, whom he loves, for his brother, whom he loves, and for us, whom he loves. His concern is all with others, not with himself. How sad that such a goodhearted lad must die for no other crime, really, than simply being too goodhearted.

But this will come a little later, in some way no doubt already planned by Aye and Horemheb. For the moment they must make one last attempt to bring the Good God back to reason, before they can finally feel themselves free to proceed as they must.

"Does Your Majesty mean to strip me of all my powers and duties as Councilor?" Aye inquires at last in a low and trembling voice.

"I have told you," Akhenaten replies, obviously with a great effort but unrelenting: *"Go!"*

And so, after a few further seconds of uncertainty, Queen Tiye, still weeping, gestures us toward the door. Aye is weeping, Horemheb (quite genuinely, I believe) is weeping; I, too, weep for them all, for tragedies past and tragedies yet to come.

At the door I cannot resist a quick glance backward.

There on their thrones, holding one another in a desperate grasp whose terrible desolation communicates itself to me like a blow, the two mighty Kings of the Two Lands are weeping too.

How strange and terrible can families be, whose members sometimes do such awful things to one another.

We go to the beautiful little palace of the Great Wife on the bank of the Nile, there to set in motion the fate the gods have decreed for him who thought he could destroy the gods.

Merytaten

I do not know what happened when they all met last night, because Smenkhkara will not tell me. All I know is that this morning he is moping about, bursting into sudden tears, uttering unintelligible sounds, acting like a sickly girl, which I often think he is. I have never understood my father's infatuation for him: to me he has always seemed the weakest—if, no doubt, the prettiest—of the Family. I have suffered him as husband because that is what the needs of the Dynasty require, but I am glad to say I have never let him touch me—even had he wanted to, which he has not.

I have suffered him also because it is not only the needs of the Dynasty that concern me. If my father dies, as his poor health and uncaring ways with food—I doubt if he eats enough now to keep a bird alive —may soon guarantee, then my puling child of an uncle-husband will become the only King, supreme in power and authority, omnipotent Pharaoh of the Two Lands. No one will dare challenge him, no one will dare control him, no one will rule the ruler—save one.

I will. And presently, when he has served my purposes sufficiently— when with his spineless agreement I have removed my mother and my grandmother forever from any power in Kemet—maybe even removed them from life itself, if the gods do not soon do the task for me—then I shall consider what to do about *him*. After I have accomplished that, Kemet will have another Hatshepsut (life, health, prosperity!) to rule and strengthen the Two Lands anew.

I can do it. I have the strength. I have the courage. I am capable of it all. They tend to dismiss me as a domineering, unpleasant, interfering girl, but they do so at their peril. None of them will be safe from the Pharaoh Merytaten (life, health, prosperity to me!) when the time comes for me to strike. . . .

Thus do I dream, particularly on days like today when my pathetic stick of a husband shows himself in all his pretty weakness. I despise him. I despise them all. Maybe what I dream is nonsense but I do not think so. Everybody around me is weak except my mother and my grandmother, Aye and Horemheb. What nature does not dispose of, I can, if I plan carefully enough. And I will. I have little else to do but think about it all day long. I am quite capable of it. They will see.

Now I think I hear him coming: there is a sniffling in the hall. Yes, here he comes, still wiping his eyes with the back of a hand. But he has stopped crying, I think. In fact, he looks quite excited and, surprisingly, of a sudden quite happy. He is not alone. Peneptah, the bearded new scribe who has entered my father's house, is with him. I have noticed Peneptah for some time. He appeals to me. He too, I think, is very strong. He is also very manly and exciting in that way, too. Hatshepsut (life, health, prosperity!) had her Senemut as builder, councilor, lover and strong right arm to smite her enemies. Why should not Merytaten (life, health, prosperity to me!) have her Peneptah?

But now the weakling speaks.

"The Great Wife has sent me a beautiful scarab by this messenger!" he says excitedly. "Good Peneptah has brought it to me as a proof of her love! She does not hate us after all!"

"I did not know she hated you," I say coldly, though I cannot resist a quick, secret, amused little glance at Peneptah, who returns it with equal humor, and as furtively.

"You were not there last night," Smenkhkara says, and for a moment looks as though he might burst into tears again. But he is too excited by this bauble from his mother, which to me means nothing but to him, in the context of their apparent quarrel, seems to mean everything.

"So she has sent you a scarab," I say, letting my voice become mocking. Peneptah again gives me a secret little smile behind my uncle's back.

"Yes, here it is!" he says, still sounding like an excited child, and opening his hand, reveals it to me. It is indeed a beauty, large and finely carved, made of carnelian with inlaid wings and eyes of lapis lazuli. I must confess it appeals to me simply for itself. It must come from her private collection, and be very old. Perhaps it was even worn by Hatshepsut (life, health, prosperity!) Suddenly I am sure of it.

"Can I have it?" I ask bluntly while Peneptah smiles benignly in the background and encourages me with little winks and nods.

"Well—" Smenkhkara hesitates, and then says doubtfully, "It should be washed, I think. It gives off an odor of some sort. It stains my hands." He holds them out to me, and indeed there is a whitish dust upon them.

"It must be simply age," I say impatiently. "I cannot smell anything. Here, give it to me!"

And obediently, of course, he does, for anyone who speaks strongly to Smenkhkara can usually carry the day.

I take the scarab in my hands, rub it between them. The same powdery stain comes off upon me. I lift my hands to my nose, take a deep breath. There is indeed, though I will not give him the satisfaction of saying so, a faint peculiar odor. Seeing me give no sign, he follows my example and sniffs his hands deeply. Behind his back Peneptah continues to smile and nod encouragement. I must see that he returns when Smenkhkara goes to my father later in the day.

"It is nothing but dust," I say scornfully.

"I suppose you are right," he agrees less doubtfully. "It must be very old. I do not think she would send a proof of her love to me that was just new-made. It can only be very—very—"

And quite amazingly he stops in mid-sentence, gives a deep gasp for breath, clutches his throat, utters a strangled and incoherent cry and falls writhing at my feet.

Instinctively I start to lean down to him, when suddenly he goes limp. I start to scream, but am dimly aware that Peneptah has leaped forward and put a hand over my mouth. Suddenly I, too, cannot breathe. He removes his hand, I struggle, I start to fall. Gently he lowers me to the floor beside Smenkhkara. Again I try to scream, I cannot, there is no air, I cannot breathe—*I cannot breathe*—my body is twisting, turning —*I cannot breathe!*

Dimly through my terrible thrashings I see that Peneptah has stepped forward, carefully scooped up the scarab in a heavy cloth drawn from the folds of his garment, and stepped back.

He begins to fade from my glazing eyes. He is in the doorway, looking thoughtfully and patiently down upon us. He is still smiling.

Tutankhaten

Criers are shouting something in the city. There is a frightened silence out there everywhere. When I look out of the windows I see hardly any moving in the streets but there is much running and whispering in the North Palace. My cousin Nefertiti is crying hysterically as though she has seen terrible things. They say my brother Smenkhkara and my cousin Merytaten are dead, struck down suddenly by some unknown disease. Now I come next to my brother Akhenaten in line for the throne. I do not want to be Pharaoh. It means terrible things. I am frightened. *I do not want to be Pharaoh.* . . .

Akhenaten (Life, health, prosperity!)

Ah! They have killed my heart. Help me, Father Aten, help me or I shall die! Why can I not die? *I want to die!* Help me die, Father Aten, for my heart is dead, they have killed my heart! He wanted to do only good—I wanted to do only good—they have killed him, Father Aten, they have killed my heart. I shall go mad. *I shall go mad!* Help me, Father Aten! *Help me!*

Book II

DEATH OF A GOD
1361 B.C.

TIYE

AYE

HOREMHEB

Horemheb

He never stirs from the Great House now: neither my father nor I see him once in a month, probably. Yet the governing of Kemet somehow goes on because it has to go on. It goes on because we *make* it go on . . . and because there is no one else to do it.

When Smenkhkara died (as he had to die, and I feel no regret for that: he was the willing fool of his brother, and deserved it), the heart seemed to die as well in Akhenaten. This of course was what we intended. For seventy days he did nothing but hover, weeping, over the embalmment and burial; I think even the precious Aten was forgotten during that time. He acted as one paralyzed, lost in grief, uncaring what went on anywhere around him, saving only that the tomb, the mummy and the coffin—those affronts to the gods and common decency!—must be exactly as he wanted them.

Therefore, of course, neither my father Aye nor myself was stripped of any honors or powers. We simply went right ahead, aided by my younger half brother Nakht-Min, whom we persuaded Akhenaten to appoint Vizier, doing what had to be done for the Two Lands, exercising our authority unchanged, giving our commands as though he had never removed us from office. Besides ourselves there were only three other witnesses to that. One died the next morning, and the loyalty and support of the Great Wife and Amonhotep, Son of Hapu, have never wavered. No one will ever know that Nefer-Kheperu-Ra cried *"Go!"* to us in that frenzied, frantic, childish way, and banished us forever from power. And he is too disheartened and broken now ever to try it again.

This we have proved by putting it to the test. The first step, of course, was to order immediately that the coronation durbar be depicted in the tombs of Huya and Meryra exactly as the Great Wife and Nefertiti wished. Now in both tombs the scene is as it should be for all time: serene on their thrones, Akhenaten and Nefertiti, surrounded by their daughters, receive the Parade of Tribute from our dutiful allies and vassals. Around them are happy games and celebrations of his assumption of power.

It does not matter that this is not the truth.

Give it a few years and it will be.

When he made no objection to this, being still too bemused by grief to countermand us—we were very careful, mind you, to go to him and announce what we had done; he merely gave a long shuddering sigh and stared at us from those red-rimmed, unseeing eyes until we shivered, in something approaching fright, and went away—we felt that we had destroyed his will as we had intended, and that he would never recover sufficient strength to defy us. We knew that we could begin to proceed—still very cautiously and slowly, for he is still Pharaoh, of course, and there still might be some last flare of rage and defiance, though we think it very unlikely—to prepare for the end of his rule, the enthronement of Tut and the return of Amon.

"The end of his rule": this we have yet to accomplish, and the means are not yet fully clear. We have broken his will and with it we have apparently broken his body, for we understand from Hatsuret, who still remains on regular duty in the Palace, that he takes little food or water, prays constantly to the Aten and to his dead brother, grows steadily thinner and weaker, and seems, in fact, to be fading away physically as well as mentally. He lives almost in a daze, Hatsuret says (fingering with satisfaction the beautiful carnelian and lapis scarab, long since cleansed of its impurities, which he hangs about his neck on a gold chain and loves to fondle as he talks), and his end cannot be too long delayed. But how long is "too long," and how much longer can we afford to let Kemet suffer the indignities that everywhere beset her?

My father and I, aided by clever Tutu the Foreign Minister, now handle Pharaoh's correspondence with our allies and vassals—and a sorry correspondence it is. They used to beg for gold: now they beg for salvation. The Hittites, pushed back and held firmly in place by Tuthmose III and Amonhotep II (life, health, prosperity to them both, great builders and savers of the Two Lands!), are on the move again, raiding down under the leadership of their new King, Supp-i-lu-li-u-mas, into Mittani, Syria, Byblos and beyond. With them conspires Aziru of Amurru, playing a double game which is obvious to Aye and myself, though even now I do not quite dare send out armies on my own command: I am still paralyzed by the simple fact of Pharaoh. It is Pharaoh they want. *They want the Living Horus at the head of his troops* to save them, and they are right: nothing else can do it now. Things have reached such a pass of demoralization in our northern territories that only his actual presence could produce the necessary magic: and he is in no condition at all to go.

We do not feel guilty about this, nor do we take responsibility for it, since even when he had the strength he had no inclination. The Empire has been crumbling for a decade and he has done nothing about it even when he could. He would never have changed even had we left him in health. He has always been hopeless in this regard, as in so many others. He has had himself depicted in the friezes and statues smiting the enemies of Kemet like any other Pharaoh, but in his heart he has not had the will or the energy to lift a finger. It is only one in the long catalogue of his sins.

So the letters come in. They still address him as "the King, my Lord, my Sun, my God." They still say, "I am thy servant, the dust of thy feet. . . ." They still tell him, "I look to the King my lord, and there is light. . . . I move not away from the King's feet. . . . On my neck rests the yoke of my lord the King. . . ." They prate, "At the feet of the King my Lord seven times and again seven times I prostrate myself upon my back and upon my breast." And they beg for help, poor dogs:

"Oh my Lord, if the trouble of this land lies upon the heart of my Lord, let my Lord send troops, and let him come. . . .

"Lord of the Two Lands, King of Kings, God-King on earth: lead your army to us in your own divine person, at the head of your vast army, with glittering chariots of gold, with warriors heavy with weapons as far as eye can see!" . . .

And from Simyra and Tunip two months ago:

"Bring help, before it is too late!"

And from Tunip two weeks ago:

"Now we belong no more to our Lord the King of Kemet . . . when Aziru enters Simyra, Aziru will do with us as he pleases, in the territory of our Lord, the King. . . ."

And from Tunip yesterday:

"And now Tunip, thy city, weeps, and her tears are flowing, and there is no help for us."

And here we sit paralyzed, while all falls!

We do not show him these letters and we do not answer them. What would be the use? He would do nothing anyway. All falls, all falls! The Two Lands dwindle and the Hittites advance. Would I were Pharaoh now, to rid us of this shame before it is too late to rebuild the Empire and make Kemet great again!

It is late, it is late!

All falls. . . .

My father counsels patience. He shrinks, I think, from further death, as does the Great Wife. From time to time Nefertiti still tries, in vain, to see her husband. Fortunately he always refuses, so we do not have to interpose force to keep her from him. If she were to see him she might be able to rally him for one last attempt to reassert his power. She is the only one who could. But he does not know this: he deliberately keeps her away. Poor Akhenaten, who has always cut himself off from everyone and everything that could help him! I might weep for him, in some other world—indeed, I have wept for him, in days past. But he receives no tears from me any more. It is all too late for that.

Almost a year has passed since the death of Ankh-Kheperu-Ra. Still he grieves, shut away in the Great House. When my father and I visit, the windows are shuttered, incense burns, priests of the Aten, by his order, still chant dirges in the corridors: all is dark and gloomy. He has stopped wearing his regalia to greet us. Now he wears only a shabby old linen shift like a woman's, not even the pleated kilt of Pharaoh. He rarely bothers with a wig, his head looks dirty and scrofulous. His misshapen body is thinner, more elongated, more grotesque, if possible. I do not think he lets them bathe him very often. He is turning a little more each day into an old man, though he is barely thirty-two. Only the terrible eyes, haunted, unhappy, filled with pain, stare out at us, saying: *Leave me alone.* He curls upon his throne like an animal, wounded, resentful, dreadfully bereft. We never dare stay long. Conscience does not permit it: and it is all we can do to stand the sight and smell of him, even for a few moments. . . .

I wonder if we did the right thing?

My concern now is how best and quickest to finish the business: because if the gods did not mean for us to begin it, they should not have let us. And if they will not soon finish it for us, then we must do it ourselves.

Ramesses and Hatsuret have their orders to report to me instantly anything that will serve as excuse. Then I shall immediately confront the Great Wife and my father, and whether I receive their approval or not, it will be done.

I am determined that it shall not continue like this.

Ramesses

I hear some gossip among the soldiers that Nefertiti has selected twelve from among her small contingent of household troops and had them assigned to her as personal bodyguards. Why does she need them, I wonder? No one is attacking her.

Hatsuret

Anser-Wossett has sought an audience with Pharaoh. To everyone's amazement, he has agreed to receive her. They have already been closeted alone for almost an hour. Soldiers are posted at the door. They are Nefertiti's and will tell me nothing. I loiter close as long as I dare, but say nothing. They begin to give me strange looks. I drop back into the crowd. Why would Anser-Wossett seek audience? Why would he receive her? When she departs I am waiting near the steps. Our eyes meet, I nod toward the market-place. She gives the slightest of nods in return. I think she will meet me. Something brews. I must find out what it is. The Heretic must not be allowed to escape the vengeance of Amon.

Anser-Wossett

I approach the South Palace, trembling, on the orders of the Queen. I send in my name with the humble request that he grant me audience. Hatsuret lurks about as I wait but I never glance in his direction. I fully expect to be ordered sternly away, if not worse. When the messenger returns with word that the Good God will see me, I am amazed. I glance then at Hatsuret. He is as amazed as I, everyone is amazed. But I keep my face composed and impassive as the Queen does, and walk past them all down the long corridors to his room. Incense is burning, priests of the Aten chant soft dirges for Smenkhkara. I am announced, the doors are flung open. I sink to my knees without looking up, bend low to touch my forehead to the floor. Behind me the doors close. I look up and cannot suppress an involuntary start of dismay: he looks so awful. Of course he sees it, he has always seen everything. A bitter and sarcastic smile touches his face.

"The Lady Anser-Wossett may rise," he says, "before she falls over from astonishment at my sad appearance."

"No, Your Majesty," I stammer, "no—no—I only—"

"I know," he says in a more kindly tone, something of the graciousness he always used to show me in the old days returning. "Here, take this seat beside me, and we will talk."

"But, Your Majesty," I stammer again, overcome with awe and hesitation, "the seat beside you is—is—"

"It is an empty throne," he says bleakly. "I know. Please be seated and tell me why you come."

Still hesitantly, for what he invites me to do is really sacrilege, I slowly mount the steps to the dais and seat myself, trembling inwardly with fright at the enormity of my presumption even though he has invited it.

"Don't sit on the edge," he commands with a trace of amusement. "Sit back and be comfortable. . . . Now"—when I have obeyed, very gingerly—"how do you find me?"

He is dressed in a simple but clean linen shift; he is not wearing the pleated kilt of Pharaoh. He has put on a wig, which is clean. He looks much thinner and older than when I saw him last, really quite emaciated. There are circles under those eyes that always seem to penetrate to the very limit of one's innermost pretensions. I do not think he has bathed this day, or perhaps for several: a rank odor afflicts my nostrils. But I tell myself firmly that he is the Good God, the Living Horus, King and Pharaoh of the Two Lands, and I must do nothing that will destroy this intimacy which is greater than the Chief Wife and I had ever dared hope. So I give no sign—at least I think I give no sign. But again, with the heightened sensitivity to others' reactions to his person that he has had ever since his illness so many years ago, he knows.

"Yes," he says with a sad smile, "I am afraid I am not as cleanly as I used to be, and I am sorry if it offends you. But there is nothing now" —and again his face takes on that terrible bleak look—"there is nothing for which to keep myself in order . . . so more and more I find that I am letting myself become slovenly. Which I know I ought not to do, but"—he utters a heavy sigh—"somehow, I do not seem to care. . . . Here"—he reaches for a bottle of scented water that stands on a small table beside his throne—"let us scatter this about and see if it will make our talk more pleasant. . . . If you had given me advance warning you were coming," he goes on when he has finished and I am breathing more easily, "I should have made myself completely presentable for you. But then you might have been afraid to talk honestly to the god.

Now you can talk to one who, as you see, is but an unclean man, tired and ill and not, I think, too long fated to stay on this earth."

"Oh no, Your Majesty!" I protest. "Many, many years await you. Many good things still lie ahead, once this—this present time has passed."

"Once this present horror has passed?" he echoes with a smile so infinitely sad that it seems to turn my heart inside out for him. "Oh no, Anser-Wossett: it is not going to pass. It is going to stay with me until I die. Which, as I say, will not be long, I think. And do you know something?" He swings himself to face me fully, bracing himself with an arm against the arm of his throne. "I do not care. I simply do not care. I pray only to Father Aten that he may take me quickly, so that I may leave this ungrateful people who do not understand or appreciate me and go to rejoin the one who does."

"Your Majesty," I venture then, a terrible fear and trembling returning to my heart, for I do not know what his reaction will be: but the Queen has told me that if I am brave he will respect it and I will receive no harm. "Your Majesty, there is still one who understands and appreciates you, here on this earth. Why can you not, even now, return to her who still loves you?"

For several moments he is silent, sitting frozen as he is. I glanced away when I spoke, not daring to meet his eyes, and so I, too, sit frozen. I expect one of the sudden rages with which Her Majesty and I were once so familiar: such a rage as killed his uncle Aanen, for instance, or Amon's old High Priest Maya. May it not now kill Anser-Wossett? But when he finally speaks it is not in rage but a genuine puzzlement.

"Why did she send you to me?" he asks. "We have had no reason to speak to one another for three years. There is no reason now. She is dead to me—dead! Does she not understand that?"

"No, Your Majesty," I say, emboldened by his evident willingness to remain calm, "she does not understand that because she still loves you."

"What cause have I given her to do that?" he asks bluntly, and this time I do turn to him and face him as squarely as he faces me.

"No cause whatever, Your Majesty," I say, as bluntly as he. "In fact, much cause to the contrary. But we women are like that: it is the only explanation. She has been committed to you from a child. *She,* at least, remains true. . . ." And then, because he still does not rage but continues to look at me curiously from those strange, hooded eyes we will never get used to, I venture still further. "Is there nothing in you that remains true to her, Your Majesty?"

"Why did she send you here?" he asks, ignoring my question. "It was not to tell me of old love, surely."

"No," I say very quietly. "It was to offer you a plan to escape."

"Escape?" he asks blankly. "Are you telling me, then, that the Living Horus is a prisoner?"

"You would not be if you would still go about among the people," I say. "But Your Majesty stays always here, always secluded, always alone."

"I am alone!" he says sharply.

"They take advantage of it," I say, wondering at my own courage but feeling now that I have gone too far to stop.

"Who?"

"Many."

"Name them!"

"They are as numerous as the sands, Your Majesty," I say, trembling again inside for fear my evasion will provoke his wrath, but determined not to be diverted from the Chief Wife's purpose. "They are in your house, they are throughout Kemet, they are north in Naharin, they are south in wretched Kush, they are everywhere along your borders—everywhere. And as long as you remain here in the South Palace and do not break out, as long as you do not take the government back in your own hands—"

"Are you saying my uncle Aye and cousin Horemheb are betraying me?" he interrupts sharply.

"I say they are ruling Kemet because Your Majesty will not," I retort, and truly then I do not expect to live, for at last his face clouds and a furious expression comes into his eyes.

"You go too far, Lady," he says, his voice suddenly choked with emotion.

"I humbly beg Your Majesty's pardon," I say, and lower my head and draw my veil across my eyes, which I close in both fright and resignation, for I fully expect the next step to be calling of the guards, followed by prison or death for me.

Instead, nothing happens. I am aware of his heavy, angry breathing, I am sharply aware that the effect of the perfumed water is wearing off and the odor is returning; I am aware that I am but a humble subject daring to speak to the Good God as only the Family, I am sure, has ever spoken to him. I am aware that I am sitting, incongruously, on the throne of Kemet, a thought that almost makes me burst into hysterical laughter. I am aware of many things, but the principal one I am aware of is that he is not going to kill me, or even let his rage continue much longer.

"You speak treasonous things," he says at last, quietly, "but no doubt you believe you have good cause. Exactly what is the reason my wife sent you here?"

At this I am greatly encouraged, for I believe it has been a very long time since he has acknowledged the fact that Her Majesty is still his wife.

"She has prepared your escape," I repeat. This time he studies me intently.

"Tell me," he says, half mocking, "where does Pharaoh 'escape' to?"

"Twelve of her household troops are trained and ready," I say. "Prepare yourself. They will come tonight at midnight while all the Palace is asleep. Her Majesty will come with them. She will announce to the guards that she is coming to see you. You, meanwhile, will have told your guards that you expect her, very late, and that she is to be admitted. They will not dare challenge her if you have given the order. She will remain but a very brief while. You will then see her to the outer door, accompanied by her soldiers. Hidden around the corner in the next street will be a litter for you. You will proceed together, not in haste but without slowness either, to the litter. No one will dare challenge you. You will go to the North Palace, take up residence and tomorrow a new day will begin for the Two Lands when you go together to the Window of Appearances to announce to Kemet that you are reunited and that henceforth you are resuming active control of all Your Majesty's affairs, removing Aye and Horemheb from their offices and appointing others loyal to you."

I pause, a little out of breath from this lengthy recital. I can see that he is, for the moment at least, interested and perhaps even excited: his face shows more animation than I have seen it show since the death of Smenkhkara. For a moment this lingers, I can see him thinking about it almost as though he believed it possible. Then as abruptly as his face has begun to glow with life, the glow fades. He seems to shrink, to withdraw, to hide away into himself again; he actually seems to grow smaller and more wasted even as I watch. It is a very odd sensation I have, and it tells me before he speaks that we may have lost him. But he is courteous about it: His Majesty has always been courteous to me. And I do not intend to give up without an argument, having gone so far.

"Lady," he says, "tell your mistress I appreciate her care for me, but tell her that what she proposes is impossible. I could not leave this house where I have been happy to return to one where I was unhappy —even though I am no longer happy here. But it is here I belong. It is here I can best worship the Aten and the memory of—of him who strengthened me in all I did. I could not abandon them to return to the Chief Wife."

"I do not believe she wishes you to abandon them, Your Majesty," I say. "She worships the Aten as you do. Together you can give him new life in the Two Lands, where few now favor him. And as for His late Majesty Smenkhkara"—he flinches at the name, but I go bravely on as Her Majesty would wish—"I believe Her Majesty fully respects your grief for him, and would not resent your expression of it. Her Majesty," I conclude quietly, "has suffered much, and learned much, in these last three years. I think she will be happy only to have you returned to her side, and well again."

"Yes," he says gloomily, distracted and as if to himself, "I am not well. . . ."

"Then come to the North Palace, Your Majesty!" I urge. "Come back to those who will love and care for you! Do not remain here where you are so unhappy and alone. They do not really care for you here—no one does. I think Your Majesty knows this, in his heart."

Again I have dared greatly in saying such candid things: but I feel I must. And it appears that I have been right, for now he turns finally, draws himself back in his throne and again looks me full in the face.

"It would be nice," he says, so forlornly that it wrenches my heart, "to be where someone cared for me again."

"Then return to the North Palace tonight!" I exclaim. "Give the orders! Receive Her Majesty! Leave here with her! And restore yourself tomorrow to the power that grief has driven from your hands!"

He looks at me thoughtfully for a very long time, during which I hardly dare breathe for fear I will wrongly affect his decision.

"Well—" he says at last.

"Return to those who love you, Majesty!" I dare exclaim, encouraged by his hesitation.

"Aye and Horemheb would be much upset," he says in a faraway tone, and I can see him considering—rejecting—accepting—rejecting—accepting again—"but if it were done swiftly and without warning—if they did not know until I appear tomorrow at the Window of Appearances what my intentions are—if I perform wonders again for Kemet, my people—"

"Then Your Majesty will do it!" I cry joyfully.

He reaches out a long, thin hand and clutches mine with a desperate grasp like one drowning in the arms of Hapi.

"Go and tell my wife," he says in a hurried, almost frightened voice, "that I will receive her at midnight tonight and we will go to the North Palace!"

"Majesty!" I cry, and leaving the throne of Kemet, where I had never expected to sit in all my life and of course never will again, I kneel at his feet, lift the hem of his garment and press it to my lips.

He places a hand gently on my head.

"Go, now!" he says with an excited urgency. "The Lady Anser-Wossett has served the Two Lands well this day!"

"Thank you, Majesty," I say humbly, backing out of his presence. The last I see of him is the misshapen figure leaning forward intently on the throne, the long, narrow eyes wide with thought, the mind far away —but alive again now, no longer dull, no longer dead, as he contemplates with an evident excitement what will happen this night and to-morrow.

I have succeeded beyond the wildest hopes of Her Majesty and myself. Acting entirely on Her Majesty's intuition, we have caught him at that exact moment at which even the deepest mourning becomes boring and it is time for life to resume.

As I leave the Palace I become aware that Hatsuret is signaling me insistently from the small crowd of watchers that always idles about the gates. He wants me to meet him in the market-place. He, too, has an urgency about him. I consider for a second whether it can do harm. I know I will tell him nothing of what has occurred—and perhaps I can find out something from him that will be helpful in furthering Their Majesties' plans. With the slightest of movements I return his nod.

When my carriage reaches the market-place I order the driver to stop and wait in a shady corner. I dismiss my escort of soldiers and send them on their way back to the North Palace, asking their captain to tell Her Majesty only: "The Lady Anser-Wossett has good news." Then I compose myself beside a vegetable vendor's stand and pretend to inspect his offerings while I wait for Hatsuret.

Presently, he comes.

Nefertiti

Word has reached me from the captain of the guard that "The Lady Anser-Wossett has good news," though she has not yet returned from the market-place to give it me herself. She likes to go to the market from time to time, though it is not necessary for her to do so, since my steward Huya oversees the buying for the North Palace. (Poor Huya! He has been cowed since the decision to depict the coronation durbar in his tomb as the Great Wife and I desired. But I have told him nothing was his fault: he and Meryra simply got caught in the midst of a family argument, and all is well. Nonetheless, he still finds difficulty meeting my eyes sometimes.)

So Anser-Wossett has not returned but her message indicates that our wildest hopes must have come true. He is going to accept my plan: he is coming back to me, and the world will begin anew, for me and for poor threatened Kemet.

For this I have dreamed and planned and plotted for a year, ever since the murders of Smenkhkara and Merytaten. I did not know, for a time, whether I could recover from those two deaths, which were in considerable measure due to me. When I mentioned Smenkhkara's name that night during our family conference, I did not contemplate that he would be removed so swiftly and so violently: I had thought some gentler means, such as banishment to wretched Kush or the Red Land, might be used. But I suppose my father Aye and Horemheb had no choice: he would not have gone, Akhenaten would not have permitted it, and nothing would have been achieved.

So, though I cried wildly for a time when I heard the news, for my hapless, well-meaning cousin and even for my shrewish, unnatural daughter—but most of all for myself who had been party to such a dreadful thing—I did not cry overlong. I thought the principal obstacle to my husband's rule (and my own happiness) had been removed, and that we could now go forward to a better day for all of us.

I did not contemplate how terribly he might be shattered, for I had refused to believe the signs that revealed how deeply he cared for his brother—and I had also grievously misjudged the determination of my father and the true nature of my half brother Horemheb.

I am now desperately afraid of them both; and so, I think, is Queen Tiye.

We have not discussed it very much, but when we have she has spoken with a profound and still grieving sadness of the son whose murder she had to agree to in order to save, she thought, the son who must be saved if he was to continue to wear the Double Crown and discharge the great responsibilities of the Two Lands.

Except that her plan, too, went awry: he still wears the Double Crown but he has retired almost entirely from the rule of the Two Lands. It rests now with Aye and Horemheb; and I sense that Horemheb, in particular, is growing ever more restive as he exercises many of the rights of power without the sanction of power.

This the Great Wife senses as well as I; and both of us, now, are coming to perceive how iron is his will and how ruthless his determination. We know what his ultimate ambition is, because Sitamon, embittered by his refusal to marry her, recently told the Great Wife. Yet he cannot possibly be Pharaoh, for poor little frightened Tut comes next, and soon now he will be married to Ankhesenpaaten, which will sanctify his full claim upon the throne; and where does Horemheb fit then? We cannot see: yet we know he dreams of it, and we know that such a dreamer is dangerous indeed to Pharaoh.

So both Queen Tiye and I have come to realize that what we were responsible for has not worked out at all as we thought it would. Just yesterday when she was visiting me—having finally come down from Thebes to spend a few days in her palace here and see for herself what all reports have told her—we admitted this to one another. Finding that she agreed with me, I decided to put into effect at once the plan that is apparently going to save the Good God and the Two Lands, at last.

(It is now nearing dinnertime. Ra is sinking in the west. The Nile has turned to copper. Across on the other bank the cultivated lands that serve Akhet-Aten, and the distant mountains beyond, are becoming purple and misty in the dying light. Anser-Wossett should be back by now. I shall send very shortly to find out where she is, for she must report to me in detail all that she said to my husband, and all that he said to her.)

Actually I did not need the approval of the Great Wife for my plan, because I have become determined to do it. And actually she did not say in so many words that she does approve. But I could tell from her expression that she was relieved to know that I was going to accomplish what we have both desired so desperately in this past year: the beginning of the campaign to restore Kemet to all her glories, which will be long and hard because of Akhenaten's almost complete uncaring for it in these recent months.

For me, of course, it will mean even more: the return to my side of him whom I have loved since a child and still love, despite all the insults and indignities he has heaped upon me and the coldness with which he has treated me since he put me aside to take Smenkhkara in my place.

It has not been an easy time for me—sometimes I have thought I would die of it, so bitterly has it hurt my heart—but I have been strong and I have persevered, as becomes a daughter of Aye and Chief Queen of the Two Lands. Now it is all going to come right at last, as I have always felt it would if I could just be brave enough to withstand the bur-

den that might have crushed me completely were I made of weaker
stuff.

But most of all, I hope and believe, it will mean happiness for him
who has had so little in his tense and lonely life. As a boy, before his
ailment, when he was Crown Prince, handsome, vigorous, joyously active with all the world waiting for his rule, I know he was happy. I think
that perhaps for six years after we were married, while our six daughters were entering the world and our childhood love for one another
was ripening into maturity, that he was happy with me. Then he began
to lose heart because his worship of the Aten, even though he built this
great city in the Sole God's honor, was not spreading to the people.
He destroyed Amon and the other gods, he abandoned me, he turned
to Smenkhkara. Perhaps he was happy with his brother, but I do not
believe it, for still the Aten failed to win the people, and still his dreams
of a universally loving world under a universally loving god did not ma-
terialize. And even if he was happy with Smenkhkara, that, too, only
lasted three years—could not last more, for Kemet's sake. All his young
beauty lost, all his dreams frustrated, all his plans gone wrong: I do not
think Nefer-Kheperu-Ra has been very happy with his life. It has made
me love and pity him the more. . . . Even when he turned against me I
could not stop.

In this past year word has come to me through my father, through
Horemheb and through Anser-Wossett—in just a moment I will send
for her, I am anxious to know that all is ready for my plan—of how
completely he has abandoned physical pride and self-respect. It has
been obvious to all of Kemet that he has virtually abandoned civil government, but since he has kept himself mostly hidden in the South Palace in the past twelve months only the Family and his immediate servants have been aware of his personal deterioration. Anser-Wossett
from time to time sees Peneptah, the bearded scribe who assists
Amonhotep, Son of Hapu, and from him she has brought me stories of
little things that the others have not known—the lateness of the hour at
which he rises, the listlessness with which he shuffles about the Palace,
the growing disinterest in eating, the frequent nocturnal passages when
he cannot sleep but goes, driven by demons—or the vengeful gods—to
wander the corridors alone and unbefriended. These things have made
me weep many bitter tears and have made my heart cry out to him . . .
though when I have tried to convince him of my continuing love and
my desire to help he has refused to see me and has continued on his
desolate way.

But now all that will change: I shall make him happy again at last.

He is coming back—I still cannot quite believe it! I do not know what prompted me to organize my plan, to realize by some blessed instinct that now might be the time when he would respond—but somehow *I knew.* So I formed my household guard of twelve men, giving no explanation to my father or Horemheb, both of whom were curious but did not quite dare ask me outright. I tested their loyalty, I waited until I was sure I could trust them completely—and then I sent Anser-Wossett to him today, and all has fallen into place beyond my dearest hopes.

I shall not truly exult until all has been safely accomplished. But for the first time in many years I, too, believe I will once again be happy, which in my darkest moments I thought had been denied me forever.

It is nearing time to go to my formal banquet room for dinner, and Anser-Wossett must come to me. We have much to talk about.

I rise from the bench before my mirror, where I have been thinking these things, hardly daring to acknowledge the growing hope and excitement I have seen in my eyes (which still are beautiful, though very sad—but much less sad now, and very soon, I hope, not sad at all), and go to the door, open it and clap my hands for a servant. For a moment none are about, the busy palace seems unusually quiet; but presently I see one of my lesser ladies in waiting coming toward me down the long painted corridor.

Amazingly, she weeps. What can it mean?

What can it mean?

My heart feels a sudden terror, I do not know why. But very soon, in a voice racked with sobs, she tells me, and I do.

I know now where Anser-Wossett is. Her battered body was tossed off at the palace gate a few minutes ago by a chariot that fled away, its driver masked and unrecognized. It was obvious she had been tortured before she died. So all must be known to someone who wishes us ill.

My poor Anser-Wossett who has been with me so many years! Oh, my heart grieves, it grieves! Good, faithful, loving, loyal—ah, such evil, such evil! May the Aten help us now! . . .

For many minutes I stand like stone while the lady weeps beside me. I am too stunned to weep, two stunned to think . . . for a while.

But presently I do.

I am not a daughter of Aye and Chief Queen of the Two Lands for nothing. My heart which has known so much sorrow can stand a little more.

I shall harden myself, I shall meet what comes without fear. Right now there is just one thing to do: go to my husband and rescue him.

I call the captain of my guard, I give him the orders, I prepare myself hastily to leave. I wear my golden shift and my Blue Crown, for I go as a Queen with my head held high and my face once again—as always when my people see me—commanding and composed.

I am Nefertiti and I will not be denied.

No one sees us leave the Palace and start across the city whose many thousands, all unknowing of the events that are occurring in their midst to affect their lives forever, are placidly eating before their peaceful hearths.

A chill wind is driving off the Nile now that night has truly come. It is turning winter and soon it will be cold: but not for Akhenaten and Nefertiti.

We will win this battle and, with Father Aten's help, regain in happiness our full rule and glory.

He has made many errors: no doubt I have. But from now on we will do all things right for the Aten and for our beloved kingdom and people of the Two Lands.

Aye

Now is this hour of final reckoning, before Horemheb and I go to my sister to secure her compliance in the terrible thing we must do, I seek a balance between the good I have known of my nephew Akhenaten and the evil he has brought upon our beloved kingdom and people of the Two Lands. I must also, if I can, accept the fate that very likely is about to fall equally upon my beautiful, misguided daughter, who has suffered so much and whom I have loved so much as things have spun down and down with increasing rapidity for them both.

Of my nephew Nefer-Kheperu-Ra, what is one to say? I loved him as a handsome child before his malady overcame him, I loved him as a young, misshapen but well-meaning Co-Regent, I still loved him as an increasingly willful and headstrong King; but each stage of love has been less than the one before, and steadily my dismay and mistrust have grown. I have forgiven him so much: we all have forgiven him so much. The balance finally drawn must, I fear, come down against him.

We could accept, I think, the early attempts to establish the Aten— the murder of my brother Aanen, who asked for it—the attempt, for which I was directly responsible, to give the Aten equal stature but still maintain Amon and the other gods. We could even accept his desperate and pathetic attempts to achieve the son Nefertiti could not give him by marrying his three oldest daughters, and by them having three daughters, all puny and mercifully now dead. But none of us has been able to accept these years just past when all the gods were destroyed, and when amiable and foredoomed Smenkhkara shared the throne, met his fate, and left his brother to decline ever more swiftly into the almost animal squalor we now see when we visit him in his haunted palace.

Smenkhkara, I know, made some earnest if ineffectual attempts to keep the government going during the period he shared the throne, while Akhenaten became ever more lost in his fading dream of the Aten. Horemheb, my other son Nakht-Min and I did what we could to help, an assistance Smenkhkara accepted gratefully, for he was very young. But it did no good: the whole thing continued to slide both within Kemet and on our borders, until the awful night when Nefertiti inspired us to kill him, and his mother, my sister the Great Wife, agreed.

We thought then, foolishly as it turned out, that the shock of his brother's death would drive Akhenaten out of his lethargy and, after a period of suitable mourning, bring him back to active rule. We also thought it would make him compliant to our growing conviction that Amon and the other gods must be restored, if not to their full power, then at least to a position befitting their place in all our ancient traditions. But neither, alas, was meant to be.

Instead we have the lonely and haunted recluse to whom we report the formalities of our rule in his name, but whose slovenly person we can hardly bear to look at, and whose intelligence, while still great, is increasingly far away in the depths of mourning and the pointless worship of the Aten.

Or so we had thought until tonight. Suddenly tonight he has revived and with my daughter's aid threatens to resume with all his old demanding persistence the power of the Double Crown and the active and unrelenting pursuit of his sacrilegious Sole God.

For perhaps an hour after Horemheb came to me with the news Hatsuret and his hidden acolytes had tortured out of poor Anser-Wossett (a violence I would never have condoned had I known about it, unless it were absolutely necessary: I think frightening her with it would have been enough, though she was always fiercely loyal to my daughter and it might not have been) I remained silent in my chair, staring blankly at the wall while a thousand things raced through my mind.

I dismissed Amonhotep, Son of Hapu, who had been with me discussing matters of government, and ordered him to tell no one. He looked deeply hurt and offended, for it is the first time in many years that we have not sought his wisdom in our family councils. But I told him that the responsibility now rested solely on my sister, myself and my son Horemheb. Wounded, he went away. For a moment I had a pang of uneasiness and regret; then I put it aside. We can count on his loyalty, we always have. He will tell no one, and it is better that on this final dreadful occasion he not be directly involved. It is truly our responsibility alone, for we, even more than his old tutor, have made Akhenaten what he is.

So I sat and thought, while patiently Horemheb sat with me. He made no attempt to influence me, he spoke no word. He simply watched me with a complete and controlled attentiveness.

He is very shrewd, Horemheb, very determined and very astute. There is no way for him to reach the place he would like to fill but he is an invaluable assistant to me in all that must be done to save the Two Lands.

So a few moments ago I finally turned to him and asked:

"What would you suggest, my son?"

"There can be only one solution," he replied in a somber voice.

"I shudder to contemplate it," I said.

"So do I," he said calmly, "but we have no choice."

"Can we not somehow banish him?"

He looked at me long and steadily before he replied with a quiet certainty:

"Father, you know perfectly well it would not work. Nefer-Kheperu-Ra perhaps has nothing left but his stubbornness, but he does have that. The wound must be cleansed completely, and it must be cleansed immediately, now the opportunity has presented itself. We must close our hearts, harden our resolve, ask the blessing of Amon and the gods, and strike without mercy, leaving no possible chance that he could ever return to power."

"To kill the Living Horus," I almost whispered, so awful is it to contemplate, even now, "is no light thing, my son."

"I do not approach it lightly," he said with the same implacable calm. "I approach it as the thing that must be done to save the Two Lands from utter and final destruction, both within and without."

"Tut should be told."

"Tut is a child," he said with a sudden harshness. "We will tell him when it is over. It will be time enough then for him to know that what he fears has happened. As Regent, I will inform him in due course. First, it must be done."

"'As Regent'?" I echoed sharply. "Who said you will be Regent, my son?"

"You have just heard me say it, Father," he said, staring me impassively straight in the eyes. For a second I was so taken aback by his sheer effrontery that I could not speak. Then I replied in the cold tones that have made many men tremble at the wrath of the Councilor Aye:

"*I* shall be Regent, and there will be no further discussion of it!"

"You are old, Father," he said, "and I am still in my forties, still relatively young and vigorous. And I have the army at my back. It would ill become us to engage in an unseemly battle for control of the King."

"You have *some* of the army at your back," I said, for it is true, he has many divisions loyal to him, "but I also have many members of it who still stand in awe and complete loyalty to the Divine Father-in-law Aye. Is it civil war you wish us to fall into over the corpse of your cousin Akhenaten? If so"—and my voice was as steely and unrelenting as I have ever made it—"I am ready."

He paused then in his headlong flight toward insane ambition and studied me for a very long time, very carefully, while my expression remained stern and never yielding. My eyes met his with an icy sternness as I thought: *This is my son. What have I created? . . . But I shall ever be stronger than he, and he knows it in his heart.*

And presently I could sense that with an obvious great effort of will he was acknowledging this to himself and abandoning his insane bluff to replace the one man whose consistent strength through more than thirty years has been the true salvation of Kemet in all her troubles.

"Very well," he said at last, very quietly, still not taking his eyes from mine. "But I shall be King's Deputy, then."

"You may be that," I conceded, for our strengths are so nearly equal that, though I did not show it, I feared a battle between us as much as he. "We shall proclaim all from the Window of Appearances in due course."

"After the occupant of the Window of Appearances is no more," he said softly; and though I shuddered again at the enormity of it, I agreed with equal softness, "It is the will of the gods. . . . However," I added firmly, "there must be no harm to Nefertiti."

"She has already been warned," he said, "and if she is as intelligent as I know her to be, she will already have abandoned her pathetic plot and be even now preparing herself for graceful widowhood."

"Are you sure of that?" I demanded. For the first time in our interview he smiled, a slight, wry smile.

"No, I am not sure of it, Father. You have bred a family of lions, and as one of them I cannot vouch for what one of the others may do."

"Your sister must not be harmed," I said again sternly. He responded with a cold indifference. "That is up to her. I hope she will not be."

I made it an order:

"You will see to it!"

He gave me a steady look and shrugged.

"It is up to her," he said again; and turning the subject with a sudden briskness, "We must yet have the approval of the Great Wife before we act. Do you wish to go to her alone, or shall we go together?"

"Together, I think," I said, and repeated, again with a shudder at the enormity about to engulf us: "The murder of the Living Horus is no light thing."

"Good!" he said, leaping to his feet. "We must go to her at once, for the time is very short in which to catch him unprepared at the Palace."

"Yes," I agreed, and also stood up. As I did so there came a frantic pounding on the door. Without announcement or apology Ramesses burst in, wild-eyed and desperate.

"The Queen has left the North Palace!" he cried. "We must stop her at once!"

"Yes!" Horemheb exclaimed, starting for the door. Then he paused in mid-step and said slowly, "No, let her come to him. . . . We will meet her there."

"No harm to her!" I shouted in a terrible voice that made Ramesses turn pale at my fury. But Horemheb gave no sign.

"Go to the Great Wife and send me word at once, Father!" he yelled over his shoulder as they crossed the threshold and started running down the hall. "Tell her it is too late to stop the just vengeance of the gods!"

"I will!" I shouted back. "But again, *no harm to your sister!*"

But they were gone at the turning of the corridor and there was no answer. I flung a robe around me against the cold and hastened shouting through the house for a chariot.

And now I am at the gates of the lovely little palace my nephew built for his mother in happier days, and now they are escorting me to her private chamber. And now together we must agree upon our last, awful act for the sake of Kemet and the millions who, all unwitting, plunge with us tonight into a future I believe not even the greatest gods can foretell.

Akhenaten (Life, health, prosperity!)

Can it be hope I feel, after all these awful months? I can scarcely imagine it. Yet do I still have sufficient faith in the word of Nefertiti that I believe it must be so. . . .

Only you and I, Father Aten, know the agonies I have gone through since they came to me with word of my brother's death. The reason was never officially discovered, but for the two of them to die so swiftly and so horribly there could be but one explanation. Someone saw fit to poison them: someone very close to me. I scarcely dare admit to myself it was at the order of my mother, my uncle and my cousin Horemheb, yet there is no other sensible conclusion. Is it any wonder I have retreated into myself to nurse my awful pain and loneliness as best I could? I have not dared do other, for daily I have lived in fear that presently they would come for me.

The Living Horus, Great Bull, Son of the Sun, He Who Has Survived, Living in Truth Forever, Nefer-Kheperu-Ra Akhenaten, King and Pharaoh of the Two Lands—cowering like a thief in his own palace, terrified of his own family! Father Aten, it has been dreadful for me. Still, I could do no other.

For the seventy days it took to embalm him, I ventured out only to supervise the process. So terrible was my obvious grief that no one ventured to speak to me, let alone harm me, then. I was enwrapped in grief, engulfed in grief, drowned forever, it seemed to me, in grief. I do not recall now whether I even knew when Ra rose in the east and set in the west during those endless interwoven days and nights: it seems to me only a long, gray blur in which I came and went between the House of Vitality, where the rites went on, and the Palace. Priests of the Aten accompanied me wherever I went, chanting their dirges for the dead. Frequently, for hours at a time, I could not even move, but only lay weeping on the floor before the sculpture of that beloved head that Tuthmose completed for me only a week before he died. I could not believe he was gone, my little brother who grew to be such a comfort to my heart and such a strength to my being. But he was: he was.

The mummification of Merytaten I left to others. I scarcely knew when it was completed, gave to Nefertiti and my mother (how could she have the courage, the effrontery and the heartlessness?) the task of presiding over her final going beneath the ground in the Royal Wadi in the eastern hills of Akhet-Aten. I was notified that it had occurred, but that was only a day before I had to preside at my own grief-filled ceremony. I barely noticed: my daughter's going moved me very little. I never liked her particularly. She was simply a convenience who, like her mother, could not even bear me a son. She was useful to keep the domestics of the Palace in line: that was all.

To Smenkhkara, however—even now it cuts me like a knife to say that name—I gave the most tender and most loving entombment he could possibly have desired. The memory of his sunny nature, always open, generous, undemanding, comforting, supported even as it devastated me. I got through it somehow and arranged it so that all who come after will know how much he meant to me.

I used one of the coffins originally prepared for Merytaten, for there had been no time to prepare one suitably ornate for him. Around the head of the one to whom I had given Nefertiti's name of Nefer-neferu-aten and the title, "Beloved of Akhenaten," I caused to be placed the sheet-gold vulture that usually bedecks the crown of a Queen: the golden wings will protect him forever. His body I caused to be mummified, not with arms crossed over the chest like a King's as though to carry scepters, but as a Queen with his left hand closed upon his breast and his right arm stretched along his side: thus will all know the position he held in my life. And at the foot of his coffin I caused to be inscribed, as if from him to me—as the God who will someday raise him from the afterworld—the prayer I composed myself in one of those occasional curious periods of detachment that come in the midst of deepest grieving:

"I shall breathe the sweet air that issues from thy mouth. My prayer is that I may behold thy beauty daily, that I may hear thy sweet voice belonging to the North Wind, that my body may grow young with life through thy love; that thou mayest give me thy hands bearing thy sustenance and I receive it and live by it; and that thou mayest call upon my name forever and ever and it shall not fail in thy mouth."

Thus will all know how tenderly and eternally he touched my heart.

Then I came away to return here to the Great Palace and resume the seclusion from which I have not, from that day to this, gone forth.

At first I took no interest at all in government. Aye, Horemheb and Nakht-Min came to me as in a recurring dream, their words meaningless, their reports incomprehensible. Somehow Kemet continued to be governed, by them but not by me. I knew this was wrong, that I should bestir and reassert myself, but a great lethargy held my heart.

And in spite of what I sensed about their part in the murder of my brother, I felt that I could trust them: I was still the Living Horus, and none, not even they who had wounded me so deeply, would dare betray me.

More lately, I have not been so sure: but still the grief and lethargy have held me prisoner. I have eaten less and less, grown thinner and more grotesque. With increasing carelessness I have allowed my physical appearance and cleanliness to decline. Again, I have known this was not right, that pride and the dignity of Pharaoh should require me to do otherwise. But again, the great pain and dullness have made me listless and uncaring.

So it has gone until a few short days ago. I do not know exactly what inspired the turning point, unless it was my surviving brother and now my heir, who came to me with a childish concern because he had not seen me for many months. Timidly he came alone in his chariot, surrounded by soldiers, from the North Palace where he lives with Nefertiti. Timidly he sent in word that he was here and asked to be admitted to my presence. My first instinct was to say no, as I have refused, until today, all requests from my wife. Then something made me relent, some memory of my own childhood, a realization of how little, how lonely and how lost he must feel in the midst of all these violently unhappy grownups; and so I reconsidered and bade them bring him in.

"Brother," he began, after he had prostrated himself dutifully at my feet and I had raised him up, "Your Majesty—how are you?"

It was asked very simply and directly, as befits a child; and it revived with a sudden rush all the affection I have always felt for little Tut, who was such a happy baby and now has been made tense and over-old by all that has happened in his eight brief years.

"I am not well, Brother," I responded, beckoning him to sit beside me on the empty throne—the first of the only two I have so honored— "but your visit makes me feel better."

"Oh," he said, eyes wide and earnest, "I am *so* glad. We have all been worried about you."

"Have you?" I asked with a smile, though I hardly believed it—at least not of my mother, Aye and Horemheb. "You are very kind."

"I have brought you a present to make you happy," he said, and held out a brown little hand, clenched tight. Slowly he unfolded it, eyes gleaming with excitement, to reveal an exquisite pale blue faïence pendant of the god Thoth in his aspect of the baboon. I still have a liking for Thoth, whose priesthood in the old days was quite small and never any real threat to me; and besides, he is the god of wisdom, scribes, learning and the arts, all of which I have respected and encouraged all my life. But I did not at once accept the gift, for through my mind there ran a sudden terrible warning:

Beware! They killed Smenkhkara with poison. Perhaps they have sent this innocent child to wreak their evil upon you. Beware!

"It is beautiful," I said, keeping my voice calm but not for the moment taking it from his hand.

"Why don't you take it?" he inquired in a puzzled tone, his eyes concerned. "It will not hurt you."

"Are you sure?" I asked, unable to keep the concern from my voice.

"Look!" he said. "It does not hurt me."

And he lifted it, turned it over, shook it, placed it next to his face, sniffed it, licked it—all with a deliberate and knowing air that made me realize sadly that even at his age he must have come to understand the evil of his elders and the method they used to wreck my life.

"No," I agreed, smiling as I took it from his hand, "it does not hurt you and you have bravely proved that it will not hurt me. I shall treasure it and wear it on a gold chain around my neck as evidence that there is one of my family, at least, who cares for me."

"We all care for you," he said earnestly, upset by my bitter tone; but I am afraid too much has happened for me to conceal my bitterness.

"You are generous to think so, little Tut," I said, "and I pray you may never have cause yourself to think otherwise. But I must warn you to be careful, as I must be careful, for the Son of the Sun has many enemies."

"I know it," he said, looking suddenly quite as old as his apparent knowledge of the dangerous world in which we live. "It is very hard being Pharaoh, is it not?"

"For me," I said somberly, "it has been very hard. But for you, when it comes your time, I hope and believe it will be better."

"I am frightened," he said in a wistful little voice that caused me to take his hand quickly and give it a reassuring squeeze.

"You must not be," I said firmly.

"They say you may die soon," he said in the same remote little voice, "and that then I will have to be Pharaoh. And I am frightened."

"I do not intend to die *yet*," I said, sounding more positive than I often am about this: often it seems I may die naturally at any moment, even if they do not succeed in making me die unnaturally. "It will be many years before you must assume the Double Crown. By then you will be a man, big and strong, and no one will dare frighten or do harm to the new Son of the Sun."

"I hope so," he said in the same wistful fashion. "Oh, Brother, I hope so!"

"It will be as I say," I told him emphatically. "You must be brave and patient and never fear; and when your time comes, you will be a good Pharaoh and do great things for Kemet. I know it."

"Are you sure?" he asked, eyes big and desperate in his search for reassurance.

"I am sure," I said with a flat certainty I indeed was far from feeling: for the evil that threatens me may yet consume him. "I, Nefer-Kheperu-Ra Akhenaten, Living Horus, Son of the Sun, decree it!"

"Well," he said with a sudden relieved sigh that told me my firmness had been accepted, "I'm glad of *that.*" His manner became suddenly grave and dignified, he rose from the throne and bowed low. "Now I must return to the North Palace, Your Majesty, if I may have your leave to depart."

"You may, little Brother," I said with equal gravity. "Come to me again when you wish to talk."

"I will," he promised solemnly, and added, with an innocent emphasis that told me much, *"I* like you."

"Thank you, Neb-Kheperu-Ra," I said, formally using the name the Family has agreed he will take when he does come to the throne. "You are always welcome in my house."

"Good!" he said with a quick smile that lighted up his face. "Be of good cheer, Brother, and do not worry. All will come well for you."

"And for you too, little Tut," I said, "and do you never doubt or forget it."

"I will try not," he said, falling abruptly solemn again. "But at times it is not easy."

After he had gone the glow of his earnest and loving little being stayed with me for a while, a bright, even if troubled, note in my weary life. But I was deeply disturbed by the fears he revealed to me. Even its youngest member, apparently, is haunted by the ghosts of the House of Thebes.

Later I reflected that he had not even mentioned Nefertiti. I wondered if this might not have been her deliberate design, to send him as a reminder of her presence that would work upon me and make me weaken toward her. But I did not weaken, for at that time I was still too gone in grief and resentment, and the things that had caused me to put her from me in the first place.

But presently I began to think; and in these past few days I have found to my surprise, with a growing inward excitement, that I am beginning to dwell a little less upon the past and a little more upon the future. In some subtle way I cannot quite define, my heart and mind are coming to life again after their long, dark passage.

And so today Anser-Wossett, with her never shaken loyalty to Nefertiti and her honest concern for me, opened the way. She was the key, as I know Nefertiti hoped she would be. The door is unlocked and I am ready to come forth.

I do truly believe that this is hope I feel at last, O Father Aten, you who have sustained me in all my troubles. Together—and together with Nefertiti, too, who I now realize possesses a love for me that nothing can ever shatter, which revives in me my love for her—we will resume our rule of our dear Two Lands.

I have given the order. All is ready. The guards are expecting her, they will let her in, we will go to the North Palace and from there, tomorrow, to the Window of Appearances to announce the resumption of our rule. It is now three hours to midnight. I have only to wait patiently, here on my throne where none will dare disturb me, and very soon I will see her again. And then, Father Aten, perhaps your son Akhenaten will find some little happiness in the world once more.

With excitement and anticipation growing eagerly in my heart, I am told that Amonhotep, Son of Hapu, would see me. I send word that he is to be admitted. I shall not tell him our plans, but he is my old, dear friend and teacher, and his presence will entertain me for a little while I wait.

I arrange myself upon the throne, put on my wig which I have not worn for days until my visit with Anser-Wossett this afternoon, straighten my linen shift, prepare to greet him with the smile of old friendship and affection. He appears in the doorway, face distraught, eyes filled with great agitation . . . and hope, which I now know I should never have allowed to bemuse me, dies.

"Majesty!" he cries with a frantic urgency. "Flee, Majesty! Flee! They are coming to do awful things! You must flee, I beg of you! Flee! Do not hesitate, do not delay—*flee!*"

"Who is coming?" I demand sharply, my voice succumbing to its damnable emotional croak. "Who is coming to my palace? *Tell me.*"

"Horemheb, Ramesses, Hatsuret and their troops."

"For what purpose?"

"I do not know, Nefer-Kheperu-Ra," he says, using my name with old familiarity, "but I know it bodes no good to you and Her Majesty. She has left the North Palace. They seem to know she is coming here— *they* are coming here. Please! Please, I beg of you as a father which I have almost been to you all these unhappy years—go! Please go! Immediately!"

"Where can I go that they will not find me?" I ask him bitterly; and suddenly I reject it all, him, them, everything—except my dear wife who is riding to me swiftly through the night, her plan apparently exposed, her life in jeopardy as I now know mine is.

A great calm and radiance settle on me, Father Aten, coming from you to your son Akhenaten. I know what I must do.

"Her Majesty is indeed coming here," I tell this old man who is almost a stranger to me now, so remote does he seem in his terror. "She is being very brave. I can be no less brave. I shall go to the gate and greet her. They will not dare harm us."

"They will, Majesty!" he cries in anguish as outside we hear the distant approaching sounds of many men and many horses. "They will! Son of the Sun, *you must go!*"

"No," I say quietly, "I will not go."

And I start toward the door, noting with disdain that Amonhotep, Son of Hapu, that great sage whom we have looked up to and revered all these years, is clinging desperately to my sleeve, weeping like a woman. He is but a poor thing, after all.

I go armored in our love for one another, and for you, Father Aten.

I am Nefer-Kheperu-Ra Akhenaten.

She is Nefer-neferu-aten Nefertiti.

And we will prevail.

Amonhotep, Son of Hapu

He tries to shake off my hand with a furious impatience, he hobbles ahead of me along the corridor as fast as he can. He is like one possessed—but of a weird otherworldly serenity I am unable to penetrate. They are coming to kill them both, and he will not listen to me while there still is time. He could flee—even now, with luck, they could manage to escape and flee together—and from some hidden place seek friends to rise and put down their enemies . . . but he will not flee, for he knows, as I know, that they no longer have any friends and their tragic story is at last played out.

So I weep as I cling to him, seeking even now to hold him back. As we near the entrance he turns upon me with a sudden violent movement, eyes still remote but blinded briefly by a savage rage.

"Let me go!" he snaps, yanking his sleeve finally from my grasp. *"Get back!"*

Furiously he stares at me, helplessly I stare back. Outside the sound of approaching troops comes nearer.

"Yes, Son of the Sun," I murmur at last through my tears, "I will let you go." He turns instantly and resumes his shuffling, stumbling run toward the great wooden doors where servants stand wide-eyed with terror, waiting to fling them open at his command.

"Open!" he shouts with a terrible urgency. They obey, tumbling over one another in their fright. We look out upon a garish scene. A wild wind is blowing off the Nile, great torches hiss back the night. There is a jumble of horses, troops, men—and a single beautiful woman, standing straight and composed in her chariot as it pauses on one side of the courtyard to confront that of her half brother which has just drawn up on the other side.

For a moment we are all frozen in one of those awful spells that last forever in memory and, perhaps, in time. Over Akhenaten's shoulder I can see them staring, first Nefertiti and Horemheb at one another, then the two of them at Akhenaten—he looking from each to each and back again, revealing nothing in a face that now is as composed as hers, serene and unafraid.

A breathless silence fills the world. The wind blows, the torches flare; only the restless shifting of the horses and the dry rustling of the palms keeps us in tenuous touch with reality. We are figures of stone, awaiting the word that will start us to life. It comes at last from him, in a voice that miraculously rings clear and commanding through the square.

"Why do you come here, Cousin? What business have you with your King and Pharaoh at this strange hour?"

Horemheb stares at him, he and Nefertiti at Horemheb. Finally Horemheb speaks, his face working with emotion but his voice filled with a terrible determination.

"We have come to arrest Your Majesties and remove you forever from the rule of the Two Lands," he says, and a great shuddering sigh goes up from the trembling soldiers, the terrified servants and the few late wanderers of the city who have been attracted by the unusual commotion.

"You speak treason, Cousin," Akhenaten says quietly, his face betraying no emotion other than a calm conviction that he will prevail. Abruptly his voice rises in sharp command: "Arrest him!"

There is a stirring among the troops, an uneasy movement, the exchange of many awed and frightened glances—but they have had their orders and although most are simple peasant lads confronted by the awesome age-old mystery of their Pharaoh, they stand firm. Horemheb is their leader, and commands the world.

"Arrest him!" Akhenaten shouts again, his voice now croaking with a furious anger that is frightening in its intensity . . . but they do not move.

"ARREST HIM!" he shouts for the third time . . . and still they do not move.

The silence returns. Our dreadful paralysis has enveloped us again. None stirs. A stillness as of death lies on us now.

"Your Majesties," Horemheb says at last, face still filled with emotion but voice implacable, "had best come quietly so that no one will be hurt."

"No!" Nefertiti cries, her voice as implacable as his, ringing firm and fearless in the chilling wind. Calmly she takes the reigns of her chariot from the trembling hands of her driver and turns to Akhenaten, standing rigid on the topmost step.

"Husband," she says, still in the same clear, untroubled voice, "come with me and let us leave this traitorous dog to eat his vomit as befits him. *Come!"*

And she slaps the reins across the backs of her horses, who whinny and start forward.

Instantly the world goes mad.

"Stop her!" Horemheb shouts in a terrible voice.

"Let her through on pain of death and the eternal curse of Pharaoh through all time, forever and ever!" Akhenaten shouts in fury equally terrible.

For the slightest of moments the world hangs suspended. Then the terrified but obedient soldiers tumble forward, her chariot is surrounded, the horses scream and rear high as someone stabs them and their entrails begin to spill upon the stones. Wild shouts mingle with the horses' screams as the soldiers seek to strengthen one another's resolve. The dust swirls up and hides the dreadful scene for several moments. When it is hurried away by the racing wind, the melee emerges again in all its awful excitement. At its center stands Horemheb, holding the reins of the dying horses. Straight and proud, eyes fierce, expression fearless and enraged, Nefertiti stands at the front of her chariot. Behind her stands Hatsuret, a glistening battle-ax raised high above his head.

For what seems an eternity but can only be a moment she stays so in the wildly flickering light of the great bronze-shielded torches, beautiful, brave, indomitable and unconquerable.

"Now!" Horemheb shouts. Hatsuret raises still higher the gleaming ax.

So fast the eye is unable to follow, it flashes for a split second and comes down to cleave forever that perfect, timeless skull.

A heavy, unbelieving groan comes from the stunned soldiers and the watching crowd, a wild animal scream from Akhenaten. Desperately I clutch his arm, with a strength I did not know my old bones could muster I drag him back inside before any can emerge from the blood-sick stupor that engulfs them. Frantically I shout at the servants, frantically they leap to slam shut and bolt the massive doors.

"Majesty!" I cry. "You must flee! Oh, my dear son, I beg of you, please, please, *please,* come with me!"

He is in a daze, he does not know where he is—but he obeys. Blindly he staggers away with me down the corridor. At our backs we hear the first heavy crash of the battering rams.

Somehow I hurry him, half falling, half stumbling, leaning on me for support I am almost afraid I cannot give, I am so desperate and frightened and my heart hurts so as I struggle to breathe, down the seemingly endless corridors to the private entrance at the back. Miraculously Horemheb has not thought of this: perhaps he could not imagine her death would not deliver the Good God helpless in his hands. Only Akenaten's troops are on guard, and they have as yet had no word of what has transpired in front.

I stand for a moment irresolute, and in that moment he comes back to me.

"Chariot," he croaks. *"Chariot!"*

"Yes!" I cry, and give the command. Sped by my haste and agitation, the guards spring to obey. In a moment a chariot with two horses stands before us. In the next, the back gates have been swung open. With a strange, startling agility, calling upon who knows what reserves of strength and terror, he leaps up as I have not seen him do since he was a child and grasps the reins tightly in his long, thin hands.

"Majesty—" I cry, and start to clamber up with him. But savagely he pushes me back—savagely, but, I think, quite impersonally, for I know he hardly realizes I am there.

"No!" he cries. "I go!"

And lashes the horses, who leap forward, and vanishes in the night of the still sleeping, unsuspecting city.

I know where he is going in his blind grief and desperation and I know that they will find him there.

I bow my head and weep bitterly for Nefer-Kheperu-Ra Akhenaten, tenth King and Pharaoh of the Eighteenth Dynasty to rule over the land of Kemet, whose living body I know I shall never look upon again. . . .

Some time later—some little time, though to me in my utmost agony of soul it has seemed very long indeed—I hear the crash of the great doors going down, a swirl of soldiers jangling through the halls. Ever nearer comes the voice of Horemheb. I sit upon the ground and draw my robe over my head and wait humbly for his coming: for I know that for me as well he means Death.

But amazingly it does not come. I am aware of a sudden quiet, I am conscious that he is standing over me. Slowly I draw my robe away and look up with tear-filled eyes into his strained and ravaged face.

For a long time our eyes hold in silence. Then at last he reaches down and gently draws the robe back over my head. I prepare myself instantly for the end of life. But again he astounds me.

"Do not feel too badly, old friend," he says softly, "and do not think I will blame you for what you have done this night. You have done what you believed you had to do"—he pauses and his voice grows infinitely sad, with a depth of feeling I had not known was in him, my bright and clever "Kaires" who came to us so long ago—"and so, I think, have we."

With an abrupt harshness he cries, "Bring my horse! I go alone to the Northern Tombs!" There is an obedient jumble of response—and he is gone.

I draw my robe tighter over my head, I lock my hands around my knees, I rock back and forth in desolation for our poor lost Akhenaten and our beautiful Nefertiti.

Akhenaten (Life, health, prosperity!)

Far below me the city sleeps. Here where I have come so often, I rest in you, my Father Aten. You are my protector, my friend; you open for me the peaceful ways. For your son Akhenaten you will set all things right and make the world to sing again. You will restore to me my beloved wife, who has not died, and my dearest brother, who has not died, and together we will rule in happiness and love for all our people, forever and ever, for millions and millions of years.

It seems to me that somewhere, but a little while ago, there was horror in the night. I cannot remember exactly what it was, I remember light and voices shouting, there seems to be a great terror—and then it eludes me. I cannot understand, I no longer remember, I forget and with a smile of infinite peace I think again upon your wonderful and loving grace to me, my Father Aten.

You know, my Father Aten, how long and faithfully I have loved you, and how earnestly I have sought to make my people understand your joyous kindness to the world. I have labored diligently in all things so that they might know how you have made the world to be a beautiful and happy place, and how you love all men and keep them safe, O Sole God who rules the universe. I have tried to make them see that they must not be afraid of other gods, that they must not fear the powers of magic, of evil and of darkness—that they must love only you, who are all things good and kind, in whose holy light all men, women, birds, animals, living things are blessed and sheltered and made whole.

This I have tried to do, Father Aten—only you know how hard I have tried. I think I may sometimes have made mistakes, for though I am a god I am also human; but they have been mistakes grown of loving you, and not from evil in my heart. I know my people have not understood me always, and perhaps I have not understood them as much as I would wish; but I have tried to serve them, and to save them, as best I could with the benison of your loving guidance. For you I married my daughters, that I might have sons to carry on my line and spread your gospel to all the lands and oceans, not only of Kemet but far beyond our borders, for all men need your loving help. For you I put aside my dear wife Nefertiti for a time and took to my side my dear brother Smenkhkara, who represented to me all that was happy and hopeful in my own youth that was so sadly ended when I fell ill: in his love I thought I might find the strength to help me strengthen you. For you I destroyed Amon and the other gods, so that nothing would stand in the way of your dominance of the world.

I have wanted only love, for you, for myself, for everyone. Dimly I seem to remember that there was opposition—bitterness—I have a vague feeling that some things were unhappy and did not go right for me—I try to remember, but my mind is tired tonight, Father Aten, and I cannot. Nor do I wish to or need to, protected as I am by your love, resting in peace within your loving arms.

It may be all has not gone as I would have wished, it may be I have been wrong about some things. But I have loved you, Father Aten, and I have loved my kingdom and its people, and for them I have sought only happy things. I have tried, Father Aten—I have tried: only you know how hard your son Akhenaten has tried. . . .

Far below I see the tiny spark of a flickering torch, twisting erratically in the wind. I thought the wind might be cold up here, for somehow I seem to have come without my robe, clad only in my linen shift; but I am warm and comfortable in the glow of your love, and I do not feel it. Somehow all the world seems bright and filled with happiness tonight, and all bad things are gone. . . .

I believe it is a single horseman who comes: the torch rocks as in the hand of one who rides a galloping steed. He has started up the long stone ramp that leads here to the Northern Tombs. His progress slows as his mount takes the steep incline. But he is coming, Father Aten, and to greet him I believe that I will sing to him once more my Hymn that I wrote to you, which I have sung so often to sustain me through all our years together. I do not know who he is who comes: but I think that he can only be moved, as all men are moved, by the loving beauty of what I sing to you.

I rise to my feet—I seem to have been lying prostrate on the ground, though I cannot remember why—and I move to the edge of the terrace that fronts the tombs. I spread my arms wide to embrace my city, my beloved kingdom and the glorious shining world. It is filled for me tonight with a marvelous all-conquering peace in the beauty of your love, and I sing to you:

"Thou arisest fair in the horizon of Heaven, O Living Aten, Beginner of Life. When thou dawnest in the East, thou fillest every land with thy beauty. Thou art indeed comely, great, radiant and high over every land. Thy rays embrace the lands to the full extent of all that thou hast made, for thou art Ra and thou attainest their limits and subdueth them for thy beloved son, Akhenaten. Thou art remote yet thy rays are upon the earth. Thou art in the sight of men, yet thy ways are not known.

"When thou settest in the Western horizon, the earth is in darkness after the manner of death. Men spend the night indoors with the head covered, the eye not seeing its fellow. Their possessions might be stolen, even when under their heads, and they would be unaware of it. Every lion comes forth from its lair and all snakes bite. Darkness is the only light, and the earth is silent when their Creator rests in his habitation.

"The earth brightens when thou arisest in the Eastern horizon and shinest forth as Aten in the daytime. Thou drivest away the night when thou givest forth thy beams. The Two Lands are in festival. They awake and stand upon their feet for thou hast raised them up. They wash their limbs, they put on raiment and raise their arms in adoration at thy appearance. The entire earth performs its labors. All cattle are at peace in their pastures. The trees and herbage grow green. The birds fly from their nests, their wings raised in praise of thy spirit. All animals gambol on their feet, all the winged creation live when thou hast risen for them. The boats sail upstream, and likewise downstream. All ways open at thy

dawning. The fish in the river leap in thy presence. Thy rays are in the midst of the sea.

"Thou it is who causest women to conceive and maketh seed into man, who giveth life to the child in the womb of its mother, who comforteth him so that he cries not therein, nurse that thou art, even in the womb, who giveth breath to quicken all that he hath made. When the child comes forth from the body on the day of his birth, then thou openest his mouth completely and thou furnisheth his sustenance. When the chick in the egg chirps within the shell, thou givest him the breath within it to sustain him. Thou createst for him his proper term within the egg, so that he shall break it and come forth from it to testify to his completion as he runs about on his two feet when he emerges.

"How manifold are thy works! They are hidden from the sight of men, O Sole God, like unto whom there is no other! Thou didst fashion the earth according to thy desire when thou wast alone—all men, all cattle great and small, all that are upon the earth that run upon their feet or rise up on high, flying with their wings. And the lands of Syria and Kush and Kemet—thou appointest every man to his place and satisfieth his needs. Everyone receives his sustenance and his days are numbered. Their tongues are diverse in speech and their qualities likewise, and their color is differentiated for thou has distinguished the nations.

"Thou makest the waters under the earth and thou bringest them forth as the Nile at thy pleasure to sustain the people of Kemet even as thou hast made them live for thee, O Divine Lord of them all, toiling for them, the Lord of every land, shining forth for them, the Aten Disk of the daytime, great in majesty!

"All distant foreign lands also, thou createst their life. Thou hast placed a Nile in heaven to come forth for them and make a flood upon the mountains like the sea in order to water the fields of their villages. How excellent are thy plans, O Lord of Eternity!—a Nile in the sky is thy gift to the foreigners and to the beasts of their lands; but the true Nile flows from under the earth for Kemet.

"Thy beams nourish every field and when thou shinest they live and grow for thee. Thou makest the seasons in order to sustain all that thou hast made, the winter to cool them, the summer heat that they may taste of thy quality. Thou hast made heaven afar off that thou mayest behold all that thou hast made when thou wast alone, appearing in thine aspect of the Living Aten, rising and shining forth. Thou makest millions of forms out of thyself, towns, villages, fields, roads, the river. All eyes behold thee before them, for thou art the Aten of the daytime, above all that thou hast created.

"Thou are in my heart, and there is none that knoweth thee save thy son, Akhenaten. Thou hast made him wise in thy plans and thy power!"

Triumphantly I conclude, my voice loud and clear in the silent night, ringing over the city, the Nile, Kemet, the world; and as I do, the horseman reaches the edge of the terrace, dismounts and walks slowly toward me. I see that it is my cousin Horemheb and that he is carrying a battle-ax . . . *and suddenly I remember. I know.*

Great terror for a second fills my heart, but then you come to me and place your hand tenderly upon my shoulder and strengthen me, O Father Aten, and all is peaceful and serene again with me. You are like unto a great light, a Nile of Niles that floods my being.

I do not fear him. He will not harm me.

I am the Living Horus and I stand armored in your love.

"Ah, yes, Cousin," I say quietly as he advances. "Somehow I knew that you would come for me."

Horemheb

From afar I hear his high, wild keening, whipped to me on the wind as my horse struggles up the long incline to the Northern Tombs. Dimly above me in the blustering night I see his gaunt, ungainly, white-clad figure, arms outstretched as if to bless the world with the obscene mouthings of his empty Aten.

To him his words may make sense. To me they mean nothing. Only the measured cadence tells me what he thinks he is chanting. From his mouth there issues only gibberish.

Upon his face as I approach there shines a light unearthly: it frightens me. He is in some other world, gone from us for good, leaving us at last forever, poor, sad, pathetic Akhenaten. I am filled with horror of what I have done and still must do: yet I tell myself that it has to be, for Kemet, for the Dynasty, and for him.

He looks to be at peace at last. It is peace that I am here to bring him.

Suddenly lucidity returns and he says the only intelligible words that I have heard:

"Ah, yes, Cousin. Somehow I knew that you would come for me."

There is in his voice such a calm acceptance, in his eyes such a look of humble yet tranquil submission, as of a wounded animal awaiting with pain yet a marvelous serenity the blow it knows will end its world forever, that almost it turns my legs to water.

It brings to my heart such terror and such grief for what I must do that almost I turn and run screaming from the necessary horrors of this dreadful night.

Almost it stays my hand.

Almost. . . .

Tiye

I sit in the window of the little palace he built for me and look my last upon the Nile, my beloved Two Lands and all the lovely world that once was so kind and generous to me. I have done my duty and I can live no more.

An hour ago they came to me, my brother and Horemheb, faces ravaged, eyes filled with tears, yet calm with the calmness of men who have accomplished what they believed they must.

"It is finished," Aye says, his voice shaking with emotion, yet firm. "Both are dead. All is over."

Though I had given the word, I yet cry out, a terrible shrieking wail that echoes down the corridors.

My heart dies within me.

Two sons I have sacrificed to Kemet and all my life of care and devotion for the Two Lands has ended in horror and ruination. Perhaps, as they tell me, it has ended in a new birth for Kemet, a great change that will be for the better after all these sad past years.

So do they believe. So would I like to believe. So, perhaps, I can make myself believe.

But however it has ended, it has ended for me.

After I have wept for a time, my body torn with such savage sobs that they look at me with fright, I tell them that I wish to be buried in the Royal Wadi beside my sons and Nefertiti. Both pledge me this, and I do not think they will betray me.

Then I tell them I wish to be alone for a while, and dismiss them. Weeping also, but strong in the certainty that what we have done must be right, they leave me.

I sit alone at my window and look my last upon all the lovely things that make life so happy on this earth for those blessed with the good fortune to enjoy them.

I have not been so blessed in many years.

The poison gleams beside me in the glass; I am taking it with wine so that I will not be aware when it goes down.

Presently I shall cease my looking, and go to sleep.

Aye

My mind staggers with horror, my hands reek with blood: I think they shall never be cleansed again.

Yet what could we do, for the Two Lands' sake?

If only we had not . . . if only he had not . . . if only . . . but we did.

I must think no longer thus. I shall weep forever for my beautiful daughter and lost unhappy Akhenaten, for my sister and for us all. But a new day has come for Kemet.

Tutankhaten is King.

I must put away the past that kills my heart and help my frightened little nephew restore the Two Lands to *ma'at* and their ancient glory.

Tutankhaten (Life, health, prosperity!)

I weep so long and so sadly for my mother, my brother and my beautiful cousin. They were all so kind to me.

Who will be kind to me now?

Beside me Ankhesenpaaten, who will be my Queen, weeps softly too.

We are alone in all this world.

Though but a child, I am King and Pharaoh. But whom can I trust?

What will happen to us, now that the grownups tell me I must rule this sad land of Kemet?

Book III

LIFE OF A GOD
1358 B.C.

King of   Neb-Kheperu-Ra,   Son of the Sun,   Prince of Thebes,
the North   TUTANKHAMON
and South,

Hatsuret

He is a pliant lad. If he continues as we desire, he and Amon will enjoy many long years together.

Tutankhamon (Life, health, prosperity!)

Today is the day we must leave the city of my brother and return to Thebes.

All about me is bustle, confusion, last-minute packing and preparation, the final hours of readiness in which everyone rushes about, worries, checks to make sure all is right, hopes to forget nothing, tries to remember everything. All over the city I can hear these sounds as Ankhesenpaaten and I stand at the window and stare for the last time at the gleaming white rooftops, the golden-spired temples, the miles of once-crowded streets, gardens, parks, alleyways that he called into life the year I was born and which, on this day thirteen years later, must now begin to die.

On the river the great barges wait, filled to overflowing with household goods, gold, jewels, the wealth of what was once his capital and for these past four years has been a favorite one of mine. A vast flotilla jams the Nile from the southern boundary to the north: all the officers of the Court, the nobility, the civil servants, their families, servants and slaves are packed and ready to leave. We sail at noon, my gold-painted barge in the lead, followed immediately by that of my uncle Aye and then by my cousin Horemheb. All the rest will jostle into place and the long journey upstream will begin amid the hectic shouts of pilots and oarsmen, the heavy rhythmic slap of paddles on water, the snapping sounds of sails as Shu the wind god bellies them out, the excited shouts of those who look forward—and perhaps, underneath, the quiet sobbing of those who look back . . . desperately muffled, of course, because this is supposed to be a happy day and no one is supposed to feel regret.

As we push out from the landing stage at the foot of the long ramp that leads from the now empty North Palace—all its bright hangings stripped from the walls, all my dear cousin Nefertiti's statues and objects of art removed, all furniture stacked on the barges, even the kitchens emptied totally of pots and pans—trumpets will blow, banners will fly, a last dwindling shout will rise wistfully from the small official guard and the handful of poor who remain to serve them. All others have been removed in these recent weeks, sent away to start new lives in villages far from here. The city will stand deserted save for its lonely guardians. It will be lonely too.

It is time to say farewell: to Akhet-Aten, to him, and to the dream. . . .

Or so, I think, would they have me believe. And so, I think, would I have them believe, for only if they believe it will my Queen and I be permitted to live. . . .

I go in deathly fear of my uncle Aye, my cousin Horemheb and evil Hatsuret, who now rules triumphant as High Priest in the fast-rebuilding temple of Amon at Karnak. All goes happily now for him, the monster who killed my brother Smenkhkara, my cousin Merytaten, and last and most awful, my beautiful Nefertiti. At his side with cold confidence my uncle and Horemheb work their will upon me and, through me, upon the Two Lands.

Once I believed they did this because they really believed it to be best for Kemet.

Now I wonder if it is not just their own glory they seek.

When I first became Living Horus, Son of the Sun, King and Pharaoh, I cowered, a child just turning nine, in the dark night of murder and horror that ended the life of Akhenaten, Nefertiti and my mother the Great Wife. Hers was the death of duty, I realize that now: she did what she felt she had to do for the Two Lands and then bravely paid for it with her own life, and I honor and respect her for it, terrible as it was. But there was no need to kill my brother, no need to kill the Chief Wife. They could have been taken prisoner and sent away somewhere, if that was deemed best for Kemet—and perhaps it might have been. I can see that argument now. But there was no need to murder them just at the moment they seemed at last to be returning to one another. There was no need to kill my poor brother, driven insane as he was by all that had happened to him: no need to kill my "second mother," my sweet Nefertiti whose only crime was loving him. They could have been allowed to enjoy in peace whatever happiness they could salvage from the wreck of the bitter past. . . .

You will say these are heavy thoughts for a youth of thirteen. But I wear a heavy crown, and because of it I am old beyond my years.

So I cowered, not knowing whether at any moment I might not be next. I did not really think so, for I was indeed the Living Horus then, I had the blood, the Double Crown was mine by right. These things had not saved Akhenaten, but I thought they might save me, whom they thought untainted by his "heresy." Beside me trembled my loving Ankhesenpaaten—my niece and four years my senior, but ordained from childhood to be my wife: we thought she too might face the ax of Hatsuret before the night was ended, for now she bore the final right of legitimacy to the throne. So we jumped and screamed and clung to one another fiercely when the door suddenly opened. But it was my uncle Aye and Horemheb, and their words were loving and sweet, and we believed them, and relaxed.

"Son of the Sun," my uncle said gravely, "we come to tell you that you have succeeded to the glorious throne of your ancestors. The House of Thebes, in you, will be restored to glory. Through you Kemet will once more flourish and be happy. Dear Ankhesenpaaten, you will rule beside him as Chief Queen of the Two Lands, and from his loins and yours will come many fine sons to serve the kingdom and preserve our Dynasty. Do not be afraid, for we are your servants and your friends, and it will be so."

And Horemheb, his hands, though I did not know it then, just washed of the blood of my brother, agreed with equal gravity:

"Son of the Sun, it will be so."

And because we were so frightened and wished so desperately to believe them, we did. And presently our trembling ceased, though not our tears for those who were gone; and soon Queen Kia appeared, her face as sad and ravaged with weeping as ours, and led us away to her quarters, hugged us and rocked us for a while and put us finally to bed, where we fell asleep in one another's arms while she crooned a gentle song all night long to soothe our restless nightmare dreams.

(Dear, kind, gentle Kia, Nefertiti's faithful friend, and ours! Where is she now? I do not know. When I went to Thebes for my coronation she was here; when I came back she was gone. When I asked my uncle where she was, he said vaguely, "She wished to go and live in the Delta, far from this place." But secretly I had the three I now regard as my only true friends—my much older sister Sitamon, young Maya, my schoolmate and now supervisor of the necropolis at Thebes, and my cousin, the Vizier Nakht-Min—try to find her for me. They have never been able.)

Very soon thereafter we were taken to Thebes for the ceremonies that would sanctify my place as Pharaoh. Somewhere I heard dimly that there had been a hasty embalmment of Akhenaten and Nefertiti, not the ritual seventy days but more like ten or twenty, and that their rotting, half-prepared bodies had then been hurried away in the dead of night to the Royal Wadi here in Akhet-Aten and there been hastily and furtively buried. Only my mother the Great Wife received seventy days and full honors, and now is buried beside them. Meanwhile throughout the length of Kemet—on our borders—in embassies sent to King Tushratta of Mittani, King Supp-i-lu-li-u-mas of the Hittites and such other few remaining friends and allies as my brother left us—it was being announced that he, my mother and the Chief Wife were dead "of a natural fever" and that I was now the Living Horus and soon to be married to Ankhesenpaaten.

So all proceeded as my captors wished. It was a great shock to me to realize that this is what they were, my uncle Aye who had always been so fatherly and kind to me, my cousin Horemheb with whom I had played so happily so many times as baby and child—but I learned it fast, as I have learned much else fast in these four years of my imprisonment on the throne. Ankhesenpaaten and I were helpless and alone: the game proceeded as they said it must.

So there came the great day; and I will admit that for me, as a child, and for Ankhesenpaaten, who was allowed to watch nearby through dazzled eyes though we were not yet married, it was, although at first almost a disaster, in final impact an awesome and powerfully moving thing. It was only later that we came to realize that ambition, evil, corruption and death underlay it all. For the moment it became a spectacle as overwhelming to us as it was to all who crowded Thebes to witness the triumph of Amon, returning to power through the medium of his small, bewildered, nine-year-old pawn.

I had not slept much the night before, falling at last into fitful dozing not long before my uncle came to waken me. So I felt, at first, sleepy-eyed and queasy at my stomach. After I retired to relieve myself, he gave me strong tea, followed by wine mixed lightly with water: the first shocked me awake and quieted my stomach, the second seemed to put me into a dreamlike and happy mood. I forgot all that had brought me to this hour and thought only of what lay ahead. A great excitement began to fill my heart.

Next there entered to me four white-robed priests of Amon, who under my uncle's supervision stripped from me my nightclothes and washed my body thoroughly in all its parts. (A little too thoroughly at times, I thought. I like not priests: they make me uneasy on many counts.) They anointed me with unguents which they told me were sacred to Amon. (Only eight days before, when my brother was alive, the unguents had been just unguents. Now the priests said mumbo-jumbo over the sticky stuff and it was suddenly sacred to Amon. I was not too bemused to miss the irony of this, but gave no sign.)

Then they placed about me only the pleated kilt of a Pharaoh, in my case very small, of course, for I was still but a skinny child. They placed nothing on my head, no sandals on my feet. Naked save for the kilt, I was escorted into the first courtyard of the temple of Karnak (its battered doors still scoured by the fires of my brother) and there joined the solemn procession—headed, of course, by Aye and Horemheb, who fell into step just behind me, and after them by Hatsuret and his highest aides. Following them came many priests and priestesses, not only of Amon but of all the other gods. (How quickly, in but a week's time, had they reappeared from hiding to seize anew their long-lost power!) These last were shaking sistrums, clashing cymbals, beating drums and blowing on the long bronze trumpets whose mournful mooing must sound like Hathor the cow goddess when she has a bellyache.

In response to their sudden raucous noise there came from beyond the walls a great, deep, roaring sound which startled me so that for a moment I turned back in fright to my uncle just behind me.

"Be happy, Son of the Sun," he said, placing a soothing hand on my naked shivering shoulder—shivering more from chill than fright, actually: it was sunny but cold that day in Karnak. "These are your people, and they love you."

And I believed him, and still do: for they *are* mine and they *do* love me, and Ankhesenpaaten as well. It is not their fault that they are unable to know who really rules them.

So we moved solemnly forward through the first pylon, erected by my father Amonhotep III (life, health, prosperity!), and suddenly I was greeted by sights such as I had never seen up to then, but have seen only too much of since. My uncle had tried to forewarn me, but his words had not really prepared me for such a startling spectacle.

Priests masked to represent the gods descended upon me from every side, dancing and cavorting and whirling about, uttering welcoming shrieks and, to me, unintelligible ritual cries. All this was entirely new to me because, having been raised in the Aten, I had never known these grotesque masks and ceremonies. They did not perceive it then, nor do they realize it now, but in that moment I thought with a sudden blinding flash: *But how absurd! They are children playing children's games!*

And instantaneously thereafter the thought which only Ankhesenpaaten knows, and shares: *My brother was right. It is nonsense, all this.*

None of this showed upon my face, for by nine I had learned very well how to keep my feelings hidden. I submitted placidly when a priest wearing what I now know to be the falcon head of Horus of the Horizon seized me by one hand, and another, wearing the old man's mask of Ra in his form of Atum as he sinks in old age into the West, seized me by the other. So excited were they at thus being back in power again that they almost yanked me forward through the second pylon built by my great-great-great-great-grandfather Tuthmose I (life, health, prosperity!). My naked feet barely skimmed the stones of the courtyard as they hustled me along. Behind me Aye and Horemheb, Hatsuret and the rest had to puff to keep up.

All this happened very quickly, you understand, and it ended very quickly too, because suddenly I saw where they were dragging me and I cried out sharply, *"No!"* and let myself go limp in their hands so that my sacred body touched the ground and they had to stop in sheer horror of their own profanation of my person.

Before me I saw a pool of water, with four masked men standing around it at the points of the compass. Later I learned, of course, that this represented the division of the world into four parts according to the ancient creed of Heliopolis. But to me, a child seeing a mask of an ibis (Thoth, of course), a dog's curved muzzle and square-cut ears (Seth), and two more falcon beaks (Horus of Behdet, and Dunawy) apparently about to plunge him into a pool of water, only one terrified thought could come: *It is like my distant brother Tuthmose! They are going to drown me as they drowned him!*

And again I shrieked, "No, no, *no!*" and sagged upon the ground.

Outside the loving roar continued. Inside all was consternation.

Instantly my uncle stooped down, angrily ordered the frightened priests aside, scooped me into his arms. Soothingly he murmured in my ear, quieted my trembling, which now was quite genuinely caused by fear, and patiently explained once again the significance of the four who confronted me. Since I could see that they were obviously as terrified of me as I of them, utterly confounded and confused by my reaction, I soon believed him and regained my composure. I slipped out of his arms, stood straight for a second and then marched sturdily forward, head held high. After that I felt no fear and the ceremony proceeded without further difficulty.

Reassembled in their positions around the pool, these child-men, in what I now felt more contemptuously than ever to be their child-masks, poured water over me from four golden jars. This water—which (I thought as before) up to Akhenaten's death eight days ago had been only water—now was presumed to splash the divinity of the gods upon me. Why this was necessary, since I am divine by birth, I did not understand; but having now resolved to see it through as befitted the Pharaoh I intended to be, I submitted quietly.

I was then led on to two chapels between the second and third pylons, one representing the "House of Flame," the ancient northern sanctuary of Amon, the other the "Great House," or ancient southern sanctuary. In the first were more priests, more masks: Horus, Neith, Isis, Buto of Lower Kemet, Nekhebet of Upper Kemet, Nephthys and many others (most of whose names I learned later: they were, as I say, mostly new to me) chanting my solemn praises. Noisily they accompanied me forward to the second chapel, pausing in its doorway as I went within.

A priestess representing Amon's daughter, the snake goddess, loomed out of the shadowy interior, around her head a great linen cobra's hood held stiff by bands of gold. Before I knew what she was doing she had enveloped my body with hers. Her bosom was suffocating and her perfume overpowering. I almost gagged from the strength of it but managed to distract my throat by pretending to cough. This stinking embrace was supposed to represent my being acknowledged as the heir to the throne—Amon's hidden hand supposedly guiding his daughter's hood to rise behind my head. To me it was simply being crushed by an offensively smelly woman. But I had made up my mind, and accepted it solemnly.

Next came a priest named (I learned later) Inmutef, accompanied by other priests, each bearing one of the crowns of Kemet (recovered from my brother's palace at Akhet-Aten, I learned later: he had not quite dared destroy these ancient symbols). Quickly they were placed in turn upon my head and as quickly removed—the combined white miter and red mortar-cap that represent the Double Crown of the two goddesses Buto and Nekhebet, meaning the Two Lands, Kemet itself; the *atef* crown of Ra, the *seshed* headband, the ibis crown of Thoth, the blue leather *khepresh* crown, the diadem of two tall plumes similar to those worn by Amon, and the great golden wig, its flaps resting on my chest. Then the khepresh was returned to my head and I was led on through the third pylon to another shadowy chapel (it is as my brother said: Amon is always cold, hidden and unhealthy) where I knelt before a rose granite shrine originally dedicated by my great-great-grandfather Tuthmose III (life, health, prosperity!). There in ringing tones from behind me Hatsuret announced that Amon had confirmed my wearing of the khepresh and henceforth I had sway over all the dominions of the sun. To prove this, he announced, I would feel the hand of Amon touch my neck. A cold hand immediately did, making me jump with its iciness.

I knew it was the hand of Amon, all right: the hand of Amon that had killed my brother Smenkhkara, my niece Merytaten and my dear cousin Nefertiti. But with great effort I managed to show none of the awful revulsion that withered my body at his touch, and all in attendance breathed a sigh of satisfaction as I rose again to my feet.

There followed the conferring of all my titularies and names, including my coronation name of Neb-Kheperu-Ra that the Family long ago selected to be mine if I should become King. I was also hailed, in a great shout that allowed of no rebuttal, "Tutankh*amon!*" Not my real name that honors the Aten, but *their* name that honors *their* god: "Tutankh*amon!*" There was nothing I could do but outwardly accept, though inwardly I made a promise to myself about that. I was then led on to the most ancient innermost sanctuary of Amon where the golden idol, released from his long hiding in the passageway off Horemheb's tomb at Sakkara, once more gleamed and glittered mysteriously in the gloom.

I looked into his hooded eyes and joined as best I could in the prayers chanted by Hatsuret and the rest; but between the hooded eyes and my own there passed a message that I think the hooded eyes understood. No one else saw it—no one to this day save Ankhesenpaaten is aware—but between the god and me there is no secret.

We are not friends, and he knows it.

Then I was led back through the pylons to the first courtyard, which had now been thrown open so that between its walls and as far as my eye could carry, to the very banks of the Nile itself, I could see my people, thousands upon thousands upon thousands of them, waiting to watch me go through once again, in public, the full traditional coronation ceremony that they had not seen since the crowning of my father, more than forty years ago.

Now the great roar welled up to greet me in person. And now it suddenly all became real to me, and to Ankhesenpaaten, too, who was brought forward to sit at my right hand, her chair a little back as became one soon to be, but not yet, Queen. Now I was to be united with my people in a bond of affection and love that nothing could break. The union with the god, restored with such desperate haste so that he might assert his claim on me as I was inducted into kingship, had been a cold, confusing and repellent ceremony to me. The taking of my crown again before my beloved people of my beloved Kemet was a thing so warm and marvelous that Ankhesenpaaten and I could only smile at one another in the wonderment and joy we shared in it.

The first part of the day was ridiculous—empty and horrid, as far as we were concerned. The second was love, in whose arms we have rested ever since, and upon whose endless kindness and unshakable loyalty we still hope to base our rule.

I was seated on the ancient throne of coronation, so old that its origins are lost in time. Before me the masked priests danced and chanted in the bright sunshine, somehow no longer chill but soft and warm with the magic of love. The khepresh was removed, the Double Crown was placed upon my head. Priests masked as the spirits of the Nile twined the lily and the papyrus, representing the Two Lands, around a pillar to symbolize their union. I then rose and made my ceremonial run around a square marked out upon the sand: this ancient rite represented the way my distant ancestors millennia ago ran around the boundaries of our first capital of Memphis to symbolize their assumption of rule.

There was more chanting, long and solemn, to which the vast crowd listened respectfully. Finally I returned to the throne, stepped forward and lifted my arms for silence. I was aware of consternation around me, sudden startled looks from my uncle Aye and Horemheb, Hatsuret's uneasy turnings: this was not part of tradition. Akhenaten inaugurated it, this revolutionary direct contact with the people: they thought they had destroyed it, with him. I could see memory in their eyes, fear of what I might say, and I knew I must banish it at once. Indeed, I never intended else.

"My dearly beloved people of Kemet!" I cried, and my fluting child's voice no doubt sounded thin and reedy in the utter silence; but they loved me for it, and their love came up to me in waves.

"Much of sadness and of ill has fallen upon us in recent years. Many were to blame"—for I would not blame *him,* ever, who strove for love and died for it, though I could sense the silent protests around me because I did not—"and all must now work together, to repair what has been done and make the Two Lands whole again. I will restore *ma'at,* I will bring back happiness. All will be again in Kemet as it was before. You and I, my dear people, together with our dear Queen, Ankhesenpaaten, will work to restore our beloved land.

"We will help one another, you and I! We will make all come right again for Kemet! Great will be her glory hereafter, forever and ever, for millions of years!

"I, Neb-Kheperu-Ra"—for a split second I hesitated, for the new name did not yet come easily to my tongue: then I decided it best to be clever and appear to accept—"Tutankh*amon*"—a joyful roar broke the silence to the very edge of the Nile, for they have never loved my brother's Sole God of love, so I repeated it slowly—"I, Neb-Kheperu-Ra Tutankh*amon,* do so promise it!"

And turned back to resume my seat for the ceremonial games, to find my uncle, Horemheb and Hatsuret nodding and beaming with great relief and approval. They need not have worried: it was not at that moment I would choose to defy them, a child of nine only. How on earth could I?

There followed a procession through Thebes that lasted all afternoon, at which those who had been unable to crowd around the temple were able to shout to me and Ankhesenpaaten, borne high in our gold-painted baldachins, their exited, happy greetings. We then crossed the river to Malkata and attended the traditional ceremonial banquet for an hour or so, after which we were sent off to bed in charge of Ramesses and his wife Sitra, who are kindly people if a little dull.

It was high time for us to leave, in fact, because by then nearly all the top officials of the Court, including even Horemheb (though not my uncle Aye), were becoming very drunk, and other things were apparently soon to happen. On such occasions in Kemet—including the banquets that traditionally follow funerals, and particularly at the great Festival of Opet, which has now been revived and lasts for two weeks while Amon is brought from Karnak to visit his temple at Luxor—the ladies wear cones of perfumed wax atop their wigs. As the wax melts, the perfumes run down over their bodies. This combines with a great deal of wine that everyone drinks, and presently things occur that are rather far from the stately, dignified life recorded on the walls of our tombs and temples. Ankhesenpaaten and I soon learned, in fact, that such occasions often conclude with most of the guests rutting like animals in a communal orgy which disgusts us so that we have banned it from our own banquets. But it goes on all over Kemet, all the time. Next day, of course, everyone is dignified again and serene as a temple painting, if a little hollow-eyed.

We went to bed with the howls of our own guests—and from across the river the howls of the common citizens of Thebes, who always pour into the streets in a drunken mass on the slightest pretext to mimic their betters in every naked particular—ringing in our ears. With a wryness that came to me even at the age of nine, I reflected that the coronation of the King and Pharaoh Tutankhamon was indeed being suitably celebrated by his countrymen. When we said good night before being led to our respective chambers, Ankhesenpaaten and I agreed that this would never happen in our own palaces again. This is one thing, in spite of some grumbling by those who consider us strait-laced, that we have been able to achieve.

After that I lingered for a few weeks in Thebes, while Aye and Horemheb gave orders to Amonhotep, Son of Hapu, and to Tuthmose, our chief sculptor, to start the rebuilding and redecorating of all the temples. I then made a triumphal coronation progress to Memphis, to Heliopolis, Hermonthis, and finally back to Hermopolis, across the river from Akhet-Aten; and so from there back to this city that today we abandon. Here I have had one of my principal seats of government, though I have spent much time, too, in Memphis and in Thebes. Thebes in particular I like, because that is where I first became aware of life, in the Palace of Malkata; and now that we are being forced to leave this city that holds so many unhappy memories—and yet, for me and Ankhesenpaaten, as children growing up mostly in the palace of Nefertiti while my mother the Great Wife spent much of her time in Thebes, many happy memories, too—it is to Thebes that I will go. I told my uncle recently that I wished to add to my titles the words "Ruler of Southern 'No,'" which means Thebes; and there was happy agreement from all, because they thought it meant I wanted to be near Amon, whom I appear to love so much. Actually I want to reoccupy Malkata, which of all my palaces, save the North Palace here which we must now abandon, I like the best.

Six months after returning here, Ankhesenpaaten and I were married in a lengthy ceremony, its first rites held in the House of the Aten, its second half held in the small temple of Amon adjoining what used to be my mother's palace, now standing empty beside the Nile. Our desire to give the Aten such renewed prominence of course greatly disturbed Horemheb and Hatsuret, but to their surprise it was Aye who said firmly it should be so. It was he, in fact, who encouraged us to request it in the first place.

"We do not wish to destroy the Aten altogether," he said to Horemheb when the two of them argued it out in my presence.

"Why not?" my cousin demanded bluntly.

"Because Aten is still a sacred aspect of Ra," Aye replied with equal bluntness. "And while we have restored Ra's other aspects, and given back their power to Amon and the other gods, we cannot simply pretend the Aten does not exist. The key to change in Kemet, my son, is 'gradual'—*gradual*. Even though *he* (Aye does not name my brother if he can possibly avoid it. He does not go so far as to call him "the Heretic" or "the Criminal," as Horemheb and many others do, but he will not say his name) is gone, still for a time the Aten *was* supreme. The god can only be reduced *gradually* to a lesser role."

"Well, see that he is!" Horemheb said tersely, at which my uncle came as close to open anger as I have ever seen him display with my powerful cousin, whom I think he even then was beginning to fear.

"You do not order the Regent to do anything!" he snapped. "I shall proceed in moderation and sense, as I have done all things."

"Including—" Horemheb began sarcastically, but his father cut him off with a terrible fierceness.

"Do not raise old ghosts with me! There is guilt enough for all and blood enough for all! Be satisfied with your portion, and be still!"

For quite a long time Horemheb stared at him, apparently unabashed, while I, frightened of their anger, almost hesitated to breathe. But Horemheb apparently was more intimidated than he showed, for presently he turned away with a sullen "Let us not do too much honor to the Aten, then!"

To which my uncle replied, more calmly, "We will not, you may rest assured of that. But neither will we invite too much comment and concern by being as violent toward the Aten as *he* was toward Amon and the others. It is balance Kemet desperately needs now. *Balance!"*

Horemheb made no reply as he departed, and my uncle turned back to me, still breathing a little hard, to say quietly, "Son of the Sun, do not be alarmed by these arguments between your cousin and me. Though a mature man, he is still too rash and impatient in some respects. I know in his heart he sees my wisdom, as I hope you do too. Do you not agree with what I say?"

So dutifully I said (because it conformed so well to my own desires, in any case), "Yes, Uncle. Your words make sense to me."

And thus we had our wedding, blessed at least in part by the Aten, as we wished; and thus began the small defiance—never daring very much, for we are still so young and our hold on the people and on the army is not yet strong enough—which has allowed us to keep our hearts at rest and feel that we are being true to those who watch us from the afterworld, expecting us to keep faith with them. It is for this reason also that, until this day, I have continued to use both my names, signing myself sometimes "Tutankhamon" and sometimes "Tutankhaten," so that both appear on my official documents.

Now I have been told that as of this day this will no longer be permitted: from now on all must be "Tutankhamon." It will also be "Ankhesenamon" instead of Ankhesenpaaten. But they cannot change what we call ourselves in our hearts, or what we call one another in the privacy of our chambers. Between ourselves, at least, we will continue to do what we feel to be our duty.

On this day also, before we depart, I must set my seal—"Tutankhamon"—to the text of the "restoration stela" that Horemheb has drawn up for me. He proposes to have it inscribed on two tablets, one in the temple of Karnak and the other in the temple of Luxor to provide, as he says, "a suitable celebration of your return to Thebes." In them he wishes me to describe for eternity how I have restored to Amon and all the others their rights, prerogatives and privileges. He also wishes me to condemn my brother. This time my uncle and even my friend and cousin Nahkt-Min are agreed. I do not wish to do it, but these are the words I must endorse for them:

"Now when His Majesty [myself] appeared as King, the temples from one end of the land to the other had fallen into ruin; their shrines were desolate and had become wildernesses overgrown with weeds; their sanctuaries were as though they had never been; their precincts were trodden paths. The land was in confusion, for the gods had forsaken this land. If an army was sent to Asia to widen the frontiers of Kemet, it met with no success. If one prayed to a god to ask things of him, he did not come. If one supplicated a goddess, likewise she did not come either. Their hearts were enfeebled because what had been made was destroyed."

I know that in large measure this is true; yet I do not like the tone of criticism of my brother, who was kind to me—*he was kind to me.* He may have done bad things to Amon and the other gods, but did they not do bad things to him? He did not turn upon them until very late, when he felt he could do no other. Is he to be blamed to eternity for that?

Apparently he is, for when I showed signs of demurring (this was handed to me unexpectedly after dinner last night when I was of course entirely unprepared for it), I was threatened that if I did not sign we would not be allowed to return to Thebes, and there would be public disgrace for me. I am still too young, as I say, to have full power, so I decided to dissemble. I said that, while I regretted what they seemed to regard as the necessity to attack a Good God (they winced at that title, as I desired they should) who could do them no further harm, still I could see that Amon perhaps needed to be appeased, now that they had made him so strong again. They did not like this reminder very much, but since I was conceding they could say no more about it. So with silent apologies to my brother I agreed to the rest of it as well.

I related (in Horemheb's words—he, being a scribe, is very good at words, of course) how I was speaking from the domain of Tuthmose I (life, health, prosperity!) at Akhet-Aten (where my brother had built our distinguished ancestor a small honorary temple). I said I must congratulate myself on what I had accomplished for Amon and the other

gods so far, and stated my determination to put an end to evil and
cause the ruined temples to flower once more as "momuments of eternity." I also promised to build Amon "an august image of pure gold"
inlaid with lapis lazuli and other precious stones, greater than he had
ever received—it would take thirteen stretchers to carry it, in fact,
which I reflected silently ought to be enough to make Hatsuret dance up
and down the obelisk of Hatshepsut (life, health, prosperity!) in sheer
glee. I also related how I had "gathered in priests and prophets, children of the notables of their towns, each the son of an eminent man
whose name is known," to form the revived priesthood of Amon (all of
them carefully selected by Aye and Horemheb, of course, even though
officially appointed by me) and told how I had endowed the temple at
Karnak with treasures and filled its warehouses with male and female
slaves to wait upon them.

I also described how I intended to rebuild Amon's barges with cedarwood of the finest quality and gild them with gold so that they might
glitter upon the river as of old, and provide for them male and female
workers and singers to assist them in their task—all this for the delight
of all the gods and goddesses, who loved me and were filled with delight
by my care for them (as indeed they should be, for it is all being
handed back to them on a golden platter).

For this, I concluded, the gods had already repaid me a hundredfold,
particularly kindly old Amon, who now "loves better than ever his son
Neb-Kheperu-Ra, Lord of Karnak, Tutankhamon, him who satisfies all
the gods."

To this I affixed my seal—"Tutankhamon"—but not before I asked
my cousin Horemheb, "Is this how you would achieve balance between
Amon and Aten, Cousin? To me it seems you would put Amon again
on top of the world."

"It is not so, Son of the Sun," he said, rather more vehemently than I
think he intended. "It is simply a matter of redressing the wrongs that
have been done him."

"Well, be sure you do not lift him too high," I said, "for he has been
known to cast down even Pharaohs whom he does not like."

He gave me a startled look, flushed and growled, "Well, it will be
done correctly. Do not worry, Majesty. He will not cast you down, for
he loves you—as you," he added, suddenly peering at me, sharp and
shrewd, "love him. Is it not so, Son of the Sun?"

"It is so, Cousin," I said calmly, "with all my heart. Does not everything you require me to do give proof of it?"

"I require of you nothing you do not grant willingly out of your deep
love for the god!" he said. "Is that not also true, Son of the Sun?"

I saw from his expression, and my uncle's that it had better be, so I laughed and said, "Certainly, Cousin, certainly! I would not have it otherwise. *Never* would I have it otherwise!"

"I hope not," he said, while at his shoulder my uncle looked as intent as he, "for to do so would only bring new sorrows upon the Two Lands. And that we *all* wish to avoid, do we not?"

"You have the proof of it," I said cheerfully. "My seal is affixed to your writing. You hold it in your hand. Certainly even for one as suspicious as you, Cousin, that should be sufficient."

"He is not suspicious," my uncle said gravely, seeking to turn aside the contest he sensed beneath our words. "He is simply careful of the kingdom."

"And I am not?" I demanded, suddenly stern, drawing myself up to my full height, which of course is not yet full-grown: but impressive enough, I guess, for they both stepped back a little as though from a physical impact, at my regal presence. "Do you dare tell me *I* am not?"

"No, Majesty," Aye said hastily; and, "No, Son of the Sun," echoed Horemheb with equal haste. And, "Very well, then," said I. "Take your paper and have your stelae carved. I, Neb-Kheperu-Ra Tutankhamon, have agreed to it, so let no more be said!"

"Yes, Majesty," they said as one; bowed low; and backed out while I still stood stern and imperious before them. Behind me I heard a giggle: Ankhesenpaaten had been peeking through a slit in the curtain that conceals my private passageway to the throne.

"You have them scared," she said, coming out and taking my hand in hers.

"Not really," I said. "*I* am scared of them, and so should you be, until we are powerful enough to bend them to our rule."

"Yes," she agreed, suddenly somber, for we agree in all things, and particularly this. "The time is not yet."

"Not yet," I said, "but it will come."

"Yes," she said softly, kissing me as she often does, for we have found great happiness and are very close now that I am old enough, "it will come." Her eyes looked suddenly fierce. "I swear it by the blood of my mother and my father!"

"I swear it by the blood of my brother and my cousin!" I said with equal fierceness: and then we clung to one another very tightly for a very long time, for in reality we are still children and today we are being forced to leave our favorite city under the command of others, and we are, in truth, unable to do the slightest thing about it.

But the time *will* come, it is simply a matter of getting through these next few years without antagonizing them too much or revealing to them too clearly what our real thoughts are. For the present, I intend to do one more thing, using the "restoration stela" as my excuse, which I think I can do in the guise of maintaining that "balance" my uncle talks about. I will tell them about this when we get to Thebes. If they protest too much I shall abandon it—for now. If they do not I shall go ahead, regarding it as one more small step on the long road we must go to return Kemet to the only balance that can truly restore her glory, the balance of love.

Now the trumpets are blowing, there is bustle in the corridors. They are coming to get us. It is time to say good-by to Akhet-Aten.

We stand together for a last moment at the window, arms about each other's waists, eyes suddenly filled with tears as we look our last upon the ghost city to which we will never, in all probability, return. They are with us achingly now, our own special ghosts. One shuffles awkwardly down the hall. One gives us a steady glance from serenely beautiful eyes. One, older and harried by her cares for Kemet, looks at us absentmindedly yet with love as she vanishes from us down an empty street.

We have not left you, dear ghosts.

By us you will be remembered and revenged.

I, Neb-Kheperu-Ra Tutankhaten, so decree it.

Amonemhet

You will remember me, Amon-em-het the peasant who lives beside the Nile and watches the grand ones pass up and down on their way to death and disaster? Well, I am still here, a little older now: and lots of them are not. So I guess I can't complain, even though life has never been easy for us here in the village, and I have just about given up hope that it ever will be.

Tonight the village is being greatly honored, so we are told, because the procession of the new Good God, our boy-King Tutankhamon, has graciously decided to tie up along our shores on its way to Thebes. What this "honor" means in fact is that hundreds of oarsmen, priests, slaves and servants will soon swarm ashore to chase our women and children and buy up every bit of food we have—or steal it, if they can't buy it.

When I first heard they were coming—horsemen rode ahead to

spread the word, followed by the sound of many trumpets on the river, far off—I ordered my wife and our six children (yes, we keep at it, though it means more mouths to feed—but also, you see, more hands to feed my wife and me when our mouths grow toothless again, as theirs first were) to take away our precious little hoard of grain, our two cattle, our two donkeys, even our dog and the cat—and hide them several miles from here in a secret cave we know at the place where the Black Land ends like a knife edge and the Red Land begins. I told them to remain there, for evil visitors sometimes want more than food, and my wife is still comely and we have three girls, and poor peasants have little appeal from the whims of nobles, thugs and city men.

I then left our hut wide open, the rough stone table and benches where we eat and the round stone where we grind the grain left in place, our sleeping pallets stacked in one corner of the room, our earthen pots and pans in another. I hoped this would discourage any would-be evildoer off the boats who might happen to look in, and with a silent prayer to Amon that all would be well with my family and our house, I went forth into the village to learn what I could learn.

The thing I learned, to my pleased surprise, was that this visit was different from the last such one we had, when the Good God's father, Amonhotep III (life, health, prosperity, and may his memory be blessed forever, good father to us that he was!) decided to tie up here many years ago on his way to Memphis. That time it did go just as I said. I was but a boy at the time, and even I was not safe from drunken strangers. The village was stripped of everything we had, there were screams and scuffles in the bushes, many of us children learned things that night we had not known before. The great ones passed through like a plague of locusts and we cursed their memory (except for the Good God, who remained on his golden barge and could not have known what went on) for many years thereafter. It was this that made us all rush our goods and families away at sundown when we heard the new Pharaoh was coming.

And for a little while, as I entered the market square and greeted my friends with worried glances—all of us standing about uncertainly, trembling and fearful of what might happen as the noisy visitors approached—it seemed the old pattern would be repeated. And it seemed that it would be approved by Pharaoh and by Amon himself, for it was one who announced himself as Amon's High Priest who strode first into the square, stabbed the pole of his flaring torch into the sand with a scornful authority, and cried out:

"Draw near and give up your goods for the comfort and well-being of Pharaoh, who blesses your humble village with his sacred presence this night! And provide you also those who will give *us* comfort! So say I, Hatsuret, His Majesty's High Priest in the most sacred temple of Amon at Karnak!"

At first none of us said anything, being too afraid to move.

"Well?" he cried out again, his voice becoming furious and demanding. "Well, well? Do not stand there like stones, but do as I say! Move!"

And, turning, he gestured imperiously to the several hundred men, some of them already swaying drunkenly, who stood behind him, many armed with clubs or spears. Slowly at first, but gaining courage from one another and from his fearsome presence, they began to stumble toward us, weapons raised.

Desperately we looked about, not knowing what to do or where to turn. I found myself crying out in my heart with a frantic anguish, "Somebody *do something!*" And abruptly, not knowing what impulse pushed me or where the courage came from, I found that I was.

"Sir!" I cried, my voice shaky but determined, stepping forward while my friends gathered behind me in a tight, protective group. "Great Sir, I beg of you, we are but humble peasants here. We have only the goods you see on our backs. We have little for the comfort of Pharaoh, but he is of course welcome to what we have, it is our greatest honor to give it to him. Take it, please, Great Sir, but spare us, his loyal subjects, from the wrath you show, for we have done nothing to deserve it!"

A murmur of agreement came from my friends behind, an angry jumble of impatience from the mob in front.

The High Priest tore his torch from the sand and jabbed it in again with a mighty force. As if observing from some other world, where I expected very soon to be, I noted that he had a long black beard, quite unlike most of us in Kemet, who are clean-shaven. I also saw that it was plaited with gold thread, which made me realize that Amon must now be very powerful again indeed. We had heard this in the village, but now we saw it.

"Scum!" he shouted. "Scum and double scum! Give us your goods at once *and provide us other comforts,* or you will not look long upon your village because it will no longer be here! And *you* will not be here to see even its ruins!"

And he strode forward suddenly and grasped me around the throat with his hairy, powerful hands, forcing me to my knees, my head back, my breath stopping, my throat trying helplessly to gag, my eyes beginning to bulge from my head. All began to swirl and swim, a blackness was creeping fast upon me—and suddenly there was a single high-

pitched angry shout, the High Priest threw me to the ground and leaped
back, a great silence descended on all the world.

Two of my dear, brave friends placed their trembling hands beneath
my arms and raised me up. Slowly the world came back into shape.
Ours was the only movement, the only sound my deep, sobbing gasps
for breath. All else was frozen.

Behind the mob, which now had turned in fear to witness him, there
stood a youth of perhaps twelve or thirteen, naked to the waist. He too
carried a long torch, almost twice as tall as he. He wore a pleated kilt of
golden thread and on his feet gold-painted sandals, and around his
shaven head a thin gold band with the hood of the cobra goddess Buto
raised to strike his enemies. There could be no doubt who he was, and
when he cried one single angry word—*"Down!"*—we all, his high-and-
mightiness the High Priest as hastily as the rest, fell groveling to our
knees.

"Hatsuret!" he shouted, his light boy's voice cracking deeper now
and then on the edge of manhood (but none, none, dared laugh, for
this was a god). "Do you return at once to your vessel, and do you take
this rabble with you! *At once!"*

For a moment it seemed Amon's prophet might defy him—a strange
dark glance shot from his eyes to those of Pharaoh, which glared back
at him furious and unafraid. Their duel lasted but a second. Without a
word the priest rose slowly to his feet, disengaged his torch and started
back to the Nile, his awe-struck gang slinking off behind him. He
walked wide around the Good God, who gave him not a glance, nor he
one at Pharaoh. There was something almost contemptuous about his
walk, but our brave little King, for whom a great love was filling our
hearts, gave not the slightest sign he noticed. He stood absolutely still,
stern and unyielding, a gleaming handsome little god in the flickering
light of his torch.

"Men of this village," he said at last, his face softening as he looked
down upon us, "rise to your feet. . . . You! What is your name?"

"Amon-em-het, Your Majesty," I said humbly, my throat terribly
raw but managing to get it out clearly. "Your faithful and loyal subject,
as are all of us here."

"So I see you are," he said gravely. "And I see that you, Amonemhet, are a brave and honest man. I must humbly beg your pardons for
the actions of the High Priest and those, unhappily for them blinded
with wine, who have disturbed your peace this night. The High Priest, I
think"—and his voice trailed away a little as some inner thought engaged him—"is becoming a little too high. . . . But that," he added
more briskly, "is my concern, not yours.

"To you I say this: Your Pharaoh loves you and wishes all to go well with your village. You will receive no more visitors this night, nor will you ever again be disturbed in your peaceful pursuits. To see that this is so, I do name you, Amonemhet, to be the Chief Headman and Leader of this village, and I do charge you to come to me at any time, in Thebes or Memphis or wherever I may be, if you need help with any of your problems. Do not hesitate, for I am your friend and you are mine. In proof of this, I give you this ring which is mate to another I have—" and he took from his steady finger and placed upon my shaking one a simple gold band bearing on its top what I could not read, but knew from its long oval shape must be his cartouche, worked in gold upon the carnelian. "I charge you to wear it always as the symbol of your office. If you ever need my help, bring it with you when you come to me and you will always be admitted. If I ever need your help, I shall send its brother to you. Do not lose yours or sell it or let it be stolen from you, for with it will go the powers with which I have endowed you.

"Men of this village! I charge you to guard and protect this ring and with it Amonemhet your Chief Headman and Leader, who will in turn protect you with my love forever and ever, for millions and millions of years.

"I, Neb-Kheperu-Ra Tutankh"—he hesitated very slightly—"amon, so decree it. And I wish you good night, and may the gods be with you always."

He lifted his torch, bowed gravely to us as we all fell prostrate again, and started to turn away. Abruptly we could sense him pause; and peering up furtively through narrowed lids, we could see that in his path stood another gleaming figure, this one a man in his forties with a sharp, shrewd face, crossed now by a frown. We could see he must be someone very great, for his fabrics gleamed with a richness smelling of wealth and power.

"Ah, Cousin," Pharaoh said (and we knew with a thrill that this must be the famous General Horemheb, King's Deputy and leader of the armies, about whom we have heard so much, even in our humble village), "have you come for me?"

At this simple question, which to us seemed straightforward enough, a strange expression, twisted and odd so that it seemed almost to be filled with some deep, mysterious pain, shadowed the face of General Horemheb. We did not know why: it frightened us. Hastily he disguised it with a cough, raising his hand to his mouth; when it came away his expression was calm again. But it was very strange: very strange. Apparently it puzzled Pharaoh, too, for he repeated:

"I said, Cousin: have you come for me?"

"They await you at dinner, Son of the Sun," General Horemheb said. "It grows late, and we did not know where you had gone. We were becoming fearful."

"I have been talking to these friends of my faithful village," Pharaoh said pleasantly. "I have been in no harm from them. On the contrary. But I must speak with you about Hatsuret."

"Yes," General Horemheb said, his frown returning. "I met Hatsuret on the way. He did not seem happy."

"Nor am I," Pharaoh said, still pleasantly but with a firmness in his voice that boded, we fervently hoped, no good for his high-and-mightiness Hatsuret. "We must talk about that."

"In good time, Son of the Sun," General Horemheb said comfortably. But His Majesty was not to be diverted.

"No, I think tonight," he said. "I had thought not until we get to Thebes, but now I think tonight. Come, Cousin," he said before General Horemheb could utter the protest that clearly started upon his lips —yet why protest? We could not see the reason, but of course we are simple peasants and we do not know the things that trouble the great—

"Give me your arm, and let us go."

And he turned once more to wave us a kind farewell, gesturing that we should rise. We leaped to our feet with a rousing shout that brought a sudden happy smile to his face. We realized then that, for all that he is Pharaoh, he is still really but a boy; and we shouted again, with encouragement and loyalty and a warm, deep love linking our hearts to his.

He said no more, but waved once again and turned upon the arm of his cousin and walked gravely away. We watched until they disappeared among the palms, watched even longer until we saw their torches emerge at last upon the riverbank on the other side of the grove and then ascend and disappear into his great golden barge; and even then we did not stop looking, but stood staring long and hard, straining our eyes as though we could somehow command him back again so that we could see him always with us in our village, our dearly beloved little King who now leads the Two Lands and cares for us in his heart.

So, as I said, you can see I am still here—and doing very nicely, thank you. Much better, in fact, than I, Amonemhet the peasant, ever dreamed in all my days that I would do. I have His Majesty's ring, I have his appointment to run the village—soon after he left, some question arose as to where we should place the new cistern and I said, "Over here," and my friends echoed eagerly, "As you say, Amonemhet, over here"—and I have his permission to come and see him if the need arises. I know that I shall do everything I can to help His Majesty and I shall do anything he desires, for he is a wonderful Good God. Long may he rule over us, with his kindness and his goodness and his love!

Now I am leaning against a palm tree in the darkness of the grove, chewing on a piece of sugarcane as I watch the glittering scene before me. Our families and goods are back, our animals are tethered for the night, the village mostly sleeps. Only a few of us are still out here watching what goes on, for it is probable that we shall never see its like again.

All along the river the great flotilla rocks gently at anchor on Hapi's black swift-flowing bosom. Many of the smaller boats are dark, their occupants already sleeping, but from others sounds of drunken singing and revelry still come. Shadowy figures stand and fall and tumble about against one another. Now and again one topples in the river with a whoop, his friends pull him out with shrieks and roars of laughter. Thank the gods Pharaoh forced them to find their amusement with each other and not with us!

Most of the ten great state barges are still blazing with light. Some aboard must be eating late. Others must be busy with matters of government, which I suppose, for the great ones, continue even at night. Pharaoh's barge gleams brightest of all, though its curtains are drawn and we could not see in even if we were closer, which we do not dare to be. No drunken voices rise from his barge. Only sweet sounds of music come from the upper deck.

A singer begins, accompanied only by a single harp and the occasional gentle shaking of a sistrum. His voice rises pure and clear like silver in the night. The other boats gradually fall silent to listen. He concludes with verses we have all known from childhood, for it is a very ancient song and even the villages know its sweet yet melancholy message:

"Bodies pass away and others come in their place, since the time of them that were before.

"The gods that were aforetime rest in their pyramids, and likewise the noble and the glorified are buried in their pyramids.

"They that build houses, their habitations are no more. What hath been done with them? . . . Their walls are destroyed, their habitations are no more, as if they had never been. . . .

"None cometh from thence to tell us how they fare, to tell us what they need, to set our hearts at rest until we also go to the place whither they are gone.

"Be glad, that thou mayest cause thine heart to forget that men will one day glorify thee at thy funeral. Follow thy desire, so long as thou

livest. *Put myrrh on thy head, clothe thee in fine linen, and anoint thee with the marvels of life.*

"*Increase yet more the delights that thou hast, and let not thine heart grow faint. Follow thy desire and do good to others and thyself. Do what thou must upon earth and vex not thine heart, until that day of lamentation cometh to thee—for He With The Quiet Heart, Great Osiris, heareth not lamentations, and cries deliver no man from the underworld.*

"*Spend the day happily and weary not thereof!*

"*Lo, none can take his goods with him!*

"*Lo, none that hath departed can come again. . . .*"

Softly his voice dies away. The harp shimmers one last note, the sistrum rustles into silence. A melancholy touches us all, we in the grove and they on the great boats. One by one the lights begin to go out, the revelry falls away. Soon it is no more. Only on Pharaoh's barge the lights still burn behind the curtains: the Good God does not yet sleep.

Silently we steal away. A wind is rising from the Nile, in all too short a time the first fingers of Ra will creep up the eastern sky and we will have to resume our lifelong burdens.

May His Majesty sleep well! May all go well with him! May he rest secure and happy in our love! May all go well with him, forever and ever, for millions and millions of years!

Amonhotep, Son of Hapu

They face us now across the polished cedarwood table sent from Lebanon years ago as gift for his brother when gifts were still being given: two defiant children in the soft flickering glow of the oil burning in the alabaster lamps that hang from hooks along the cabin walls. The curtains are drawn tight against the night, outside the singing and revelry are at last beginning to die down. The crew of the royal barge is sleeping on the shore. No one is near to disturb the six who are still awake at this late hour: Aye; Horemheb; Hatsuret; the two children; and myself, who am still permitted to attend their councils, because Horemheb has kept the word he gave me that horrible night: he forgave me. Miraculously our friendship, and my trusted place with the Family, continue unchanged.

It is apparent that His Majesty is very angry, and that Ankhesenpaaten (the new name "Ankhesenamon" does not yet come easily to me) shares his feelings fully.

"I have asked you here," he begins, his boy's voice breaking now and again with adolescence, but his intensity such that he ignores it save for an occasional impatient shake of the head, "because I am much displeased. I would have the cause of my displeasure—removed."

"What is the cause of your displeasure, Son of the Sun?" Aye asks gravely. Tut almost interrupts with his scornful answer, which startles us all, it is so unlike him heretofore: this must be an anger genuine indeed.

"You know what it is, Uncle!" he says sharply. "I have no doubt they have told you all about it long since. It is the High Priest and his rowdies who break the King's peace and harry his people!"

"I am sure there was no intention—" Aye begins, but this time Pharaoh does interrupt.

"Oh, there was intention," he says coldly. "I was there, Uncle. I saw the intention." He turns sharply on Hatsuret, who is still standing near the door because Pharaoh has deliberately not asked him to be seated. "What did you intend to do to that poor man had I not stopped you, Hatsuret? Is the High Priest of Amon a murderer?"

Hatsuret starts as though struck a physical blow in the face. His eyes narrow with anger, but he knows he must control it, and he does.

"Your Majesty," he says quietly, "I was but teaching him a lesson."

"What kind of lesson?" Pharaoh demands. "And what had he done to warrant such a lesson? Speak! I would know!"

"He and his village were insolent," Hatsuret begins. "They defied me when I asked for goods for Pharaoh—"

"I arrived before you think, Hatsuret," Pharaoh interrupts. "I know what was said."

"Do you accuse me of lying, Your Majesty?" Hatsuret demands with a sharpness he would not have dared show a grown man. Perhaps he should not have dared with this.

"Do you accuse *me*, Hatsuret?" Tut asks, his voice suddenly soft and dangerous with an emotion we have never heard in it before.

Hatsuret is obviously taken aback but, for a moment only, he holds his ground. Then his eyes drop and he says sullenly:

"They were insolent. They would not have given me what I asked for Pharaoh."

"Amonemhet offered it!" Pharaoh says. "And you did not ask only for me. You asked for yourselves and they knew, as I knew, what you wanted. You do lie, Hatsuret. I should have your head!"

"Perhaps it were best," Ankhesenpaaten says clearly before any of the rest of us, shocked, can reply. "It might remove a painful thorn from Your Majesty's side."

"The 'thorn' is Amon!" Hatsuret retorts angrily. "Would you remove Amon again, Your Majesty, as the Heretic did?"

"The 'Heretic,'" Tut begins in a blaze of anger, "was my brother," he finishes, more quietly. "I do not intend to debate that with you now, Hatsuret. You are back in power, Amon rules the land with us again. But I am determined it shall be a fitting rule, and not the threatening ways you displayed in my loyal village tonight."

"Amon has done all things fitting so far, Son of the Sun," Horemheb remarks quietly. "On every side the people welcome him. Are you not pleased that he has returned to bless our House and help it lead the Two Lands to happier times?"

For a second—longer than he perhaps intends, long enough to stir uneasiness in our hearts—His Majesty hesitates.

"I am pleased that Amon has been restored," he says carefully, "and I am pleased that he wishes to aid our House. I desire only that he do so in ways that will truly benefit the Two Lands. I did not see those ways tonight."

"I am sure the High Priest will take your desires into account very seriously," Horemheb says smoothly.

"And I am sure," Aye says, "that we will all forget the words that have been spoken in anger by you both, and by Her Majesty. Only in the closest trust and confidence can Pharaoh and the gods work together to save Kemet. And all that really matters is to save Kemet, do you not agree?"

"Yes, Uncle," Pharaoh says with what appears to be a sudden submission, though now, startled by his most unusual display of defiance, we can no longer be sure. "I agree. Hatsuret, go now. Guide yourself better and serve us well, and you shall have no more complaints from me."

"Thank you, Your Majesty," Hatsuret says, bowing low so that the carnelian scarab at his neck swings loose on its golden chain and gleams and glitters in the light. "It will ever be my pleasure to serve you well, O Son of the Sun—if Her Majesty," he adds with another bow, so low that we cannot be sure whether it is respectful or not, "will permit me."

"Your own actions will permit you or not permit you, Hatsuret," she says, her determined young voice and cool expression rousing sharp and uncomfortable memories of her mother. "It is for you to decide."

"Yes, Majesty," Hatsuret says, his eyes for an instant dark again with anger; but he recovers smoothly. "Such will ever be my earnest intention."

"Go then," Tutankhamon says, "and sleep well, for tomorrow we arrive in Thebes and great will be the ceremonies thereof."

Once again Hatsuret bows low to them both; bows to us; and leaves. We hear his footsteps pass above us across the deck, we hear a muffled exchange as some of the sleeping crew rouse to hand him down. We look at one another and our real council begins.

"Uncle," Pharaoh says, "I do not like that man."

"Nor I," Ankhesenpaaten agrees calmly, and her words are so bold that there is no doubt at all whose daughter she is. "He murdered my mother, my sister and my uncle, and he helped you both in an even greater crime, the death of Pharaoh, for which the gods will not forgive you or cease to harry this House unto its last generation."

"Your Majesty knows why this had to be done!" Horemheb says sharply, his face flushed with anger.

"I have heard your reasons," Ankhesenpaaten says, indifferent to the point of insolence.

"They are sufficient!" Horemheb snaps.

"So we are told," she says in the same cold way.

"It is done," Horemheb says, breathing hard, "and never will I discuss it more with Your Majesties."

"Perhaps we would discuss it with you, Cousin," Tut suggests softly, but at this a curtain of rejection seems to fall across Horemheb's eyes. His face sets in stubborn lines.

"Perhaps you would, Cousin," he says evenly, "but I am afraid that will not matter."

"Well," Aye says hastily, for all of this tonight—Tut's defiance, Hatsuret's anger, Horemheb's deliberate insubordination—has brought the true situation so suddenly and glaringly into the light that he, like myself, is deeply upset by it. "Well, now. I do not think there need be any cause for controversy among us. We are agreed that Amon and our House must work together to return Kemet to glory. There is no place for argument in that. There is no need for falling out about it. Tomorrow we land in Thebes and Your Majesty's rule, in a sense, will truly begin at last, there in the place where Amon lives, the place that you and Her Majesty enjoy so much. The past is dead with those who peopled it: what the gods have taken away cannot be returned. We must look forward now, no longer back. The good of Kemet requires it."

"The 'good of Kemet'!" Pharaoh echoes. "You always talk of 'the good of Kemet,' Uncle. How much it has excused, in your mind!"

"Only what has been necessary," Aye says, his face grave. "And you should thank us for it, Neb-Kheperu-Ra, because had it not been so you would not now wear the Double Crown."

"Is it your thought I enjoy the Double Crown, Uncle?" Tutankhamon asks, and he looks as young as he is, strained and worried with his burdens. "I should be happy, I assure you, were it to rest upon some other head."

"It cannot, Your Majesty," Aye says quietly, "for you alone have the blood."

"And I!" Ankhesenpaaten reminds him sharply. He bows in apology.

"And you, of course, dear Niece," he agrees humbly. "Indeed, without you the Double Crown would not rest easily upon the head of Neb-Kheperu-Ra."

"It does not rest easily, Uncle," Pharaoh says with a wryness beyond his years, "but it rests. . . . Tell me, then: what are we to do about this troublesome priest?"

"I shall vouch for him," Horemheb says firmly. "I was not present in your village tonight until it was all over, so I did not see for myself. But," he adds quickly as Tut's eyes begin to narrow, "I believe Your Majesty, of course, as to what happened. I agree it was ill thought out, ill considered, evilly done. Even priests are human sometimes."

"They should not be," Tut says. "Particularly the Priest of Amon. He should be above the desires and passions of ordinary men. Otherwise how can he serve me and the god?"

"I shall speak to him," Horemheb assures him.

"I have already spoken to him!"

"I shall reinforce your words," Horemheb says smoothly. "It will not hurt to have all of us speak to him."

"I, too," Aye says. "With your permission, Majesty, of course."

For a moment Tut hesitates, obviously considering whether to tell us something. The decision is apparently negative.

"Very well," he says, seemingly mollified. "If you give me your words. I cannot have him trouble me and my people thus." And suddenly he yawns, a great yawn, rubbing his eyes with his fists, reminding us of the boy he really is.

"I give my word," Aye says.

"And I," says Horemheb, and moves quickly to take advantage of the moment. "And now, Majesty, had we not best seek sleep, as you yourself suggested? It grows very late and Thebes awaits us tomorrow. It will be a very long and tiring day."

"I think so," Pharaoh says, yawning again. "I have much to do tomorrow, as you say. I shall announce my plan tomorrow, then."

"What plan is that?" Horemheb demands sharply, and his father and I suddenly find ourselves listening very intently.

"Oh, just a plan," His Majesty says lightly, but between him and his wife passes a look that stirs unhappy memories and makes our blood run cold. We have had enough of secret "plans" between a Good God and his Chief Wife. Surely the gods will not permit it again!

"Can we not be told," Aye suggests quietly, "so that we, unlike your people, may be prepared to assist you in it?"

"I hope you will assist us in it, Uncle," Tut says with a smile growing sleepy either naturally or deliberately, we cannot decide which. "But I have now decided that tomorrow will be time enough. You are right: we must sleep. Good night, Uncle. Good night, Cousin. Good night, Amonhotep. Rest well in the arms of Nut the night, for tomorrow will be, as you say, a busy day."

"No, wait—" Horemheb begins, but before he can go further His Majesty gives way to another tremendous yawn.

"Ay-yai!" he says, blinking hard. "I am *tired*. Are we not, wife?"

"We are," Ankhesenpaaten says and, rising, goes to the door and opens it. There is nothing to do but bow and leave.

As we step out upon the deck a lone singer is sounding a last farewell to the day. All about are either asleep already or silent listening to his song. His closing words are familiar: we have heard them all our lives. But never, perhaps, with quite the melancholy chill that Aye, Horemheb and I feel now, as we realize that our young King and his young wife have suddenly and unexpectedly become as elusive and mysterious as those we have known before.

"Increase yet more the delights that thou hast," the singer urges, his voice lifted high on the silken sheen of a harp, his words given emphasis by the gentle rustle of a sistrum. *"Follow thy desire and do good to others and thyself. Do what thou must upon earth and vex not thy heart, until that day of lamentation cometh to thee—for He With The Quiet Heart, Great Osiris, heareth not lamentations, and cries deliver no man from the underworld.*

"Spend the day happily and weary not thereof!

"Lo, none can take his goods with him!

"Lo, none that hath departed can come again. . . ."

We cross the deck, are handed down by two sleepy crewmen. We pause for a moment on the bank. All is finally quiet. Only the light in Pharaoh's barge still burns: the children must still be talking about their disturbing mystery.

"Do what thou must upon earth and vex not thy heart," Horemheb murmurs softly.

"For, lo, none that hath departed can come again," Aye replies with equal softness.

"Good night," we say abruptly to one another, and go swiftly to our separate boats. But not to sleep for a while, I think. Certainly not I, and not, I am sure, the Regent Aye nor the King's Deputy Horemheb.

Sitamon

Far down the Nile we hear the trumpets blow. The great crowd waiting on both banks stirs and shouts with excitement. Faintly beginning, growing ever louder as the flotilla advances, comes the swelling roar of love that greets Pharaoh and his Queen as they approach their capital of Thebes. Not since my parents' day has there been such a welcome for a Good God and his wife. My little brother and our niece are well launched upon the path the Family wishes them to take.

I say "the Family"—and yet what of us is left? I, the Queen-Princess Sitamon, settling ever more rapidly into lonely middle age while my dream of marriage to my cousin Horemheb fades as surely as the evening glow on the Western Peak . . . my uncle Aye, doing his best, with guilty hands and fierce, unhappy conscience, to restore to Kemet the *ma'at* and order for whose sake he had to violate *ma'at* and order so dreadfully himself . . . Horemheb, troubled by it all but not, I think, troubled as much as he used to be, now that the fires of his ambition have truly begun to consume him . . . my youngest brother Tutankhaten (pardon me: Tutankh*amon*) . . . Akhenaten's and Nefertiti's third daughter Ankhesenpaaten (forgive me: Ankhesen*amon*) . . . Nefertiti's odd little half sister Mutnedjmet (still accompanied everywhere by her always chuckling, faintly sinister dwarfs, Ipy and Senna), and her brother Nakht-Min, children of Aye's second marriage, to gentle Tey, who also still survives . . . and that is all.

Where are we now, the great Eighteenth Dynasty? How fast has dwindled the House of Thebes!

My mother and father gone . . . my younger brother Smenkhkara dead of poison . . . our little sister Beketaten, always sickly, dead of a fever . . . Akhenaten and Nefertiti dead of the ax . . . their daughters Merytaten, Meketaten, Nefer-neferu-aten Junior, Nefer-neferu-ra and Set-e-pen-ra, all dead, Merytaten of poison, the others of that fragile

health that has taken every product of Akhenaten's loins save Ankhesenamon . . . all their children by him dead, too . . .

Cursed are we, I begin to think, cursed by fate and the anger of the
gods, brought upon us by poor, foredoomed Nefer-Kheperu-Ra and his
lost dream of the Aten.

All, all dead. And of the eight remaining, only Aye, Horemheb and
Nakht-Min really have influence in the Two Lands; and of them only
Aye and Horemheb really have the power; and of them, which will win
in their duel over the helpless persons of my little brother and my
niece?

Because duel it is, and make no mistake about it. They would have
you think otherwise, covering all with sweet words for one another and
shows of unity. But the words grow increasingly tense and the unity
shows signs of cracking, to those like myself who watch it most closely.
Beneath their public display the old lion and the younger contest for the
bones of Kemet. Two defenseless children only keep them from one another's throats. Only in the balance of their contention lies safety for
my brother and our niece.

I pray for them that they may have many sons, and swiftly; for only
by this means can the Dynasty be restored and Kemet and the Family
truly returned to glory, and only by this means can they hope to live
long and bring peace and stability to the Two Lands. I understand they
have lately begun to live together as man and wife, and perhaps
Ankhesenamon will soon have a son. I pray so, I pray so. We have had
enough of deaths and killing in the glorious Eighteenth Dynasty.

I speak so bitterly because I think it need not have been so had there
been, at various points along the way, more understanding here, more
restraint there, more imagination somewhere else. Yet all have been
trapped in the stately ritual of the kingship of Kemet, which requires of
those who would keep the Double Crown a steady obedience, and of
those who would acquire it absolute loyalty and endless patience for the
will of the gods to work itself out. My brother Akhenaten overturned
all, of course; but before him our father had begun to let things slide;
our mother had tried valiantly but without much success to hold them
together; Aye had sought desperately to keep a balance, only to be
thwarted; and soon the misgivings of the Family, the ambitions of
Horemheb and the vengeance of Amon combined to bring blood upon
our House as chaos swept the land.

Somewhere there must have been a key, but it was never found. I believe Akhenaten tried to show it us: to him, however strangely he expressed it, the key was love, by One God, for all men. Perhaps he came
too early, perhaps *he* was too strange to make us understand, since he

and his weaknesses loomed so large before us, to the exclusion of the dream. But he may have been right . . . he may have been right. Except, of course, that it could not succeed in Kemet as Kemet has always been; and as Kemet has always been, so Kemet must always be, if the Two Lands are to come again to happiness, serenity and peace.

Perhaps order, to us, means more than love.

Perhaps that is our triumph.

Or perhaps it is our curse.

It may be we will never know.

Now the roar is becoming steadily louder. As I watch from my vantage point atop the first pylon at Karnak—waiting to join them for worship to Amon, whose now triumphant priests have assisted me up the sharply winding secret stairway inside the great stone mass to this commanding overlook—I begin to catch a glimpse of many banners, crimson, purple, gold, orange, green and blue, sparkling in the sun. I see the rhythmic glistening of oars as they plunge in and out of the water, I see white sails billowing in a favoring wind, I see boats as far as my eye can reach, more boats upon the river than I have seen in many years. Trumpets are blasting now in almost continuous frenzy, the heavy throbbing of drums is beginning in the courtyard below. Great excitement seizes all. And I pray for my little brother and our niece, whose golden barge I can now see coming ahead of all the rest, that they may have the happy and fruitful role that their gentle hearts desire.

One of the assistant priests comes for me—dark Hatsuret, harsh instrument of unhappy destiny for some of those I loved, comes upriver with the rest from Akhet-Aten—and I am led down the stairs and transported in an open, jewel-hung litter to the landing stage.

I am greeted with a special affection by the wildly happy throng, for they have always loved me, and—I am very happy to be able to say— still do. The Queen-Princess Sitamon has always fortunately been someone a little apart, somehow separate from the rest of the Family in their minds: this has been my intention, which they reward with their love. I am a living memory of past triumphs and past happiness for the land. I take them back to the old days of my father and the Great Wife, for which they still secretly yearn in their hearts even as they desperately hope that this reign will eventually make all right for Kemet.

At forty-two I am an established symbol of the past.

Which is all right with me: I don't mind. In fact it has been my deliberate purpose ever since it became apparent to me that my mother, Aye and Horemheb were becoming determined to rid the land of Smenkhkara and Akhenaten. I stayed away and thus was spared any responsibility or guilt when Hatsuret, who had his orders to abduct Smenkhkara and Merytaten and transport them to permanent exile far to the south in wretched Kush, instead took it upon himself to murder them. I was not privy to the anguished counsels and tortured reasoning by which Aye and Horemheb persuaded my mother to approve the final removal of Akhenaten and Nefertiti, nor was I inside the mind of Horemheb when he, too, exceeded his mission and decided to kill them and so remove them once and for all from their disastrous rule of Kemet—and quite incidentally, of course, from the path of his own ambitions. I was not involved—if anyone was, except possibly gentle Tey —in the agonized process by which my uncle Aye made his peace with all this and decided to go on to what may yet become a final contest with his son for possession of the Double Crown. I am not among those who even now, I am sure, are studying how best to remove my little brother and so open the way for themselves to full power and kingship in the Two Lands.

And praise all the gods there are, I do not want to be. Thank them all that I am out of it! But give me strength to come to the aid of the children if I have to, for I am one of the very few real friends they have left—though the sound of love and greeting that now fills the world would make you think they had millions. So they do, while they ride the golden barge and sit the golden throne. But tomorrow, if need be, the crowds will shout for someone else and give their docile worship to whoever has the power to claim it. Right now the love is genuine enough for the two brave little figures who dismount and come smiling toward me while the heavens break with sound; and no doubt it would be quite genuine for someone else tomorrow. After all, it has to be: such is the place of Pharaoh in our world that the people have no choice.

"Sister," he says cheerfully, greeting me with a kiss whose obvious affection draws a special roar of approval, "it is good to see you again. It has been long since you came to our capital of Akhet-Aten."

"And long since you will go there again, I take it," I murmur in his ear, for Aye and Horemheb are coming up swiftly behind him.

His eyes flash at mine and he murmurs quickly back, "I will not have it dishonored, though. I shall tell Kemet about that before this day is over."

"Good," I say, and turn to Ankhesenamon, standing quietly by his side.

"Niece," I say formally as the others arrive, giving and receiving an affectionate hug, "I trust your journey was a pleasant one."

"We accomplished much," she replies easily, and over her shoulder I can see Aye and Horemheb exchange a glance in the interested silence that has fallen on the crowd as we momentarily pause, a glittering and apparently close-knit family group, on the landing stage.

"I am glad you are returning to Thebes," I say truthfully. "It has been lonely for me here, much as I love Malkata. I have rattled around the compound like the old bag of bones I am."

"Aunt!" she says with a laugh. "A better-preserved bag of bones I have yet to see. Yes, we shall join you in"—she hesitates, then gives me a quick wink—"rattling around the compound. After all"—and she raises her voice deliberately so the others can hear—"we will have nothing better to do."

"You will have the Two Lands to rule," I take the cue stoutly, and give my uncle and Horemheb look for look as they prepare to greet me. "That will be enough occupation for the Good God and his Chief Wife, surely."

"Indeed it will!" Tut says with equal stoutness. "And in this endeavor, Sister, I want you always with us to counsel and assist, for you are very wise and *your*"—a slight emphasis, but noticeable and almost openly defiant—"counsel we will value and rely upon."

"I shall be happy to help in any way I can," I say calmly and, turning to my uncle and Horemheb, give them the ritual kiss of greeting on both cheeks, thereby forcing official cordiality from them in return and causing their eyes to lose, temporarily at least, the sharpness with which they have been observing us.

"You look well, Niece," Aye says. "It will be good to be a united family again, now that we are all returned to Thebes."

"Yes," Horemheb agrees gravely.

"If you can stand it, Cousin," I say dryly. He smiles in a way that tells me it really is all over. Horemheb is enwrapped in his own purposes now and I obviously no longer figure in them.

"I can stand it, Cousin," he says politely. "If you can."

"Let us go to the temple and worship!" my brother says sharply, as one might almost add: *"and get it over with!"* The cautious and carefully observing look returns to the faces of my uncle and my cousin. Something obviously happened on the journey from Akhet-Aten. I will find out presently from the children. In the meantime it is obvious their elders fear yet more will happen. It is obvious that my brother and my niece have come to some determination that it will.

They are very young, however, he nearing fourteen, she soon to be eighteen. But they come of tough-minded stock, he of the Great Wife and she of Nefertiti. It will be an interesting contest, if it has to come to that. In it, the Queen-Princess Sitamon has already chosen *her* side. I, too, am a child of the Great Wife and I, too, can be tough-minded if I have to be. In the cause of my little brother and Ankhesenamon, I may have to be.

The moment passes. The roar of the crowd begins again as the children step into their gold-painted baldachin and are hoisted high on the shoulders of the bearers. I follow with Mutnedjmet, who returned to Malkata a week ago in advance of the royal party, complete with Ipy and Senna—*"Must* you take those two characters everywhere?" I snapped this morning as we prepared to come to Karnak. "Yes!" she said with a defiant chuckle, echoed by two squeaky little ghosts of laughter from her half-sized familiars. Then come Aye and Tey in their own baldachin, as befits the Regent and his wife, followed by Horemheb and Nakht-Min in theirs. The rest of the Court, including Ramesses, Amonhotep, Son of Hapu, and Tuthmose, chief sculptor since the death of faithful Bek, follow on foot.

We leave the landing stage and proceed down the long avenue. It is lined with priests of Amon, elbow to elbow, rigid at attention all the way.

Ahead of us all Hatsuret walks, his High Priest's leopard skin flapping around his stocky brown legs, his carnelian scarab and his glossy beard glistening in the sun, his stride confident and commanding.

How high have you risen again, O Amon, I think to myself as we rock along on the sturdy shoulders of our bearers. *Be careful you do not fall anew from too much pride and arrogance.*

It is obvious from the set of Hatsuret's head and shoulders that there is no limit to his pride and arrogance, and that he has no intention whatsoever of ever permitting Amon to fall again.

The crowd pours out its adoration and excitement in a constant loving roar as we approach the first pylon. The trumpets have resumed their bellowing, the great drumbs throb. Pharaoh has come home to Thebes, and on two little figures dressed in cloth of gold now rest the hopes of Kemet.

Tutankhamon (Life, health, prosperity!)

My wife and I understand fully now what is expected of us in Amon's temple, and as we dismount inside I bow gravely to the masked priests who dance their rituals around us. They chant. Ankhesenamon and I respond. We move through the stations of the temple, making at each its proper oblation. In our wake the others dutifully copy.

Finally I proceed alone to the inner sanctum, the holy of holies.

There he is, eyes hooded, the single ray of sunlight falling through the slit in the roof, the solid gold of his figure glowing softly in the gloom. He is standing in a new Sacred Barque, only four years old but polished and rubbed and hand-worked every day until it now has the look and patina of the original: one would think it had been there for centuries.

He looks at me, I look at him. Again we understand each other, though those at my back see only my dutifully bowing figure. "The enemy of my life," Akhenaten called him once, to me. *Beware, O Amon,* I tell him privately now, *lest brother follow brother and you find yourself with enemy again.*

He gives no sign, but our eyes hold for long as I lift my head and stand before him proudly and unafraid, staring up as sternly as he stares down. We almost enter into a trance together, it would seem, until presently outside I hear a murmuring amongst Aye, Horemheb, Hatsuret, Nakht-Min. I shake my head as if to rid it of some heavy burden, which indeed I have begun to feel pressing down upon me almost physically in the last few seconds, and turn solemnly to lead them out.

Ankhesenamon keeps me company at my side, behind us Sitamon walks alone, head held as high as ours. I realize with a sudden rush of love for my big sister that she is our ally and our friend in a world that holds very few. After her come my uncle, my cousins and Hatsuret. We return through the columns and statues, we emerge again into the long processional way flanked by priests, we come again to the landing stage, we turn to the left and enter the field beside the temple. A platform has been set up. I intend to say some words to my people upon this my formal day of return. I shall then be taken in triumphal procession through all Thebes, worshiping at Luxor as well, going across the Nile to visit my father's mortuary temple and there worship his memory and my mother's, and all my illustrious ancestors' back to Menes (life, health, prosperity!) of the First Dynasty, two thousand years ago.

Then there will be great rejoicing, drinking and roistering all over Thebes, far into the night. By then I hope my wife and I will be soundly asleep in Malkata with Sitamon. By then we shall be thoroughly exhausted by the day's ceremonies.

But those who roister, and my uncle and Horemheb as well, will, I hope, have reason to pause and think of me sometimes as the day and night wear on. For in what I will speak from the platform now I am about to give them what my brother used to call "wonders." I do not call them wonders, because for me there is no wonder about it: they are simply the things that in fairness (and for the protection of my crown) should be done. It is well I have waited for this moment, because it will not be easy to challenge me now.

I think the journey from Akhet-Aten has been very good for me. Somewhere along the way I seem to have found a sudden new confidence, the confidence I must have if I am to be a good King and Pharaoh to the Two Lands. I think it began with my facing down of Hatsuret in the village: I was so angry with his bullying of innocent peasants that I did not even stop to think of the fears that used to hold me silent in his presence. It continued to grow in my argument on the boat with my uncle and Horemheb. I perceived that when Ankhesena-mon and I really stood firm—my anger apparently continuing to give me strength—it really cowed and frightened them. They did not argue back, they slunk away. For quite a while thereafter we were too excited to sleep, but lay side by side in our golden bed reviewing all that had been said. I told her how it began, of my friend good Amonemhet in the village, and all that followed after. We congratulated one another that we had won a significant victory. From now on they will begin to obey. From now on we will not be afraid to assert ourselves and do what we think is right for Kemet. The love we have received every-where from the people confirms us in this.

What is right, I think, is the restoration of a balance. I think I let Horemheb persuade me to go too far in my "restoration stela." He gave it all back to Amon and, being only nine, naturally I was unable to think it through very clearly or do anything about it if I had. I was their prisoner in Akhet-Aten—in fact, I still felt myself to be so just a week ago on the day we left—and I submitted easily to Amon then. It is different now. It is amazing how fast one's feelings can change as one grows older. I no longer feel their prisoner today.

I think it is time for Amon once more to be brought to heel—Hat-suret represents him well, as Ankhesenamon and I commented to one another when we saw that arrogant figure swinging along so confidently before us into the temple. It is time to make it walk humbly again. I took his measure in Amonemhet's village and I won. I feel now that I will continue to win.

We reach the platform, take our places. The Family, Hatsuret and the rest sit in a row of gilded chairs along the back, Ankhesenamon and I side by side on our golden thrones in front. (The back of every chair and the backs of our thrones carry carvings of the head and enormous double plumes of triumphant Amon. There, too, I think I will restore a balance.) I am continuing with Ankhesenamon the custom of my father

with the Great Wife, of Akhenaten with Nefertiti: my wife is my partner and almost, as nearly as tradition permits, my equal. We love one
another and we will share our power for all the years we are given to
rule the Two Kingdoms. This will be very many, for we are young and
long lives stretch ahead for us in the service of our beloved Kemet.

The trumpets give a final blast, there is a final long roll on the drums
—and silence. It is time for me to speak. I rise and move to the edge of
the platform. My people stretch as far as the eye can see. I begin to
speak and, happily for me, my voice seems to have stopped cracking
with the unexpectedness of youth. (Maybe my voice has grown up in
this past week too! I hope so, for it is embarrassing to be steady one
minute and squeaky the next.)

"My beloved people of Kemet!" I cry. A great roar of love comes up
in response. Then they are swiftly silent, listening intently to what I
have to say.

"It gives Her Majesty and me great pleasure to be back in Thebes
again!"

Another roar of approval, another quick silence.

"Here and in Memphis will we re-establish our capitals, but it is particularly here that our hearts will rest. For this reason I am this day
adding to my titles the words 'Ruler of Southern No,' 'Ruler of Thebes'
—and I am restoring to Thebes her ancient name of 'No-Amon,' City
of Amon, which lately has been known by another name. [My brother's
"No-Aten," of course—"City of the Aten"—but I am determined not
to name him or blame him.]

"These changes, signifying my close friendship with Amon, do I,
Neb-Kheperu-Ra Tutankhamon, decree."

There is another great shout, including applause from Aye and
Horemheb, who knew I intended this, and approve; though I think they
are uneasy concerning what I may do next. I will show them.

"People of Kemet," I continue while all fall still again, "you know
what I have done and am doing for Amon, here and everywhere in the
Two Lands. You know I am restoring his temples, replenishing his
wealth, returning his priesthood to its ancient glory. You also know I
am doing the same for all other gods. You have read my Restoration
Stela and with your own eyes see everywhere about you in Kemet
the living truth of it. I am doing as I have promised, for my word is
good and I do what I say I will."

Once more, approval, loud and fervent. I turn for a quick downward
glance at Ankhesenamon, who gives me an encouraging smile: we are
no longer afraid of my uncle and Horemheb, or of anybody. So I pro-

ceed to jar them a little—not too much, I think, but enough so that they will know that Neb-Kheperu-Ra lives—and rules.

"Though I return to Thebes and to Memphis," I resume—and suddenly it is very still indeed, particularly behind me—"I do not wish to destroy or take vengeance upon those who in recent years have sought some other faith than Amon.

"I wish my rule to be one of conciliation, of happiness and of peace. I wish to bring all of you, my dear people of Kemet, and all our great gods, together once again in harmony and love. I wish to restore *ma'at* and do justice to all, in all things."

A little uneasily, for they do not know what to make of my frank reference to the Aten and to recent unhappy years, my people applaud me. Aye, Horemheb and Hatsuret are listening very intently now. It is exciting to know that in their eyes the child King has become truly Pharaoh at last. Suddenly I am someone who can make things happen, and to whom they must listen because he is the Living Horus and sole ruler of the Two Lands. I like this.

"So that all may know that peace and conciliation are my purpose, I wish it known that I do not desire the destruction of the temples of the Aten at my city of Akhet-Aten, nor do I wish punishment to be visited upon any who may still wish to worship, in the privacy of their own homes or in his temples, that particular god."

I sense a tense, uneasy stirring at my back. But I go firmly on.

"It is my desire that the Aten shall resume the honored place he had before recent unhappy years came upon us. [Again I refuse to name or blame my brother, who was always kind to me.] The Aten shall not be supreme, neither shall he be inferior. He shall not dominate, neither shall he be dominated. He will return to his rightful and traditional place among the gods, and we will continue to honor him as we honor Amon and all other gods. This, too, do I, Neb-Kheperu-Ra Tutankhamon, decree."

Applause and approval come, but thinner and more uncertainly now, as many eyes look past me to my uncle, to Horemheb and to Hatsuret. I, too, turn and look at them. Their faces are a study in many things, but sternness is the chief. I stare at them with equal sternness and presently they look away. Suddenly I *know* I can do everything I wish to do to make Kemet a happy and prosperous land again.

"My beloved people," I resume, and in the silence that has returned my voice rings clearly across the vast crowd, "in addition to the preservation and maintenance of the temples of the Aten at Akhet-Aten, for which I shall dispense suitable funds from the coffers of Pharaoh, it is my will that the temple of the Aten here at Karnak shall be enlarged and extended, so that it may be suitable for the god as he resumes his rightful place among us.

"To you, Amonhotep, Son of Hapu, builder and maker of so many great things for the House of Thebes, do I give this responsibility. And you, Tuthmose, chief sculptor to Pharaoh, do I charge to assist him in this task."

There is a murmuring, an uneasiness. But I am only being fair and restoring justice. I continue unperturbed.

"I charge you also, Tuthmose, to make for me another set of scepters, a golden crook and flail similar to these I carry"—and I raise and show them to my people, for these are things they regard with an awe almost as great as that with which they regard my own person. "These bear the name of Amon. I wish the second set to bear the name of the Aten. Thus will Amon and Aten both be served, and confirm me in my rule."

Again the uneasiness. They do not know whether to applaud. They know they cannot protest.

"And finally do you, Tuthmose, build for me a second golden throne, equal in size to this one on which I sit today. And do you place on the back thereof pictures of Her Majesty and me, and do you place above, blessing us, the sign and cartouches of the Aten, so that in this, too, we may restore balance and *ma'at* to the gods."

Once more, murmuring and uneasiness. I do not look behind me at my uncle, my cousin and hateful Hatsuret, for I do not wish to be distracted by what I assume to be their disapproving stares. I am doing exactly what is right: I am not threatening Amon, I am not exalting the Aten: I am in fact reducing the Aten. If I am still keeping him great enough to give Amon pause, well, then, so be it. Ankhesenamon and I are agreed that this is the only way to restore the health of the Two Lands.

"My beloved people of Kemet!" I conclude solemnly, and now the whole world seems hushed and listening. I have their attention forever now. Never again will the King be considered just a boy, I can tell that, and I am glad of it, so that happiness suffuses my whole being though I do not discount the difficulties and do not fool myself that my path will be easy.

"It is my desire that from this time forward the Two Lands and all their gods shall truly be united again in love and tolerance for one another. It is my desire that you shall live together, one with the other, forever and ever, for millions and millions of years, in harmony and joy. It is my desire that all our gods shall live together, one with the other, in this same way. Thus, and only thus, can our beloved Kemet be whole again.

"Join me in this, I say to you, people of the Two Lands! Join me in this, I say to you, great gods of Kemet! And together we will enter upon a new day when old bad things are swept away and the land sings again with happiness and peace!

"So do I, Neb-Kheperu-Ra Tutankhamon, decree it!"

And I bow low to them and turn to Ankhesenamon, who rises and comes forward to stand beside me. Now the great shout of love and loyalty wells up again. I have puzzled them a little, made them think, convinced them, I hope, that they must forget the past, be compassionate with one another, move forward together for Kemet's sake. I may even have disturbed them a little—certainly I know I have disturbed my uncle, Horemheb and Hatsuret, who have other ideas. But now all is forgotten in our physical presence before them, our living proof that the Good God and the Chief Wife are with them and working for their welfare always, which we truly are. Their love for us engulfs the world.

For many minutes their shouts go on, until at last we turn away to prepare for the great procession. First we shall return to the temple to relieve ourselves and eat a hasty bit of food to sustain us during the long afternoon. Then we shall remount our baldachins and the procession through Thebes, across the Nile to my father's mortuary temple, to the Valley of the Kings, and so finally to Malkata, will begin.

We give the Family an easy, smiling look as we step from the platform. Aye, Horemheb and Hatsuret preserve a careful politeness. Nakht-Min, Amonhotep, Son of Hapu, Ramesses and Tuthmose dare to look friendly and pleased. Sitamon steps forward fearlessly to kiss us both, and on some sudden impulse as startling and inexplicable as most of the things she does, funny little Mutnedjmet does the same while Ipy and Senna bounce about, shrilly crowing and applauding, somewhere down around our kneecaps.

"Majesty," Sitamon says in a voice she makes deliberately clear and carrying, "I agree entirely with what you said. It means a great new day for Kemet. We have had enough of separation, bitterness and hate."

"I, too," Mutnedjmet says happily, "I, too."

"And we!" Ipy and Senna flute with their customary privileged informality. "And we!"

"Thank you, Sister," I say gravely to Sitamon, and, "Thank you," gravely to the rest. "My wife and I will do our best in all things for our beloved Two Kingdoms."

"You may rely on me," Sitamon says in the same emphatic way as I take her arm and Ankhesenamon's and we begin to walk toward the temple.

Behind us the others fall in line. No word comes from my uncle, my cousin or the dark and dangerous priest. But I do not care.

I am truly Pharaoh now, and I do not care.

Hatsuret

The day draws toward its close and I no longer lead the procession. I led it all through Thebes, walking ahead triumphantly as the High Priest of Amon should, sanctifying by his presence the god's blessing and support of Pharaoh. But when we crossed the Nile and were about to land on the west bank he turned to me and said firmly in the presence of the Family:

"Hatsuret, I wish that you take your place somewhere behind us now. On that bank of the Nile I let you lead through Thebes as a sign of my respect for Amon. Here I wish you to let me lead as a sign of Amon's respect for me."

"But, Son of the Sun—" I began smoothly, confident I would have the support of the regent Aye and General Horemheb in my objections to this sacrilegious order.

"We so wish it," he said evenly, and turned his back on me to point out to Her Majesty the distant towering colossi of his father which guard the mortuary temple, and the gracefully ascending stairways of the mortuary temple of Hatshepsut (life, health, prosperity!), far off against the tawny cliffs.

"But—" I began again; looked around in consternation at the others; found them also too taken aback, apparently, to speak; found myself inadvertently staring into the coolly amused eyes of the Princess Sitamon, who is not my friend and had best not become too clever with me; and was forced to subside in angry silence and confusion until the royal barge touched the landing stage.

There I made a last attempt, starting to step forward as though the conversation had not occurred.

"Hatsuret!" Pharaoh said, and his sharp young voice cracked across my face like a whip. *"You heard me!"*

"Obey His Majesty," Aye said calmly, "for it is not worth disrupting this day."

"It is not important," Horemheb agreed.

"It is important to *me*," Tutankhamon said; and I almost replied with equal arrogance, "And it is important to *me*." But I did not quite dare, particularly since my allies seemed for some reason to be abandoning me.

I said no word but waited for them to disembark and then took my place behind Horemheb and Nakht-Min. As I did so Horemheb turned and shook his head slightly with an expression as if to say: *Do not worry. We will tame this cub.*

But we had thought he *was* tamed! Suddenly he does not seem to be, any more.

Well: this does not frighten me. Three times now I have done the work of Amon and the House of Thebes. Smenkhkara—Merytaten— even that great proud beauty who scorned Amon in all her pride and arrogance, that spoiled one who thought she could live forever but could not, Nefertiti. I killed them all for Amon and for those who, like myself, sought the restoration of the god and a rebirth of *ma'at* and justice in the Two Lands. I will not be afraid to kill again for the same reasons, if we all decide it necessary.

Today I sense the thought has begun to enter the minds of Aye and Horemheb. Certainly it has entered mine. For four years the boy King and Ankhesenamon have appeared to be docile tools in our hands as we have restored the old religion and begun the long task of bringing back the ancient order of Kemet out of the chaos left by the Heretic. The task is far from complete: we have much farther to go. Years of patient work still lie ahead to repair all the damage the Criminal of Akhet-Aten left behind.

Two stubborn children cannot be allowed to stand in our way.

We reach the mortuary temple of Amonhotep III (life, health, prosperity!). The procession halts, the Good God and the Chief Wife are lowered to the ground. They walk into the temple to do worship to his father.

Horemheb drops back a step. I whisper urgently, "We must discuss this!"

He nods.

"Tonight I shall talk to my father."

"Where shall I meet you?"

"*Alone!*" he snaps, and starts to turn away. Then he hesitates and turns back to murmur more courteously, "Do not press, Hatsuret. You

will be advised in due course. Rest assured all things will come right for
Kemet and for Amon."

And for Horemheb, I think, but this I would never, ever, dare say to
anyone. He, too, can kill for his purposes as I have killed for mine. We
are allies and must remain so. The welfare of Amon depends on it.

I convey my understanding with one swift look, bow impassively,
raise my staff of office and move off as he leaves me to approach
Ramesses, standing at the foot of one of the Colossi. Every line of his
body as he walks away speaks determination and power.

I must always remain his friend.

I sense it is becoming very dangerous to be his enemy.

Ramesses

He is greatly troubled. He calls me aside as Pharaoh and the Chief Wife
go into the mortuary temple of Amonhotep III (life, health, prosperity!) and demands in the peremptory tone he uses more and more frequently now:

"Ramesses, what do you make of this?"

"It seems to me," I say cautiously, "that Their Majesties wish to restore harmony and peace to the land."

"So he says," Horemheb agrees, skepticism heavy in his voice. "So he
says."

"What do you think?" I ask, still cautiously, for I have learned that
there are times when it is best to approach Horemheb slowly and let
him do the talking.

"I think," he says, and his eyes narrow, "that though he pretends to
lower Aten, he still means to leave him in place high enough to threaten
Amon. I think he means someday to restore the Aten altogether."

"Oh no!" I say, shocked into speaking loudly enough so that soldiers
and priests waiting nearby shift uneasily and glance at us as openly as
they dare. *"Oh no!"* I repeat, hastily whispering. "He would not
dream of such a thing. He knows the evil Nefer-Kheperu-Ra—"

"The Heretic," Horemheb interrupts sternly, and dutifully I amend:

"—the Heretic—brought upon the land. He knows how thankful
Kemet is to be rid of him. He has seen how speedily in these past four

years, under your magnificent leadership—(it does no harm, these days, to flatter Horemheb)—"the Aten has been reduced and Amon raised again to his supreme and rightful place. His Majesty would not dare reverse this process!"

"I am not so sure now as I was a week ago what His Majesty will or will not dare," Horemheb says dryly. "I think His Majesty is beginning to fancy his majesty. I think we must be on guard against him, lest he overturn all our work. He took us by surprise today. He must not be allowed to take us by surprise again. I wish you to make it your special charge to know all that he does, at all times. Starting immediately after the procession. You and Sitra have guarded the children before. Do so again tonight. Take Seti with you—they like Seti. Arrange it so that you become their intimates. Insinuate yourselves. Watch. Listen. Report to me everything."

"What if he objects?" I ask, knowing it is probably a stupid question, but then I have never pretended to be clever. Ramesses is only a simple soldier—a very good one, but not brilliant like Horemheb. Or like my son Seti, whose mother must have been embraced by Amon, for the boy certainly does not get his brains from her or me.

"He will not object," Horemheb says with the obvious patience he sometimes shows me when I fail to grasp his intentions immediately. "I said, take Seti with you. They both like Seti. Work through him. Officially, I will have you assigned as Head of the King's Household. The rest will fall into place."

"But suppose he does object?" I repeat, again rather stupidly, I am afraid: but after all, the Good God is reaching an age, as he showed today, when he is beginning to get his own ideas. And he *is* the Good God.

"He will not object," Horemheb says, a certain harshness entering his voice. "How can he object? He is only thirteen."

"But he is the Living Horus—" I begin.

"He is not going to fly yet awhile," Horemheb says with a sudden grimness in his voice. "We will see to it that his wings remain clipped. Do not worry about things that do not concern you, Ramesses. Do as I say. Tell Sitra and Seti to be prepared to move into Malkata tonight. From now on you are Head of the King's Household and they are the King's friends and helpers."

"They *are*," I say truthfully. "So am I. Will that not make it difficult for us to—"

"Ramesses," Horemheb says, placing a hand like iron on my arm and lowering his voice in the way that has made me a little afraid of him, of late. "I have never had cause to question your friendship or your loyalty in all these years we have fought and worked side by side. Do not give me cause now."

"No, Horemheb," I say hastily. "Of course not. We will do as you say."

"Good," he says, releasing my arm and lightening his tone so that those few who had dared glance our way glance no longer. "Look! The Good God comes!"

And from the mortuary temple the two children emerge blinking into the softening afternoon sunlight and the procession prepares to resume its stately progress to the Valley of the Kings, and from there to Malkata. I search for my wife and son in the crowd, finally find the bright and handsome lad of ten who belongs to me.

"Go find your mother, Seti," I direct, "and tell her that we are moving into the Palace of Malkata tonight."

"Why?" he asks blankly.

"Because your 'Uncle Horemheb' decrees it," I say, "so no argument. Get along to your mother!"

"But only Pharaoh 'decrees'—" he begins; and then abruptly stops. His eyes widen thoughtfully: all children around the Palace in these recent years have become old before their time. He apparently sees something I do not understand.

"Very well, Father!" he says briskly, and runs off, leaving me standing puzzled in the sun.

"Ramesses!" Horemheb shouts as the procession begins to move slowly forward toward the barren rocky gorges where a special altar has been set up for the Good God's worship of his ancestors.

"Yes!" I shout back as I hurry to catch up. "I am here, Horemheb!"

Horemheb

I move them about like black and white pieces on the checkered board of the game of *senet,* and they jump to my command. Many things in Kemet, now, jump to my command. And why should they not, since I am the principal power and moving force therein?

Or so, at least, it says in my titles. . . .

"King's Deputy" was given me by my father at my insistence, you will recall—which he did not relish too much—when he assumed the title and position of Regent. Since then, with his agreement, sometimes willing, sometimes grudging, I have added many more:

"The King's Elect . . . the Administrator of the Two Lands . . . The Greatest of the Favorites of the Lord of the Two Lands . . . the Two Eyes of the King of Upper and Lower Kemet . . . The True Scribe, The Well-Beloved of the King . . . Chief Intendant . . . The Confidant of the King's Special Confidants . . . The Greatest of The Great . . . The Most Powerful of the Powerful . . . High Lord of the People . . ."

Thus the titles, which I have adopted to impress *all* the people—and which, I suppose, impress *some* of the Court.

Others, particularly my father, know that essentially they mean something less than half what they say. He controls the other half, and more.

The Regent Aye is still the most powerful man in Kemet, though his son presses him hard on every count. We manage to work in reasonable harmony—for now. But inevitably the day is coming when one or the other must yield. As between a man seventy-one and one fifty-one, time, if nothing else, is on my side.

Much else, of course, is also on my side; but much is on his side, too. The Regent Aye is now the longest continuing link with what Kemet regards as the golden age of Amonhotep III (life, health, prosperity!), exceeding even Sitamon, who fancies herself in the role—as she has fancied herself in other roles that she will never occupy. She apparently thought she was going to be my wife. In all honesty, for quite a long time I thought so too. But things change, plans change. Mine no longer include such a position for her. It is unfortunate, probably, but there it is. Womanlike, she now refuses to see me at all, which I consider rather foolish. We have always been friends, always enjoyed one another's company: she is an intelligent woman, I value her opinions and advice. She has turned against me, however, and today she has made it quite clear that she intends to side with the children against me and my father. This is not wise on her part, but she knows the risks and, I suppose, being a daughter of the Great Wife, has the character to meet them if they come. I hope so, for her sake.

In any event, Aye possesses still an influence in Kemet that I can only challenge, not defeat; and I dare not challenge it too openly, either. The day will come, but it will be awhile, I think. Meanwhile we work together in uneasy tandem, a tension between us that could explode into action when Tut goes if not before.

How naturally I use the phrase "when Tut goes"! Tut has been on the throne only four years, he has not yet reached majority, he could conceivably live and rule for another thirty, forty, fifty—yet somehow I do not think he will. Already, in fact, I have accepted in my heart the possibility that he, too, may eventually have to be removed from the throne as his brothers were before him, if Kemet is to flourish and prosper again. And that Kemet flourish and prosper again is my sole desire. I feel this even more deeply, if possible, than I did on the day I came to Thebes as eager young "Kaires," so many long and bloody years ago.

All I have witnessed since, all I have been party to, simply confirms me in what I thought then: that I care more for the Two Lands and their welfare than even the occupant of the Great House. And now that I see opening before me the possibility that I myself may someday be the occupant of the Great House, this motive is even more insistent in my being . . . particularly when the present occupant already shows signs of being as stubborn, as inflexible and as unmanageable as the Heretic himself.

I do not know what has inspired the boy to become so suddenly independent. A week ago he was a willing child of thirteen, shy, compliant, almost timorous in the way he acted in the presence of my father and me. You would have thought we were keeping him prisoner in some fashion, instead of aiding him in every way we could to restore the Two Lands to *ma'at* and glory. There were times when I almost thought he was afraid of us. Yet all that we have done we have done for Kemet. Surely he must see this.

Now he no longer seems afraid. I believe it began with the episode in the village when Hatsuret, who is an ambitious fool and sometimes a drunken one (with him, too, I may someday have a date to keep), tried to lead his stupid foray against the peasants and ran afoul of the King. I think Tut was so shocked and angered by what he found Hatsuret trying to do that he lost any lingering belief he might have had in Hatsuret's pose of priestly piety. He also lost the fear of him which he has felt ever since Hatsuret performed for us those terrible but necessary errands that helped put an end to the rule of the Heretic.

In those, of course, he was acting upon the orders of the Great Wife, my father and myself. He exceeded them in the case of Smenkhkara and Merytaten, but in case of Nefertiti and in my own rendezvous with Akhenaten, we did, viewing it now in retrospect, exactly what had to be done. I had not intended that we go that far—permanent arrest and secret imprisonment somewhere in the Red Land was my original thought—but Nefertiti provoked me beyond endurance, and so ended all.

"Husband," she cried to that awful scarecrow he had become, "come with me and let us leave this traitorous dog to eat his own vomit as befits him!"

Me, her own brother, her friend from childhood! This she said about *me*, in the presence of all those witnesses, thinking herself too proud and too powerful to suffer the fate of those who flaunt the gods too brazenly and too long!

Something broke inside my head. A blinding flash of fury drove all before it. Behind her Hatsuret stood with ax poised. *"Now!"* I cried, and it was done. And having caused that awful thing, I knew then there was but one thing only left for me to do, and that was end the whole sad shadow show once and for all, forever. And so I followed him to the Northern Tombs and did it.

When my father and I met again a few minutes later, we did not know at first how we would face the Great Wife and tell her. But it was done, all done: there was nothing remaining but to move straight ahead. We told her with pain and weeping, we thought we convinced her that the final steps had been inevitable and necessary—because by then we were convinced of it ourselves: it had to end, they could not have been left alive, it would have meant nothing but chaos for the Two Lands. She appeared to agree, we left her. In the morning they found her sitting dead by the window, her head propped against pillows so that her sightless eyes could still gaze upon the eternal Nile and the kingdom she had loved and served so well.

Still there was nothing to do but move forward. It was done, all done. My boy cousin was on the throne, a new day had dawned for Kemet. A child of nine could not rule, it would have been ridiculous. The reins fell into the two pairs of hands strong enough to take them up. My father and I began our uneasy but inescapable joint rule of the Two Kingdoms.

I suppose it was understandable that my little cousin should consider himself a prisoner after that, because naturally we had to make decisions in his name, we had to repair the sad state of Kemet just as rapidly as we could. It was imperative that we restore *ma'at* and justice, bring back Amon as the principal element of stability among the people, place Pharaoh firmly once more in his position of partnership with all the gods. I wrote the restoration stela setting forth the things that must be done and proclaimed it in his name so that the Two Lands would know that this was his plan and intention. And the rebuilding of a shattered society began.

Never have I worked so hard before, never has my father labored so diligently—and neither of us has ever been a sluggard. The chaos in which Akhenaten left this land was unbelievable. We are only just beginning to see some orderly pattern developing again, only just beginning to perceive the possibility of re-establishing a sound and stable future—and suddenly Tutankhamon betrays us all by maundering off once more about the Aten!

Is it any wonder the Regent and I have been astounded and upset this day? Is it any wonder we feel as though the ground had been cut suddenly once more from beneath our feet? Is it any wonder that, whereas it took me years to come to the bitter conclusion that Akhenaten must be removed, and years after that to actually do something about it, it has taken me only a few swift hours to acknowledge and accept the very real possibility that Tutankhamon may have to be removed too?

I do not know what ultimate dream possesses the boy, what secret plottings go on between the two of them—for I suspect that she, like her mother, is probably the constant encourager and supporter of her husband's follies. But I do know that it cannot be permitted to continue. I do know that if the heresy, which we thought dead with its creator, is to be revived in the person of his youngest brother, then this time there can be no long, spun-out unraveling of the years to bring it to conclusion. We are only just beginning to find our way out of the tangle left by Nefer-Kheperu-Ra. For the very sake of Kemet, we cannot permit Neb-Kheperu-Ra to drag us back into it with our work only half completed.

Oh, I know he talked about "reconciliation," "harmony," "peace" and "love." I know he talks—*now*—only of making the Aten a friendly partner with Amon. Those are pretty words—pretty words. Perhaps he is sincere in them. But we have heard their like before.

Was not Akhenaten sincere too? And did not sincerity lead very fast to fanaticism? And did not that in turn make inevitable Kemet's troubles? And does that not mean that we have no choice but to stop it *now* before it becomes again a ravening serpent in the land?

Would that I were Pharaoh *now,* and there would be none of his nonsense ever again in Kemet! Would that I could seize power *now* and set things right once and for all!

No man deserves it more—none has worked harder or waited more patiently—none would be a more worthy servant of the Two Lands. The Pharaoh Horemheb (life, health, prosperity to me!) is needed by this kingdom. Amon and all the gods know it as well as I. . . .

I must talk to my father about this. I have sent word that I will meet him in his audience chamber here in Malkata an hour from now when Ramesses tells me that the children are finally asleep, and when, from the Court to the farthest reaches of Thebes, the world will be filled with drunkenness and roistering and no one will notice our quiet conferring.

I have been patient for many, many, years—all my life, it sometimes seems to me. All that I have done I have done for Kemet. I am getting no younger. Now Tutankhamon suddenly threatens all. The Regent Aye and the King's Deputy Horemheb must decide the future before he becomes old enough to take full power and thwart us, as his brother did, when we seek to do what is right and best for Kemet.

Aye

He has sent word to me, my patient son—now suddenly impatient. We must talk of Pharaoh and the kingdom, and at once. I understand his urgency. I feel something of it myself after this surprising day. But I am not, I think, quite so anxious as he to leap to a conclusion that could only mean more unhappiness and horror for the House of Thebes and for the land.

It seems to me that all my life I have been mediating between the violent and the peaceful elements of both. Sometimes I have been successful. More often, I suppose, I have failed. Yet even though I now am reaching substantial age and showing a little in my physical reactions, there is nothing slowed yet in the heart and mind of Aye. I see through impatient Horemheb. What Sitamon told me years ago is truer now. He seeks to be Pharaoh, and it has, I think, become in him an obsession that rationalizes all he may feel necessary to achieve the goal.

This is a very dangerous state to be in. It can lead to a fanaticism of a kind different from, but no less devastating than, the fanaticism of his cousin Akhenaten. I grant to Horemheb his oft-proclaimed motive that all he does he does for Kemet; yet I think in his own strange way Akhenaten was trying to do the same. He sought to approach it on the spiritual plane of the Aten, hoping, as I understood him, to spread the goodness downward to the people. Horemheb approaches it on the practical plane on which he has always lived, seeking to make sure that goodness reaches the people by a route more direct: *he will command them to be good and kill them if they aren't.* As between the two, given the sad condition of the Two Lands, I suppose for the present (and perhaps always in our long history) Horemheb's way is the better and more certain of success. Yet I cannot escape the lingering feeling that in Akhenaten's method there may have been some key to it all that we failed to grasp—but could have, had we but possessed a vision and a selflessness as great as his: even though with him, as I say, it soon became a fanaticism we could not follow.

There may have been a moment—just a moment—when, had all come right, we could have joined him in his dream and made it work. The traditions of Kemet were too strong. They had held us to a steady course, save for the Hyksos invasion and a few times of dynastic turmoil, for almost two thousand years. It was easy for us to turn back to them when doubt assailed us. And with Akhenaten, doubt assailed us early and often. He proclaimed love, but doubt ate up love. The fault was equal: Akhenaten lost his grip on reality long before we suspected, I believe. The tragedy had to play itself out to the end.

But it does not need to be revived.

All of that, we thought, was past. Yet tonight we face a new condition. The Aten is not dead with his unhappy prophet. He lives anew in a boy of thirteen, who says he seeks a balance between the gods to restore the Two Lands.

This, I know, is why Horemheb comes to me in anger and alarm. Knowing him and the methods he has resorted to increasingly in the past four years, I think the Regent Aye will have to employ all his resources to prevent further tragedy. And when all is said and done, the Regent Aye's resources come down to just one thing: the Regent Aye.

I am seventy-one, last link, save for Sitamon, who has the people's sentimental love but no power, with the great days of my sister and Amonhotep III (life, health, prosperity!). Like Horemheb, I too have many loyal friends in the army, many staunch supporters among officials of Court and government throughout the Two Lands. If it came to open war between us I do not know which could command the greater strength in the field: probably my son, for he is younger, more vigorous, more careful about keeping such alliances strong and fertile by a constant policy of pressure and reward. But he is weak where I am strong: my strength is in the hearts of men, and on that subtle but often decisive battlefield I am very strong.

After the deaths of my sister, my nephew and my daughter (no one will ever know the agonies it cost me to accept Nefertiti's murder, even though I understood how it all happened in that terrible moment of fury, dismay and final disillusionment between brother and sister) there was a great revulsion in the kingdom, a great turning back. From it I emerged, as I knew I would, the one revered leader whom all elements respected and around whom all could join. Thus it was relatively easy for me to reject Horemheb's too quick presumption in seeking the title and power of Regent: we both knew the country would not stand for it.

So he deferred to me, grudgingly but practically. Our contest was over in a moment, for essentially it was no contest: he would have been regarded as usurper, and all he attempted would have been sapped and subverted thereby.

Therefore we began our joint rule of Kemet uneasy in our partnership but aware that it was all that could save the kingdom. Behind the symbol provided by my youngest nephew, that sunny child who too soon grew sadly old in the shadow of his unhappy elders, we began the rebuilding and restoration of the Two Lands. Horemheb traveled constantly from Napata to the Delta, up and down the river, ceaselessly prodding, goading, directing, exhorting, commanding in the King's name the rebuilding of temples, the re-establishment of justice, the restoration of *ma'at* and social order where it had so universally collapsed. In Memphis, Thebes and in Akhet-Aten, where we believed it best to remain for a while until the country had become fully accustomed to the idea that we would presently return to the ancient capitals and abandon Akhenaten's city, I too worked tirelessly on the endless details of civil government and foreign relations, seeking to bring back an equal order to a system that had virtually died in Akhenaten's last dreadful year. (In that time, also, we had worked in harness toward these same ends, only to find ourselves thwarted by the presence of a mature Pharaoh who had lost the will to live and the desire to govern— in whose name we did things, but hesitantly, tentatively, not knowing when his interest might suddenly revive and we might find ourselves facing punishment for things we had done in good faith and love for Kemet because he would not.)

With Tutankhamon—until today—we have had no such problems. He has been a malleable and apparently contented child, appearing to look with approval on all that has been accomplished in his name. He has obligingly given his seal to all that we asked, conferred on us the titles and powers we have requested. (Horemheb, I think, has requested a few too many, but I have acquiesced in this, since he seemed to need them for reassurance. I have known his reasons, and my bland agreement has in itself been a kind of triumph for me, as he is aware with a chagrin he strives to keep secret from me, but which I know as I know many things.)

So we have kept Tut happy, given him the first traditional coronation in more than forty years, married him to my granddaughter Ankhesenamon, a child almost as beautiful, and fully as shrewd, as her mother; taken him on lion hunts and expeditions, shown him to the people on regular inspection tours which both he and they have seemed to enjoy, arranged for envoys to bring him interesting gifts from far places, done all we could to keep him entertained and happy while we have done the necessary business of government in his name. The education of both children has been entrusted to Amonhotep, Son of Hapu—what would we have done in the House of Thebes without that wise contemporary of mine!—and everything has been ordered to make sure that he would grow comfortably into the eternal mold of the ideal Pharaoh, steady, reliable, predictable and sure, as most of his great ancestors have been before him.

Until today and his surprising remarks on his official return to Thebes. I had been disturbed by our argument on the journey from Akhet-Aten but I had no real idea until he spoke today that another independent mind might have been developing under our very noses, so clever have both children been at concealing their real feelings. I am still not convinced of it, though I suspect Horemheb is.

It is nearly midnight: I go to the window and look across the Nile at Thebes. It is still brightly lighted with the flares of welcome and rejoicing. Across Hapi's dark surface, covered now with many hundreds of boats riding at anchor while their owners, crews and passengers celebrate ashore, comes a steady hum composed of rollicking music, good-natured shouts, coy screams and raucous laughter. I have never been one to join in the drunken revels that always accompany our great state occasions—or indeed any other occasion, for that matter, since in Kemet high and low alike have a great fondness for wine and all that frequently happens in its wake—but tonight I almost wish, rather wistfully, that I did.

It would be nice, sometimes, to simply let go and forget the cares of government. It would be nice to be a common drunkard like everyone else. It would be nice to let the heart and mind reel happily down into that spinning forgetfulness that is the solace of so many lesser men.

It can never be. Duty is the life of the Regent Aye, duty is the burden of his family. Duty killed my sister the Great Wife, duty—as he saw it —killed my brother Aanen, duty killed my daughter Nefertiti, duty sometimes almost kills me.

But it will not occur yet awhile. I am the last survivor of the elders, and my course has a time to run before it is over. That I know, and Kemet can be thankful for it—as many signs of public gratitude show me Kemet is.

There is a knock on my door, furtive but firm. I say softly, "Come!" and turn to face my son.

I can see at once that he has worked himself to a pitch of anger and determination, and I can tell that he, too, has been fortified by wine. I decide it will do no harm for me to have one, and much to my advan-

tage for him to have possibly two or three more, so my first move after
he has bowed and kissed my hand (he is always very circumspect about
observing the courtesies due the Regent) is to offer him a cup.

Surprisingly, he refuses.

"I have had too many already," he says. "But you have one, Father,
if you like. It will help you celebrate the unveiling of our new Akhenaten."

"My son," I say, taking my ornate chair of office, itself so elaborately
gilded and decorated as to be almost a throne, "seat yourself and discuss this with me without dramatics, if you please. I do not propose to
let myself be disturbed by a thirteen-year-old boy, particularly since I
do not believe he intends at all what you anticipate."

"How do you know?" he demands, not accepting the invitation for a
moment, but going to the window himself to stare moodily across at ri-
otous Thebes. "Listen to them! They would not care if he re-established
the Aten full scale and began the whole business over again."

"Oh yes, they would," I respond sharply. "They are forgetful now but
tomorrow they will remember. They were made very uneasy by his
words today."

"And you claim you were not?" he demands with equal sharpness,
turning to seat himself. "Tell me truthfully, now, Father."

"I was surprised," I admit carefully. "Unprepared—startled—unsuspecting. But not, as I said, disturbed. Or alarmed."

"You should be both," he says moodily, "for he means no moderation though he babbles of it."

"Your cousin does not 'babble'!" I snap, for I learned long since it
does no good to disparage without admitting the stature of one's opponent. ("Opponent"? Do I already consider him so? I must not think
such things even to myself, else Horemheb will have me off balance
and on his side before I know it.) "Neb-Kheperu-Ra is a fine and
thoughtful lad, and what he said showed much deliberation. Wherein
lie your fears about it?"

"Where any intelligent man's lie," he says. "In the ghost of the accursed Aten."

"Accepting the fact that I am of course very unintelligent," I say
dryly, "I cannot find myself as frightened as you of a simple boy."

"I apologize for the word," he concedes, "but he is no longer a boy,
and he is not simple. I am beginning to believe that in his heart Tutankhamon is as complex as the Heretic."

"I know you like that designation," I say, again sharply, "but I prefer
to let the past go. He is dead and can harm us no longer. He is Nefer-
Kheperu-Ra Akhenaten to me, and will always so remain."

"He is dead," Horemheb says, "but I do not agree that he can harm us no longer. He is still alive in the hearts of his brother and his daughter, and he can still do his hateful work through them."

"He will not," I say calmly, "for I will not permit it."

"You think I will?" he demands. "I am as sensible of what the kingdom needs as you, Father. That is why I am with you now."

"I am Regent," I remind him coldly, "and need no lecturing on my duty to the Two Lands."

"Lecture not and be not lectured," he retorts, and for a moment a genuine hostility flares between us. But before the moment becomes irrevocable his eyes drop and he says more calmly, "I am sorry, Father. But I *am* much disturbed by this day, and I do not think it wise to let ourselves think that it had no far-ranging significance, for I feel it does."

"What did he say?" I inquire, making my own voice reasonable. "He said he wished to restore a balance between the gods. He said he did not want to exalt either Amon or Aten at the expense of the other, neither did he wish to take from one to reduce the other. He said he wished his reign to be one of reconciliation, harmony and peace for all the people of Kemet and for all the gods. He said he wanted love to rule again in the Two Lands, as it used to do. He said he wished all to be at peace with one another. I see nothing so unreasonable or frightening in that."

"And he decreed—he *decreed,* Father, the first time he has ever dared use the word—that the temples of Akhet-Aten remain unspoiled and open to worship, that the temple of the Aten at Karnak be extended and enlarged, that Tuthmose make him a new crook and flail bearing the name of the Aten, and a new throne bearing on its back himself and Ankhesenamon being blessed by the Aten, together with the Aten's titularies and cartouches. Quite a lot to say in a 'reasonable' address!"

"I will admit he may have gone a little far—"

"A little!"

"—a little far in his attempt to be conciliatory, but essentially there is no harm in any of these, is there? I hope you have not contemplated diverting the funds and energies of the kingdom to destroying the temples of Akhet-Aten when there are so many more pressing things to be done! Leave them alone and they will be forgotten. Shu will blow the sands of the Red Land over them soon enough. You will see."

"But," he says, his face stubborn, "funds and energies will have to be diverted to enlarging the temple at Karnak, will they not? How does that fit your complacent picture of it?"

"I am not complacent," I retort, "I am simply practical. It is true that if we do that—and I for one think we must, for he is the Living Horus and he has given the direct order, and it is no great thing, and I will not be a party to a struggle over something so minor—it will take some funds and some number of workmen to do it. But neither will be great, I am sure of that. He will be satisfied with little. It is a gesture of policy on his part: I do not for a moment believe he wishes us to empty the treasury to satisfy it. If worst came to worst, I should simply refuse, in any event. There is nothing he could do. I think even at thirteen he is wise enough not to contest it. We can afford to bend a little."

"And the new set of scepters, which are unneeded and an unnecessary flaunting of the Aten in the face of Amon? And the new throne, which is even more so?" He shakes his head. "No, Father: there is a purpose here that reaches far. It must not be allowed to grow."

"It will not be. But there is no need for it to come to open battle."

His eyes narrow and he looks back down the years. I know what he sees and brace myself for his next remark.

"I remember other times when you said that. I remember other times when you counseled temporizing and compromise. And I remember what happened then, how finally it all ran on too long and got out of hand, and you and I had to—"

'Stop!" I cry harshly, but he continues inexorably to the end.

"—when you and I had to countenance, and finally commit, murder—"

"Stop!"

"—*murder,* because we did not act soon enough. . . . And, Father" —his voice becomes low and he looks at me unblinking with the iron of my own soul in him, but many years younger—"we must face *now,* unafraid and unhesitating, the possibility that it may have to come to that again."

"No!" I cry desperately. *"No!"*

"Cut down the young shoot now before it becomes a great tree, Father," he says, voice still low but implacable. "Cut it down *now!*"

For several moments I am unable to answer him, so hurtfully and with such searing force does my breath tear through my lungs, so wildly does my heart pound within my breast, so deeply do I crave that sanity return to this conversation which has suddenly become so grim. Too many ghosts surround us now—too many! I am not sure, for a little, whether I can muster strength to reply to him.

But presently my breathing calms, my heart subsides, a lifelong steadiness returns to the Regent Aye. When I speak at last it is in my customary calm and measured tones.

"There will be no more killing in the House of Thebes. Neb-Kheperu-Ra will not be permitted to go too far, neither will any man, least of all in his own family, be permitted to raise his hand against him. All will proceed according to *ma'at* and justice as has been the immemorial way of Kemet. Only thus can the Two Lands be served. And do not forget, my son: it is the Two Lands *we* serve, not the Two Lands that serve us."

He looks at me for a long time, his emotions clear but his courage still not great enough to make the final challenge that both of us know he inevitably will someday. I return him look for look and never flinch, though it calls upon all my reserves to do so, and my reserves are also growing older now. But thank the gods they are still sufficient! It is his eyes, not mine, that finally yield.

He looks away again toward still roaring Thebes, whose wild hilarity sinks scarcely yet upon the night.

"I pray to the gods," he says finally, his voice still very low, "that you are not making a terrible mistake, Father."

"I pray that you will help me do all things right for Kemet," I say gravely, "and that neither of us makes a mistake."

"Good night, Father," he says: bows low, kisses my hand; and straightens to go. His eyes once more meet mine and I read the message clear in them: *Watch yourself, Father. I am waiting.* And mine reply: *Watch yourself, Horemheb. I have outwaited shrewder men than you* . . . though I know in my heart what I now will never tell him: there are very few shrewder men than my son Horemheb.

I know, in fact, only one.

After he has gone I leave my room and walk slowly—hands locked behind my back—head bowed—brooding, brooding, brooding—for perhaps an hour along the sleeping pathways of Malkata. Only an occasional sentry greets me with hushed respect. All else is quiet in the Palace.

About my legs three dear little boys run and frolic, laughing, calling, racing, jumping, begging me to "play horsie," "play ball," "tell us a story!"

Ghosts accompany me—too many ghosts.

Across the river the drunken shouts of the happy kingdom still reverberate.

The Living Horus has returned to Thebes and all rejoice.

I shiver, and go in.

Tutankhamon (*Life, health, prosperity!*)

In the room adjoining, kind Ramesses and gentle Sitra snored; on his
pallet against the wall young Seti, exhausted by our excited chatter of
the glorious day, lay at last asleep, curled upon himself with occasional
little gruntings like a puppy filled with dreams of hunts and chases.
Very gently I reached out my hand and touched Ankhesenamon. As
silently as I, she leaned close to me as I whispered, "I think I heard
Horemheb speak to Ramesses a little while ago."

"I, too," she whispered back. "Ramesses said, 'They are asleep,'
Horemheb, 'I go to him now.' Ramesses, 'They will hear nothing.' What
do you think it means?"

"I think we should go and find out. Will you come with me?"

"Of course."

Very carefully we rolled off the bed, our feet touched the floor without a sound. I slipped into my pleated kilt, she into her transparent
gold-embroidered linen shift. Seti stirred uneasily, groaned, whimpered,
turned and snuggled comfortably against the wall: his back was to us.
At first softly, then with a deeper, steadier rhythm, he too began to
snore.

The door was half ajar. We slipped past Ramesses and Sitra,
drowned now in sleep like Seti. Very carefully we opened the door to
the corridor: thank the gods it is well oiled and does not squeak. We
were in the corridor, the door was closed behind us. All was silent. We
clasped hands tightly: we were trembling but unafraid. We began to tip-
toe along the corridor. Perhaps the gods directed our steps. Without
word, without conscious decision, we found we were on our way to the
rooms of my uncle Aye.

We took a turn in the corridor, bumped squarely into a sleeping
guard. He staggered awake with a muffled exclamation, spear instinctively raised high. Instantly he saw who we were. I glared at him with
my finger across my lips. He shrank back humbly against the wall.

"You will be silent!" I hissed. "You will tell no one!"

"Yes, Son of the Sun!" he whispered, trembling. "Oh yes, Your Majesty!"

"Good!" I whispered in return. "You will be rewarded well tomorrow."

"Thank you, Majesty!" he whispered. "Oh, thank you, Son of the Sun!"

"Shhhhh!" I hissed again sternly. He nodded with desperate earnest and we passed on.

Outside the audience room of my uncle Aye we heard their voices. We crouched close to the door. We listened, staring at one another wide-eyed in growing terror. When we realized Horemheb was about to leave, we turned and raced back as quickly and silently as we could. The guard gave us an elaborate wink and pretended he did not see or hear us: I really will give him some gold tomorrow.

We sneaked past deeply snoring Ramesses and Sitra, past deeply snoring Seti. Trembling we slipped back onto the bed; trembling we clutched one another tightly; trembling we fought for sleep that would not come. Across the river Thebes still roared—for us.

Seti

They thought I was asleep but I fooled them. I heard them whispering, I heard them slip out, I rose and followed them as far as I dared, until they met the guard; then I dared go no further, I turned and raced back to my pallet. Now they have returned and lie again within their golden bed. I can hear it shake with their trembling but I do not think it is love. I think they are awfully frightened of something.

Tomorrow I shall tell my father.

Book IV

ORDEAL OF A GOD
1353 B.C.

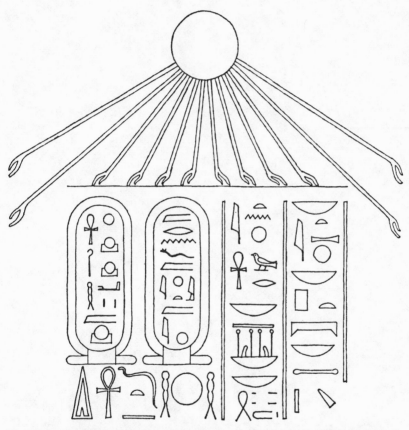

Live, Ra, ruler of the Horizon, rejoicing in the Horizon, in his role of light coming from the Sun's Disk, giving life forever and to all eternity, Aten the living, the Great, Lord of Jubilees, Master of all that encompasses the Sun's Disk, Lord of the Heavens, Lord of the Earth,

THE ATEN

Hatsuret

They move more and more toward the Aten, the two clever ones who have pretended to be such mild and humble children. They have made their dutiful tributes to Amon, they have begun to restore his temples and add to his riches, they have tried to persuade us they believe fully in his restoration to his rightful place at the right hand of the King . . . but with his left hand the King does other things.

The Aten's temple at Karnak has been extended and enlarged. His priesthood, while reduced, remains active in many places. The temples at Akhet-Aten, now almost deserted save for a few squatters who grub out their meager existence amid the crumbling mud walls of empty homes and ruined palaces, are still kept up. He uses the Aten's crook and flail in public ceremonies almost as often as he uses Amon's; and the special throne with its arrogant flaunting of the Heretic's god conferring his blessing upon their ostentatious domesticity is carried with them, and used, wherever they go up and down the length of Kemet.

The Aten is not dead in the Two Lands, he is not even lowered as Pharaoh promised. He is simply being kept in reserve, and may be brought out again at any time to overwhelm us.

This I think Tutankhamon intends, and this I think the Queen encourages him to do. Tomorrow he turns eighteen and assumes full power. Will he seize the day to re-establish the heresy?

I say to you, O Amon, your High Priest Hatsuret will not permit it. I say to you that the Regent Aye will not permit it. I say to you that Amon will rule and reign forever, supreme among his fellow gods, bowing to no one, yielding to none, as he is meant to do, through all eternity.

This do I, Hatsuret, who have labored so long and hard to save Kemet from the evil and the unbelieving, pledge to you, O Amon.

I have not hesitated heretofore to bring vengeance in your name.

I shall not hesitate, be it necessary, to do so again.

Tutankhamon (Life, health, prosperity!)

Around us the hordes of Amon grow more overweening day by day. It is not enough for dark Hatsuret, that hateful priest, to lord it over the temple at Karnak and parade himself up and down the land in all his pomp and glory. Always he is about the palaces, always he mixes in: suffered and assisted, of course, by my cousin Horemheb, who likes to have him present as threat to me, as I am bondsman (he likes to think) to him.

Well: tomorrow all that changes. All, all changes. Ankesenamon and I have been prisoners for nine years. Tomorrow we will be prisoners no longer.

After our return to Thebes we were forced to resume our humble pose: the conversation we overheard that night outside my uncle's door terrified us so that for a time we feared constantly for our lives. Indeed, we still do, though after a while apprehension becomes such a burden that it dulls of its own weight. We had to go on living, of course. We had to continue performing the rites and ceremonies and duties that fall upon Pharaoh and the Chief Wife. We could not hide away, though at first we wanted to. We confided our fears immediately to Sitamon and through her intervention were able to secure from her own household guards a few we could trust to attend our progress and safeguard our sleep—in addition, of course, to Ramesses, Sitra and Seti, whose wards, you might say, we have remained: not minding that too much, since they are kind and loyal people. And because he seemed, that night, to be far kinder and fairer than we had thought him to be in recent years —and because Sitamon told us she also believes in his loyal determination to protect our rights and preserve us on the throne against the ambitions of Horemheb—we began cautiously to renew our trust in Aye.

We remembered that he was always a loving uncle to me and a loving grandfather to Ankhesenamon when we were little. We gradually forgave the years after I first came to the throne, when I was still a boy and he seemed to us an eager usurper of powers I was too young to exercise. Maturity brought with it a kindlier view of him. In retrospect he began to seem what we now suspect he has always been: the steady anchor of the House of Thebes, the one unswerving constant through all the troubled times and tempests of my father's later years and my brothers' tragic rule.

Concerning Horemheb, we have other ideas. Influenced partly by Sitamon, partly by his actions, but most of all by his really frightening threats to our lives in that dreadful overheard conversation, we have no faith at all in him. Sitamon says, "I believe he began by truly caring for Kemet and wishing to make her great again. I believe he still has this desire. But I also believe he now desires to make Horemheb great along with Kemet. And which of those desires is the greater . . ." Her voice trails away and we all reach the same conclusion.

We all mistrust Horemheb. We have mistrusted him ever since the most dreadful night of all, the night he ordered Hatsuret to kill Nefertiti and himself murdered Akhenaten: though we eventually managed to understand how these awful events might have come about through a genuine desire to save the Two Lands from further disaster. But the memory has always made us fearful of him—more so as the years have passed and he has gathered to himself increasing power which I know he will not yield without a struggle.

Well: I am ready for him now. Tomorrow all changes, and with it Horemheb. Otherwise, I will have his head. I am the Living Horus and after tomorrow none will dare say me nay.

Aye I intend to keep close to my side, however. We have finally returned without reservations to the feeling that in him we have a genuine friend, one whose only desire and ambition really *is* to serve the Two Lands. He will no longer be Regent, of course, and I do not think I will make him Co-Regent, for there is no need for that. It is true that Ankhesenamon has already had one stillborn daughter, not the son we fervently hoped for; but she is pregnant again, scarce two weeks from delivery, and this time, if Aten and the gods agree, the Crown Prince will be born. Someday when he is old enough I will create him Co-Regent. Meanwhile, tomorrow I am eighteen and all power returns to my hands. I shall be very slow and cautious about whom I let it out to hereafter, even to Aye. But we have decided that he will continue to be my most trusted adviser—as counterweight to Horemheb and Hatsuret, and for many more good reasons, principally his own integrity, loyalty and care for our beloved kingdom which is only now, nine years after the death of Nefer-Kheperu-Ra, beginning to recover some semblance of order from his chaotic rule.

There are other things I must do after tomorrow, also. I must see to it that the bodies of the Great Wife, my brother Smenkhkara, Merytaten, Meketaten, Nefertiti and Akhenaten are returned with suitable re-

spect and ceremony to the Valley of the Kings to rest beside our ancestors where they properly belong.

I think of them often, lying in the Royal Wadi at Akhet-Aten: how
very lonely they seem, so far away from us in the now deserted city.
One thing I have constantly asked Aye and Horemheb to do, and I think
Aye in particular has obeyed: make sure that those graves have not
been disturbed and that all is safe and secure there. They assure me it
is and, having no word to the contrary, I assume they are telling me
the truth. But it is time for my family to come home now: the reasons
of state that have made my uncle and cousin reluctant to return them
here will be canceled when I take full power. I have told Aye this, and
he agrees. It is time for the dead to rest easy, even poor Akhenaten,
who brought such disaster on us all—*particularly* Akhenaten, who will
find in our plans, I think, much with which he might agree.

We feel that he and dearest Nefertiti are watching us from the afterworld and supporting us in what we intend to do.

Because, look you: Amon is becoming too great again. He is never
content, that one, particularly when his forces are led by such as Hatsuret, that ravenous, ambitious priest. Amon is pushing us again, growing too strong, meddling too much. Once again, like my father and my
brothers, I am faced with the greed of Amon. He wants land and he
wants gold, much of which Horemheb returned to him in my name
years ago when I was too young and helpless to prevent it. But above
all he wants power. And while Aye has worked with him reluctantly,
and while Horemheb, I am sure, thinks he could work with him completely, I know that I, Neb-Kheperu-Ra Tutankhamon, cannot.

Every time I go to the temple at Karnak it seems to me the messages
I exchange with those hooded eyes, gleaming from the golden head in
the single ray that illuminates that somber sanctuary, grow more threatening and more hostile. Amon has never been my friend, from the first
day I saw him as a child of nine: and he knows well what I think of
him, too. Our exchanges, never friendly, are now almost openly hostile,
although since I alone face him while the others remain respectfully
outside the inmost chamber, they do not know. But *he* knows and *I*
know: Amon must be reduced again, before he swallows me up.

There is another reason, too. Amon and the gods have been restored
for nine years now, and dutifully and earnestly Ankhesenamon and I
have sought to understand them and try to appreciate their role in the
life of the Two Lands. And we have concluded this: they are not
bringers of happiness and joy to our people. Mostly, they frighten our
people. They are simply weapons in the hands of ruthless priests and

those, like Horemheb, who use the priests to impose their will upon the kingdom.

We will grant you that some are lovable like Hathor, amiable and wise like Thoth, gravely impressive like Sekhmet, stately and commanding like Horus. But none says, "I am Love. I want to love you and have you love me. I want you—*all of you*—to be free from superstition and fear, happy in our love for one another."

None says this—save one. And so Ankhesenamon and I find ourselves coming back more and more to the god in whose faith we were reared, the god we are told we must continue to reduce and, ultimately, forget.

But we cannot forget, and him we do not wish to reduce. He is too bright, too happy, too loving—too *comforting*. Comforting, we think, is what we and our people need now, more than anything.

That is why we have preserved his temples in Akhet-Aten, enlarged his temple at Karnak, used as often as we dared his crook and flail and the golden throne emblazoned with his image blessing us. And that is why I think I begin to see in the eyes of Amon lately something of the fear he always tries deliberately to create in others.

That is why it will please me to do what we plan. But it must be done slowly and carefully, step by step. I must not make my brother's mistakes. I do not think I will, because I do believe he was truly a fanatic and I am not. But that does not make my purpose less firm nor my will less determined.

I shall be careful, I shall be clever, I shall follow the rule of my uncle Aye we have heard him express so often: if change is to succeed in Kemet, it must be gradual.

Gradual I will be, but I will not be deflected. Our minds are made up and we are determined to do it. We have learned craft in our nine years as the prisoners of the Palace. We have also learned tenacity.

Tomorrow we will be prisoners no longer. Things will begin to happen as we wish them to happen. Gradually, Uncle, as you recommend: but inexorably, nonetheless.

Aye

Hatsuret complains and Horemheb mutters of dark things; and I must confess that I am not as easy as I profess to be when I answer them. Nor do I approach this occasion of my nephew's full assumption of power with any less apprehension than they. But as I stand now in my room in Malkata while the servants dress me in my robes of office to attend the ceremonies soon to begin in teeming, excited Thebes across the river, I know that I must remain calm and steady whatever happens. Because upon the calmness and steadiness of the Regent Aye depends, I think, the future of what remains of the House of Thebes.

I am old, and I am tired; but I am not ready yet to yield to others less selfless than I the control of this kingdom, this beloved land. I have labored too long for Kemet, rescued her too many times from disaster, given her my heart and strength too often. I have connived in terrible things for the Two Lands—only because I thought I had to, only because I could see no other way out, but terrible nonetheless. And terrible in what they have done to me inside, too, though I have survived them—for one simple reason, I think.

Someone has had to survive.

Now two clever children are about to come to power; and what will that mean, for me and for Kemet? Hatsuret fears a restoration of the Aten, Horemheb fears a permanent impediment to his ambitions: I fear I shall be called on once again to stand in the middle and hold off contending forces by sheer strength of character, for that is about all that is left me now. I command great respect from the people, no one is revered as I am—but in Kemet it is not the people who decide what happens in the Palace. It is those within. And there the Regent Aye possesses means that dwindle as the years close in.

Yet in a profound though somewhat negative sense I think it is the people who are indeed my strength: because thanks to their support I do not believe my son quite yet dares challenge me openly. The people are not capable of giving me power, but the massive weight of their reverence for me is sufficient to prevent anyone from taking it from me. Not even the army, which Horemheb commands and has rebuilt to some reasonable degree of competence since Akhenaten's death . . .

not even, I think, my youngest nephew, who today is eighteen years of age and moves, as he rightly should, to claim his full inheritance.

It is my duty as Regent to make sure that the transition is peaceful and occurs without incident. I shall then lay the seals of my office at his feet, which he will wish me to do in any event, and offer myself for whatever further service he may feel an old man can render. I shall be very much surprised if he continues me as Co-Regent, for he wishes to be King alone, as he should, and my granddaughter is soon to give birth to a son who in due time will become Co-Regent, as *he* should. But I shall also be very much surprised if he does not keep me at his side as principal councilor and adviser, for the only alternative to me is my son. And I know Neb-Kheperu-Ra fears my son as I do, and will never give him such authority.

I do not know exactly how I know this, for both children are always very circumspect about Horemheb, even in their private conversations with me; but I do know it. It shows through. They dislike and fear him, whom once they looked up to as a kindly older friend of their childhood days. He has been very astute about concealing his ambitions, having only slipped once years ago in talking to Sitamon; but that was enough. Everything he has done since has been suspect, to her, to them and to me; and increasingly in recent years his actions have confirmed what those few inadvertent words foreshadowed. During my regency he has had enormous power, second only to mine; and he has used it to strengthen himself everywhere he could, with the army, with the people (through fear, however, not the love they bear me and Pharaoh), and through the priests of Amon whom Hatsuret leads once more to triumph in the land.

It is age, I suppose: but with increasing clarity I find myself remembering those many conversations with my sister and Amonhotep III (life, health, prosperity!) in which we deplored the steady inroads of Amon upon the power and prerogatives of the Eighteenth Dynasty. I can remember their attempts to stop this, I can remember how their failures drove my brother-in-law to dedicate Akhenaten to the Aten, I can of course remember all else. So much tragedy and so much pain as a result of this! And now it seems we have come full circle to find ourselves facing the same problem again—this time, because Horemheb believes he sees in the swarming priests of Amon the surest road to power.

He will be defeated in this, as I believe he must be—for under his patriotic exterior he has become too arbitrary, too harsh, too stern to rule easygoing Kemet—*providing* he does not have assistance from another quarter. *Providing* my last surviving nephew does not play directly into

his hands and the hands of Amon. *Providing* there is no foolhardy
attempt to revive the god whose diminishment has been necessary in
order to restore *ma'at* and justice and the fragile balance of the Two
Lands.

Bitterly I argued Tutankhamon's defense, that night after Pharaoh
had returned to Thebes and proclaimed the counsels of moderation
which I myself had originally proposed to him; sternly I ordered
Horemheb to abandon his wild ideas that "the young shoot must be
rooted out before it becomes a great tree." Horemheb was close to hys-
teria then, I think, and actually I was more uneasy than I cared to
admit to him, myself, not being prepared for the forthright firmness
with which my nephew stated propositions that had been simply
diplomatic suggestions on my part. But I realized that this was in all
probability youth's enthusiastic tendency to overstate; and since next
day he appeared to have relaxed to a more comfortable and less urgent
frame of mind about it, I knew I had been right to face down my son
and block his foolish exaggerations. Since then we have moved gradually, as I desired, to restore Amon, gradually to reduce the Aten. Tut
and Ankhesenamon have seemingly been quite content with the placid
flow of their days, the round of ceremonies and entertainments, their
lingering sentimental allegiance to the Aten while the formal re-associa-
tion of the Double Crown with Amon has proceeded under my careful
guidance. All has appeared to go smoothly . . . until today. And today,
I must most earnestly hope, the mood will continue and nothing drastic
will be done. . . .

I seem to have fallen into a dreaming study as the servants dress me,
because I become aware that one of them is pulling gently at my arm to
get me to raise it and slip it into the gold-threaded robe he holds. I
start, and apologize with a smile. He returns it with the worshipful air
they all show me: I still have much respect to rely upon.

"It is almost time to go, Excellency," he says. "The barges are ready
at the landing stage."

"I will pay attention and help you complete this speedily," I promise,
and bend myself to it as he holds out to me the seals and symbols of
office. . . .

Horemheb will be defeated in his ambitions, as I say, providing Neb-
Kheperu-Ra does not do something foolish this day. I think all of us in
the Court have known that he and my granddaughter continue in their
hearts to favor the Aten, that for them both there is an extremely strong
emotional pull in the memories of Akhenaten and Nefertiti, that it is
quite understandable that they should remain loyal to the faith in which
they were reared. But I have done all I could to ease and moderate this

during the nine years of my regency, and with their co-operation (for they are very far from fools) I think I have done very well. The Aten has been preserved—for, after all, he has been a god of this dynasty for the better part of two hundred years, though never such a one as Akhenaten tried to make of him—yet he has been gradually reduced to a more reasonable position. There was never any thought in my mind, and obviously none in Tutankhamon's or Ankhesenamon's, that he should be banished altogether. That has been Hatsuret's idea, of course, and I suspect Horemheb's, but that is not how Kemet functions. We have not lasted almost two thousand years by going to extremes: we have lasted by moving gradually. So it has been with the Aten since the death of his most fanatic worshiper. Not so, alas, has it been with Amon since his restoration.

There, of course, is the danger: that action will provoke reaction, that Pharaoh will move too strongly and too fast to counteract the renewed dominance of Amon which he rightly fears. I have cautioned him repeatedly, directly when he was a child, more indirectly and diplomatically as he grew older, that all things must be in moderation, all must be gradual. Politely he has listened, but I have learned to mistrust such politeness from the young. My daughter and my other two nephews were always very polite to me too—and then went headlong to their destruction. I pray to Aten, Amon and all the gods that this will not be the case with Neb-Kheperu-Ra. For, if so, sad and dreadful again may become the burden and the duty of the Regent Aye. . . .

I am dressed and ready to leave. Trumpets sound, drums beat. From across the Nile comes the swelling roar of excitement that always heralds the royal progress from the Palace of Malkata.

I leave my rooms and walk, preceded by heralds, through the busy corridors to the landing stage. It is January. The sky is filled with scudding clouds, the wind whips sharp off the river. Sitamon, Horemheb, Nakht-Min, my second daughter Mutnedjmet (and of course her two annoying little people) are there already. Pharaoh and the Chief Wife have not yet emerged.

The others are to precede us. Only I am to ride with my nephew and Ankhesenamon. This is significant and not lost upon Horemheb, who looks annoyed and upset and for a moment appears about to protest. I stare him down and he embarks, casting a dark glance back at the Palace as he goes. It is not a good omen for the day.

It is time for a boy of eighteen to be very, very clever. I do not know whether he has it in him, though I have tried as much as I could to impart from my years and wisdom the conviction that it is very, very necessary.

Amonhotep, Son of Hapu

Normally I would ride with the Family, but Aye has asked me to wander among the people on the east bank in Thebes and tell him of their reactions to what Pharaoh does this day. None of us knows what this will be but all are apprehensive. We have witnessed so many of these state occasions at the temple of Karnak. Far more often than not they have meant trouble for the Two Lands and further unhappiness for the House of Thebes.

Yet we have done all we can, the Regent and I, to try to make sure that today will not be such another as those many that have gone before. We have been dealing with a bright and gentle lad, whose intelligence lies somewhere between the extremes of Akhenaten's erratic brilliance and Smenkhkara's amiable dullness and whose common sense, we hope, far exceeds them both. Since his return to Thebes, when he startled us all by the generosity of his gestures toward the Aten, he has subsided into an apparent acquiesence in all that has been done for Amon and the other gods. He has been content to make his point from time to time only by a gentle but persistent encouragement of the enlargement of the Aten's temple at Karnak, by a fairly frequent display of the Aten's crook and flail, and by his employment of the Aten's throne, which he takes with him everywhere and uses whenever he can. He has also insisted that the temples at Akhet-Aten be protected and has refused to permit reprisals against the steadily dwindling Aten priesthood (many of whose members discreetly disappeared immediately after Akhenaten's death, anyway, so that now only a handful openly remain).

In these things Aye has encouraged him, and when Tut has sought my advice I have counseled the same. I know our policies have disturbed Hatsuret, I think unduly (for surely Amon cannot honestly complain about all that has been given back to him!). I know they have made Horemheb uneasy, sometimes dangerously so, to the point where his father has on occasion been forced to warn him forcefully about it. But the Regent and I speak from the wisdom of seventy-one years, now, and we know our way is best. At least moderation has prevented another open clash between the Living Horus and Amon; and this is a clash we know must never occur again. None of us—the Two Lands, this House, none of us—could survive another such.

So it is with some trepidation that we await the full assumption of power by Pharaoh today. Yet I detect none of this among the people as I wander through the odorous alleyways and crowded streets of Thebes, jostling along with the enormous crowd that makes its way eagerly toward Karnak. There is a holiday mood in the air, a happy excitement: Pharaoh and the Chief Wife are very popular among the people, certainly the most popular pair to occupy the throne since the days of Amonhotep III (life, health, prosperity!) and Queen Tiye. Whatever dark doubts disturb the inner circle in the Court, they are not transmitted to the streets. There Neb-Kheperu-Ra and Ankhesenamon rule supreme. If the streets decided such things in Kemet, these two would reign for many years. So they may—I for one devoutly hope they will—if His Majesty is shrewd. Not even Horemheb will be able to do anything if His Majesty is shrewd. But from this moment on none of us who favor him can really help him set the course. It rests entirely now in what lies behind that handsome young face, which of late has begun to lose its youthful roundness and acquire a withdrawn, uneasy expression as its owner looks into a future that now belongs to him.

Slowly yet inexorably, like some vast oozing jelly, the crowd fills up the banks of the river and all the public space around the temple, pushing me along on its surface like a bug until I come to rest finally where I want to be, beside the landing stage near the foot of the platform that has been set up for the Good God's address to the people. (He favors Akhenaten's custom, and knows he is effective at it.) Ramesses is in charge of the guards this day, and through the crowds he recognizes me and sends two soldiers to escort me. I do not mind this assistance now, for I am in truth getting old and it has been a lengthy walk from where I first put ashore at the temple of Luxor. He provides a chair for me, which I thankfully accept, and then stands beside me for a time while we watch the people continue to come, and hear from upriver the first long-rolling shouts that greet the beginning of the royal procession. I have little to report to Aye that he does not know: Kemet loves his nephew and granddaughter; and upon their own shoulders rests their fate.

This I think even dull but reliable Ramesses senses (he is the perfect foil for lightning-quick Horemheb, which I am sure is why Horemheb has made him his most trusted lieutenant all these years) because, after watching the crowds for a moment, he asks me in his usual amiable, half-bewildered fashion:

"What do you think His Majesty will tell us this day, Amonhotep?"

"I think he will tell us he is happy to have full power," I answer promptly, "and that he will use it only for the good of Kemet. Which is what all of us who have power must do. Including," I add, for with Ramesses one must spell things out, and I intend the word to get back, "Horemheb."

"Oh," he says, "I think Horemheb intends always to do only that."

"Do you?" I ask, speaking frankly, for I am indeed very old and Horemheb's possible annoyance does not trouble me any more. "Would I were so sure."

"Why are you not?" Ramesses asks, squatting on his heels at my side and lowering his voice so that we will not be overheard by the pressing crowd. "What troubles you, Amonhotep?"

"Horemheb grows impatient about many things, these days. Too many things."

"Only those that threaten the kingdom," Ramesses says stoutly, and I nod.

"Granted. But only as Horemheb sees them."

"Who better? Horemheb is very wise."

"And very ambitious."

"Ambition is not a crime in a man. It has given him power to save the Two Lands, many times."

"He has done much for Kemet," I agree, "but now I think it time for him to relax a little and let things take their course."

"But what course will that be?" he asks, coming back to his original point—Ramesses is not always as dim as one is inclined to think. "Is that not what we must learn from His Majesty? And is it not worrisome a little, since we have had so much misgovernment from the House of Thebes, and now know not what its youngest son may do?"

"You must not speak treason, Ramesses," I say sternly, and though he looks a little taken aback he does not yield much. He is also stubbornly loyal and unafraid, which is another reason Horemheb values him.

"I mean not treason," he says, "as you perfectly well know, Amonhotep. But this lad, like his brothers, worries me. He appears to be a good King but so for a time did they. Then something changed. Could it not change with this one? And would that not be a sad day for the Two Lands?"

"It would be if it came about," I agree, "but it will not come about because he is not his brothers. He is himself."

"But he has the blood," he persists. "And he has the wife to match it, daughter as she is of the Heretic and the Beautiful Woman. It could be a bad combination for the kingdom. I worry about it."

"I know you do," I say, as around us the roar increases and distantly we see the first golden prow splitting Hapi's waters, "and I know your friend does too, and so you worry twofold. But I tell you, Ramesses, this Good God you must not worry about. He has been well-trained, he is an amiable lad, he is possessed of common sense."

"I hope so," he says, his eyes widening with a bleak thoughtfulness I have never believed him capable of, "for I should hate to see more killing in the House of Thebes."

"There will be none if all of us—*all* of us," I say more loudly as the roar of greeting begins to overwhelm us, "who have any direct part at all—including you, Ramesses, you are as responsible as the rest of us—agree and make certain that all will go well. *You* must not be party to any killing."

"I do not want to be," he says with a shudder. "You know that is not my nature, Amonhotep, except as a soldier in the field, where it is all impersonal against the Two Lands' enemies and does not matter. It is not my nature as a friend to all in the House of Thebes."

"It is not the nature of most of us," I say, hesitating for a second but then deciding to spell this out, too: "It must not be the nature of Horemheb, either."

"It will not be," he says, rising to his feet with a wince for muscles aching from his awkward posture at my side, "if the King keeps his part of the bargain and does not do anything foolish."

"He will not do anything foolish," I say firmly as he prepares to return to his post at the landing stage to assist the royal debarkations. "Believe me, Ramesses, he will not!"

"I believe that as you do, Amonhotep," he says with an unhappy smile that robs his words of some of their sting but not their significance. "Pray to the gods our trust is not betrayed."

"Go to your post," I say, dismissing him with a wave. "Do what you can to restrain your friend, should it be necessary."

"Pray with me it will not be necessary, Amonhotep," he says as he turns away. "My heart would break should they of the House of Thebes turn again upon one another."

And so would mine, good Ramesses, I think as he departs. So would mine. And you pray no more fervently than I about it.

Yet for a while all appears to be going well. (Indeed, looking back now in this night electric with horror, it still appears that all went well. With what insanity did the gods drive Horemheb to do the thing he did?)

First comes Sitamon, serene and gracious as always, receiving from the city which is more truly hers than anyone's—since she never really abandoned it during Akhenaten's reign but always stayed as much as possible at Malkata—the loving tribute she always does. With her comes Mutnedjmet, small clever face almost submerged in a huge black wig. On either side her two little familiars laugh and chatter in their squeaky, privileged voices. To her the crowd gives an amused yet affectionate welcome: she long ago became the official jester of the House of Thebes, her eccentricities emphasized by Ipy and Senna, whom she has had about her for fifteen years and more. The people like an eccentric in a royal house, it gives them something human and comfortable to laugh about amid the pomp. Mutnedjmet has deliberately courted it. She has never married and probably never will; was one of her half sister Nefertiti's closest confidantes in the last, tragic years; and now goes about among the people doing great good with many charities. She is much shrewder than most realize but is content to hide it behind the public character she has carefully created for herself. How such a one could be daughter to Aye and half sister to Horemheb must intrigue the people, too, they are both so stiff and proper in all their public doings. But Mutnedjmet goes her own way quite successfully and, aside from her friendship for Nefertiti, has managed to stay out of the unhappy events that have afflicted the Family.

Following Sitamon and Mutnedjmet comes Horemheb, riding with Mutnedjmet's brother, his half brother, the Vizier Nakht-Min. (It is interesting to note that at the moment, until Ankhesenamon produces living issue, the family of Aye now outnumbers the House of Thebes.) Nakht-Min is his usual smiling, imperturbable self: he too has managed to stay relatively free from the Family's agonies. Horemheb is dark-visaged, self-absorbed, somber, stern. To Nakht-Min's smiles and waves the crowd responds with friendly cheers: he is well liked and much approved, managing as he does to moderate some of his half brother's more stringent approaches to things.

For Horemheb, who makes no gestures, offers no smiles, scarcely looks up from the brooding study he appears to be in, there is but a scattering of applause, few cheers, no warmth. He gives none: he gets none. The people are afraid of him, which is sad indeed when one thinks back over four decades, (alas, so fast does time rush on!) to happy young "Kaires," and when one pauses to reflect upon how driven the mature man is by what he sincerely conceives to be his duty to the Two Lands. Duty to himself, yes, because he has come to feel that he and Kemet are synonymous and that only he can restore her to her fullest glories; but duty to Kemet most of all, I do believe. I give him that: but the crowds, seeing only the increasingly stern, public appearance, knowing only the gossip and the whispers of the things he has done—

hearing of them only, not understanding the inner agonies which prompted his actions and took their bitter toll from him when he responded—are not so charitable. They may approve in their hearts of what he did to rid the kingdom of Akhenaten and Nefertiti, but they seem to feel that he should at least smile at them about it. Then they could comfort themselves with the feeling that it was really all right . . . and they could get over their instinctive apprehension that they themselves may yet suffer equally from such an iron will, should he ever have the unchecked power to turn it upon them.

Much, much rests on the shoulders of Neb-Kheperu-Ra and Ankhesenamon. The people's prayers, moved by a certain underlying desperation, are with them, and now from up the river comes the proof—that long, rising roar of love, whose deep, almost animal fervor cannot be matched in memory unless one goes back to his father and mother in their greatest days.

Neb-Kheperu-Ra Tutankhamon, Great Bull, Living Horus, Beloved of Goddess Buto and Goddess Nekhebet, the Two Ladies of the North and the South, Lord of the Two Lands, Great in Splendor, Sacred to Amon (and friend to Aten), twelfth King and Pharaoh of the Eighteenth Dynasty to rule over the kingdom of Kemet, comes.

The greeting grows, swells, takes over the world. In the midst of it two small golden figures step down from their golden barge and stride sturdily forward to the first pylon where dark Hatsuret and his masked priests wait. After them comes Aye, face as always calm, mien impressive, receiving from the people that special sound of deep respect and humble worship that his advanced age and unique place in their hearts always guarantee him: his tribute and, one suspects, his shield against the ambitions of his son. He accepts it with a dignified but smiling bow —he has taken to smiling in public in the last few years, as part of his subtle campaign to hold Horemheb in check—and, as always, the crowd is delighted at such humanity from one who most of his life has appeared basically kindly but outwardly unbending and severe. He decided some time ago, apparently, to let Horemheb be the one to look unbending and severe if he so desires; and since Horemheb obliges without the saving grace of also being kindly, it is Aye who profits in their contest for the trust of the people. One would think Horemheb would perceive this and moderate his own severity accordingly; but Horemheb, like all in this powerful, headstrong group, goes his own way.

Pharaoh and Ankhesenamon move on to the first pylon. Behind them the rest of us fall in line. I hate to give up my comfortable chair but now my presence is expected, so I must comply. I wince like Ramesses from aching muscles as I take my place. We move on into the temple, where Hatsuret presides in his usual imperious fashion over the rites of Amon which are designed to sanctify this day.

These completed—Pharaoh and Ankhesenamon going through the rituals with impassive faces that reveal nothing to their closely watching elders—we return to the platform set up in the open field beside the temple. I am able to sit down again, this time with the Family, and a welcome relief it is. I am seated beside Sitamon, who greets me with kindly concern and presently murmurs, "Come to me tomorrow at Malkata. I have an idea for you," which leaves me puzzled but intrigued. She is a generous soul, Sitamon, bearing well, after an initial period of bitterness, her disappointment that Horemheb apparently will never marry her. I think she is better off, myself, and I suspect she has concluded the same.

When we are all arranged, the crowd having finally quieted its restless pushing and shoving and the occasional renewed bursts of cheering with which it has relieved its boredom while we have been inside, an attentive silence settles over all. Tutankhamon rises and moves forward to center stage. The silence, if possible, grows deeper.

His arms are crossed beneath the robe he wears against the cold: he is holding crook and flail. The two sets are so nearly of a size that one has to look closely sometimes to tell which he is carrying. The crowd cannot see, but we can: today it is the Aten, and with a wry little smile visible only to us seated behind him, he turns and hands them to Hatsuret, standing at the side. Hatsuret looks for a second as though he would like to crack them over his knee, but of course he has no choice but to accept them. He passes them hurriedly on to a younger priest behind him: so hurriedly that Pharaoh again smiles the slightest of smiles as he turns back to face the crowd.

"My people of Kemet!" he cries, and his voice rings clear and strong over the blustery gusts that sweep off the river. "I greet you on this day when I come fully to my heritage. I thank you for your kind attendance on these ceremonies, and I want you to know that on your loves I rest my rule as King and Living Horus."

It is a graceful opening, received with great applause and gratification. He has made himself one of them in these warm initial remarks, and he binds them even closer with his next.

"In honor of this day and so that all here may suitably celebrate with Her Majesty and me our happiness in your loyal loves I am ordering that the granaries be opened so that each among you may receive a goodly share of food this day. And I am further ordering that from the Treasury the Grand Vizier Aye"—there is a stirring among the Family,

for now we know what he intends for Aye, a title and office supreme
and unusual, if not entirely unknown, in our history—"shall distribute
to each and every one who comes to him between now and the time
when Ra-Atum sinks to rest behind the Western Peak one weight of
gold apiece with which to celebrate this day, or feed his family, or do
with what he will."

Now the response is joyous indeed: he has appealed to their loyalty,
their stomachs and their greed. So far it is a very skillful performance.
Now he moves on to deeper things.

"My people of Kemet," he says, and he lowers his voice deliberately
so that they must now be absolutely still and strain with all their attention if they are to hear his words, "it is now five years almost to the day
since the Chief Wife and I left our capital of Akhet-Aten to return to
our capitals of Thebes and Memphis. In that time, as you know, much
has been done to rebuild the temples of Amon and the other gods, to
restore civil order to the land, to strengthen our defenses against our
enemies of the Nine Bows who threaten our borders, particularly King
Supp-i-lu-li-u-mas of the Hittites, who wars against us. Much has been
done to restore to the Two Lands peace where peace, for a time, did
not exist.

"Much, however"—and a certain sternness enters his voice which
makes the silence, if possible, more profound—"remains to be done.
Amon has been restored, the Aten has been reduced. A balance has
been sought. Yet the Two Lands do not yet know the full and universal
peace Her Majesty and I would like to see. For this reason we would
propose new plans and policies for the kingdom."

Now the apprehension we have been feeling in the Court as we
neared this day springs back full-blown in all our hearts. What "new
plans," what "new purposes"? Others announced new plans and purposes from this same spot: disaster was the child of their intentions.
Pray it may not be so with Tutankhamon! Aye, Horemheb, Hatsuret,
Nakht-Min, Ramesses, Mutnedjmet, Sitamon, myself—no common
subject listens more intently than we.

"First, however," Pharaoh continues calmly, "I would tell you of the
new officials of my court. The Councilor, Divine Father-in-law and Regent Aye, our most dear and trusted adviser, will hereafter be what I
have already told you, the Grand Vizier. To him will report, assisting
him and obeying his orders in all things connected with the internal
affairs of the kingdom, our cousin and faithful friend the General
Nakht-Min, who will continue in his present post as Vizier of Upper
Kemet." There is a wave of applause. They are pleased to have popular
Nakht-Min remain with them. "Also working with the Grand Vizier

and subject to his orders"—we all tense anew, for now comes the dangerous one—"will be our cousin and faithful servant, the General Horemheb, who in addition to his title of Vizier of Lower Kemet will bear the title 'King's Defender of Lower Kemet.' To him, working with the Grand Vizier Aye, do we entrust the defense of our borders against Suppiluliumas and the Hittites and against all others who dare to challenge the power of Pharaoh, wherever they may be."

Again applause, more perfunctory yet curiously relieved. They are glad to have Horemheb far away to the north, and busy. So, obviously, is Pharaoh.

Furtively we glance at Horemheb, demoted thus abruptly from his treasured post and powers of King's Deputy and, in effect, banished, at least for a time, to the Delta. He loves the Delta, loves Memphis, loves the role of warrior-defender of the Two Lands: but obviously not on these terms. His face for several seconds is a study as he first flushes, then pales, then flushes again. But there is nothing he can do and he knows it. Our pliable youth of eighteen is pliable no longer. He is assuming his powers with the firmness that is his right. Horemheb would be well advised, I think, to accept, obey and reserve his ambitions for another day.

Until, that is, Neb-Kheperu-Ra does what we who love him have feared. Suddenly now, without warning, he responds to the urgings of his blood (or perhaps of his wife, who knows)—tries to be too clever —behaves like his brother—goes, we are almost immediately aware, too far.

"Through these good and trusted servants," he announces, while all again fall silent, "I shall presently announce to you in detail the new plans and purposes Her Majesty and I propose for the Two Lands. They will seek to bring about a more perfect balance between Amon and Aten, and all the gods; to put an end to lingering factions within the land who favor one or the other; to permit, above all, freedom to all our people to worship whatever gods they please, openly and unafraid, placing not one above the other nor lowering them likewise. We have wished for this since the day we came to the throne; it has happened only partially. From now on the Chief Wife and I are determined that it shall be the true and universal state of our dear Two Lands.

"To symbolize this unity we desire for all the gods and all our people, I am ordering this day the start of my mortuary temple. It is to be built on the west bank of the Nile on that rocky spur which, slightly north of the mortuary temple of the Good God Hatshepsut (life, health, prosperity!) curves toward the river. There do I decree to the Grand Vizier and to my faithful sculptor Tuthmose and to all my loyal artisans and workmen, these things:

"Halfway up the ridge, there shall be hewn a circular level platform which it will take three hundred men with linked hands outstretched to encompass.

"Around the edge of this platform there shall be raised a hypostyle hall of columns entwined with lotus and papyrus symbolizing the unity of the Two Lands.

"There shall be over these columns no roof, nor anywhere above the circle within them any roof; and they shall be open to the rays of Ra forever and ever."

Sitamon and I exchange a disturbed sidelong glance. There is a restless stirring down the line of chairs. Something familiar and frightening is creeping toward us in the windy day.

"In the center of the circle there shall be a single stone shaft, circular in shape, the height of a man and the breadth of a man. It shall bear upon it no sign or symbol of any god or anyone, save at its base, in small, the cartouche of myself, the Pharaoh who built it; but on the altar itself there shall be no sign or symbol of any god.

"Thus will it be a place for all the gods, where all people may come and worship freely as they wish."

Now Horemheb and Aye are looking at one another with growing alarm and comprehension; and over the others a frozen stillness comes. In front of us the crowd listens attentively but without noticeable change. They follow a step at a time, as he intends them to, and do not put it all together. The people are innocents who go where Pharaoh leads them. They do not look ahead, as we who have trod this tragic path before find we are suddenly looking ahead.

Serenely Pharaoh continues, while at his side Ankhesenamon looks up at him with approving adoration in her eyes. Have they really no concept of what they do?

"Down from the point of this holy circle which is nearest the Nile," Tutankhamon says, his voice ringing clear above the sharpening wind, "there shall radiate twelve broad stairways descending to the plain. In the center at the foot of each there shall stand the figure of a god, beginning with Amon and the Aten at the two innermost stairways, followed on either side successively by Ptah, Horus, Thoth, Hathor, Isis, Sekhmet, Buto, Nekhebet, Ma'at and Ra-Herakhty.

"Thereby shall all be equally honored, and so may each who worships choose the stairway that suits him as he starts his climb to the holy circle of my mortuary temple above, there to find peace, love and comfort for his own heart."

The circular platform—the circular row of columns—the unadorned altar—the twelve radiating arms . . . *the Aten.*

But so mesmerized are the people as they listen, so pleased are they by the honors to be given all the gods, so unable are their simple minds to visualize these symbols as though from above and to see them in one coherent whole as Pharaoh has cleverly described them step by step, that we can tell they do not perceive this. Instead they exclaim with wonder and pleasure and burst into prolonged and happy shouts; while Tut and Ankhesenamon, never indicating by so much as the flicker of an eyelash that they do indeed know exactly what they are doing, smile serenely out upon them.

"Thus," says Tutankhamon firmly when the applause and excitement have finally subsided, "do I decree, and thus do I charge you, Grand Vizier, and all my loyal servants of the Court, to see that it is well and speedily done. . . .

"Good people," he concludes, "dear children of our dear Two Lands: may all the gods keep you and comfort you, and may they give us many long years to rule over you that we may answer with our love the love you bear for us.

"And now let there be rejoicing until the last man has fallen to sleep!"

And he waves to them and then he and Ankhesenamon glance at us with pleasant, apparently innocent smiles, as the shouts and jubilation well up again and they begin to walk toward the golden litters in which they will be borne high through Thebes in the slow triumphal procession that will not end until many hours from now when they cross the river and return to Malkata.

Clamorously the people press forward toward Aye, who rises, wraps his robe about him and, with inscrutable face, gestures with his staff toward the Treasury and the granaries standing side by side on the road to Luxor. A roar goes up, dutifully they fall in behind: he goes to keep Pharaoh's promise. Horemheb, his face set in sternly formal mold that reveals nothing of what he must be thinking, strides somberly toward the landing stage, looking neither to right nor left; the people open way for him in fear-tinged respect and close again silently behind him as he passes. He apparently intends to return at once to the Palace, there to take counsel of who knows what thoughts. Nakht-Min, looking troubled but managing to maintain his usual amiable outward aspect, chats for a moment with Ramesses, who also looks disturbed but as though he is not quite sure why he should be. Nakht-Min then offers his arm to Mut-nedjmet and they too move toward the barges. Ipy and Senna skip squeaking along beside, receiving their usual amused catcalls from the crowd, replying with shrill and sometimes ribald rejoinders.

Sitamon and I are left to bring up the rear. For a moment we simply stand silently looking at one another, while around us our escorting guards wait patiently, and beyond the crowd surges away after Aye and the Good God's promised bounties.

"Well," she says finally in a voice low so that only I can hear. "We face the legacy of Akhenaten rather sooner than I had thought."

"We must help Pharaoh before it is too late," I say, my teeth chattering both from the cold rattling my old bones and fear of what the future may hold.

"So we must," she agrees firmly, "and in this you and I must be allies, Amonhotep. Come back with me now to Malkata and we will talk."

Gratefully I accept her invitation and we are escorted to the remaining royal barge that waits for us at the landing; not knowing that by then, of course, it is already too late.

Aye

He has come to me, stayed for ten minutes and, raging, gone. I am left to put the world together again one last time—if it can be done.

The day passed in parades and ceremonies. At last, as the Nile turned bronze and purple light began to fall upon the Western Peak, Pharaoh and Ankhesenamon returned to Malkata. Tey, Sitamon, Horemheb and I dined with them—early, for it had been a wearing day. Then they retired, he to their regular bedchamber, she to a special one arranged for her down the corridor some way from his. The birth of the Crown Prince being so near, they do not for the present sleep together, because she is having some difficulty with this pregnancy and is up much, and restless, in the night: it is better she be attended by nurses and by Tey, who watches over her with loving care. And he of course has his harim if he wishes to go there; though, being deeply in love with the Chief Wife, I believe he very rarely does.

On this night, for the first time in many nights, he drank a little more wine than he usually does. It was, he said, the exhaustions of the day

which caused the indulgence; and the importance of tomorrow, which
he wanted us to be sure to understand.

"I wish to sleep soundly tonight, Uncle," he said to me, "because tomorrow we begin my mortuary temple and announce the new laws for
religion, with which you must assist me. Much will be done for the Two
Lands tomorrow, much will change. I wish to be fresh and ready for
this. I am very tired right now."

"I, too, Son of the Sun," I admitted; adding automatically, "But I assume the changes will not be too great, as I do not believe the Two
Lands to be quite ready yet for anything sensational."

"Not ready 'yet,' and not ready ever, Son of the Sun," Horemheb said
gravely. "The kingdom has had enough of violent changes. So we hope
you do not plan any such."

"Only what will be best for Kemet, Cousin," Tutankhamon said, a
certain iciness entering his voice. "You may be assured of that."

"I hope so, Majesty," Horemheb said, standing his ground. "Good
kingship requires no less."

"I am a good King!" Tut exclaimed, blazing up with a temper that
was suddenly, chillingly, reminiscent of his older brother. "You need
not instruct me in my duties as King, Cousin!"

"Such was not my intention, Majesty," Horemheb said, still calmly,
though I could sense his growing anger beneath the enforced blandness.
"It was a reminder only."

"I do not need reminders!" Tut snapped. "Give me more wine!"

And he held out his cup imperiously to Horemheb, who accepted it
with impassive face, brushed aside the servant who stepped forward automatically to assist him, went to the wine jar in the corner and dipped
a portion, full running over, which he brought back and placed, still
with impassive face, at Pharaoh's hand.

"Now!" Tut said. "Drink with me, Cousin, to tomorrow and a better
day for the Two Lands!"

For a moment Horemheb did not raise his own cup, but stared, still
with the same impassive air, at the King. Finally he raised his cup and
bowed.

"Very well, Majesty. I drink to that."

"And I!" Tut exclaimed. "And let there be no more nonsense about
it!"

Across the table Sitamon stirred instinctively as the cups met their
lips, and so did I—both of us, I know, seized by a sudden fearful apprehension.

But of course nothing happened. Both drank deep and replaced their
cups on the table. The moment passed without incident. In a second I

was telling myself, and I am sure Sitamon was too, how absurd it was to have imagined for a moment what I know we both did imagine. Not even Horemheb—how sadly easy it has become to say, *"Not even Horemheb,"* when calculating degrees of evil!—would dare anything so desperate and blatant in the presence of us all.

We relaxed, the meal went on. Tut, growing more talkative from the wine, changed the subject, began reminiscing about the early days here at Malkata. Soon we were all recalling pleasant things—carefully avoiding Akhenaten, Smenkhkara and Nefertiti, of course, but still finding much to talk about concerning my sister and my brother-in-law and their great days on the throne—and so it all passed amicably until Tut finally announced in a voice slightly fuzzy from his unusual imbibing, "I am sleepy, and my wife should be in bed too, taking care of the Crown Prince. You will excuse us. Come to me at noon tomorrow, Uncle. We have work to do."

"Yes, Majesty," I said as we all arose, Ankhesenamon awkward with her pregnancy but looking beautiful with it, too.

"Good night, Sister," Tut said, kissing Sitamon affectionately, a gesture she returned with a sudden fierceness that surprised him a little, though I could understand the reason for it: neither of us, still, was quite convinced we had been mistaken a few minutes before.

"Good night, Cousin," he said pleasantly to Horemheb, offering his hand to be kissed, which Horemheb did gravely without change of expression. "You, too, I will see tomorrow, for there is much to be done to carry out my desires for your new post in Lower Kemet."

"Yes, Son of the Sun," Horemheb said. "Sleep well, for tomorrow's sake."

"What mean you by that?" Sitamon asked sharply, her worries breaking unexpectedly to the surface. Horemheb looked at her with a blank surprise and then responded with a calm, half-humorous air.

"Why, Cousin, I mean naught but what I said: he should sleep well, for tomorrow's sake. He himself has said much depends upon tomorrow. I agree. What did you think I meant?"

And under his bland stare her eyes finally dropped and she murmured, "I do not know, Cousin. I suppose you meant what you said."

"I suppose so," he said comfortably. "I can think of nothing else I might have meant. But send word to my quarters by a servant later, and tell me, if you think of something."

"I will," she replied with a sudden flash of anger. "You may be sure I will send a servant to your quarters later, Cousin. I hope he will find you there."

"He will find me there," Horemheb said serenely. "I have no other plans this night."

"What is this?" Tut demanded with a puzzled half laugh. "I do not understand all these riddles you propound, Sister."

"She does not understand them herself," Horemheb said in the same comfortable way. "Do you, now, Cousin!"

But she did not reply, only giving him a long stare, finally shaking her head and turning away. As she did so her eyes caught mine and a message shot from them as if to say, *I am counting on you, Uncle: control him!*

And so I think I still may be able to do, though at a price I do not yet wish to contemplate, so fiercely does it harry me in this once more haunted night for the House of Thebes.

After we had all said our farewells the party broke up. I could see that Ankhesenamon, too, had been troubled by Sitamon's remarks and the hidden contest, whose nature she did not understand, with Horemheb. But she also was tired, too tired for her normally quick perceptions to function at their best; and by then she was also feeling as she said, a little ill, so she gratefully accepted Tey's sustaining arm and they went off together to her bedchamber. Pharaoh, after once again bidding us all good night (a repetition he apparently did not realize, now that the wine was really beginning to claim him), went off to his, where faithful Ramesses and lively Seti still guard his doors each night—though this, too, I think he may change . . . or would have changed . . . I must now remind myself. . . .

What will happen to me! I have dipped my hands in horror so often for the sake of Kemet, and do not know now when, if ever, I will get them clean! Too many things have crowded me over the years. Too many . . .

I bade Horemheb good night and proceeded alone to my bedchamber. There my servant helped me undress, clothed me in my sleeping robe, lit a small fire in a brazier in the corner against the chill of the winter night. I dismissed him and prepared myself for bed. I was about to extinguish the lamp when sharp knuckles struck the door in a fashion not to be denied. I knew who it was instantly. My heart began to pound, my hands to tremble. I made them stop, took deep, deliberate breaths to steady myself, moved with a deliberate slow dignity toward the door. Once again the knuckles struck, louder and more imperative. I thought: *He is not afraid of being heard.* It was not necessary for my son to tell me what this meant, though he did so as soon as I had let him in and closed the door tightly behind him.

"I put a sleeping powder in his wine," he said harshly and without preliminary. "Soon he will sleep a sleep like the sleep of the dead. I suggest to you that he must never be allowed to waken."

"You cannot—" I said, wondering that I could speak at all. "You cannot—"

"I can and I will," Horemheb said sharply. "He has revived the Aten this day and intends to revive him further tomorrow and the day after —and the day after—and the day after—until all the land suffers again from the madness. *It must not be.*"

"You *cannot!*" I said, trying to hold my voice to a near whisper but becoming almost shrill in spite of myself. "There must be no more killing in the House of Thebes. You *cannot.*"

"I can and I will," he repeated in the same harsh voice, "with or without your permission, Father. It will be done this night."

"No!" I cried. "No!"

"Yes," he said with a steady quietness doubly devastating in contrast to my frantic protest. "Yes, Father. There will be no more turning back, no more tolerance for that which will destroy the kingdom if we let it grow again. The consequence I warned you of five years ago when he returned to Thebes has come. As a youth he toyed with the Aten and you allowed it with your policy of 'compromise' and 'toleration.' As a man he now seeks to restore the Aten fully, and that you cannot allow. *You cannot permit Kemet to be ravaged again.* It would be unconscionable."

"It is unconscionable what you propose," I managed to get out. "He has done nothing to deserve this. His gestures to the Aten have been harmless these past five years—"

"Not harmless!" he snapped. "He has kept the Aten alive, and very much alive. The throne, the crook and flail, preserving the temples at Akhet-Aten, enlarging the temple here at Karnak—they have not been harmless. And they have not been done with a child's innocence, for Neb-Kheperu-Ra has not been a child since the Heretic's death. He has known exactly what he was doing, and so has she. Now today, with their clever trick of a 'mortuary temple' that is nothing but the Aten in giant form, they move to begin the full restoration. Tomorrow he says there will be 'new laws for religion.' That can mean only one thing. It must be stopped. *Father!* Surely you can see that?"

"I can see only more horror for the House of Thebes—" I began, and I am afraid my voice broke and trembled and sounded very old: I *am* very old. He interrupted me without pity. This night Horemheb has gone beyond pity.

"I can see only more devastation for the Two Lands," he cried, his voice suddenly filled with a great anger. "It is enough, enough, *enough!*

I will have no more of it! Father!"—and he dared put a hand like iron on my frail old arm, a grasp so fierce I thought it might crunch the bone were I to endure it long. *"Father!* With . . . you . . . or . . . without!"

And he glared into my eyes with an anger so consuming that I think he barely knew I was there.

"We will hold him to the mortuary temple and nothing else," I began —feebly, I am afraid, but I was almost at the end of my strength. "We will not permit him—"

"Not permit him!" he cried. "He is the Living Horus, Son of the Sun, full in his power as of this day! We will 'restrain' him? What nonsense! One restraint only is possible now. *Father!"* And again his painful grip tightened on my arm, his eyes stared furiously into mine, he spoke very slowly and distinctly. "You *know* I am right. You *know* he intends to do what I say. You *know* what this means for the kingdom. You *know* we cannot stand it again. . . ."

Abruptly his voice became very soft and very adamant.

"With you or without you, Father. With you or without."

For what seemed many minutes he held me so, his grip unrelenting, his eyes boring into mine, his face implacable. And at last, of course, I told him what he wanted to hear: because, in truth, I felt him to be correct and I, too, was terrified of the chaos into which the last of my three ill-fated nephews might once again plunge the Two Lands.

"Very well," I whispered huskily, shuddering and turning away as he instantly released me, covering my head with my robe and not looking at him again. "Very well. Do what you must."

"Good!" he said—one short, sharp, explosive word—and was gone, leaving me to weep, as I have so many times before, for three dear little boys, running and laughing down the sunlit pathways of Malkata . . . three little boys who became great kings and betrayed their trust, and so had to die to save the Two Lands, for whose sake we of this House have seen and done and suffered so much, in all these recent dreadful years. . . .

I weep: but I will go on because I am Aye, and the Two Lands depend upon it.

Tutankhamon (Life, health, prosperity!)

The wine is creeping gently upon me. It makes me feel pleasantly dizzy
—relaxed, peaceful, happy—wonderfully happy, because now I am
Pharaoh in all the fullness of my powers, now I am the Living Horus
beyond the hand of any man to stay, not even trusted Aye, not even
mistrusted Horemheb whom I have now, I think, brought finally to
heel. Now I can do all the great things I wish to do for my beloved people and our beloved Two Lands.

Down the hall my dear wife sleeps, and with her sleeps our son who
will soon be born to stand beside me and someday wear the Double
Crown. She shares in all my plans as her mother shared with my
brother and as the Great Wife shared with my father before them. We
are agreed on what we will do and we know the gods will assist us, because what we plan is good for all.

Great Amon will be lowered once more to his proper place, great
Aten will be lifted once more to sit beside him: about them all the other
gods will be peaceably disposed in friendly rank. Equal honor, equal
tribute, equal love will go to all. Worship will be freely given by those
who wish to give it, to whatever god they may wish to honor. Peace and
good times will prevail in the villages, including the village of Hanis of
my friend Amonemhet, who regularly sends me simple gifts of fruit and
grain—which I appreciate more than jewels, for I have many jewels
and much fruit and grain, and I know his gifts represent real sacrifices
of friendship, and I value them. . . . All, all, will be happy and peaceful again in Kemet, and the years will unfold in glorious harmony for us
all as I father many sons and restore our borders with many brave bat-
tles, and the House of Thebes brings back the land again to happiness
and love.

This do I wish for many reasons but most of all for the sake of my
brother and dearest Nefertiti, who sought to do great things but went
too far. I shall do them patiently, shrewdly, earnestly, with great love in
my heart for all men—for such, I think, are becoming my principal
qualities.

I will be a good king.

I, Neb-Kheperu-Ra Tutankhamon, Living Horus, do so decree it.

My eyes grow heavy behind their shuttered lids, my brain begins to swim away along some glorious river where I go to dream of happy days for beloved Kemet . . . our beloved people . . . our beloved House . . . I drift . . . I float . . . tomorrow will begin the glories, tomorrow will begin the love, tomorrow all men will know what a truly Good God I am . . . tomorrow all will come right . . . tomorrow . . . tomorrow . . .

Ramesses

He came to bed an hour ago, eyes drowsy and dulled with wine. He gave us a sleepy smile, amiable and untroubled.

"Good Ramesses!" he said, giving my back an affectionate slap. "Good Seti!"—tousling the hair of my sturdy fifteen-year-old with an affectionate hand. "What would I do without you two fearless guardians of my gate?"

"We attempt to keep them safe, Your Majesty," I said, pleased with his familiarity.

"Not even great Horus could enter here unchallenged!" Seti assured him with an easy grin.

"Wonderful," he said, holding out a hand to brace himself as he staggered slightly against the doorjamb, his words slurring a bit. "Wonderful, to know I am so loved."

"You are by us, Son of the Sun," I said stoutly; and Seti, who after all is only three years younger and so really a friend of both Their Majesties, nodded vigorously and said:

"Always, Son of the Sun."

"Good," he said. "I love you both. Keep me safe. Good night."

"Good night," we echoed together, and watched with fondly approving smiles as he righted himself with careful dignity and went within. Because it is true: we do love His Majesty and he does love us. It is also true that we report faithfully to Horemheb on all they do, but Horemheb does not misuse it and loves them as we do . . . or so we thought until just now, when suddenly all has grown dark and frightening so that we crouch together trembling, knowing nothing but fearing awful things, while in His Majesty's room there occurs—what?

It began scarce five minutes ago. We were almost asleep ourselves, when abruptly we were jolted awake by the sounds of someone softly approaching—very softly, but not softly enough to get past our trained ears, which woke us even before the visitors rounded the turn in the corridor.

"Who comes?" I demanded quite loudly, for I knew His Majesty was sleeping the sleep of the wine-drowned and would not easily be disturbed. Both Seti and I had sprung to our feet, spears raised and ready.

"I come," Horemheb said, and his voice was cold and remote as if from some far distance, which frightened me, who have been his friend and intimate for so long: but sometimes of late I do not know Horemheb.

"And I," said the accursed priest, who lords it over us all now that Amon has been restored. "Does His Majesty sleep?"

"His Majesty sleeps," I said.

"We would go in to do business with His Majesty," Horemheb said.

"But—" we both began in automatic protest. Hatsuret started to give us his usual pompous glare, but it was unnecessary: Horemheb's cold expression was enough.

"Stand aside, good Ramesses and young Seti," he said softly. "Our business with His Majesty will be brief."

"But His Majesty is sleeping!" I blurted, I am afraid sounding as stupid as I know he thinks me; but a great fear was beginning to seize my heart and I could tell from Seti's white-faced, wide-eyed look that it was beginning to seize his too.

"*Aside!*" he said, and it was so harsh and so violent that I, who have always thought I knew him but wonder now if I ever did, shrank back against the wall, shielding my son, who shrank back behind me. The gesture must have touched Horemheb in some way, for his expression softened for just a moment and he said more gently, "Do not be afraid, either of you. We come on the business of Kemet, and all will go well. Do you move down the corridor and take up your stations by Her Majesty's room until we are done. Please."

This appeal I could not deny—indeed, I could not deny him in any case, but for a moment or two this gentleness somehow seemed to make it better—so both of us mumbled some word or two of agreement and started to move away, looking back fearfully as we went.

Horemheb stood for a long moment facing the door. Then he took a deep breath, squared his shoulders, opened it very quietly, and went in. Hatsuret followed, but not before giving us a lofty and contemptuous look—to which Seti, I am pleased to say, responded with the most vulgar street gesture his hand could perform.

But our moment of pleasure at this stopped immediately the door closed behind them. Awful fears were in our eyes as we looked at one another. We crept away down the corridor to Her Majesty's door, where now we stand, looking back in terror at the door we have left.

It is very hushed, very still, in the Palace of Malkata. What have we done, to yield up our charge so easily? What could we have done, in the face of such a demand, from such a source?

It is very quiet, very still. Presently we both become conscious of a clicking noise. It is our teeth chattering, though it has taken us quite a while to become aware of them.

Horemheb

He lies on his right side, face flushed, breathing sonorous and steady. Perhaps the powder was not necessary: the wine might have been enough. Anyway, there is no chance of failure now.

The once round and rosy cheeks have become a little hollowed, the brow is not quite so serene and unlined as it used to be; the years are already beginning to take their toll of Neb-Kheperu-Ra. It may be as well there are none left.

Hatsuret leans above him like the dark, avenging falcon he has always fancied himself to be. The long thin spear gleams like a needle in the light of the single candle that gutters low in the alabaster lamp by the bed. Slowly he lowers the spear, gripping it tightly in both hands, toward the tender skin near the left ear. He shifts a little, seeking exact position, lowers it still further; pauses, takes a deep breath and looks up at me. I nod.

Without a sound the spear sinks into the skull, driven with all the force of his muscles and his hatred. Blood spurts, the dying body gives several convulsive leaps . . . quivers, jerks, trembles, shakes . . . subsides. The frantically strangled breathing stops. The God Neb-Kheperu-Ra Tutankhamon has rejoined his ancestors.

Hatsuret withdraws the dripping spear, straightens, looks at me with the start of a triumphant smile. It lasts perhaps a second before my knife drives between his ribs. His face has time for a wild, horrified look, instantly erased by death, before he falls spread-eagled across Pharaoh's body, their blood commingling on the finespun golden sheets.

Noisily I run to the door, fling it open with a crash.

"Help, Ramesses, help, Seti! Help, help, all!" I shout at the top of my lungs as dutifully down the hall my two faithful friends begin to stumble toward me. "The priest of Amon has killed the Living Horus! Help, help, all!"

Sitamon

So horror has come again to the House of Thebes. I am almost too tired to think about it, too tired to do anything but sit in my room and stare blankly at the wall, lost in tragedy beyond tragedy, despair beyond despair. What does it all add up to, what is the purpose, what is the point? . . . except that I know, well enough. The purpose is to put Horemheb on the throne and the point is that he believes he, and he alone, is sufficiently strong of character and determination to restore the Two Lands to all their ancient power and glory.

And he may be right . . . he may well be right. I can see his argument. But at what a cost!

When the Palace was awakened last night, not long after we had all retired, there were great cries, shouts, uproar throughout the compound. People raced through the corridors and along the paths, there were shouts of "Guards!" and the sound of arms. I arose hastily, clothed myself—my pleasant, incompetent ladies in waiting had already hurried across to the main Palace, too excited and too curious to help me—and also hurried out, not knowing what had occurred but sensing that, whatever it might be, I should undoubtedly have a part to play. And so I did, and much yet lies ahead for me—who, with my uncle Aye and aunt Tey represent, I think, the last islands of sanity left in Malkata this day.

Brushing aside my squealing, fluttering ladies, striding imperiously past the frightened guards who themselves were so curious, frightened and confused that Suppiluliumas of the Hittites might well have invaded us without challenge at that moment, I came swiftly to the room of my niece. Beyond it down the hall I could see a crowd gathered at the door of the King. I recognized Horemheb, Ramesses, Seti and my uncle, saw from their expressions that something awful must have occurred; but before I could proceed further was compelled into my niece's room by a long-drawn recurring howl, almost animal in nature. I knew at once what was going on and where I was needed most. I turned instantly and went in.

On her bed Ankhesenamon was writhing in premature childbirth, her eyes blank with pain as she repeated her continuous cries. One hand tightly clenched gentle Tey's, the other ripped the cloth-of-gold sheets in frantic agonies. All around hovered nurses, bringing hot water and compresses, uttering soothing, crooning sounds: here, at least, instinct was compelling all to do efficiently what nature demanded. Outside the men's tumult in the corridors continued; in the Queen's room we had our women's work to do and could not be bothered.

Tey looked up at me with tear-filled eyes and said gratefully, "Thank the gods you are here, Sitamon. His Majesty has been slain by the priest Hatsuret, himself killed by Horemheb, and this—this is the result. They did not even tell her gently, some soldier rushed in and shouted it out. She went immediately into convulsions. Pray with us that we may save her and the Prince."

"Yes," I said; gave her a hug of encouragement; laid my hand for a moment on Ankhesenamon's sweat-drenched, unheeding brow; and then took my place in the line of ladies who were bringing buckets of hot water and compresses from a huge kettle boiling in the corner.

For three hours we labored so. Time blurred, shrank, expanded, passed. Outside the noise gradually died away; when I could think at all, I assumed that my poor nephew's body must have been taken already to the House of Vitality to begin the seventy days of embalmment. Now and again I found myself weeping convulsively for him who had been so gentle and kind and young. Then Ankhesenamon would utter some particularly rending cry and I would be called back to the only reality we knew in that room, her reality. Once, at some point I cannot fix now, there was an imperious rapping on the door. I knew that impatient sound and said quickly, "I will go," before anyone else could respond to it. On the threshold stood Horemheb, his face looking drained and, either sincerely or artfully, ravaged with pain.

"What do you want, Cousin?" I demanded coldly, for even then I knew instinctively what had happened, I knew he was no longer friend or lover to anyone save himself. "We are busy here."

"How are Her Majesty and the child?" he asked.

"They are well," I lied, "and no concern of yours."

"They are of concern to everyone," he said, "for Her Majesty is now the sole ruler of the Two Lands."

"And will so remain if I have anything to say about it!" I snapped, and with all my strength flung the heavy wooden door shut in his face, having time only to catch a glimpse of the sudden naked rage that replaced the pious sorrow. If I had any doubts left as to what had occurred in Tutankhamon's room, they vanished then. And not fear but a cold fury wiped away the last lingering traces of any love I might once have mistakenly felt for my cousin Horemheb.

Back I plunged into the ceaseless yet orderly activity in that overheated, fate-filled chamber. Again time did strange things, shrank, expanded, blurred, faded, re-emerged, became a jumble, passed. Finally there was a last dreadful shriek and my niece fell back, eyes closed as if in death. Hastily we ascertained that she was all right, then turned to the child which lay on the bloodied sheets before us. Frantically Tey and I washed it, slapped it, breathed upon it, shook it, sought with cries and supplications to bring forth some sign of life. There was none.

The last child of Tutankhamon and Ankhesenamon had been born dead. And in one last cruel joke of the gods, it was not the Crown Prince we had all so confidently expected, either. The last royal child of the Eighteenth Dynasty was but one more of those puny foredoomed girls who, save for unfortunate Merytaten and Ankhesenamon herself, have apparently been destined to curse forever the line of poor Akhenaten.

Now twelve hours have passed and Ankhesenamon is in my small palace at the far end of the compound of Malkata, the palace I have occupied ever since my marriage to my father forty-six years ago. She is sleeping the sleep of utter exhaustion in the bed that has been brought in next to mine. In the next room dear Tey also sleeps. In a room on the other side the four nurses sleep. I have not been sleeping: I have been on guard. And as much as one woman can who is also a Queen and Princess of the blood of Ra, I have made sure that we will be safe here.

I have my own household guards, completely loyal to me, and these have been placed on post all around my palace. I have organized them into regular watches: only a handful of servants whom I trust are permitted to come in and out with food and water. I have established my own small armed camp. No messages have reached us from others in Malkata, with the single exception of Aye, and I have sent none to them. Aye's message said: "Keep her safe. I trust you." My reply said: "I shall guard her with my own life. You have my trust also." As indeed he does, and between us I think we may make some sense of this, though I do not yet see how.

I said we have had no messages from others in Malkata, but we have had one visitor, an hour ago. A guard came to tell me, in considerable agitation: apparently the demand for entry had been as imperious as the night before. Tired as I was, I could be imperious too. I had the guard show the visitor to my audience chamber and went to confront him alone.

"What do you want?" I demanded sharply before he had a chance to speak. "More victims?"

"Do not be too clever, Cousin," he said angrily, "or I may find one."

"That would be three in twelve hours," I snapped. "I must congratulate you on your taste for blood, Cousin. It is beginning to become you."

At this he had the grace to flush. With what I could see was a great effort, he managed to make his tone more reasonable.

"I am here to inquire for the safety of Her Majesty," he said, "and to take her to the main Palace where she may be placed under suitable guard and made safe while she recovers."

"I would not let you have Her Majesty were you Menes himself!" I said. "*You* place Her Majesty under suitable guard? *You* keep her safe? Why, Cousin, I dare say she would be as safe with you as her husband was. You have given him the greatest safety of all, the grave. How kind of you to wish the same safety for Her Majesty!"

"*Cousin—*" he began, a furious anger rising in his eyes and voice. But I simply gave him a contemptuous look and started to turn away. He reached forward and placed a restraining hand on my arm and said, "No, wait," in a suddenly pleading voice. And fool that I am, something—old love, old hate, old habit—made me respond to the appeal and turn back. At least I heard his rationalization of what he had done, anyway, and I was glad to have that, for now I know that it will justify anything for him, and so I know better what we face.

"Well, Cousin?" I said coldly. "What is it?"

"To begin with," he said, "Hatsuret killed Neb-Kheperu-Ra. I did not."

"How could Hatsuret have been in his bedchamber if you did not take him there?" I demanded. "How could he kill him in your presence if he did not have your approval?"

"I killed Hatsuret instantly the deed was done," he said. "I revenged His Majesty instantly."

"You do not answer my questions, Cousin," I said, "because you know you cannot. You took that pretentious priest—who, incidentally, is no loss to Amon or the Two Lands, I give you credit for that—and you told him to kill my brother. And then you killed *him,* to cover your crime and make it appear to the people that the Priest of Amon had murdered Pharaoh. Thus you removed Pharaoh and rid yourself at the same time of one who knew all your crimes. And thus you, too, Cousin, sought to lower Amon in the eyes of the people. Even you, proud

Cousin, are afraid of Amon! Two ducks fell together at the slingshot of that great hunter, Horemheb. How skillful, how noble! I would congratulate you, were it not—were it not—" at which point, being a woman, though a strong one, and very, very tired after the dreadful night, I began to cry, quietly enough but without being able to stop. The rest of our conversation took place to the steady fall of my tears, which only seemed to make him more anxious to justify himself.

"You must understand me, Cousin," he said quietly, shifting his chair closer to mine and taking my hand, which at first I sought to remove but then allowed to remain limp in his, for what was the use? I was too overwhelmed suddenly with grief to end a contact I now despise. "You must understand about Tutankhamon and about Hatsuret, for on your understanding of them depends your understanding of me, which I hope I have always had, and will always have."

"Oh, you have always had it," I said bitterly through my tears. "And never more than now, I assure you, Cousin."

"I think not," he said, flushing again with a renewal of anger, but forcing himself to remain calm. "You know as well as I that our little kinglet was well begun on his plan to restore the Aten. You *know* that was what he intended. You *know* that yesterday when he announced his so-called 'mortuary temple,' that joke upon all of us who thought the Aten in disgrace, he was already starting down the road that would bring him back inevitably to Akhet-Aten. You *know* the Two Lands could not have survived this again. You *know* he had to be removed, as Hatsuret, that priest grown too big of a priesthood also grown too big again, had to be removed. My father agreed with this: why do you not see it?"

"I do not believe he agreed with it," I said, "except under the pressure of your persuasions."

"He agreed with it," he said grimly, "and so it was done, because he knew there was no other way."

"There are always other ways than killing and more killing!" I said, an anger of my own breaking through my tears. But he only shook his head somberly.

"No, Cousin. Sometimes there are not."

"And so now you want Her Majesty!"

"She is the ruler of the Two Lands, last bearer of the legitimate right to the Double Crown," he said simply. "I must see that she is safe."

"*I* will see that she is safe," I responded sharply. "I have received the charge of Aye that I do this and I shall obey him, *for I trust Aye.*"

"When did Aye speak to you?" he demanded.

"He sent me a message," I said, "and I replied that I would guard her

with my own life. And so I will, brave Cousin, so raise your spear and
stab me in the head or in the heart or wherever your great concern for
Kemet tells you to strike me if that is what you wish to do!" And fling-
ing off his hand, I stood up and pointed to the door. "Begone, Cousin! I
do not wish you to come here again without invitation. My niece
remains with me and I will yield her only to Aye. Work on the old man,
if you can! But I do not think you can. So go, Cousin. Just *go!*"

He, too, stood up, and for several moments our eyes locked furiously.
My tears were forgotten now, I seethed with an anger as great as his.
For a second I thought he might indeed raise his spear and run me
through: I wondered with a strangely distant curiosity whether anyone
would hear my dying scream. Then I found the words to vanquish him
. . . at least for the moment.

"In the name of Aye," I said, "who now truly rules the Two Lands,
go!"

"He does not rule the Two Lands!" he shouted. "I—"

"You do not, Cousin," I interrupted in a voice that somehow managed to be so cold and level that it stopped him in mid-utterance. *"She*
does, and through her, *he* does, because that is how we have decided it.
And unless you would slaughter us all this day in one great final blood-
drowning of the House of Thebes, *you will be gone from my sight before I call my guards and have them throw you out, O great Vizier of
Lower Kemet!"*

For another long and furious moment he glared at me; and then with
an inarticulate, strangled cry of rage he spun on his heel and left; and
womanlike, I sank back in my chair and gave way once more to tears,
trembling all over but with a resolve as hard as stone in my heart.

I know now why my cousin Horemheb wishes to gain possession of
Her Majesty, and I know now why we must truly be prepared to die so
that he may not have her. She is indeed the last bearer of the legitimate
right to the Double Crown. He thinks far ahead, does Horemheb, but
farther yet thinks the Queen-Princess Sitamon.

I returned to my room and resumed my patient vigil at my niece's
side, so tired that I could barely keep my eyes open. But I knew I must
keep them open until she awakened so that we might talk of this and
decide what to do.

Another hour has passed since then. Now at last she stirs and opens
her eyes. They wander, then focus: she knows me. Abruptly her eyes
fill with sadness and terror as she remembers.

"My husband!" she says, and begins to cry. Patiently I wait until she
remembers something else.

"And the Crown Prince?" she asks. And then we cry together as I give her, as kindly as I can, the second blow the gods have decreed she must accept.

We do not cry for long, however. Into her eyes there comes presently a cold and steady resolve. She is not Nefertiti's daughter for nothing. She smiles, wanly but gamely.

"I am hungry, Aunt," she says in a weak but steadily strengthening voice. "Have them feed me, and then we will plan what must be done."

"Yes, Niece," I agree thankfully. "He has not defeated us yet."

"No," she says, not bothering to ask who I mean because she knows. "Nor will he, while I am Queen and Lord of the Two Lands."

Aye

Two days have passed since the horror. Hatsuret's body has been burned on a traitor's pyre, his ashes thrown into the Nile. Neb-Kheperu-Ra lies in the House of Vitality, the long process of embalming begun. We have sixty-eight days in which to decide the kingdom.

It is only now that I have begun to think clearly again. I know that I must, for Kemet's sake, and I know that I will. I have suffered great regret, great anguish, great despair, in these past two days: many times I have not known whether I would come through with my sanity intact. It has been a terrible ordeal for a man of seventy-six. But I have survived and now it is time for me to move on, since someone must. More than ever, I believe, Aye is the only element of stability that stands between the Two Lands and chaos.

Ankhesenamon and Sitamon summoned me two hours ago to Sitamon's heavily guarded palace, to whose protection I have added substantial numbers of my own household troops. They told me of their plan, which is unknown in our tradition: but these are not traditional times. At first I demurred, aghast: never before has such a thing been done in all our history.

"I will not order you to support me, Grandfather," Her Majesty said, "but it will be much easier for me if you do."

I said I wanted to think and they were silent and let me think. Finally I began to understand their idea in all its clever ramifications. At first uncertainly, then wholeheartedly, I endorsed it and pledged my support. With her first genuinely happy smile since the horror, my granddaughter embraced me, called a scribe, dictated her will that I should hold the title, powers and privileges of Co-Regent until the burial of Neb-Kheperu-Ra and told me to publish it immediately from the Delta to Napata.

Scarcely had I returned to my chambers here in the main palace than my son came to me with his own ideas for the future. They were more conventional and in their vaulting ambition hostile to the careful compromise that must be worked out. They were also personally repugnant to me, as I know they would be to my granddaughter. He wished my support. I temporized, which angered him. He was angered even more when I told him I was Co-Regent, but there was, for the moment, nothing he could do. He went away planning, no doubt, further things.

Instantly I called in a team of scribes, dictated a proclamation announcing my appointment as Co-Regent, announcing that I will remain so until Tutankhamon is buried, announcing further that Her Majesty will not choose a husband to be successor to the King until that day. Then I dispatched many horsemen and many river craft (for I am taking no chances on how many Horemheb may be able to stop when he learns of their departure) to carry the proclamation throughout the Two Lands.

I then sent word to my granddaughter and Sitamon, repeating my pledge to co-operate fully with their plan and telling them that I have already, in fact, sent word to him who is the key to it, so that he may be swiftly on his way.

No doubt Horemheb will wish to kill us all when he learns of it. But I am still the Co-Regent Aye, last remaining link with the golden age of the Eighteenth Dynasty; and my niece and my granddaughter still guard between them the legitimate right to the Double Crown; and not even he, I think, would dare.

Amonemhet

Now all is sadness in the land of Kemet and all is fear here in my village of Hanis which I have led faithfully and well for His Majesty since the night five years ago when he made me Chief and Headman. I have sent him many gifts of food and grain, he has sent me and the village many gifts in return, doubling our gifts with his, protecting us from hunger and guarding us always, as his friends.

Now His Majesty lies dead in Thebes, scarce eighteen years of age; and it is given out that he was murdered by the priest Hatsuret, that evil one of Amon, "in a fit of madness that took him suddenly at the sight of His Majesty." We do not believe this in the village, nor is it believed by any of our friends in the other villages, nor, I think, by anyone in all the Two Lands. The rumor that runs along the Nile says he was murdered at the orders of his cousin the General Horemheb, that crafty, glittering one who stood beside him that night in all his array of pomp and power; and great is the fear that we feel now for what will happen next in the land of Kemet.

No one, however, knows the fear I know, because apparently I have been chosen to play a part in what is going on in Thebes. I do not know why, unless it be that I was His Majesty's friend and was known to those he trusted in the Great House as another he could trust. Never did I go to him with the ring he gave me to ask help, though he told me I might; and never did he send to me for help, though I would have left all else and gone to him at once had he so requested. But now his ring has been sent to me secretly together with four fine horses (hidden in the safe place we know on the edge of the Red Land), a bag of gold, two rolls of papyrus, and a letter from the Co-Regent Aye. Imagine me, the peasant Amonemhet, receiving a letter from the Co-Regent Aye!

I cannot read it, of course, but my oldest son, who is studying to be a scribe, says he will read it to me. So now I sit in my hut as in a daze, while before me the two rings gleam side by side on the table in the flickering light of the taper, and against the wall my wife and our other eight children huddle together and stare at me with frightened eyes while my oldest son clears his throat importantly and begins:

" 'The Co-Regent, Councilor and Divine Father-in-law Aye, in Thebes, to the Headman Amonemhet, in his village of Hanis, greetings. May all go well with you and with your village, which was ever dear to the heart of Neb-Kheperu-Ra, may he live forever young and happy in the afterworld!

" 'The Co-Regent Aye is empowered by Her Majesty Ankhesenamon, Queen and Lord of the Two Lands, to request the Headman Amonemhet as follows:

" 'For the love you bore His Majesty and the love and duty you bear Her Majesty, the Queen and Lord of the Two Lands, Her Majesty desires that you take these four horses and this bag of gold, together with one other you can trust to assist you, and ride secretly at once to

His Majesty Suppiluliumas, King of the Hittites. Go at your greatest haste for her sake. Take with you this ring of His Majesty which I send you, and show it to them that guard the borders of Suppiluliumas to prove that you truly come from the Great House. Present to them also the roll of papyrus bearing the ribbon of blue. This is Her Majesty's commission to you. It names you as her envoy and requests safe passage be given you to her royal brother, Suppiluliumas of the Hittites.

" 'When you have been brought safely to the presence of His Majesty Suppiluliumas—' "

"But there is war with the Hittites! What if his border guards take the ring and kill you and you never see the King!" my wife wails suddenly, and our five girls dutifully start mewling along with her like a nest of kittens.

"Silence!" I thunder, very loudly, for I, too, of course, am quite aware of all the possibilities: but they don't have to make me more frightened than I am, with their caterwauling. When silence has been restored I say as firmly as my trembling voice will allow, "Now be still and let our son proceed!"

" 'When you have been brought safely to the presence of His Majesty Suppiluliumas,' " he resumes, his voice also shaking with excitement and fear, but striving to maintain that grand detachment they teach him as a scribe, " 'do you deliver to him the second roll of papyrus, that which is bound by the ribbon of gold and sealed with Her Majesty's seal. Her Majesty wishes me to trust you by telling you that this is a letter from Her Majesty to King Suppiluliumas. You are not to read it, but you are to guard it with your life and see that it gets safely to his hands alone.

" 'Then do you wait upon King Suppiluliumas for his answer; and do you then return at your greatest speed to Thebes and deliver his answer directly to Her Majesty, who will be awaiting you anxiously each day and praying constantly to the gods for your safety.

" 'Her Majesty and I know this is a long, hard and dangerous journey, full of many perils for you. But we know of His Majesty's love for you, and yours for him, and we remember well that he often told us what a brave and loyal subject you are. Therefore Her Majesty trusts you with this great mission, upon which rests the fate of the kingdom of Kemet and the ancient glory of the Two Lands.

" 'Go with the gods, good Amonemhet! Go with our love! Perform your noble mission bravely and successfully, and Her Majesty and I will give great rewards to you and your family!

" 'This do we swear upon the name of him who loved you, faithful servant, and whom you loved, Neb-Kheperu-Ra Tutankhamon, he who has gone to live forever young and happy in the afterworld, forever and ever, for millions and millions of years!

" 'So speaks the Co-Regent Aye, in Thebes, to the Headman Amonemhet, in his village of Hanis.' "

My son stops reading and an awful silence falls upon us in our little hut (somewhat larger now, though—we have been able to add two more rooms as the family has grown. I have prospered as Headman of the village.) For a long time no one says anything; we just stare at one another and at the two gleaming rings, like birds hypnotized by the cobra. It is my son who finally speaks.

"Father!" he says, his eyes gleaming with excitement. "May I go with you?"

"No!" his mother wails. "You are the oldest, we need you to help us if—if—"

"Silence!" I thunder again, I am afraid not a very convincing thunder, for they all start shouting at once, even the baby beginning to scream in the midst of the chaos. *"Silence!"*

Eventually they obey me and I try to speak as calmly as possible, though I too am seized with fear, excitement and also—yes, because the honor and the danger and the challenge are all beginning to work a powerful magic upon me, I must admit it—with a sort of terrible eagerness.

"I will go," I announce flatly. My wife and the girls sob, the boys look solemn-eyed with fright. "Young Amonemhet"—I pause as they watch me fearfully, all save he, the scamp, who I can tell regards it now as a great lark—"will go with me because—*because,*" I go on firmly over my wife's anguished cry, "I am an ignorant, unlettered man, and he is young and clever and learning to be a scribe, and he can help me if I have to read anything. He can also help me with the border guards and, yes, even with His Majesty, King Suppiluliumas, if need be. His brother is almost fifteen and already a fine, sturdy lad. He will be a good guardian to you all if—if—"

I pause as my second son stands up, happy, proud and confident. I almost choke with the sudden emotion that sweeps me as I realize how much I love them all, and love my village, and how it may be that I will never see any of them again, for this is great danger into which we go.

"So let there be no more squalling about it. Wife! Children! Get food and water ready for us at once! We leave immediately on the mission of Her Majesty, in the memory of him who loved us and whom we loved, Neb-Kheperu-Ra Tutankhamon, Lord of the Two Lands, may he live forever young and happy in the afterworld, for millions and millions of years!"

And so presently we are on our way under cover of Nut the night, whose grasp still lies firm upon the land. It will be several hours yet before Ra's first faint fingers begin to mark the eastern sky.

We are muffled in heavy wraps against the winter cold. Our horses, loaded with water and food hidden under piles of straw, are muzzled so they will not whinny. In careful silence we skirt the village, keeping to the edge of the Red Land as we will do every night of our journey at other villages. During the days we will travel the public road like any other peasants bound on normal business, so ordinary in appearance that I think not even the great General Horemheb will find us among Kemet's millions. And when we get to the border of the Hittites—well, I will think about that later when we have to meet it. I am frightened enough as it is, right now.

But bound against my body I carry the rolls of papyrus, wrapped in old rags so they look like nothing; and on a leather thong around my neck the bag of gold and the ring, resting warm and snug against my chest; and in my mind's eye a small golden figure, head held high and eyes filled with love and kindness for me and my village, defying his evil cousin and the evil priest—bright and brave and young and good, as he will always live in our hearts, even as he lives forever in the afterworld.

And I know that I will give whatever is asked of me, even life itself, to help her whom he has left to keep the kingdom, if she can.

Ankhesenamon (Life, health, prosperity!)

My grandfather has chosen our messenger well, one for whom my husband always felt deep trust and fond regard. He is a simple man of absolute integrity, loyalty, honor, a peasant who can disappear among other peasants so that no one will notice his passage as he goes swiftly on my mission. I pray to the Aten and the other gods—not to Amon, for Amon, like Horemheb, would stop him if he knew—that he may come safely to Suppiluliumas, and that Suppiluliumas will swiftly respond.

I had never thought to do such a thing, never dreamed that I would find it necessary. But I did not dream of my husband's death either: and it came. Now if I would save the Two Lands from my grasping cousin I must do what I am doing. My aunt, my grandfather and I see no other way.

At first, of course, I saw nothing. When the soldier burst upon me with his dreadful news, I fainted as if I too had died. When I returned to the world I found my body tortured with pain, my child already on the way; I had no time or ability to think of anything else. Then that ended, I fell into a deep, unknowing sleep. When I awoke I remembered: dread, terror, grief for my gentle husband flooded my heart. Sitamon, trying her best to be kind, for she is very kind, told me of the death of the Crown Prince—who was not the Crown Prince at all, thanks to the vengeful gods. Again grief consumed my being, but not for long: again I had no time.

Now I carry in my heart a crying for Tutankhamon, our lost prince and our lost chances, which I shall never lose though I live to be the age of Aye; but there has been little or no time to give to that. I realized that I was sole ruler of the Two Lands, that I had to strengthen myself for many things: grief had to be sternly conquered and swiftly put aside. Now though I weep ritually each day for Pharaoh, I do not really cry inside: I suspect it will be a long while before I do. Someday I know I will, but not now. Now a cold resolve resides in my *ka* and my *ba,* in the very soul and essence of my being. I think only of my plan, and of what I shall do when it has been accomplished. First I shall take vengeance upon Horemheb. And then I shall restore to Kemet all that has been taken from her in these past sad years, using the power which will be fully mine when the answer comes from Suppiluliumas.

That I should appeal to him was Sitamon's idea to begin with, but I was quick to embrace it when I looked about the ruins of our House and saw what was left after the horror. The gods have always denied me sons: even to the end, I could bring forth only girls, all dead—all three dead, even the last, when the Good God and I wanted so desperately to have a son. Had I been so delivered, and had the child lived, I should have ruled the kingdom as Regent until he was old enough to take the throne, and no one, not even Horemheb, would have dared challenge me. But it was not to be. And so I am forced to do a desperate thing, strange and unknown to our history, but the only thing left for me to do.

My cousin has not yet approached me formally for my hand but it will come: it will come. Sitamon tells me so and logic tells me so. I am the surest road to the Double Crown for Horemheb. We think he will not dare try it until Pharaoh has gone beneath the ground, but surely he will try it then. And by then, I hope, I shall have answer for him.

Meanwhile I remain in Sitamon's palace and refuse to give him audience. Why should I? As surely as though he used the spear himself he killed the Living Horus, as he killed the Living Horus before him; and not I, nor anyone in Kemet, I believe, accepts his feeble tale of how he surprised Hatsuret at it and killed him to revenge the King. As Sitamon says, that is transparent nonsense. Why should I give audience to such an evil one?

I am ruler of the Two Lands and I am but a girl of twenty-two. Yet am I daughter of Nefertiti and Akhenaten, and strong must he be who bends to his will the child of that union. I may yet have to flee, he may yet kill me: but while I live, I, Ankhesenamon, Queen and Lord of the Two Lands, will do all I can to keep my kingdom safe from such a one. . . .

When we were young— *When we were young!* Were Tut and I ever young?—my husband and I dreamed always of the day when we might bring to Kemet the rule of love and universal happiness that my father and mother tried to create. They did many wrong things, particularly my father: this we can all see now. But at least their hearts were good, and they wanted only good for the Two Lands and our people. In the Aten, the Sole God, my father thought he had found the key; and this did my husband and I also believe, and now it is I who am left to believe it alone—I and to some degree my grandfather and Sitamon. All else has gone back to jealous Amon.

Yet even so there was no need to do what Horemheb has done. Tutankhamon and I were not going to overturn the kingdom again. We planned nothing violent, we, too, wanted only love. We did not even wish to turn again upon Amon, though Amon, we knew, was always ready to turn upon us. We simply wanted all the gods to live, like all our people, in love and harmony. We wanted to favor the Aten, as we intended to do in the mortuary temple which would be his symbol. Yet even there, particularly there, we would have given all other gods, including Amon, a rightful and worthy place.

Now it is not to be: Aye does not think it wise to proceed with the project at this time and I agree with him. Perhaps later, he says, and I think later I will hold him to it. But right now all energies and effort must be devoted to digging Tutankhamon's tomb in the Valley of the Kings. He had not ordered work begun on it himself, because he wished to construct a single huge family tomb in which all of us, my father and mother, the Great Wife, Beketaten, Smenkhkara, Merytaten, Meketaten, our other sisters, ourselves and all, might be gathered together to lie in one place. Thus Tutankhamon did not order his own individual tomb, and so now his friend Maya (who supervises the necropolis as his father Pani did before him), the sculptor Tuthmose and our good cousin Nakht-Min are supervising the crew that is working frantically night and day to dig his sepulcher. It will be hurried and cramped and small, but in it he will be buried with full honors and with all the riches of funerary furniture, jewels and equipment that befit a Good God. Because that is what he was, my earnest young uncle and husband, whom I came to love and whom my bad cousin has taken from me: he was a *Good* God, and he would have been a great one had he lived. But it was not to be. . . .

Meanwhile, loyal Amonemhet hurries on his way to Suppiluliumas, and in Sitamon's palace in Malkata I await his word. May the Aten grant him safe passage and a quick return.

The days pass slowly for me, but they pass. I am determined to do this thing and when I have, though I have husband, it will be I, Ankhesenamon, who truly rules the Two Lands. Then will there come finally to Kemet the love and peace and goodness that my father, my mother and my husband all failed to bring about.

Tradition—superstition—jealous gods—the ambitions of others—all defeated them.

I am determined they will not defeat Ankhesenamon, last direct descendant of the Eighteenth Dynasty, last member of the House of Thebes.

Suppiluliumas

I do not know what I have here. They appear to be two brave, if frightened, peasants; yet in the papyrus which I hold in my hand as they stand trembling before me I find that Her Majesty the Queen of Kemet (if so strange and unheard-of a document can indeed come from her, which I doubt—and yet who could forge such a thing, and for what reason?) refers to the older, obviously the father, as "the Lord Hanis." What does this mean? Is he in disguise as a peasant? Is he really one of her nobility, sent on mission to me? What does it mean? And why to me, who am at this very moment ravaging the borders of her collapsing empire and raiding deep into her territory? We are at war with one another, does she not know that? Can it be she has sent him and his son to sue for peace? And what of her husband Biphuria, whom they, I believe, call Tutankhamon? Does he know of this? Is it done with his knowledge, or is she appealing to me behind his back? Would she dare such treason? What use can I make of this to gain my own advantage? It is all very puzzling to me.

I peer down from my throne upon "the Lord Hanis," who stops trembling and straightens proudly beneath my glance; still obviously frightened, but brave, as I said: brave.

"You are the Lord Hanis?" I inquire in a mild tone of voice, for I do not wish to harm my chances of getting to the bottom of this by disturbing him even more.

"I am?" he responds blankly; and then, as his son nudges him sharply in the ribs, repeats hastily, "I am! Yes, Your Majesty, I *am!* Bringing to you the greetings of Her Majesty Ankhesenamon, Queen and Lord of the Two Lands, as you see, may it please Your Majesty."

"Oh, it pleases me," I agree, exchanging a wry glance with *my* son Mursil, who stands at my right hand, vainly trying to conceal his baffled amusement at this strange scene. "Welcome to the land of the Hittites, O Lord Hanis."

"It is my pleasure," he says loftily, "to be here. Particularly," he adds, "on the business of Her Majesty. Poor girl!"

" 'Poor girl'?" I echo sharply. "Why 'poor girl'?"

"You have not heard then," he says, suddenly cautious; and then, shrewdly (I still think he is a peasant, but no matter: I will play the game until I find out its meaning), "Perhaps it is in Her Majesty's letter."

"Perhaps it is," I agree, "but it is not in this one you have given me. This one says only that you are the Lord Hanis and his body servant" —at this "Lord Hanis" gives his son a superior glance and his son grins cheerfully and not, I am afraid, too respectfully, at his lordship—"and that I am to welcome you as though you were Her Majesty herself and receive from you her message. Why does this not come from His Majesty Biphuria? Do you carry another letter for me?"

"Perhaps," said Lord Hanis, and I say—suddenly stern, for I do not want him to think he is too clever—"Do not joke with me, Lord, or I shall have thy flesh served me on a platter, which you know we do here in the land of the Hittites."

(Of course any civilized man knows we do no such thing, but it has helped us militarily a good deal to spread such rumors. I can see "Lord Hanis" and his body servant have heard them, for both he and his son turn suddenly pale and very quiet.)

"Come now," I say more reasonably. "I have no intention of eating *you,* good Lord Hanis, or your son either. But if Her Majesty has sent me another letter, give it me at once. I still do not understand why it comes from her and not from His Majesty Biphuria."

"His Majesty is dead," "Lord Hanis" says, and suddenly his eyes fill with tears and he is quite genuinely overcome. I could wish I had a few subjects who loved me as he obviously loved Biphuria. "He has been foully murdered, and that is why I come to you from Her Majesty, I believe."

"You 'believe,'" I say sharply. "Has Her Majesty not told you?"

"Her Majesty," he says grandly, recovering a bit through his tears, "does not tell me *everything.*"

Now I know he is a peasant, but the knowledge, I must say, gives me a sudden respect for Her Majesty's cleverness. Apparently there is some desperate urgency about this message of hers, and who better to entrust it to than two peasants who can pass unseen through the millions that fill the world?

"Well, come, come," I say. "Give me her other letter, now. I would read it and try to untangle this mystery for myself."

He hesitates, although I am sure he has orders to hand it to me.

"Give it to His Majesty, Father!" his son says sharply; and with a strange reluctance, almost as though he were afraid of its contents, although of course he really has no idea what they are, he draws from beneath his rags a second papyrus. This one is tied with a ribbon of gold, and upon it in wax a royal seal, which I take to be Her Majesty's, for beneath it there is also stamped in small, as though from a signet ring, the cartouche of Biphuria.

"How do I know this really comes from Her Majesty?" I ask, and again from beneath his rags my strange "Lord Hanis" takes a leather thong on which hangs a small leather bag and a ring.

"See?" he says, holding the ring next the cartouche of Biphuria. "Are they not the same?"

Mursil and I inspect them carefully. I nod.

"Hide His Majesty's ring again, my lord," I advise. "We *do* have robbers here. . . . Well then, let me see what it says."

And while my lord, his son and Mursil all watch me closely I untie the ribbon of gold, break the wax seals, open Her Majesty's letter, start to read—and, with a startled gasp that makes them jump, almost drop it in amazement.

Never have I heard of such a thing! Never have I dreamed it possible! It is *im*possible! I do not believe it! Yet here it is, I give you my word as King of the Hittites, sixty years old and aware that the world is full of wonders, but by all the gods I know of anywhere, not full of *this* kind of wonder. It is absolutely unbelievable. Yet here it is:

"Her Majesty Ankhesenamon, Queen and Lord of the Two Lands, to His Majesty Suppiluliumas of the Hittites, greetings. May all go well with you, may all be well in your house and in your country. May we live in peace hereafter.

"I say to you this, O King of the Hittites:

"My husband Tutankhamon, whom you know as Biphuria, has been slain in a terrible way by those he trusted. All the land of Kemet grieves for him. I, his widow, grieve for him. Yet I must act, O mighty King, for you know who I am and the blood I bear. I carry the blood of the Living Horus, eternal and sacred in the eyes of Ra—"

(Sometimes their pretensions in the land of Kemet amuse the rest of us; but there it is. What does this strange girl want of me? I learn soon enough, and this is when I gasp.)

"—and in me there lies the right to the Double Crown. Lo, at this moment while my husband whom you call Biphuria lies dead, I am myself the Living Horus, for no other rules now in the land of Kemet save myself.

"I am, however, but a young woman, surrounded by few friends and many enemies. Though I could continue to rule alone, yet my heart does not desire it and my enemies would seek to deny it to me. I needs must have a husband to share with me my power. That is why I write you, O King of the Hittites. This is what I ask of you:

"My husband is dead and I have no son. People say that you have many sons. If you send me one of your sons he will become my husband, for it is repugnant to me to take one of my subjects to husband.

"Thus will your son be King and Pharaoh of Kemet at my side, O Suppiluliumas. Thus will one of your House be given an honor never before conferred upon one who was not of the land of Kemet. Thus will our two kingdoms be united so that we may live in peace together forever and ever, for millions and millions of years!

"Thus do I beseech thee, mighty King of the Hittites! Send me one of your sons that I may marry him and have his help in the rule of Kemet. Heed me speedily, for Biphuria will be buried soon and on that day I must have husband to rule with me as King and Pharaoh.

"Great will be the happiness in my heart, and great the happiness between our two countries, if you accept my offer of the Double Crown, O mighty King! You know such a thing has never been done before. You know I do not lie."

But that, I think as I finish reading and slowly roll up the papyrus again, tapping it thoughtfully against my palm as I muse, is exactly what I do not know. I still cannot grasp it. It is unbelievable.

"Mursil," I say finally, "take my Lord Hanis and his son to your private quarters, dine them and wine them well. Let them sleep fully overnight until they wish to rise, for I can see they are weary from their long journey. Then tomorrow escort them yourself to our borders and let them return to Her Majesty with word that I am considering her request."

"You do not accept it, then, Majesty?" my Lord Hanis inquires hesitantly, and I shake my head.

"Not yet," I say, "but tell Her Majesty I do not reject it either. Tell her I must think about it for a time. But tell her I shall act quickly when I do."

"But—" he says, face crestfallen, voice openly disappointed. His son tugs at his arm.

"We do not know the message, Father," he says. "Perhaps His Majesty needs time to think about it."

"His Majesty," I say dryly, "would not say he needs time if he does not need time. You have a bright lad there, my Lord Hanis. I am sure he is of great help to you in your village."

"Yes, Your Majesty," he says, his eyes humble as he acknowledges my perception of his true calling, but proud also in his son, which I like because I have many sons, and they are all fine lads and a great help to me, as his to him. "He *is* a bright lad, and we thank you for your patience with us in receiving the word of Her Majesty."

"Go, then, and rest well," I say, "and tomorrow begin your return to the Queen. Tell her as I say: I shall think and then I shall act. She will receive further word from me."

After Mursil has taken them away I sit for a long time, musing. Then I clap my hands and order the servant who comes to gather before me at once the great ones who form the council of my kingdom.

To them I read Her Majesty's letter. Their amazement is like to the heehawing of sixteen donkeys at feeding time.

"Since the most ancient times," I remind them, "such a thing has never happened before."

They nod and agree and babble on in noisy amazement. None, however, dares give me advice until, as usual, I myself decide what to do.

To my chamberlain, Hattu-Zittish, I say:

"Go to the land of Kemet, bring me information worthy of belief. They may try to deceive me. And as to the possibility that they may have a prince in spite of what she says, bring me back information worthy of belief."

And then I tell my generals that I will lead a campaign against

Kemet's city of Karkemish in Palestine. My spies inform me it is ill defended and I know I can conquer it easily. I shall keep the war going for a while as I probe Her Majesty's words, just in case it is all some kind of trick designed to lull me to sleep.

Ankhesenamon (Life, health, prosperity!)

He sends back words of disbelief to me. First I receive them from Hattu-Zittish, his ambassador, who speaks to no one else but whose presence, of course, instantly interests Horemheb. He tries to demand from Hattu-Zittish what it is all about. Hattu-Zittish is an old man like Aye, possessed of great dignity. He ignores Horemheb's noisy demands and will not tell him: he speaks only to me. He sees my situation and he leaves. I send no word by him, because Horemheb would somehow extract it from him, but I know he will report truly what he has seen.

Meanwhile there also come to me, in great secrecy, my faithful Amonemhet and his son, using their peasants' anonymity to slip within the palace walls. They also report His Majesty's words. To them I entrust my written reply, and once again they begin their long journey on my behalf. I love them for it and tell them that I have already sent gold to their village and special gifts to the family, and will send more upon their safe return.

Tutankhamon has been forty days in his bath of natron in the House of Vitality. Thirty remain before he goes beneath the ground. Sitamon and Aye counsel me not to worry, that all will come right. But time grows very short. How can I not worry?

Suppiluliumas

Before me again come my stout Lord Hanis and his sturdy son. Her letter this time is short and sharp:

"Her Majesty Ankhesenamon, Queen and Lord of the Two Lands, to Suppiluliumas, King of the Hittites: greetings.

"Why do you say, 'they are trying to deceive me'? If I had a son, should I write to a foreign country in a manner humiliating to me and to my country? You do not believe me and you even say so to me!

"He who was my husband is dead and I have no son. Should I then perhaps take one of my subjects and make of him my husband? I have written to no other country, I have written only to you.

"They say that you have many sons. Give me one of your sons and he will be my husband and lord of the land of Kemet.

"So say I, Ankhesenamon, to you, Suppiluliumas."

And so, in truth, said Hattu-Zittish just yesterday when he, too, returned from the land of Kemet. And so, having taken the city of Karkemish meanwhile, and being in a position to be generous, and seeing also, as she so cleverly said in her first letter, that together we may combine our two countries into one vast empire that will control the world from the Fourth Cataract of the Nile to the borders of the Mongols, I have decided to send my youngest son, Zannanza, who is fair and favored and whom I love, to wed this determined lady and through her become King and Pharaoh of the Two Lands—a thing I never thought would happen in all those millions and millions of years they are always talking about.

Horemheb

She has sent out mysterious packages from Sitamon's palace to some place along the river. We do not yet know where, though I have a hunch. Ramesses and his men are upon it and soon we will find out. Some instinct tells me that when we solve that mystery others will be solved as well.

Amonemhet

We have good news for Her Majesty and we sing as we leave the border of the Hittites and approach the border of our own land. Her prayer—which His Majesty kindly told us, saying, "I can trust two stout men of the land far better than I can my own nobles, my good Lord Hanis"—will be answered. The Prince Zannanza and his party will depart secretly for the Two Lands tomorrow and will arrive in Thebes two days before the Good God's burial. Thus all will be ready in good time for Her Majesty's wedding and an end once and for all to the evil ambitions of General Horemheb.

The Prince Zannanza and his party will come pretending to be peasants—as I have gone pretending to be the Lord Hanis! I, Amonemhet, "the Lord Hanis"! Yet I will be, and you may believe me or not when I tell you. You had better, because it is true. Her Majesty gave me her word on it just before we left this last time.

"My good Amonemhet," she said, looking more beautiful and determined than any lady I have ever seen, "dear to Neb-Kheperu-Ra and dear to me: when you return safely from my second mission, and when all is settled happily as I know it will be, I shall come to your village of Hanis and there my new husband and I will officially proclaim you what I have named you to His Majesty Suppiluliumas. You will truly be 'the Lord Hanis,' forever and ever, and your son and all your family will rise and go far in the service of our House. This do I pledge you on my word as Queen and Lord of the Two Lands."

So, you see, I *will* be Lord Hanis after all. Who would ever have dreamed such a thing of the peasant Amonemhet! If I had not been brave on the day His Majesty came to Hanis, and so begun his love for me, it would never have happened.

Beside me my son is singing, too, as we see in the distance the guard-house on the border of our beloved Two Lands. It will be good to be home, good to stop adventuring, even though "Lord Hanis" will come out of it. It has been very exciting for us to be involved with the great ones, but we will be quite content to return to our village and lead our simple lives—though now, I guess, this will not be possible since we will be called, as she has promised, to the service of Her Majesty in the

Great House. Well, I shall do my best as I always have, and so will the rest of my family. We are simple folk but sturdy. Kemet rests on the likes of us. We carry the burden and do not complain.

Now we are within hailing distance of the guardhouse. There seem to be more soldiers than usual there, but this does not alarm us. I shout and wave and they shout and wave back. It is not until we are almost upon them that I see that they are carrying bows and spears at the ready and that their greeting is not meant to be friendly.

"What is your name?" their captain demands in a loud voice.

Suddenly trembling inwardly, though I try to remain outwardly the dignified "Lord Hanis" I soon will be, I give him my title.

"Where have you been?" he goes on, still in the same loud voice, while the soldiers encircle us, and my son, suddenly terrified, clings tightly to my hand.

"On business to my brother in the Red Land," I say as calmly as I can.

"That is a lie!" he cries, and he gestures to the soldiers, who suddenly move to seize us both.

Desperately my son breaks away and begins to run. Before I can even cry out one of the soldiers draws his bow. An arrow flies. I do not know which is louder, my anguished cry or my son's dying scream. I see him fall—I struggle frantically but helplessly in my captors' arms—I begin to sob wildly as horror closes in upon me.

"Now, Peasant Amonemhet," the captain says in a terrible voice, "you have upon you a ring and we intend to find it; and you have been to certain places, and we intend to hear about them; and you know certain things, and we intend to learn them. Will you tell us of your own desire or shall we make you tell us, as we made your wife and family?"

The world is spinning away, spinning away, spinning away, very fast: soon, I know, it will be gone. But with one last ounce of strength I summon what I can from my parching mouth and spit it straight in his face.

He does not hit me—he is, I suppose, General Horemheb's man, and General Horemheb's men do things with grace, for they are soon to rule the world. He simply wipes his face very carefully with his robe. Then he gestures to my captors and suddenly I am pinned down spread-eagled on the ground. "Now," he says softly from somewhere above me as I feel the cold iron touch my private parts, "tell us things, Peasant Amonemhet."

I try as long and hard as I can not to, but I do: I do. And death, when it comes at last an hour (two hours? three?) after he has begun, is a blessing of the gods for the great Lord Hanis.

Aye

I have received a message from Suppiluliumas of the Hittites declaring war upon us for the murder of his son Prince Zannanza, surprised upon our borders on his way secretly to marry my granddaughter. I do not know how actively he will pursue this, or how far he will get into our territories, but I do not blame him: I do not blame him. Horemheb has volunteered to muster a force and go at once to meet him, which I suppose is right. Horemheb manages both effects and consequences, these days, and it is only fitting that he should now attempt to settle what he has begun. Also his work on this has given him an excuse to be absent from my nephew's burial, which has now started with ceremonies here at the temple of Karnak on a bright, sunny day, in the soft winds of spring. This saves us all from embarrassment, for I doubt that Her Majesty could look upon him without open hatred and I doubt that I could without showing the dismay and revulsion I feel.

As surely as Akhenaten ever did, Horemheb is moving away from us. I shall tell him so someday before I die. He deserves to be forced to face the parallel before it is too late: because sooner or later, somehow or other, he is going to take the Double Crown. It is still not clear to me how this will come about, particularly after this latest episode, but I have no doubt of it any longer. The will is too strong and the ambition too fierce. Having done so much, he will not blink at more. It will come.

It will not come, however, without one more struggle on the part of the Co-Regent Aye to preserve the order of Kemet. If it has to come, it will come in a legitimate and orderly way. I am as fiercely determined as he on this point. I will sacrifice myself, actually throw myself on his sword if need be, to stop him from stealing the throne and thus overturning the very *ka* and *ba,* the very soul and being, of the Two Lands.

At my granddaughter's suggestion I have recently added to my titles a new one which describes me as *"Aye, who is doing right."* And so I shall continue, as long as the gods give me breath. My son's will is fierce but mine, for all my seventy-five years, is still the fiercer. I do not know how events will proceed from this day forward, but I am not afraid to face them, whatever they may be. I shall do right until all ends for me, as I have all my life for Kemet. I cannot change now.

Not, mind you, that it will be easy, or that I see my way clear to save the land from being ravaged by Horemheb's ambition. But it will come to me, I think. I am giving it much thought, assisted by my grand-daughter, by Sitamon, and by my oldest living friend, Amonhotep, Son of Hapu, that faithful one who continues, like myself, to serve our House in his final years. We are discussing many plans, considering many possibilities. It is not only Horemheb who plots, these days. He is forcing us to plot, too.

Meanwhile, the ceremony proceeds. The beautiful coffin of solid gold, bearing the likeness of my dear nephew as he used to look before the years began to harry him, round-faced, youthful and serene, rests on the platform before us. At its head presides the new High Priest of Amon, one Nefer whom Horemheb and I selected together: probably our last compromise, as he wanted one loyal solely to himself, I wanted one beholden to no one in the Court. We settled finally on Nefer, hitherto a minor priest in the temple of Amon in Memphis; a weak and elderly man who will last my time. After that Horemheb may do as he pleases. But while I live Amon will not take sides in the struggle for the Double Crown.

Now Nefer intones the ancient phrases, goes through the ancient rit-ual. Tut, I think, would have liked to be buried in the Aten faith, but this I did not quite dare attempt. Had I done that, I too would have been guilty of upsetting the balance. I would also have invited reprisals from Amon and fierce demands from Horemheb, whom Amon would then support even more openly than his priests do now.

Instead I decided, with Her Majesty's approval, that we would use the rites of Amon. But in return for that concession we have made sure that in his tomb there have been placed the cross and flail of Aten, the throne of Aten, and many other things of Aten including wines from Aten's vineyards and scarves from the linen mills of Akhet-Aten marked "Year 8" and "Year 10" of Akhenaten's reign. And on Tut's shaven skull there rests a beaded uraeus with four raised cobra heads, each bearing the cartouches and titularies of the Sole God.

Into the tomb also, small, cramped and limited, prepared as it was in great haste because of the tragically sudden nature of his death, we have been forced to jumble together without much order some two thousand other things—some taken from the tombs in the Royal Wadi at Akhet-Aten (where I am preparing, as he wished, to move the bodies of my sister, Akhenaten, Nefertiti and the rest back here to lie beneath the Western Peak), some newly fashioned just for him—some taken from the storehouses that hold funerary items originally prepared for other royalty but for one reason or another never used. Included also are the mummified remains of two of their stillborn daughters, and mementos of two of the Queen's dead sisters, an ivory palette bearing the name of Merytaten and an inlaid box that once belonged to Nefer-neferura. Maya offered a miniature of the King on his bier, Nakht-Min five *ushabtis,* tiny figures of the King wearing various crowns. Smen-khkara's cartouche is on one of the coffins, and there is a gold pectoral that belonged to Akhenaten.

It is a great huddle of things, but all do suitable honor and will be ready for him when he awakens in the afterworld. We have made up in riches what we have lacked in space.

Nefer has finished now. The bearers lift the coffin to its baldachin, Akhesenamon, Sitamon and Mutnedjmet (and, of course, Ipy and Senna) begin their ritual wailing; Nakht-Min, Amonhotep, Son of Hapu, and I follow gravely after. We, too, are lifted into our baldachins. Slowly the procession begins.

Before the temple, through Thebes, along the east bank of the Nile, the vast crowds stand silently as we pass. Now and again someone bursts suddenly into a cry of sorrow, quite genuine; each time this happens a low, sympathetic groan passes from one end of the enormous crowd to the other. It is an eerie, yearning, wistful sound: they loved Neb-Kheperu-Ra, they wished him well, and now they fear a future without him.

Slowly, slowly, we pass through Thebes to the beat of muffled drums, the muted mourning of trumpets, the repeated regretful groanings of the people. Slowly we come to the landing stage, slowly we board the golden barge, slowly we set out across the Nile: once again, as so many times before, Hapi bears the burden of the House of Thebes.

The world is silent now; only the splash of oars breaks the stillness of the river. Behind on the east bank they watch us go, our gleaming banners fluttering at half mast in the gentle wind of spring, Ra high overhead as this, his latest Son, returns to him.

We reach the west bank, are greeted by more priests of Amon. We are taken to the necropolis, move slowly toward the entrance to the Valley of the Kings. We dismount from our baldachins. The other members of our family group utter their final ritual cries, fall to their knees, bow their heads in silent farewell: they will remain where they are until we return.

Her Majesty and I go on alone behind the group of slaves who bear the coffin high, and who later, after the final rites are done, will return with the priests to place the last objects in the tomb and close its doors forever.

We move on through the barren rocky gorge, through the naked earth as raw, harsh and savage as it has forever been and will forever be. We come to the entrance to the tomb, we pass within. We reach the antechamber, turn right to the crypt. Carefully the slaves lower the gold coffin into its two enormous interfitting sarcophagi, remove the lid so that we may look down upon the mummified remains of Tutankhamon, and withdraw. My granddaughter and I draw near. She begins to weep, softly and steadily in a release she has not until now, I suspect, been able to achieve. I weep with her, as deeply as she. I have loved all my nephews: and all have come, before their time, to this.

I am clad in the leopard skin of a high priest. At Ankhesenamon's insistence I have reserved for myself—and no one, not even Horemheb, has dared challenge it—the privilege of performing the rite of The-Opening-of-the-Mouth.

Normally this honor is reserved for the successor to the dead Pharaoh. With a startled glance at my granddaughter, standing head bowed, tears streaming down her cheeks, I suddenly think: *And perhaps it is this time, too. . . .*

This is the thought that comes, at last, to me.

But I remain impassive, though my heart surges wildly with many things. I take the iron prong, I lower it gently to touch the lips of the dead boy (I shall not make the mistake of poor Akhenaten with his father and actually damage the teeth in my strain and nervousness), I cry his name three times, and I say to him with a loving gentleness, because this is how I feel for him, though I know that duty forced me to be as responsible for his death as Horemheb, and the anguish and ordeal of that decision will eat forever at my heart:

"You live again, you live again forever! Here you are young once more forever!"

Silence answers, though we know that with my calling of his name and the utterance of these gentle words the long process of coming to life again in the eternal afterworld has begun for Neb-Kheperu-Ra.

Hardly able to see through her weeping, Ankhesenamon leans down and places a wreath of fresh flowers on the mummy.

In tears, clinging to one another, we turn away. Maya, superintendent of the necropolis and close friend of His Majesty, enters with priests of Amon as we leave, to supervise the final nesting of the coffin within its gilded sarcophagi, the final placing of the funerary furnishings, the final closing of the tomb.

For some minutes we stand and watch, still holding tightly to one another while Ra looks down upon the young girl and the old man who must decide the fate of the Two Lands. Was there ever such a pair had such a heavy task?

Presently the work is done. Maya and the priests bow to us and withdraw. Only we and the slaves remain.

The slaves who, unknown to them, will see no tomorrow, begin their labors to their characteristic low-voiced chant. Plaster slaps against the heavy stone doors. Hammers pound against their edges to seal them forever.

So we lay him to rest—slain by Hatsuret and Horemheb but slain even more, I think, by the beliefs of his brother, still doing their work from beyond the grave: my darling nephew Tutankhamon, that sweet and gentle boy—safe at last for all eternity—nevermore to be disturbed by hand or eye of mortal man.

We turn, eyes still blinded by tears, and walk slowly back toward the others.

I will permit myself this night to weep.

Then I must face my son.

Book V

TRIUMPH OF A GOD
1353–1339 B.C.

King of   Ser-Kheperu-Ra-   Son of the Sun,   Prince of Thebes,
the North   Setep-En-Ra,   HOREMHEB
and South,

Amonhotep, Son of Hapu

My old friend embarks today on a dangerous course—embarks, and
perhaps comes dead ashore, in more ways than one, should Horemheb
not be as taken by surprise as we estimate he will be.

Aye (Life, health, prosperity!)

He came to me yesterday morning, plaster scarcely twelve hours dry on
Pharaoh's tomb. He spoke without preliminary, almost without greeting
save a perfunctory "Good morning, Father"—not using my titles, not
honoring my age and dignities, consumed by the force of his own obsession and his certainty that he needs but state it with suitable impatience
for it all to come about at once as he desires.

Well: this did not impress the Co-Regent Aye, though I let him
think it did. I played for time, successfully, I think; and today he will
find out that things are not as he so arrogantly assumes them to be.

"Father," he said (he did not even bow: in his mind he was my superior already, I suppose), "I come to you on the business of Kemet."

"What else, my son?" I asked mildly, because it was obvious he was
under great tension and I thought mildness best. "There has been nothing before either of us but the business of Kemet, for many years. What
aspect of it concerns you now?"

"The marriage of Her Majesty to the new Living Horus."

"Oh? I did not know she had selected a new Living Horus."

"It would not matter if she had," he said contemptuously. "The
choice rests with you and me, in any event."

"Does it, my son?" I inquired dryly. "Does Her Majesty know this?"

"She will soon enough. What can she, a helpless girl, do about it? She
will take whom we give her, and he will be the King."

"I believe," I said slowly, "that she had the Prince Zannanza in mind, did she not? Strange that he should have died so tragically en route, thereby bringing us further troubles with Suppiluliumas."

"Suppiluliumas is a bag of wind," he said harshly. "I shall drive him out of Palestine in a month's time, have no doubt of that. He had no right to send Zannanza. No foreigner should wear the Double Crown. It was right that Zannanza should die."

"His father does not seem to think so," I remarked. "Nor, I believe, does Her Majesty."

"She is a helpless girl," he repeated in the same harsh tone. "What can she do about it? She will take whom we give her to be the Living Horus."

"You have someone in mind for this honor, Horemheb?"

I gave him a bland look, under which he fidgeted. But he was not, of course, to be deterred.

"Certainly," he said. "Myself."

Though my granddaughter and I had expected this ever since Tutankhamon's murder, the sheer effrontery of it took my breath away. Here it was at last, as blunt and direct and insistent as we had assumed it would be. Yet still, now that it had come, it was overwhelming.

But not overwhelming in the way he had hoped, my shrewd, ambitious son; because, after giving him stare for stare, I said quietly, "I should have to consult Her Majesty most carefully on that."

"You will not consult Her Majesty on it for one second!" he snapped. "I, the General Horemheb, who have at my back the army of the Two Lands, the priesthood of Amon, and the people of Kemet, tell you this is how it will be!"

"You have some of the army—"

"Ramesses has secured all but a few garrisons for me!"

"—and you may have the priesthood of Amon—"

"Nefer's age makes him timid. I have them."

"—but you do not have the people of the Two Lands. They hate and fear you, my poor Horemheb. They will never accept you as King."

"The people of Kemet," he grated with a furious anger, for here I had apparently touched him straight on the quick—I had not realized until that moment that Horemheb, too, feels the need of love and suffers for the lack of it—"will learn to love whoever wears the Double Crown as they have learned many times in the past. If they do not learn of their own will, they will be made to learn. Why do you think *their* disapproval would make me hesitate, Father?"

"I have never had to look at it that way myself," I said with a thoughtful air I knew would infuriate him further, but I did not care at that moment, I was beginning to become angry myself, "because the people have always loved me. I have never had to force them. And I think they give me, still, a strength you would be hard put to challenge."

He looked at me for a long moment before he spoke. When he did he was very quiet, very calm, very firm. I knew then that words would no longer stop Horemheb, and that now only the shrewdest measures could prevent him from working his will upon us all.

"I shall have her, Father," he said, "and I shall have the Double Crown. Now: will it be with your approval and support, or will Aye, too, go the way of Akhenaten, Nefertiti, Tutankhamon, your simple Amonemhet and Zannanza?"

"You are proud of such a catalogue?" I asked with a terrible bitterness, thinking him at that moment a monster: but his answer was not the answer of a monster, and almost persuaded me to give way.

"No, Father," he said quietly. "I am not proud of the things I have been driven to do for the sake of Kemet. But for the sake of Kemet I have done them; and for the sake of Kemet I will do whatever else is necessary. So concede me my motive, if you will."

"What are you?" I half whispered at last.

"I am he who loves the Two Lands," he said simply.

"There is not one you name," I said, "save Zannanza, who did not truly love the Two Lands. How could such horrors come from love?"

"I do not know, Father," he said, still quietly. "But they have." Abruptly his face changed, his voice changed. His patience, I could see, had run out. "Now," he said harshly, "let us have no more parley. I would have you send for Her Majesty, Father—*at once*—so that we can conclude this business and be married tomorrow at the temple of Karnak. At which time Amon will crown me Living Horus, King and Pharaoh of Kemet, as the gods have ordained from my earliest youth, when a seer once said to me: 'You will come to great power.'"

"I did not know of this seer!" I said in a last attempt to hold him off.

"I told no one," he said with a bitterly humorless little smile, "else I should never have lived to see the prophecy come true. Now send for my cousin, Father. We must settle this with no more talking."

Again our eyes held; until finally I said with a little nod and a weary sigh, "Very well. I shall go and talk to her."

"Call her here! At once!"

"My son," I said quietly, "all will be as you wish. But I must be allowed to speak to her privately first, to explain why this must be, to persuade her to accept it willingly and gracefully. Surely you do not wish to see hatred forever in the eyes of your wife when she looks at you! Surely even Horemheb needs at least a little love!"

Which, as I had shrewdly calculated, was the thing that did it. His face contorted with pain, his eyes actually filled for a moment with tears. He is driven, my son, driven: differently, but as surely, as his cousin Akhenaten.

He rubbed a hand savagely over his eyes. The pain was still in them as he said:

"Very well, Father. Go to her. Say it is only my great love for the Two Lands, and the need that all become calm and orderly again as soon as possible, that compels this. But tell her it must be. And I will send word at once to Karnak—in your name—telling them to make all ready for noon tomorrow, as we are agreed."

"I shall give you my seal upon it," I said and, taking a piece of papyrus hurriedly from my table, I wrote:

"To Nefer:

"Prepare all at once for the marriage tomorrow of Her Majesty Ankhesenamon, Queen and Lord of the Two Lands, to the new Living Horus, whom she will reveal to the world at that time, so that all may rejoice in his glory, and *ma'at* and order may come again to the kingdom."

And hurriedly stamped it with my seal and gave it him; and he went away, believing all would be as he said. And I went at once to the palace of Sitamon, stopping only to bring Amonhotep, Son of Hapu, along from the small adjoining house he now occupies as steward of her estates; and in Sitamon's private chamber, conferred with her, with him and with my granddaughter, who carries the blood of Ra and with it the legitimate right to the Double Crown. . . .

Now we are again at Karnak, and again the multitudes stretch out before us. Akhenaten began this practice of speaking directly to the people and allowing them to be witness to great events; Tutankhamon continued it; it seems good to me, too. Changes in the Great House come from within the Great House, but as I near the end of my life, and as I realize that the people's love is really all that is left to me, I have come to perceive that it can sometimes be of genuine assistance.

Her Majesty and I are gambling all that it will be, today.

Again the drums beat, the trumpets blare, the banners fly. All is pomp, bustle, excitement. Neb-Kheperu-Ra is in the afterworld: it is time to move on. The people are eager and excited, filled with shouts and cries and sudden explosions of impatient anticipation as they wait to learn who their new Living Horus will be. There is an uneasy, uncertain note in much of this: many fear Horemheb.

He sits beside me, face impassive, revealing nothing to the crowd. Only we in the Family, who know him so well, can see the grim little lines of satisfaction at the corners of his mouth. He will be a fierce Living Horus, my clever son. Somewhere far back, I think, he decided that he will never receive love and so he will not deign to give it. The brief tears of yesterday were only a moment's weakness. My son is himself again. In him Kemet will have a stern father and a hard and ruthless taskmaster. The people sense this and are afraid.

Nefer dodders forward (we have previously, of course, been inside the temple to offer our dutiful sacrifices to Amon), makes a few last ritual signs, chants a last blessing upon the Queen, dodders back to his seat.

Pale, tense but perfectly composed, as icily calm and very nearly as beautiful as her mother used to be, Ankhesenamon comes forward. Her voice trembles a little at first, then steadies. Clear and determined, it rings out across the crowd:

"Good people of Kemet! I, Ankhesenamon, Queen and Lord of the Two Lands, only existing bearer of the blood of Ra, sole remaining daughter of Nefer-Kheperu-Ra Akhenaten and Neferneferuaten Nefertiti"—beside me I can sense Horemheb grow tense, for this reference is not necessary, stirring as it does old ghosts and old pains, unless she has some purpose he cannot yet fathom—"have called you together this day to receive a new Living Horus to wear the Double Crown and sit beside me as I conduct my rule of our beloved Two Lands.

"Such a one must be wise in the ways of men and of government. Such a one must be shrewd in counsel, sound in advice, fierce in war, kind in peace. Such a one must be a worthy successor to Amonhotep III, Akhenaten, Smenkhkara, Tutankhamon"—and again Horemheb tenses—"life, health, prosperity to them all! Such a one must be pleasing to the gods, to great Amon, to great Aten"—again he stirs uneasily —"and to them all. Such a one must be pleasing also to me, who am the sole surviving daughter of Nefer-Kheperu-Ra Akhenaten and Neferneferuaten Nefertiti, sole existing bearer of the blood of Ra, sole bearer of the legitimate right to the Double Crown. . . ."

She pauses, takes a deep breath. We can see through her transparent skirt that her legs are trembling, but it does not affect her voice. Daughter of my daughter she is, and proud would be Nefertiti could she hear her now.

"Such a one," she says, and her voice rises slightly, "I have already beside me in the House of Thebes. He has served us long and faithfully and well for many years. The highest posts of government have been his, the highest honors have rightfully come his way. I have known him all my life and never found him wanting. Valiant in war"—I can sense Horemheb begin to relax a little—"gracious in peace, magnanimous and wise in all things, it pleases me to marry him and thus create him Living Horus to sit beside and help me as I rule.

"My people of Kemet, hail your new Pharaoh! Hail Aye, Living Horus, Great Bull, Lord of the Two Lands, King and Pharaoh of our dearly beloved Kingdom of Kemet! May he have life, health and prosperity forever and ever, for millions and millions of years!"

The world explodes in a roar of sound. I am conscious of a strangled cry beside me, of Horemheb half starting from his seat, of Nakht-Min at his side reaching up and pulling him down again, an instinctive movement that could cost him his life but will not if Ankhesenamon and I can prevent it, and we will. I am conscious of a strange, moaning sound, like unto the insane, coming from Horemheb's lips, drowned out, thank the gods, by the ecstatic roaring of the people. Then I rise and leave him and go forward to stand beside my granddaughter and the world seems to crack wide with sound, so much do they love me and so relieved are they that she has not chosen Horemheb.

When the sound dies at last she cries firmly:

"Nefer! Do you marry us in the rites of Amon! Now!"

We turn to look at him, and for a moment poor old Nefer appears absolutely paralyzed as he stares desperately first at us, then at Horemheb, then back at us. From the corner of my eye, for I would not deign to give him open look, I too steal a glance at Horemheb. He is deathly pale, completely immobilized. There is nothing, after all, that he can do, away from his troops and in front of this multitude. My granddaughter and I have gambled, and we have won.

"Nefer!" She cries again sharply and, like a child's toy suddenly yanked by a piece of string, he jerks hastily forward and takes up his position in front of us. Four of his priests automatically attend him, two on each side. In a shaky voice—so low that Her Majesty orders "Louder!" and he obeys enough to reach the front ranks, so that we have sufficient witnesses—he begins the ceremonies.

Ten minutes later I am the Living Horus, Aye, thirteenth King and Pharaoh of the Eighteenth Dynasty to rule over the land of Kemet. . . .

Now we parade triumphantly through Thebes and everywhere we are greeted with wildest adoration. Ankhesenamon smiles proudly and waves: each wave produces a new surge of loyalty and love. Now and again she turns and smiles at me: the crowd's response grows even louder. We congratulate one another that we have done the right thing. My granddaughter has served the kingdom well with her eager acceptance of my idea—and I have received at last my deserved reward for more than fifty years of selfless service to the Double Crown.

Aye the survivor, Aye the balance wheel, has saved the House of Thebes this one last, this most important, time.

We do not fear my son's reaction, violent though he might wish it to be. He will accept this as he must, for he has no choice. If he were to try to overturn us by force now I do truly believe that for the first time in all our two millennia the people would rise and kill him for it. He knows this, and so presently, for he has much sense and is no fool, he will work with us as we wish him to do, quieting the mad ambition to which he has increasingly devoted his life.

Tomorrow we leave for almost deserted Akhet-Aten to repeat the ceremonies at the temple of the Aten, and then to Memphis where we will repeat them in the temples of Amon and of Ptah. Then we will return here and I shall plunge back happily into the never ending duty of government.

I am, after all, only seventy-five. I feel I have much time left. I feel the gods have much remaining for the Pharaoh Aye to do. . . .

Sitamon

"I feel I have much time left," he used to say to me often in his early days upon the golden throne. "I feel the gods have much remaining left for me to do." Yet Pharaoh is nearing his eightieth year, the end obviously approaches, and little that he planned has come to pass.

Horemheb, moreover, is still here. He has not gone away. He has never abandoned his ambition—his father was wishful to think he would—and his demands become more insistent every day. The latest is this demand for marriage and co-regency, which has brought us all together again in family council—the last council, I think, that the House of Thebes will ever hold . . . because soon I think the House of Aye will fully succeed at last . . . and after that, unless I miss my guess— which I seldom do—the House of Ramesses.

My uncle likes to think that it was he who suggested that Ankhesenamon marry him and thus thwart Horemheb. I have never argued it with him, but it was I who proposed it in that hurried meeting after Tut was buried. We were filled that night with furious stratagems, desperate proposals, wild starts and stops; my cousin seemed to loom like some gigantic monster just across the river, waiting to consume us all. Perhaps he was. At any rate, when we were exhausted at last by all our futile thrashings about, I looked straight at Aye and said, "There is, of course, one man she might marry whose selection would settle it all."

There was silence for a moment. Ankhesenamon was the first to grasp my meaning. "Yes!" she cried happily. "That would be it!" Then of course there was a great babble, Aye protesting, Ankhesenamon, Amonhotep, Son of Hapu, and I insisting, all of us getting more and more excited, all of us drinking much wine to celebrate, even Aye for once indulging (for we all thought we had killed the monster), so that presently it was forgotten who had really offered the idea in the first place. But I did not forget, because for me it was the settling of an old score. We were lovers for twenty years, he gave me three children whom I had to dispose of because we could not be married while my father lived; then when he could marry me he refused and went off in pursuit of other ambitions. So much, I thought that night, for *you,* my fine Horemheb, and so much for your ambitions!

But this was reckoning, of course, without Horemheb—and without the simple chances of life, which so often confound us all. To begin with, of course, there was never any question that Pharaoh and the Queen would live together as man and wife. My uncle, after all, was seventy-five then, and still devoted to gentle Tey, who over the years has been such a wonderful mother and friend to Nefertiti, to Horemheb and Nakht-Min, to me, to Akhenaten, to all of us. In official duties and on ceremonial occasions she has been his secondary Queen, because of course Ankhesenamon has the blood; but in his tomb and in other personal representations he has continued to present her as his consort. And to this Ankhesenamon, being as sensible and as practical as her mother (thank the gods the erratic heart of my poor brother did not find its way into the body of his only surviving daughter!), has readily agreed, for she too loves Tey. She did ask rather wryly once, "Grandfather, should you not give me *something* to signify this union blessed by all the gods?" So with a smile he said yes and within a week presented her with a beautiful ring bearing both their cartouches, which she constantly wears, as she told me once, "to symbolize my happily married state." But aside from this, and their public appearances for government and ceremonies, they lead separate lives—though, with her mother's determination and her father's stubbornness, she has tried repeatedly to have children from another source who could be presented to the people as children of Aye, and so be accepted as legitimate heirs who might thus revive and perpetuate our dwindling, unhappy House.

For this honor, after long talks with Pharaoh and with me, she chose Nakht-Min. He and Mutnedjmet, born within a year of one another to

Aye and Tey, are approaching middle age (how fast the years sweep over, how fast we are covered by time as by the whispering, ceaseless sands of the Red Land!) but both are still handsome and well favored. Mutnedjmet grows, if possible, even more eccentric as she ages. She still does much good among the people with many charitable ventures, and she is still much loved; but Ipy and Senna, who are also aging but somehow seem perversely eternal, continue to hop and cackle by her side, and the people still have much affectionate fun with this. Nakht-Min, on the other hand, continues with quiet dignity to serve the kingdom well as Vizier of Upper Kemet, general of the army, scribe, confidant and adviser to his father, firm friend to Her Majesty.

Therefore when she summoned him, two months after she married Aye, and told him what she had in mind, he was perfectly willing to comply—particularly since he is very fond of her, as she of him, and no fonder of his older brother than the rest of us. Indeed, he has put his faith in Aye and Ankhesenamon to protect him, and Aye and Ankhesenamon have; but this is another question that remains unresolved. I am sure Horemheb has plans for that, too, as he always does for everything. He is not Aye's son for nothing. (The generations repeat their patterns in all of us. I think I am like my mother, Queen Tiye: at least I hope I have shown something of her strength and her loyalty to Kemet. I have tried.)

Nakht-Min, in any event, has been willing; and three times in these past four years Ankhesenamon has secretly become pregnant by him— only to see, each time, her child born dead. The event has been even sadder because twice they have been boys: she could have given the Two Lands a Crown Prince at last. But the curse of poor Akhenaten still seems to hold; though now, I believe, she is pregnant again and we must pray once more for a son who will live . . . if Aye lives.

But Aye, I think—and I think he thinks—is not going to live much longer. He is failing very noticeably now. His eyesight is almost gone, he has difficulty hearing, he moves very slowly and always with a cane and on the arm of a page. There are many days when he does not rise from bed, when Ankhesenamon must come to him to secure his seal on state papers. Sometimes he scarcely seems to know she is there. Increasingly in this past year she has made decisions alone and Tey has guided Aye's trembling hand to make the necessary marks in the proper places. It is all very sad; and will not, I believe, last much longer.

He has built his mortuary temple on the west bank near my father's. He has built a rock chapel to Min and other local gods at his family seat of Akhmim. He encouraged Horemheb to mount a counteroffensive against Suppiluliumas which drove him back a bit in Palestine, though our frontiers continue in sad disrepair all through the region where we once could walk unchallenged. He has brought all the Akhet-Aten bodies save those of Akhenaten and Nefertiti back to lie beneath the Western Peak; and they will soon be also returned, now that we think the bitter passions they aroused have finally died, so that they, too, may safely rejoin our ancestors. And he has continued to lend his enormous prestige to Ankhesenamon's determination to keep the Aten officially equal to Amon, so that their uneasy balance of tension has been maintained in reasonable degree except here in Thebes where Amon again reigns supreme.

And this, in truth, is about all that one can say of the rule of Aye, who came, at my suggestion, almost too late to the power he had earned through all his long and frequently tormented years of duty and devotion to the good of the Two Lands.

Now as he comes to die—for this he is doing, there is no point in closing our eyes to it—Horemheb again seeks to take the Double Crown. And this time, I think, there will be no stopping him. He has been patient these past four years because he has had to be, but it has not been easy for him. Now at sixty there is nothing to stand in his way. He will be King and Pharaoh at last, my poor Horemheb—for whom I use that adjective as automatically as I do for poor Akhenaten. I wonder if the Double Crown will make him any happier than it did my brother?

I find that I am the first to arrive at my uncle's chambers. He has been in bed these past three days, and it is Tey who ushers me in, with finger on lips. Though we are very quiet, some signal transmits itself to the fading brain: he rouses, his eyes open, he peers up at me. I lean to kiss his forehead, he manages a feeble smile.

"Well, Niece," he whispers, "so we all meet again, for one last time."

"You must not say that, Son of the Sun," I tell him firmly. "We shall meet many times again."

"In the afterworld, dear Niece," he whispers with the trace of a smile. "In the afterworld. . . . Tey, help me. I must rise and be seated on my throne for them."

She starts to protest and I say quickly, "Nonsense, Majesty, you stay where you are. We will not respect you less if you lie abed where you will be comfortable."

"*One* might," he says with a ghost of a laugh. "But he would rather see me in bed, anyway. It will make him happier."

"Well, be that as it may," I say, "you stay where you are. We will handle *him*."

"Can anyone, now?" he asks, again with the ghost of a laugh. "It is getting less easy all the time."

And as the others arrive, very shortly thereafter, it is apparent that he will not be easy to handle this night, at all. First comes Ankhesenamon, looking tense and determined, followed by Nakht-Min, doing his best to appear unconcerned; Amonhotep, Son of Hapu, stronger than His Majesty but also becoming quite frail; and then Horemheb and Mutnedjmet, Ipy and Senna, all of whom seem to have reached the door at the same moment. This leads to immediate friction.

"You are in our way," Mutnedjmet says—flatly, for, like Nakht-Min, it has been years since she liked or trusted her half brother.

" 'Our' way?" he snaps angrily. "Must you have those two hobgoblins with you cackling like geese wherever you go?"

"Yes," she says coolly, while Ipy and Senna cling to her legs, peering up at him with a deliberately exaggerated fear that only makes him angrier. There are times when neither she nor they show any sense, and this is one of them.

"Mutnedjmet," I intervene sharply while Aye looks about in a half-bewildered way as old, sick people do, "this is a private conference with Their Majesties. Those two *will not* be permitted in here. You will remove them *at once.*"

"Well—" she begins, still defiantly, trying to decide whether to continue annoying Horemheb, whom she despises, or obey me, whom she likes and respects; while behind her back Ipy and Senna stick out their tongues at me and I come very close to striding over and slapping their silly little faces. But fortunately their mistress decides that appeasing me is more important. She leans down, whispers in their ears, and with a last insolent look at me and a leer at him they go scurrying away down the corridor—cackling like geese, exactly as he says.

"Now, Majesties," he says, breathing hard, "perhaps we can have a little sense here and get on with our business. Father," he adds almost perfunctorily, going over to lift Aye's trembling hand and kiss it, "how are you?"

"I hear them calling me from the Peak of the West," Pharaoh whispers with a wry expression, "but I am not in quite such a hurry to answer as you would have me, my son."

"I am in no hurry," he says with a scowl that does not conceal the flush that rises in his face—can there be some shame left in Horemheb? "I wish only Your Majesty's continued health and well-being, Son of the Sun."

"Yes," Aye whispers, "I know." He starts to say something else, then seems to lose the thread of it. Ankhesenamon surveys Horemheb calmly and asks:

"What would you with us, Cousin?"

"May we sit?" he asks.

"There are chairs," she says indifferently: so he decides to remain standing. So do the rest of us, save for Tey, who seats herself on the bed beside Aye and tenderly takes his hand.

"I have made no secret of it," he says bluntly. "I think it time that I be made Co-Regent to aid His Majesty, who we all pray will be with us long but who nonetheless might welcome some assistance in his burdensome duties; and I would marry."

"Why must you come to us about marriage?" Her Majesty asks, carefully avoiding the other issue for the moment. "You may marry whom you please, as far as we are concerned."

"I think not," he says, "for the one I would marry is in this room."

"But I am married to His Majesty!" she cries indignantly, even as I also cry out, with all the bitterness of the long, scorned years. "Even so, I would not have you were you the last peasant left in Kemet!"

"What about you, Lady?" he inquires, ignoring us as we stand with mouths open in amazement, realizing the audacity of his thinking—or the farseeing nature of his plan, depending on how you look at it.

Her face is a study in many things—first disbelief, then shock, then repugnance, then scorn, then a sort of wild, fey hilarity. It is finally the scorn and the hilarity that struggle for victory on Mutnedjmet's face, and eventually the scorn wins out.

"You do me great honor, Brother," she says with scathing sarcasm, "and I must remember to sacrifice to all the gods, particularly to those who may presently take our father, so that I may thank them suitably for it. But having done so, I must tell them that I have to decline with thanks. I am entirely unworthy of so great a position."

"It *will* be great," he agrees icily, "and you *will* be unworthy of it. However, I am offering it to you. You would be fool indeed not to take it."

"*She* has the blood," she says, gesturing toward Ankhesenamon, who has turned paled with both fear and anger as the full impact of his audacity sinks in.

"*He* is the Living Horus," he says, pointing to their father. "Therefore, dear Sister, the blood has passed to you." He turns sharply upon Ankhesenamon, so sharply that she jumps. "Is that not so, Majesty?"

"If I have children—" she begins, breathless with shock and anger, while Nakht-Min, fortunately standing at the side where Horemheb does not see his expression, struggles to remain impassive.

"If you do, they will be no children of his. Is that not so?"

"Go!" she cries, drawing herself to her full height. *"Go!"*

"No, I shall not go," he says quietly, "nor will anyone here be able to force me to. We will have this out now, for I have waited long and the years will soon be no kinder to me than they are to him. Father!" he says loudly, turning to Aye, who huddles back against Tey, his bewildered old eyes now wide with fear. "Give me your blessing to marry my sister! And let me help you as Co-Regent with all those duties you are no longer able to perform yourself!"

It is then so hushed in the room that it seems we hardly breathe; yet that tortured, worried, gasping sound must be coming from somewhere, and I suppose it is from all of us, though we are concentrating so hard upon His Majesty that we are hardly conscious of it.

For a long time Aye looks from face to face. At first he continues to seem bewildered and afraid; then gradually his eyes clear, his expression changes, a strange, almost unearthly calm and serenity begin to surround him. His mind is lucid and he has made it up. Even before he speaks, I for one know what he will say. Aye the survivor, the balance wheel and our rock, is about to perform his last service for the Two Lands.

"You will forgive me, Granddaughter," he whispers carefully, ignoring her sudden anguished cry of protest, "if I say to you that what he says makes much sense for Kemet. You will forgive me if I admit what he tells me, and what the gods also tell me every waking moment of every day—that soon I will awake no longer, but will go to lie with the others beneath the Western Peak. Sixty years and more have I served this House, this Dynasty, this kingdom; but now the gods beckon me and I can do no more. Soon, very soon, I must respond and go with them. What, then, of our beloved kingdom?

"It is true, my dearest granddaughter, that you have not yet had children for Kemet, and are very like not to before I go. It is true that this means that the legitimate right to the Double Crown will very soon pass to Mutnedjmet. It is true that what he has wanted for so long will very soon come to pass: the gods, too, wish Horemheb to be the Living Horus. And so he will be."

Again Ankhesenamon cries, *"No!"* Horemheb gives her a single sharp look, then his face becomes impassive. He can afford to be magnanimous in this moment of triumph, but I do not think he will be magnanimous for long. Already my mind is racing with what I must do.

"Therefore," Aye goes on, his voice becoming even more of a whisper as he imposes this long but necessary strain upon it, "it is fitting that I should now appoint him Co-Regent, which I hereby do and charge you all to proclaim it and honor it; and it is fitting that he should be married to his sister so that his right to the throne can never be challenged. To do else would be to bring new troubles and uncertainties to Kemet—and Kemet," he says with a sudden heavy sigh, "has had troubles and uncertainties enough in these last unhappy years. This is the only way to make the transition easy and secure for the Two Lands; and now, as always, that is my only concern."

He pauses and looks at Horemheb, a long, searching look that Horemheb returns unflinching.

"My son," he says, "you soon will have what you have long wanted. There will be no need for you to be harsh or cruel or unkind to anyone. That is all over now: let the past go. This kindgom needs charity and generosity and a loving hand from Pharaoh. I charge you to give it these, for soon you will have absolute power and no one can restrain you. Let Horemheb not be remembered as a vengeful man: let him be remembered as a Good God who sought always to bring peace and happiness to the Two Lands."

"So have I always sought to do, Father," Horemheb says, very low— but this time Aye seems to hear very well. Again he holds him in a long and searching look.

"So do you do hereafter!" he says, and for all that it is a whisper, it is an order: though it comes from a dying man and will be obeyed or ignored as his heir may choose.

"Daughter," he says to Mutnedjmet, whose face wears now a defiant and obstinate pout, "I wish you to be married to your brother at once. You may live as you please thereafter, and no doubt"—the last faint ghost of a smile touches his lips—"and no doubt you will. But you are to go through the ceremonies and confer upon him the legitimate right to the Double Crown so the people may know that he is their true and lawful ruler. This you will do this night, so that I may know it has been done."

Again there is a silence while she looks first at him, then at Horemheb, then back to him, then back to Horemheb. Finally, fixing her glance firmly on her brother, she says calmly:

"Very well, Father. For you, for Kemet, I shall do it: not for him." Her voice fills with a savage sarcasm. "As for you, Brother! See to it that you do not come near me after our ceremony, ever again, because those two little guardians you despise so much are always at my door. They do truly cackle like geese, as you say. That is why they have always been there and always will be—to protect me from the various madnesses of the House of Thebes. They will cackle if you come for me. And I shall also have always by my side armed guards, loyal only to me, for I shall constantly re-examine them to be sure that they are. And they will strike you dead, be you Living Horus or no that day. So beware, Brother. Keep far from me!"

I think for a second that he would like to strike *her* dead right there; but the stakes are too high and he cannot. I doubt, in fact, that he ever will. They are two of a kind. I suspect that Mutnedjmet, Ipy and Senna will live out their lives quite happily and safely, coming and going as they please, to the eternal annoyance and eternal frustration of the mighty Living Horus.

Now Aye falters, his eyes begin to acquire again their wandering look; the long strain is starting to tell. He sighs heavily.

"Go now," he whispers. "Granddaughter, give me a last kiss, for I may not see you again. I commend you to your cousin, who will be kind and gentle to you, for now he has no need to be other."

On that point we all have reservations; so after she has kissed him, weeping bitterly, and after Nakht-Min, Mutnedjmet and I have left Horemheb to talk a little longer with one who has very evidently forgotten us by the time we reach the door, I begin at once upon the plan I have devised while Pharaoh has been talking. Not to my surprise, Mutnedjmet joins in entirely.

"Call on me for anything," she whispers fiercely as the four of us stand for a moment in the corridor, clustered together away from the guards, Ankhesenamon still weeping as though her heart would break, as perhaps it finally has. "I shall always help. Sitamon—?"

"Yes," I whisper back. "I am prepared. Come, Ankhesenamon! Come, Nakht-Min! He may die tonight. Come with me!"

As I reach the far end of the corridor Pharaoh's door opens again and Horemheb comes out. Mutnedjmet has gone, Ankhesenamon and Nakht-Min have hurried ahead of me out of sight. Only he and I can see one another. We both stop. We exchange a long, unyielding stare. Neither of us gives ground. We are truly enemies now, though I, like Mutnedjmet, know I am safe. So are those I have taken under my care, if there is but time for my plan to succeed.

I incline my head, a slight, ironic bow. He makes no response. I leave him staring there, turn on my heel and hurry away. He does not follow for the moment, but he will: he will. He is the son of Aye, is Horemheb, and very, very thorough. I have until morning to do what I intend. It may just be enough.

Ankhesenamon

Ahead of us in her beautiful gilded barge goes the Queen-Princess Sitamon, traveling to visit her estates in the Delta. Following in this second barge come her household servants. Disguised among them are her
new serving maid, Mutnofret, and the latest addition to her household
guard, Seneptah. Them she intends to leave at her favorite farm near
Tanis, where, she tells them, they will find an old friend she has hidden
and protected all these years, with whom they will be safe to live out
their lives, as they wish to do, together.

Kia! *Dear Kia!* Nakht-Min and I had thought her dead these many
years. And all the time my aunt was hiding her near Tanis and keeping
her safe, as now she will keep us safe! It is but one more of the many
great kindnesses she has performed in this world: surely she will live
happily forever in the afterworld! She tells us she will visit us quite
often in Tanis. We hope so, for it will be a strange life for us at best;
bearable, with Kia, but not really happy without Sitamon—and Mutnedjmet, who tells us she, too, will visit as often as she can.

When we left my grandfather's room that night a week ago, both
Nakht-Min and I thought we would be dead within a day. I do not believe Horemheb knows that I am pregnant, but the possibility that I
could be would have been a constant threat to him: he would have had
to kill me or he never would have rested easy on the throne. There
would always be the chance of a counterclaimant; and if Horemheb is
the kind of Pharaoh we all think he is going to be, a counterclaimant
would find much support among the people and even the priesthood—
because if Amon thinks he is not going to feel a strong hand, too,
Amon is mistaken. The Two Lands are in for cold times as the new
Living Horus seeks to bring all once more within the iron bounds of
ma'at—as he sees it; and order—as he sees it; and justice—as he sees
it. His brother and I are well out of it to be hidden away in Tanis. Even
if he let us live at Court, it would be a cheerless world.

Yet even knowing this, it has not, of course, been easy to embark
upon our new lives. I did not mind giving up my fine robes and dresses,
but the jewels—the jewels! Ah, it hurt me to abandon such lovely
things! But Sitamon was right: a serving maid with jewels would arouse

impossible suspicion. Better to leave them for Horemheb to find and seize when he learned from Sitamon that we had "fled together in terror into the Red Land, not even taking food or water, so great was their fear of your vengeance. So let the Red Land claim them: they will not live beyond two days in that empty desolation!" I have kept only a small gold scarab ring that belonged to my mother, and it I do not wear upon my hand but upon a hidden chain beneath my peasant dress. And Nakht-Min has stripped himself of all possessions, too, keeping only a small jewel-encrusted dagger to remind him of past position, which he, too, keeps hidden beneath his peasant robe.

We miss the finery, we miss the power, we miss being waited upon. It is strange to know that great ministers of state will nevermore attend us, that we will never again be able to clap hands and have a dozen servants come running, to realize that we have no power at all and that now it is we who must come running, at least for show in the presence of others, when Sitamon or someone else of rank claps hands. It is strange not to have our food prepared and brought, our beds made soft and comfortable, our every wish attended instantly by a hundred willing souls whose only duty in the world was to make us content. It is strange to realize that armed guards no longer stand always between us and the unexpected, the threatening, the dangerous—to know that we are now alone and unprotected and, save of course for such safeguards as Sitamon can provide us, vulnerable at any time to the chance of exposure, capture, torture and inevitable death.

But I am not the daughter of Nefertiti and Akhenaten, and he the son of Aye and Tey, for nothing. We have chosen to live, and if possible to have our child live (and the others we intend to have, because we have decided that we are married now in fact if not in ceremony), and for that we have had to make our bargain. We are blessed beyond all measure that we have so kind and loving a friend as Sitamon to assist us, and nothing we can ever do for her as "serving maid" and "member of the guard at Her Majesty's farm at Tanis" can repay her for that.

So it is with a good heart and in good spirits that the last rightful heiress of the House of Thebes has passed forever from the sight of Kemet, and that, with an equal cheerfulness, the Vizier of Upper Kemet has vanished "in terror into the Red Land." We have each other, we have our coming child and others yet to come, we have the love of Sitamon, Kia and Mutnedjmet, we are safe from Horemheb. There is much for which to thank the gods. All of the gods—and the Sole God, who still, I believe, watches over me.

Two days ago, near noon, we passed the village of Hanis and I wept for dear loyal Amonemhet and his simple family: I never thought to bring upon them such horror and I shall remember and honor them always. And now today, just ahead of the great golden barge that precedes us, I see the river beginning to swing slowly to the east, and I know that I am come again to Akhet-Aten.

As if at a signal, the others sense it too. The oarsmen have been singing: they stop. The servants have been chattering: they stop. Only the splash of the oars, the lazy snap of a sail, the cry of Thoth the ibis along the shores, break the silence. Slowly we glide on, the river widens, the great bend appears. To my right gleam the fading towers, the crumbling palaces, the ruined houses, of my father's capital.

Do I see you once again, dear ghosts? I think I do. I see you, Mother, I see you, Father, I see you, Great Wife and easygoing, simple Smenkhkara, I see you, dear brave Tutankhamon bright and golden in sun! I see you, all our happy times of yesterday when we all were young and happy and the Sole God ruled!

Where did you make your mistake, Father? What happened to you, Mother? We lived in love, we wanted only love! Where did it all vanish? Why did it all go wrong?

Slowly we glide on, past the empty temples, the gaping palaces, the deserted houses. On the royal landing stage, rotting away and half sagging in the water, a single peasant with a donkey stands and waves at us. Through my tears I wave back. Your Queen is passing, last citizen of Akhet-Aten! Say farewell to all that here was bright and lovely, for it will not come again. Say farewell! Say farewell!

Blindly I turn and bury my face against Nakht-Min's loving and protective chest. He soothes me, his hand brushing tenderly across my brow.

"Do not look back any more," he whispers. "Do not look back."

Even if I would, my tears are so heavy that I could not see.

Where did it all vanish, where did it all go? What went wrong, Father? What went wrong, Mother? What happened to our dream?

Ramesses

What happened to their dream? I stand here with Pharaoh, both of us beginning to slow and stumble as we near our seventieth year, and I ask myself: what happened to their dream? I am not one given much to musings, but here at what remains of Akhet-Aten I cannot help but ask it of myself—though I would never ask if of him because it is against all his orders and I would not dare.

Nefer-Kheperu-Ra and Nefertiti wanted only love: and horror was the end.

I am only a simple soldier, but I cannot help but wonder why.

Oh, I remember all the step-by-step: I can still name you each mistake as it came along. Pharaoh and I often discuss it and finally say to one another, "Well: let it be a lesson to *us*." At least we know what not to do, not that either of us ever would. But still, I mean: what *really* happened? Why did it *really* go wrong?

These are questions I do not believe the Good God asks himself, even in the privacy of his own room. It is a lonely room, because he rarely has time for the harim and the Queen of course is never there— or if she is, it is only to taunt him for a while before she disappears again with her snickering little companions, who grow more obnoxious and repulsive by the year. We are all roughly of an age, but those two seem to be eternal; they do not age, they just crinkle away, sneering evilly at the rest of us, sharing some never ending private joke with their mistress. I think the joke is that he had to marry her and make her Queen so that he could be King. Something went wrong there, too, but history made it impossible to correct. She comes only to argue, and goes away.

So, too, did Sitamon until she died recently and unexpectedly at Tanis. In these later years she used to go often there, gradually almost abandoning her palace in the compound of Malkata, particularly when he was in residence. He has not been there much either in recent years, for he has always preferred Memphis and now for all practical purposes has made it his principal capital, though Thebes remains the seat of Amon and so he comes at the time of Opet and for other ceremonies. Mostly, though, he stays in Memphis.

Sitamon died of a seizure of the heart in her sixty-second year, having before then been in excellent health as far as we knew. She made her regular progresses about the country, joined Mutnedjmet in many charities, remained beloved by the people. There were many things Pharaoh was unable to forgive her, but being loved by the people, I think, was the most unforgivable of all. Nor did he like the way she too, like the Queen, never hesitated to challenge his decrees and complain to his face about his harshness. "It is necessary," was all he would grate out to her; and lately he stopped saying even that, only turning away with a black and angry face. Finally he refused to see her at all. But she still remained beloved of the people.

Now he has appropriated all her estates save the farm at Tanis, which she left specifically to three of her serving people, the maid Mutnofret and the guard Seneptah, who are married with three fine children, and an older serving woman nearer her own age, Nessamon, whom they seem to regard almost as a mother.

(Things about them were different, wigs, clothing, ways of walking, mannerisms carefully cultivated over the years; but when he sent me to inspect the property for him I of course recognized them instantly. Instinctively I bent low to kiss Her Majesty's hand—there was immediate consternation—but, having done that, there was nothing for it but to kiss Queen Kia's hand and bow low to Nakht-Min. We stared at one another: I don't know which of us was the more confused. At first they were terrified, but I gave them my absolute pledge that I would keep their secret. I have never said anything to His Majesty and I never will. They are no longer threat to him. And he is my friend: I would save him from further blood.)

Sitamon's will was very strong that they should have the farm, calling down upon Pharaoh's head the eternal wrath of all the gods if he interfered; and since it is, as he says, a rather poor and infertile place, though pleasant—and since he is not entirely sure, I think, that Sitamon could not make good her threat from the afterworld, so strong a person was she—he has decided to let them keep it. And to Amonhotep, Son of Hapu, now almost ninety years of age but still, up to her death, active as steward of her estates, he has given her palace at Malkata for the remainder of his days.

So, aside from the Queen, who is as strong as he is and whom he will never control and now very seldom sees, all has been put in order by the Living Horus. *Ma'at,* order and justice have been restored, harsh laws and punishments govern all: the Two Lands are quiet and at peace because they do not dare be anything else. Abroad the Hittites still continue to press halfheartedly, but Suppiluliumas is also dead, Mursil II is a lazy weakling, and there have been no major clashes in recent years. All is in order save one thing. He has mentioned it to me increasingly of late, and today we are here to put it right at last.

He intends to remove the mummies of Akhenaten and Nefertiti and, I assume, return them to Thebes to lie with the others beneath the Western Peak.

Or at least that was what I thought he intended when we landed here last night. Now it is night again, and I am not so sure.

We have been twice to the Royal Wadi, the first time alone, the second accompanied by the small group of soldiers we brought with us. All but those two tombs are empty and deserted like the city itself. It has been an eerie experience to be here, because only among the trees at the very fringes of the Nile do there remain four or five peasant families. All else is empty, crumbling, open to the sands, deserted. The glassworks that used to produce such beautiful blue faïence were the last activity in the city to shut down, and that was five years ago. Shortly before that the last guards were withdrawn, the last contingent—two—of the once powerful priesthood of the Aten were arrested and sent to work as common laborers in the royal granite quarries at Aswan. Nothing remains here but ruined buildings and ruined memories. I shall be quite happy to get it over with, and leave.

We surveyed all the tombs today, not only those in the wadi but the Northern and Southern Tombs. The tomb of Aye, who died two weeks after the marriage of Horemheb and Mutnedjmet, was never occupied: he was buried hastily and with scant honors in the Valley of the Kings. Pharaoh did not even conduct the Ceremony of The-Opening-of-the-Mouth: we do not know where Aye is now in the afterworld, and his son obviously does not care. The other tombs along the hills, like Aye's, were never finished and never occupied. The scenes they carried of the Heretic and the Beautiful Woman riding with their daughters about the city have been almost completely defaced on Pharaoh's orders (as he also contemptuously ordered the de-manning of Akhenaten's colossal naked statue at Thebes). Only the Hymn to the Aten has been allowed to remain intact in Aye's tomb, probably because Pharaoh even now does not want to break entirely with the Aten, who still remains among the gods, though now a minor one.

We surveyed them all and then came back again to the wadi, where the soldiers met us; and after he had stood a long time staring at the sarcophagi of Akhenaten and Nefertiti he turned to the captain and said tersely, "Proceed as I said. We will be there tonight."

"Where?" I asked, I am afraid in my usual stupid way—I am still not very bright, and I do not know why he has suffered me all these years, except that I am a good soldier and absolutely loyal to him—and for a moment I thought he was going to tell me. Then he took my arm in his usual familiar manner, his voice got its usual joshing note and he replied:

"Ramesses, as always you ask too many questions. All will be revealed. Let us go back to the barge now and have supper. You will see later."

But no surprise that comes now can, I am sure, match the surprise he gave me when we finished supper. He pushed back his chair, gave me an appraising look and said quietly:

"Ramesses, my friend, how would you like to be Co-Regent, King and Pharaoh with me of our kingdom of Kemet?"

For several seconds I must have looked even more stupid than I probably do look, because I was completely and entirely astounded. Never in my wildest dreams, never in my most unbelievable—but I am a good soldier and I am also no fool when it comes to something like *that*. An offer to share the highest position in the world is not something you hesitate overlong about.

"Son of the Sun," I said fervently, "I *accept*. But"—again it must have sounded stupid, but it was all so sudden and overwhelming I simply could not resist asking—*"why me?"*

"Because," he said quietly, "you are my old and trusted comrade in arms whose loyalty and trustworthiness I have tested many years in many places. Because I have no heir, of course, from Her Majesty"— he made a grimace both of sadness and distaste—"or from any secondary wife, or even from the harim. Because there is no one who agrees more closely with what I have done and yet plan to do for the Two Lands. Because there is no one who has more faithfully carried out my wishes or been of greater help to me. Because there is no one I would rather see assume the Double Crown if the gods should see fit to take me before my work is done. Because you are faithful Ramesses, whom I love and who loves me, our brotherhood strengthened in a hundred clashes of war and a thousand things of peace. Because I think you would be a good Pharaoh. Because I need you to help me rule." He smiled, a quizzical yet curiously tender smile, and asked in a tone once more joshing, "Is this not enough for you, O 'stupid' Ramesses? What more can I do to explain it? Must I beg you for it?"

"Oh no!" I exclaimed hastily. "I have already accepted, Majesty! I was just—just curious."

"Well, now you know," he said. "So rise, Living Horus, and come with me that I may announce it to these first witnesses who are with us, as tomorrow it will be carried to Memphis and to Thebes and to all our dominions from the Delta to Napata, and to Mittani, and to Hatti, and to the Great Green and to all the world besides."

So we went out on the deck, he had a trumpeter blow a salute and caused a drum to be beaten; and there I, Ramesses, in the presence of some thirty bewildered but soon wildly enthusiastic soldiers, became Co-Regent, Living Horus, King and Pharaoh of the Two Lands of Kemet, like unto my dear friend Horemheb by whose side I have made my way and lived my life all the days since I first met him in front of the temple of Karnak, fifty-five years ago.

I did not think there could be more surprises after that, but there was one.

"And now," he said, "we go to the Northern Tombs."

Horemheb (Life, health, prosperity!)

He is overwhelmed, good Ramesses, yet this is an honor overdue. His qualities are simple but sound, his loyalty to me and my ideas absolute. I shall have an excellent Co-Regent beside me to help me with my burdens, and when I go Kemet will have a ruler who can be trusted to keep her to the course I have set. Thus will the Two Lands prosper, which has ever been my aim.

Now I can sense him wondering earnestly as we ride along through the silent, ruined city: why are we going to the Northern Tombs, what do I have in mind? I think he may suspect, for when I turn suddenly and catch him off guard he looks worried and fearful—he is still, at heart, the simple, superstitious peasant he was when we first met at Karnak. But I think in his innermost being he knows that this is the only way: the only way, if the last ghosts of Akhet-Aten are to be laid to rest forever.

It is very still as we ride. The soldiers have gone on ahead to make all ready. About us the great city stretches, crumbling away now into earth, its vacant boulevards, empty palaces and temples, gaping houses, inhabited only by snakes and scorpions. Khons rides above in his silver boat, the sands of the Red Land whisper gently over in the soft warm wind that blows against the Nile. My cousin and my half sister had their chance: they failed. It is right that I do what I do tonight.

A hardness has come into me over the years: I am far from amiable, idealistic young "Kaires" who came, cricket-bright, to Thebes so long ago. Yet I do not know how it could have been prevented. Great wrongs were done, great evils brought upon the land. Life said to me: "These things you must do for Kemet." I did them, and the rest fell by the way.

At first it was not easy; but to some degree he made it so. He ordered me to kill our uncle Aanen, raging at him blindly in his fierce frustrations with Amon. I did so, and that was the first step. After that it gradually became easier—or if not easier, at least, shall I say, more of a habit. Killing is something one becomes inured to, I have found, even if one's *ka* and *ba* can still cry out inside in horror at what one does. It was not my nature originally to kill; I was young, I was happy, I liked the world. But presently I came to see that my duty to the kingdom was such that I might well have no choice. I fought against it for a while but then gave in. It had to be. Each time my agony grew a little less, though never has it disappeared entirely. There are times even now when I awaken suddenly in the night and see myself with bitterness and loathing. But the kingdom had to be saved, and I was the only one strong enough to do it.

After Aanen, as I say, it became easier. This was aided by Akhenaten, who left us and went far away into those mystic realms of his own where only he—and possibly Nefertiti, though I think even she did not fully understand him—could go. There he built his dream world, which she shared for a time, and then poor, foolish, easygoing Smenkhkara, who tried to please everyone and reaped the sad reward thereof. Meanwhile the Two Lands failed abroad and collapsed at home. My father, the Great Wife and I knew something had to be done. Hatsuret went too far and killed Smenkhkara and Merytaten. We thought we had Akhenaten isolated, captive, stripped of his ability to ruin Kemet further. Then Nefertiti tried to rescue him, he decided suddenly to reclaim his power: his own example with Aanen, Hatsuret's with the others, influenced me too much, perhaps. Yet, again, it had to be done and it proved best that it was. I ordered her death, in a moment of rage as blind as that in which he had me kill Aanen; yet it was necessary. After that I took the very same streets we take tonight and followed him to exactly the same place, the ledge along the Northern Tombs; and there disposed, as the gods told me I must, of that sad, sad figure that once had been such a promising Pharaoh. And that, too, was necessary.

Then came Tutankhamon, and for a time, while he was still a child, my father and I thought he could be trusted not to take us back down the same blind path that Akhenaten had followed with his sacrilegious "Sole God." But soon the signs were there. Slowly but surely, with what they thought was disguising cleverness, he and Ankhesenamon began to attempt to re-establish the Aten and once more cut Amon down. With this last motivation I found myself in agreement, for Hatsuret was not content with the restoration of Amon and the great powers we had given him: he thought to rule us once again as Amon had in the past. It was time to lower both Aten and Amon once again; but neither could be done if Neb-Kheperu-Ra and Ankhesenamon persisted in their course. So Hatsuret became again my instrument, not knowing that in doing so he was sealing his own death and the new restraint of Amon. And Amonemhet and his family were sacrificed to defeat Ankhesenamon's crazy scheme. So was Zannanza. And these things, too, were necessary.

My father continued to mumble on, sinking ever more rapidly into age. I was tempted to assist the process but he was too much beloved by the people; and in any event I knew the end could not be long delayed. Even so it was four years before the old man died, four years in which he continued to permit the Aten to flourish, modestly but persistently, under his protective rule. Only at the end did he give me the power I needed to set the Two Lands right; and it has taken all my efforts ever since to achieve even a modest start upon restoring the order, the *ma'at* and the justice that have been so sadly allowed to fall away in these last thirty years.

Marriage to my bothersome half sister, though it gave me, of course, no heirs—I never intended that it should, for who could couple with an infuriating baggage like that?—did confirm my claim to the throne. Then Sitamon removed my only remaining problem, and for that my thanks to her, wherever she may be in the afterworld. Ramesses, of course, is not my only spy: I have known for five or six years that they are at Tanis. But Kemet has forgotten Ankhesenamon, who represents the Heretic in any event, and I am so solidly in command of the kingdom that her children are no longer threat to me. They are no longer in the direct line, and my naming of Ramesses, who brings with him brilliant young Seti and, now, Seti's own lively little second Ramesses, summons further weight against them. I think they are so afraid of me, and so thankful to be alive at all, that they will never be heard from again. And, also, I want no further blood: I am tired of blood. I have never wanted blood, though blood has been my portion. They may live out their lives and be happy, for all of me.

Their happiness is all I begrudge them, because happiness, though I am Living Horus, Good God, King and Pharaoh, has not come to me.

I do not know why, exactly, except that I suppose it has been sacrificed, like so much else, to my ambition to rule the kingdom. But from the day I entered the Great House and began to realize the state into which likable but self-indulgent Amonhotep III (life, health, prosperity!) was allowing Kemet to decline, I also began to think upon the prophecy of the ancient seer who clutched my hand when I was ten and cackled, "You will come to great power!" I began to feel that in some mysterious, secret way the gods had selected me to save the kingdom. And apparently I was right, for here I am.

Yet even so, I have not known happiness. A little, perhaps, with Sitamon, until her hopes of marriage had to be sacrificed, like all else, to what I came to realize was my duty to Kemet. An occasional scrap here and there, possibly, on campaign or in the harim with some anonymous, compliant slave girl. But nothing lasting, nothing real, nothing to really stir my heart. Perhaps if I had married Sitamon it would have come to me: but if I had married Sitamon I would not be King. And so the conundrum turns back upon itself and renders its own answer. . . .

We are beginning to leave the confines of the city now. The mile or so of open road leading up to the Northern Tombs shines dimly before us in the moonlight. There are lights above on the ledge. Ramesses grows ever more silent and concerned. But it must be done. There is no other way.

It will complete the action I began five years ago when I ordered the destruction and defacement of all monuments and portraits of Akhenaten, of Tutankhamon and of Aye, and began to date my reign from the reign of Amonhotep III (life, health, prosperity!), ignoring the three who came between. Thus do all official records, paintings, sculptures and monuments now proclaim. It is not the truth, but it is the truth as I intend it to be; and as I remarked during the Family's argument over the painting of Akhenaten's coronation durbar which ended in such disaster for him, *it may not be the truth now, but give it a few years and it will be.* A generation or two, perhaps three, and it will never be remembered that I was not the immediate successor to Amonhotep.

This has been the first stage of my campaign to wipe out the Aten heresy, and all connected with it, once and for all. Tonight brings the completion of my plan. I have hesitated many years, but it must be done. There is no other way. . . .

When Aye finally died, two weeks after creating me Co-Regent, I came to the throne to find that all about was chaos, despite the best efforts of both of us during Tutankhamon's reign. Power had been too divided, I did not have a free hand to do what needed to be done. My father to the end was moderating, mollifying, conciliating, compromising. Yet the condition of the country had passed beyond those gentler things. Abroad the Empire was virtually gone. Suppiluliumas and the rest were raiding at will across our borders. Tribute from foreign vassals had fallen to virtually nothing because no vassal any longer respected us. The standard of the Living Horus no longer commanded the allegiance of our territories and the swift obedience of the "Nine Bows" of our traditional enemies. At home Amon had been partially restored, new temples had been built, corruption had been partially cleared away but still was present in every level of government and domestic life. My father, too, lived in duty to Kemet all his life, but by the time he came to the throne he was too old to be as stern as the times required; and in any event it was not in his character. I was left, and I found that it was in mine.

During his reign I organized a campaign and pushed Suppiluliumas back from his halfhearted attempt to avenge Zannanza. Mursil II made a few gestures after his father died, and them, too, I repulsed. Now the borders are reasonably secure, though the peace is tenuous and at any moment we may have to fight again; certainly I have not yet been able to recapture all the territories we have lost. I shall keep trying while I live, but I suspect it may be Ramesses, or more likely Seti, who will avenge us in the end.

Meanwhile, I have concentrated on domestic matters. Here I have been harsh, perhaps, as Sitamon always told me, and as Mutnedjmet still does when I cannot get away from her; but harshness was needed to restore the land and make it just and safe for all. Here, too, the work progresses and is not yet finished; but in my Edict I have laid the groundwork and established the rules. "Slowly and gradually," as I wryly recall my father always saying, Kemet is beginning to move my way. The Edict has been the whip with which to drive the horse.

Unlike those who went before, I do not follow Akhenaten's practice of going directly to the people. Tut followed his precedent, Ankhesenamon did, Aye did. I decided that few things had done more to weaken Pharaoh's authority and damage the mystique of the Double Crown than this attempt to speak with the people on their own level. I have never appeared before them to address them on my intentions, and I never will. I pass among them in pomp and ceremony, they see me from an awesome distance: I never step down. In distance lies the mystery of the throne, and distance I have restored. The Edict was given them by Maya, that same Maya who was superintendent of the necropolis and friend to Tutankhamon, but has yet managed with his skill and diligence to become one of my most trusted advisers. He it was who appeared before the awed multitude in my favorite capital of Memphis and read my commands.

I began by telling them (through Maya and the proclamation which was then written on papyrus and sent to every city and village from the Delta to Napata) that I had taken counsel with my heart how best to expel evil and suppress lying. I told them that I spent my whole time seeking the welfare of Kemet and searching out instances of oppression.

I told them that Maya, my scribe, would give them the following orders:

First, I ordered punishment for those who rob the poor when they bring their humble levies for the royal breweries and kitchens. I said that any officer who did this would have his nose cut off and be sent to Tharu.

I said next that if any officer finds a citizen who does not have a boat to bring his tribute of wood to Pharaoh's storehouses, then he shall find that citizen a boat and aid him to bring his tribute. And I said that if any citizen finds that his boat has been robbed, he shall not be required to pay further tribute; rather restitution shall be made to him out of Pharaoh's treasury.

I went on to say that any soldier or officer who is guilty of robbing the poor when they bring gifts to the harim or to the temples of the gods shall also have his nose cut off and be sent to Tharu.

To stop the general practice by tax collectors of seizing the slaves of taxpayers and putting them to labor for six or seven days in order to exact extra taxes which they then pocket themselves, I said that any tax collector found guilty of this would himself be put to six or seven days' labor.

I went on to correct another prevalent abuse by ordering that any soldier found guilty of stealing hides that he was supposed to be collecting for Pharaoh, and of not leaving a hide with each household as he was supposed to do, should be given a hundred blows, opening five wounds, and have the hides taken from him.

I then turned to other corruptions of tax officials that had grown up in recent years and ordered that severe punishment should be meted out to dishonest tax inspectors who connive with dishonest tax collectors to retain part of the taxes for themselves; and I also said that any official or soldier who seeks to steal vegetables being brought to Pharaoh's houses and storehouses should likewise be given many blows, opening five wounds. And I said that taxes on grain should be levied more heavily upon the rich than upon the poor, for the poor need grain to live and the rich have much grain and can afford it.

I then reminded them what I had already done (this was in the second year of my reign, when I thought it time to give them a general review of what I had accomplished for them to that point). I said that I had improved the entire land, that I had sailed it as far south as Napata, traveling the interior from one end to the other, which was true. I noted that I had found two excellent honest citizens and appointed them Vizier of the North and Vizier of the South, as indeed I had, Pera and Neferhotep. I said that I had led these two to the truth and instructed them to administer all my regulations honestly and fairly, guarding themselves against the temptation to take bribes and always working diligently for Kemet; and so they have faithfully done, from that day to this. I said that I would pay them directly and well with silver and gold from the royal treasury so that no one could obligate them with gifts; and so I have.

I then issued a strong order for punishment of any government official taking bribes; and I noted that I had appointed new priests (including young Nefer, able and my willing servant, to be High Priest of Amon on the death of his feeble old father), new prophets and new officials of the courts (to rid the land, though I did not feel I had to spell it out, of the old ones who had done so much to corrupt our society).

I reminded them that I was legislating for Kemet to improve the lives of its people; and I announced times and places when I would be present regularly throughout the land to preside (but not to speak) while my officials conducted their business for the good of Kemet. And I promised that on these occasions I would give gifts of gold and silver and grain to those citizens who had done well, and deserved it. And this, too, I have done.

I told them then that I had so far accomplished many great things for them and for the Two Lands, and that I would continue to do so with a strong hand, for such corruption and sadness had fallen upon the Two Lands that only a strong hand could rescue them; and I ended by saying (through Maya and the written proclamations):

"Hear ye these commands which My Majesty has made for the first time governing the whole land, when My Majesty remembered the many cases of oppression that have occurred before!"

Since then some five hundred noses have been cut off, the prison in Tharu has grown by three thousand, a good many hundred blows, opening a good many wounds, have been administered. But it has been necessary. This is an amiable and easygoing people, but they do need an iron hand to hold them to the course of justice. This I have provided.

I had originally prepared this Edict for Tutankhamon, and some parts of it had been published in his name. But I felt no compunction about claiming it, expanding it and reissuing it for myself, because when he was alive I was the principal administrator of it, anyway.

But, as I said, much still remains to be done. So I travel ceaselessly up and down the river—I am even now on my way to visit Thebes, after I complete the business here—and I labor each day from the time Ra's first light begins to slant across the land until the time the last purple glow fades at last from the western hills. My life is work, for I have few pleasures. I have little time for them, and the needs of the kingdom will not let me rest. . . .

We are at the foot of the last ramp up the hill to the Northern Tombs. Our horses puff and whinny, our progress slows. Above we can see soldiers, torches flaring in the gentle wind. They are formed into ranks and stand facing us, so that we cannot yet see what is behind.

We top the rise, halt the horses, hand the reins to two soldiers who hurry forward and tie them securely to a jut of rock. The rest stand im- mobile, white with fear and superstition as their captain salutes us and says solemnly:

"Your Majesties, all is ready."

Ramesses starts—he is not yet used to his new title—and I say:

"Very well, good captain. Leave us now and we shall perform the business. Remain at the bottom of the hill and when we come down I shall instruct you."

"Yes, Your Majesty," he says; calls an order to his men; they march swiftly down the ramp.

We see now what is behind them.

"No!" Ramesses cries, half turning away, his face contorted with fear and horror. But:

"Yes!" I say in a terrible voice. "You are King now, too, my friend! Act it, and do with me what must be done!"

And after a moment, with a heavy sigh and a little whimpering sound, he rejoins me and we walk forward to the great pyre of wood on which lie the broken bits of bone and rotted flesh that once were he who was known as Nefer-Kheperu-Ra Akhenaten and she who once was known as Neferneferuaten Nefertiti.

Here on the ledge where they liked to picnic, here where he loved to brood above his shining, foredoomed city, here where I, Horemheb, raised my ax and ended his pathetic life, I keep my last appointment with my strange cousin and his beautiful, unhappy Queen.

She is not beautiful now, nor is he. We have here mere ghastly tat- ters, wrapped carelessly in hasty rags. There was no time or desire to mummify them properly, they were pitched pell-mell into hurried graves. Only a few jewels sewn with desperate haste into the fraying fabric still gleam and glitter in the moonlight, and them I reach down and carefully remove, for I am a careful man and waste not what I can use.

This done, I take two timbers from the pile, hold them for a moment in the torches that flare high all around, casting a garish light upon the scene—like to the light of that wild night in front of the Palace when I saw them last—and hand one to Ramesses.

He takes it in a trembling hand. He still is inclined to whimper a bit, but my mind is made up. I strike him sharply on the back.

"Light the pyre!" I order, and plunge my own timber into it. After a frightened moment he does the same. The wood, drenched in pitch-blende, catches at once. We step back from the blasting heat. In seconds the flames are roaring toward the sky.

"So die, Akhenaten!" I cry, and to my mind come racing the words of The-Opening-of-the-Mouth, which I turn now for my own purposes in this moment of final triumph over him. "Die, Nefertiti! Die you both forever! You die again, you die again forever! Here you will never live again, you die again forever!"

Another sob comes from Ramesses at what he regards as this impiety; but I have said what I meant to say and I am not afraid. It is what they deserve, and the gods, I know, are with me as I say it.

Once more he starts to turn away. I grasp his arm and force him sternly back. We face the holocaust, in which we can discern nothing. There is one sharp pop! as of a bone, or perhaps a skull, exploding, but that is all we hear, save only the steady rush of flame that mounts higher and higher as the impregnated wood roars into ashes and takes them to ashes with it.

For many minutes we stand so while they burn. I feel great calmness, great serenity. Now they are truly gone forever, and Kemet and I can both, at last, rest easy.

Finally the flames flicker and die. Nothing but ashes remain. It is over.

We turn, untie our horses, mount and ride down. At the foot the troops await us, rigid, awed and terrified.

"Captain," I say, taking a purse from my belt, "here is much gold for you and your men, five pieces each for them and ten for you. Do you return now to the ledge, disperse the embers, rake the area, remove all traces. And be sure to spread the ashes thinly over the rock, so that the winds of the Red Land may blow them away and they may nevermore be seen."

"Yes, Majesty," he replies in a shaking voice. "We go." And fortified by my gold, they gather up their courage, put aside their superstitions and obey.

Ramesses heaves once more a deep, shuddering sigh. But I tell him calmly, "Son of the Sun, it is no matter. It was necessary for the sake of the Two Lands to put them to rest forever—we did it—it is done. Come with me now and we will go to Thebes and make you King."

He looks at me strangely as though he has never really known me, though we have been closest friends for more than half a century.

"Yes, Son of the Sun," he says at last. "It shall be as you say."

We go down from the Northern Tombs, through the ghostly city, along the empty streets and so to the river and my golden barge.

Khons rides above in his silver boat. All is quiet everywhere. No human stirs. Only a lone dog howls, somewhere along the Nile.

The city is dead.

The Heretic and the Beautiful Woman are dead.

The evil concept of One God is dead, forever and ever, for millions and millions of years.

The mad dream is ended.

The vast plain sleeps.

EPILOGUE

Amonhotep, Son of Hapu

So it ends, as it began, in Thebes. Far down the Nile I hear them coming, Pharaoh and the Co-Regent, and the Co-Regent's son, and his son.
Once more comes the familiar roar of greeting from the same familiar
crowd. The same crowd—the same enthusiasm—the same welcome—
the same pomp and circumstance—it never changes, though the faces
change. Nor will it ever change, I suppose, as long as the Two Lands
live. And that, they tell us, will be forever.

Forever is becoming a somewhat easier concept for me now, because
a month ago I attained one hundred years of age. I do not know why
the gods have preserved me so long, unless it be to have one mind that
can still remember how it all began. And one, perhaps, that can stand
aside and watch the pageant pass and reflect upon the mortality that
overtakes us all, even should we happen to be Good Gods, Living
Horuses, Kings and Pharaohs of the Two Lands of the kingdom of
Kemet.

Horemheb and Ramesses are eighty, now, and both are beginning to
show signs of it. Both have lived the warriors' life and Horemheb has
added to it the burden of all the things he has had to do since to restore
ma'at and order to the kingdom. He, I think, will go to lie beneath the
Western Peak somewhat sooner than simple, kindly Ramesses; but I do
not think *he* will be with us much beyond.

And of course it does not really matter. Horemheb has set the Two
Lands firmly on their course at last; an iron will has restored a stable, if
a somewhat iron, society. All that remains now is to recapture fully our
lost territories and Empire, and that I do not think will be too long
delayed, though I do not expect that either of the Good Gods, or I, will
live to see it. There is one who will.

The great golden barge is nearing now, approaching on the usual roar
of sound, as they prepare to disembark at Karnak to start the Festival
of Opet. Horemheb stands in the prow; behind a little, at his right
hand, stands Ramesses; and behind him stand forceful determined Seti,
now thirty-nine, and his own young second Ramesses, now twenty. I almost said "Seti I," for soon, I think, he will be. I feel in my old bones,
which have grown more sensitive to nature's winds and human weather

as I have achieved my century: the Good Gods will not be here much longer. I believe the years will be few until Seti succeeds to the Double Crown.

The House of Thebes is finished, the Eighteenth Dynasty is, for all practical purposes, over. The Nineteenth Dynasty, for all practical purposes, has begun. And now truly, such is the strong character and imperious will of Seti, the great days of Kemet will at last return.

So we come again full circle, as we have before in our ancient history of near two thousand years, from glory to collapse to glory again. It is good, as I near my own end, to know that the future shines bright once more for the Two Lands and for the wearer of the Double Crown; because grievous and many are the wounds we have suffered in recent years, and dark and dismal have appeared our chances, many times.

Now the dream is at last played out, the remaining characters soon will leave the stage; and out of it all, what remains? What of him who still haunts the plains of Akhet-Aten, who still lives restlessly in the hearts of all who knew him, even though Horemheb would like to think he banished him forever on the ledge before the Northern Tombs?

He still lives: and as much as any, and perhaps more than most, will continue to live, I think, forever and ever, for millions and millions of years.

Who was Akhenaten? What was he? Was there any true idealism and consistency in the god who raised his spear against the other gods, who sang of love and happiness and joyful worship yet married his daughters, abandoned his wife, loved his brother, ruined the kingdom, lost the Empire, sacrificed all to his lovely, futile dream?

I did not used to think so before I reached my present years; and even now I am not sure I am right to believe it. Yet it seems to me that he *was* true idealist, and so can be forgiven much; and that his inconsistencies were human inconsistencies and thereby became of themselves an understandable, and so forgivable, consistency.

Out of his hatred for the gods because they would not rescue him from his disfigurement came, with true human irony, his Sole God of love.

He was idealistic, power-loving—humble, arrogant—gentle, ruthless —practical, impractical—normal, abnormal—weak, strong—a dreamer cursed by dreams.

He was both god and man, and in both a multitude. He greatly tried and greatly failed; and though his message of a Sole God of love was not for us, I yet suspect that sometime, somewhere, it will find an answer in the hearts of men.

They are on the landing stage now, they turn to receive the tumult of the kingdom: Horemheb and Ramesses—two fast-aging gods who hold themselves determinedly erect with the pride of their position; Seti and young Ramesses—symbols, and soon to be creators, of the new day. The Two Lands are in good hands now, and before long, I suspect, will have forgotten their strange, unknowable Pharaoh and the chance of love that they had in him, and lost. But somewhere buried deep the memory will live, uneasily; and Kemet, for all that Horemheb has returned her successfully to the ways of her ancestors, will never be the same again. Nor, perhaps, will the world beyond her borders.

Now as they begin their slow progress toward the first pylon of triumphant Amon's temple—where they will stop at the litter in which I lie and bow low and greet me fondly for old times' sake and all we have been through together—two scenes are in my mind.

The first is that early night upon the ledge when he announced his Hymn to the Aten and had us join him in the flaring torchlight as he chanted. It can be found now only in the tomb of Aye and one or two others, but it lives in my heart as I suspect it does in Horemheb's, though he would never admit it:

"Thou arisest fair in the horizon of Heaven, O Living Aten, Beginner of Life. When thou dawnest in the East, thou fillest every land with thy beauty. Thou art indeed comely, great, radiant and high over every land. Thy rays embrace the lands to the full extent of all that thou hast made, for thou art Ra and thou attainest their limits and subdueth them for thy beloved son, Akhenaten. Thou art remote yet thy rays are not upon the earth. Thou art in the sight of men, yet thy ways are not known. . . .

"The earth brightens when thou arisest in the Eastern horizon and shinest forth as Aten in the daytime. Thou drivest away the night when thou givest forth thy beams. . . . The entire earth performs its labors. All cattle are at peace in their pastures. The trees and herbage grow green. The birds fly from their nests, their wings raised in praise of thy spirit. All animals gambol on their feet, all the winged creation live when thou hast risen for them. The boats sail upstream, and likewise downstream. All ways open at thy dawning. The fish in the river leap in thy presence. Thy rays are in the midst of the sea.

"Thou it is who causest women to conceive and maketh seed into man, who giveth life to the child in the womb of its mother, who comforteth him so that he cries not therein, nurse that thou art, even in the womb, who giveth breath to quicken all that he hath made. . . .

"How manifold are thy works! They are hidden from the sight of men, O Sole God, like unto whom there is no other! . . .

"Thy beams nourish every field and when thou shinest they live and

grow for thee. Thou makest the seasons in order to sustain all that thou hast made, the winter to cool them, the summer heat that they may taste of thy quality. Thou hast made heaven afar off that thou mayest behold all that thou hast made when thou wast alone, appearing in thy aspect of the Living Aten, rising and shining forth. Thou makest millions of forms out of thyself, towns, villages, fields, roads, the river. All eyes behold thee before them, for thou art the Aten of the daytime, above all that thou hast created. . . ."

And as the two elderly Pharaohs who are, and the two youthful Pharaohs who are yet to be, leave me after much kind greeting and pass within the temple of Karnak, this last thing comes to me:

That night on the river when the Court left Akhet-Aten and Tutankhamon stopped for the night at the village of Hanis; and when, on the deck of His Majesty's barge, very late, the lone singer sang, to the shimmering sound of a harp and the gentle rustle of a sistrum, his bittersweet words that speak to us all, old and young, rich and poor, greatest of the earth or smallest on it, after all the strife is over and the final word is said:

"Be glad, that thou mayest cause thine heart to forget that men will one day glorify thee at thy funeral. Follow thy desire, so long as thou livest. Put myrrh on thy head, clothe thee in fine linen, and anoint thee with the marvels of life.

"Increase yet more the delights that thou hast, and let not thine heart grow faint. Follow thy desire and do good to others and thyself. Do what thou must upon earth and vex not thine heart, until that day of lamentation come to thee—for He With The Quiet Heart, Great Osiris, heareth not lamentations, and cries deliver no man from the underworld.

"Spend thy days happily and do not weary thereof!

"Lo, none can take his goods with him!

"Lo, none that hath departed can come again. . . ."

September 1975–March 1976

S1